A NIKKI GARCIA THRILLER

COYOTE ZONE

ISBN: 978-1-68313-108-3

Library of Congress Control Number: 2017949239

First Edition
Printed and bound in the USA

Kathryn Lane photo by Mindy Harmon
Map courtesy of Alma Guerrero
Cover and interior design by Kelsey Rice

A NIKKI GARCIA THRILLER

COYOTE ZONE

BY KATHRYN LANE

For Karen,
Enjoy !
Kathryn Lane

𝓟
Pen-L Publishing
Fayetteville, Arkansas
Pen-L.com

BOOKS BY KATHRYN LANE

~ The Nikki García Thrillers~
Waking Up in Medellín
Awarded Book of the Year (2017) by Killer Nashville
Coyote Zone

Backyard Volcano

DEDICATION

To Bob—I couldn't do it without your love and support

To my mother, Frances—for your lifelong love and guidance

To Philip, Jorge, and Cristina—for the love and wise counsel you've given me

And to all the dedicated volunteers and professionals who work with victims of human trafficking

"All we have to decide is what to do with the time that is given to us."

– Attributed to J.R.R. Tolkien

The map shows the states of Mexico including: Baja California, Baja California Sur, Sonora, Sinaloa, Chihuahua, Durango, Nayarit, Jalisco, Colima, Aguascalientes, Zacatecas, Nuevo Leon, Coahuila, Michoacan, Guanajuato, Mexico State, Hidalgo, Tamaulipas, Guerrero, Puebla, Tlaxcala, Veracruz, Oaxaca, Chiapas, Campeche, Quintana Roo, Yucatan. Marked sites: Mapimi Zone of Silence, San Miguel de Allende, Palenque Maya Site.

CAST OF CHARACTERS

Nikki García – protagonist, investigator

Eduardo Duarte – medical doctor, Colombian citizen, Nikki's fiancé

Floyd Webber – Nikki's boss and owner of a private investigative firm in Miami

Sofía Lombardi – owner of a restaurant in San Miguel de Allende; Bibi's mother

Bibiana Lombardi – Sofía's ten-year-old daughter, also known as Bibi

Paolo Lombardi – Italian businessman, Sofía's ex-husband, and Bibi's father

Chiara Lombardi – Paolo's widowed mother

Matteo Lombardi – Paolo's cousin

Juana la Marihuana – bag lady, might also be a drug addict

Fígaro – Juana's dog

Sebastián – Juana's crow

Héctor Sánchez – Paolo's attorney in Mexico City

Arturo Béjar – Former federal police agent who works for Héctor and for himself; Maria's father

María Béjar – Héctor Sánchez's administrative assistant and Arturo's daughter

Fernando – Floyd's contact at Gobernación (equivalent to Homeland Security)

Charlotte – Floyd's administrative assistant in Miami

Nita Zapote – Nikki's undercover persona

Goyo – coyote; human trafficker

Petra – owner of a small convenience store in the city of Zacatecas

Antonio Enríquez – employed by Arturo

Joaquín – Colombian citizen, employed by Arturo

Bernardo – Goyo's right-hand man

Assistant – Goyo's young helper

Adelita – transvestite at Zacatecas market

Angela – teenage girl held by coyote

Florencia – child sold to the coyote

Josefina – Juana's house mate, flower grower

Santiago – helicopter pilot

Jack Levy – communications expert, investigator, and consultant

Timothy Ramos – ransom negotiator

Ana – Juana la Marihuana's daughter (also known as Juana Beltrán García)

Raimundo "Rai" Beltrán – narco from Sinaloa and Juana's former common-law husband

Father Abelardo – Catholic priest

Cristóbal Arenas – Colombian drug trafficker living in Mexico; remains offstage but has ties to former Federal agent Arturo Béjar

GLOSSARY

Bajadores – men who take by force (kidnap) the trafficker's people and/or children (whether they have gone with the trafficker by free will or not)

Birria – spicy barbecue made with meat of sheep or goat

Cagna – Italian word for bitch

Chava(s) – girl(s)

Chavo – boy

Coyote – human trafficker

Cuernos de chivo – slang name used to denote AK-47 and other automatic weapons

Estás loco, buey – You're crazy, dude

Güeritas – light-skinned, little blonde or golden-haired girls

Hijos de puta – sons of bitches

Jefe – boss

La Parroquia – The Parish

Malditos – cursed or damned

Migra – slang in Spanish for immigration officials

Oye – Hey

Pendejada – stupid act, stupidity, depending on context, it can also mean bullshit or asshole

Perdón – excuse me, I beg your pardon

Pinche – damn, or depending on context, it can mean goddamn

Pollos – slang name for people being trafficked

Puta chava – damn girl or fucking girl

Sicarios – hired assassins who perform drive-by killings

Signora – Italian word for lady or woman (Mrs., Ms., or Ma'am)

Taniche – small store

PROLOGUE

A man strolls up to a ten-year-old, golden-haired girl at a crowded, noisy, colorful open-air market in San Miguel de Allende, a paradise for retired Americans and a few Canadians snowbirding there during the winter months. The man holds his index finger to his lips as he hides his other arm behind his back. He speaks to her, opens his eyes wide, and smiles at her as he produces a cute, two-week-old puppy in the hand he has been hiding. He passes the newborn to the beautiful child. She cuddles the pup in her arms, kisses its nose, and smiles as she glances up at the man. He kneels beside her, cups his hand around her ear as he whispers to her, and points to the street. She touches the puppy's head with the side of her face and rubs her cheek back and forth on its furry little head. The man whispers in her ear again.

The child takes one step backward and looks at him for a second before glancing anxiously at a tall, slender woman standing a few feet away at a fish stall. The girl cuddles the puppy and kisses his head.

The man removes small paper cards from his shirt pocket and shows them to her. She smiles as she sorts through them and hands them back to him, keeping one. He takes her hand to study the card she selected, and he points toward the street again. He stands up, still holding her by the hand, and together they walk in that direction.

The tall, slender woman standing at the fish stall examines fresh offerings displayed on a bed of ice. She pokes and smells samples of shrimp, trout, salmon, and red snapper, pointing out her selections to the vendor. Engaged in animated conversation with him throughout the process, she takes money from her handbag, hands several bills to him, gets change back, and places it in her purse. She has a final conversation with the vendor, gesturing wildly with her hands and arms as she speaks. The vendor laughs in a friendly fashion. Before she moves from the counter, she reaches out her hand, as if to find someone. No one is there. She looks to one side, then to the other side.

"Bibi, il mio tesoro, andiamo," she says loud enough to be heard over the din of the crowd in the immediate area surrounding her. "Bibi, my treasure, let's go."

The woman scans the crowd and calls for her child again. She calls a third time. When she gets no response, she twirls like a tragic ballerina to face the full market. Taking a few steps, she goes toward a tent displaying women's intimate garments—hot-pink, purple, and polka-dotted bikini panties, fancy bras accented with lace, and a table overflowing with both men's and women's bargain underwear. She sidesteps that booth and checks the next one selling jeans, dog leashes, and pirated movie and music CDs. She rushes back to the opposite side and searches for her golden-haired daughter at a food tent offering tacos, pizzas, and tamales. A dark-haired girl of about twelve, fanning the air with a large hand-held fan to keep flies from landing on the food, stands by a table spread with pizzas, but her daughter is not there.

With tears forming in her eyes, the woman places a hand on her chest, as if to prevent her heart from jumping out of her body. She starts calling, "Bibi, where are you hiding? Bibiana, come here this minute!"

No response.

She yells again . . . with the same result.

Desperate in her search, her eyes and mouth contorted by panic, she returns to the fish stand hollering, "Help me! My daughter is missing!"

Another woman, much older, in a long, tattered dress—like a street person, a vagabond, or a scruffy trespasser—leans on her cane near a vegetable booth two tents away. She shouts and raises her cane in the air.

"Ese señor se la robó." She points toward the street. "That man stole her."

The child's golden hair is nowhere to be seen. The tall, slender woman is crying.

COYOTE ZONE

"Where is my daughter?"

Vendors and customers scurry one way and then another looking for the girl. No one pays attention to the woman pointing toward the street who keeps repeating, "Ese señor se la robó."

"That man stole her," the old woman repeats over and over again like a mantra.

CHAPTER 1

Palenque archaeological site—Wednesday, day one after abduction

"I can't believe the beauty of this place," Nikki said. "How could the Maya build temples so long ago that contain such modern-looking elements?"

Nikki slid down the sunglasses, protecting her eyes from the strong morning sun, to rest low on her nose before peering over the frames to gaze directly into Eduardo's eyes as she reached for his hand.

Howler monkeys, screaming for a mate, could be heard in the distance. The Palenque ruins sat lazily in a rainforest near the Usumacinta River in the Yucatán Peninsula on the ancient Maya trade route that ran from the Yucatán to the former Maya stronghold of Tikal three hundred miles to the southeast in the Petén region in Guatemala.

Nikki readjusted the shades over her eyes and turned her head toward the Palacio, an ensemble of archeological structures sitting atop a hill—a small hill, whose top had been sliced off to build the foundations for the edifices. Steps in a terraced walkway led up from the park's perfectly mown lawns to the ancient royal palace, a decaying relic upon the truncated hill. Slightly off-center in the complex, a square tower rose skyward with four layers, the heavier ground level supporting three layers above it. Each of the upper floors was punctuated with large open windows resembling the California mission revival style.

Eduardo put his arms around Nikki and moved in closer to snuggle. She leaned her head against his shoulder, and he followed her action by resting his own head against hers for a few seconds.

"We're living our dream," he said as he kissed her hair and then pushed it back to touch her forehead with his lips. "In Colombia, we spoke of becoming archeological junkies, traveling the world's ancient civilizations. We've made it happen."

Nikki moved to look at him. "Can we spend the rest of our lives here, breathing in this panorama? Let's move into that four-story tower. It reminds me of Gaudí's Barcelona-style rooftops."

"Great idea. It's known as the Palacio. Palenque peaked at about six or seven hundred years after the birth of Christ. Its best known ruler, Pakal, built this pyramid where we're sitting. It's called the Temple of the Inscriptions, after the discovery of tablets containing hieroglyphs describing Pakal's family tree. His tomb is in a crypt below us."

"Oh, can we see it?" Nikki asked, excited as a child at a circus.

"When we go to Mexico City. Its contents are on exhibit at the archeological museum there. The crypt below us is now closed to the public. Getting back to our tower, it probably served as an observatory for ancient astronomers by night and lookout tower by day. We can convert that top floor into a comfortable bedroom and use the Temple of the Cross, down that pathway, as our wedding location."

She loved how his soft Colombian accent made his English sound charming.

Eduardo pulled Nikki in toward him again and kissed her lightly on the lips.

"We can explore wedding venues while we're here," Nikki said, "but there are so many tourists in Palenque that we can't hold a private ceremony. Besides, not all our friends appreciate archeology like you and I do. We can honeymoon here. In our tower hideaway. So let's start decorating. We can take siestas every afternoon. We're in the tropics, you know."

"Love that idea—a siesta every afternoon." His eyes lit up as he smiled. "Now about this site, did you know Palenque dates back to about the year one hundred fifty of the Common Era?"

"You're the erudite junky. I'm just a beginner, so tell me about it." Nikki placed her elbows on her knees and looked at Eduardo with loving eyes. "I'm listening."

"This place dates from roughly the time when Christianity began spreading from the Middle East to Asia Minor, way before the Spanish set foot in the New World. I wanted to bring you here to show you some of the finest examples of Maya art and architecture. I knew you'd appreciate their ingenious use of harmony between their temples and nature. The Temple of the Inscriptions, where we're sitting, is—"

Nikki's mobile phone rang. She glanced at the screen and sighed.

"It's Floyd."

"Don't answer." Eduardo made a hands-up position, as if he were being threatened with a gun. "We're on vacation."

"He's my boss. I can't ignore him."

"Please, Nikki, don't do it. We just arrived last night." Eduardo moaned audibly as she accepted the call.

"Hello, Floyd." Her voice reflected her happiness, lilting at the end of each word. "Yes, we're having a great time."

Eduardo shook his head in disbelief as he sat there on top of the Temple of the Inscriptions. His romantic rendezvous with Nikki, the love of his life, appeared to be crumbling just as the Maya civilization had crumbled centuries before in the same spot.

"Sure, I'll be happy to fly to Mexico City or Querétaro." She listened for a few seconds. "No, no, Eduardo and I don't mind at all." She slid her sunglasses over the top of her head—like a hairband over her shiny, long, dark hair. "We'll rent a car and drive to San Miguel and I'll talk with her."

Nikki said goodbye to Floyd and turned to face Eduardo as she tucked the mobile phone into the thigh pocket of her cargo pants.

"Looks like we need to postpone decorating our love nest. Floyd wants me to investigate the abduction of a ten-year-old by her father."

"Custody battle?" Eduardo asked. His brow wrinkled into a distasteful frown as he spoke. "We're on vacation. Our plan was to visit several sites in the Yucatán. Why didn't you tell him to send someone else to cover that job?"

"I can't do that. You know I've been working for him barely a year. Besides, it's only a couple of days, and then we can return here."

"Only a few days . . ." Eduardo shook his head again.

"That's what Floyd said. It's about talking to an Italian woman who lives in San Miguel de Allende. She called Floyd in Miami. Of course, he took the case to find her little girl, who's been missing since yesterday."

"An Italian woman? In San Miguel? A tourist?" Eduardo asked.

"No. Floyd said she left Italy six years ago after a nasty divorce and settled in Mexico to avoid her ex's constant threats to take their child. The mother has full custody, but the father, a wealthy industrialist who still lives in Italy, hired a Mexican attorney to get joint custody with the mother. Looks like he's abducted the child. Floyd will email me more details."

"And what am I supposed to do while you're out happily chasing a bambino snatcher?" he asked.

Eduardo's eyes scanned the clearing in the jungle landscape from their perch on top of the Pyramid of the Inscriptions. Early morning sunlight made the whole site magnificent. Farthest away in the clearing from where they sat stood the Temple of the Cross, the one with hieroglyphs and relief sculpture Eduardo intended to study up-close. The dense, green jungle vegetation partially hid it, yet the visible part of the sunbathed limestone building reflected a luminous quality. A grand temple awaiting their visit. So grand, it rivaled Egyptian monuments.

Two young tourists, both women, started climbing the steep, narrow steps of the Temple of the Inscriptions. They took a good look at Eduardo's muscular physique while ignoring Nikki. She noticed their flirtatious glances at Eduardo.

"You'll go *with me* to San Miguel, of course," Nikki said as she stared at the young women. Abruptly, she turned to face Eduardo with an expression of surprise, as if he should know the answer.

"I could stay here and explain Maya hieroglyphs to ladies more interested in Maya culture than in pleasing their new boss." His eyes followed the two young women.

The women smiled at Eduardo as they walked past him on the temple platform when they reached the top of the pyramid.

Nikki gave him a dirty look.

"What happened to your idea of spending the rest of our lives here?" he asked as he shifted his gaze to the people in the park below. "Didn't you tell me you wanted to move into this World Heritage Site?"

"San Miguel is also a UNESCO site," Nikki said.

Vendors were arriving. A few were already setting up their wares on display for the onslaught of tourists. Eduardo glanced at Nikki and saw she wore a determined look on her face, an expression he'd seen before.

"Okay, I guess I'll play caddie and carry your luggage." His eyes twinkled as they always did when he teased her. "And since the salary is so paltry, you must provide good benefits."

"I always give you great perks," she said as she smiled seductively at Eduardo. "You'll love the town of San Miguel. My grandmother took me there when I was a teenager. It's a quaint colonial town."

Eduardo looked across the expanse of the archeological site.

"Before we leave," he said, pointing to the far end of the complex, "we must visit that pyramid. It's called the Temple of the Cross for a cross-like motif on a bas-relief sculpture on one of the interior walls. According to Maya mythology, it represents the world tree." His eyes settled on the distant temple.

"World tree?" Nikki asked. "Like in a tree of life?"

Nikki stood up and dusted her derrière with both hands. Then she extended a hand to Eduardo. He got up and, once he was standing, put his arms around Nikki's waist and drew her in close to him.

"As long as we can carve out a little fun now and then, I'll go with you," he whispered in her ear before he nibbled at her earlobe. "But tell me why Floyd wants you to give up our vacation to do this job."

"First, I speak Spanish. Second, we're already in Mexico. Third, he thinks I'll be more sensitive to her suffering since I'm a woman. I'll do preliminary work, and Floyd will fly in later to do the heavy work."

"I've heard that before."

"He's the former CIA operative, and he'll carry the big load. We'll have plenty of time for us." Nikki nestled her head between his face and his shoulder. "We'll come back here, I promise."

"I'll hold you to that promise."

"Will you take my hand so I can descend this lofty perch?" she asked as she lifted her head to face him.

Eduardo released her from the embrace. She picked up her purse—a gift from Floyd when they had been in Medellín, performing a job for Nikki's former employer, an American multi-national corporation. Floyd, who had worked with Nikki on several assignments in Europe, South America, and India, had been so impressed with her performance on the Colombian job that he hired her as an investigator for his Miami-based firm, Security Source. The job in Medellín had been a tough situation, where Nikki had investigated and uncovered a drug ring exporting cocaine to the U.S. The purse Floyd had given her—a large, brown leather handbag—actually served as working equipment. He had given it to her so she could carry a concealed handgun, a Baby Glock, in a special zippered compartment. However, when she and Eduardo packed for their trip to Mexico, Nikki had left her Baby Glock at home in Miami. Having a gun like that had saved her life a year earlier when she did the Colombian assignment, but a gun would never make it past international airport security or the Mexican Customs and Immigration authorities. Without the gun, her purse felt much lighter.

"Tell me more about the world tree," Nikki asked, repeating the request Eduardo had ignored a minute ago.

"It's a symbol," he said. "Like a tree of life that appears in a lot of the world's early civilizations. Myth states it can be found at the center of the world. It's a pillar, holding up the universe. It connects the underworld, represented by the roots, to the sky, represented by the branches. It links the underworld and the sky through the trunk of the tree, which represents the terrestrial world. Let's walk over and take a look at it before we leave Palenque. Then we'll grab our luggage at the hotel, check out, and leave for the airport."

They strolled, hand in hand, across the expanse of scrubby grass.

"We'll make our ten thousand steps today, no problem," Nikki said as they walked.

Eduardo glanced at his wristwatch in a semi-conscious attempt to check the steps he'd already taken that morning.

"How's that step tracker working in your shoe?" he asked.

"It seems pretty accurate, more than the wristband I used to wear."

"It doesn't bother your foot?"

"Don't even feel it. What's more, I love it. The training app on my phone is so easy to use. The only problem is the color of my new tennis shoes. Look how grubby they already are," she said, glancing down at her brownish-gray-colored sneakers that two days ago had been pristine white.

A young vendor, selling necklaces depicting a miniature replica of the world tree, emerged from a group of hawkers and interrupted their walk to the temple. Nikki stopped to admire the hand-sculpted pendants made of green jadeite. She discovered one with a slightly more delicate bas-relief than the others. Eduardo negotiated with the young woman, agreed to her price, and purchased it. As he clasped the necklace around Nikki's neck, the young vendor handed Nikki a small, dirty pocket mirror so she could admire her gift.

"I like it," Nikki said. She touched the world tree image as she looked at herself in the little mirror. "I like it very much."

CHAPTER 2

San Miguel de Allende—Wednesday, day one after abduction

In 1542, barely twenty-three years after Hernán Cortés formally took the territory of the New World—that expanse of land now known as Mexico—for the Spanish Crown, a Franciscan monk named Juan de San Miguel founded the present-day town of San Miguel. In the valley close to the Laja River, the monk oversaw the construction of the town near the grounds of the historical Toltec ceremonial site. The Toltecs had abandoned their ceremonial center around the beginning of the thirteenth century. After that, various nomadic tribes used the remains of the Toltec center until the Chichimecas took over and established themselves along the river. Despite the Indian tribes who settled and resettled the area for centuries before the advent of the Spanish conquest, history now credits the founding of the town as 1542. The pueblo, which had been called San Miguel el Grande, dropped the last two words to add the surname "Allende," to honor the popular national hero in the fight for independence, General Ignacio Allende. The general had been born in the town. So it became San Miguel de Allende, often referred to as San Miguel, or simply "SMA" to the expatriates living there.

Eduardo drove a Volkswagen Jetta toward San Miguel over Federal Highway 57 as Nikki slept. She had rented the Jetta at Las Palmas airport in Querétaro after their flight over from the Yucatán.

When the divided highway gave way to State Road 51, ramshackle houses with concrete block fences covered in graffiti started appearing, scattered along both sides of the highway. Eduardo awakened Nikki and drove slowly at a roundabout with a large statue depicting Ignacio Allende, completing three full circles around the monument to make sure Nikki was awake enough to serve as his navigator.

The roundabout divided the Americanized Luciérnaga shopping center, complete with a large Home Depot, from the more traditional Plaza Real del Conde across the street. Large letters on the roundabout announced San Miguel as a World Heritage Site. On his third circle of the roundabout, he slowed the car and pulled into the Luciérnaga parking lot. Nikki took her phone from her purse and opened the maps app. She copied over the address of the restaurant from Floyd's email. The restaurant belonged to Sofía Lombardi, the mother of the missing child. A British-accented male voice in her GPS guided them to the summit of a hill overlooking the town.

"Stop at the mirador," Nikki said. "The scenic overview can give us a feel for the village before we descend into it."

She wanted to see if it was still the beautiful colonial village she remembered from her teenage years. After parking the rental car, they walked to the retaining wall at the edge of a small cliff. The quaint town, nestled in a hilly expanse below, looked picture-perfect. Pink granite church towers, almost fairytale-like in appearance, dominated the panoramic view. The pink towers distinguished themselves from three domes that capped surrounding churches. Nikki pointed out a large-domed church, perpendicular to the towers, which she remembered as belonging to a cloistered convent.

"When my grandmother brought me here, that church was called Las Monjas, The Nuns. But that could have changed by now," she said.

She continued to point out landmarks she could remember. She spotted a bullring, which, on close inspection, appeared to be in the center of a city block, completely surrounded by colonial-style homes.

"I wonder how people get to the bullring," she mused.

"What a coincidence," Eduardo said. "The in-flight magazine had an article on this bullring. I think it said it's the oldest one in Latin America, over three hundred years old."

"Interesting," she said as she continued looking at the picturesque town below.

KATHRYN LANE

Glancing toward the street, she saw several vendors. One to the right side of where they stood was weaving a palm leaf into a grasshopper the size of a small cat. Another had a basket of local, handcrafted sweets. Nikki's eyes settled on a life-sized bronze figure bolted to the sidewalk. The sculpture represented a surreal design, a mixture between a demon and a human. She walked over to read the plaque and noticed the name of the artist: Leonora Carrington. Then she stepped back to the retaining wall where Eduardo still stood, surveying the town below.

Her eyes moved to the spot where Eduardo's attention seemed to be focused, and she noticed two small traditional belfries attached to chapels.

"From all the churches and chapels they built here," he said, "you can see the town's religious fixation. Man, it's hard to imagine the religious fervor of colonial Mexico."

"It's a beautiful town," she said as she rubbed her eyes, as if she could not believe the beauty of the vista. "It hasn't changed much since I was a teenager."

"That's why it's an UNESCO World Heritage Site," Eduardo said. "It's to preserve the historical aspects of the town. Like medieval towns in Europe that have World Heritage denominations."

"We'll enjoy our stay here. Then we'll return to the Yucatán for vacation." She put her arms around Eduardo's shoulders. "Shall we move on? I'd like to show you the sculpture by Leonora Carrington on the way to the car. Originally from Britain, Leonora painted, sculpted, and wrote in a surrealist manner. In fact, her life seemed a rather surreal adventure."

After looking at the sculpture, they returned to the Jetta, and Eduardo drove down the stone inlaid hill into San Miguel—its winding streets flowing over hills, and the pink towers of the church yawning at them when the vegetation or the town's colonial-style city blocks opened up to allow a glimpse. The street tapered down like a funnel as they drove past each new intersection. As they approached the center of town, the granite spires grew larger, and their details became more clearly focused with the passing of each vividly painted Spanish-style block of colonial buildings. As they approached the historic center, the street gave way to smaller cobblestones, causing the Jetta to vibrate rather than bounce over the pavers.

Following the British-intoned instructions from Nikki's phone app, it appeared they had descended into town, only to start bouncing uphill over larger cobblestones again.

"Ristorante Italiano is a few blocks away," Nikki said.

She directed Eduardo through San Miguel's narrow cobblestone streets using the map, now on mute. The accent was starting to annoy her. She glanced back and forth between the phone and the mirror on the sun visor as she combed her hair and applied lipstick, attempting to look professional before she met the Italian woman.

"We're not far from the ristorante," she said, "and there's a parking garage on Recreo Street. Take a right turn at the next corner—"

Eduardo slammed on the brakes, throwing both of them into the constraint of activated seatbelts. Nikki looked up from the map in time to see the smiling face of a child, six or seven years old, appear over the hood of the car. He'd run into the street after a soccer ball and stopped to pick it up mere inches in front of their bumper. The little urchin looked back at them, smiled, and kicked the soccer ball to three other boys down the street. He turned again, revealing two missing front teeth as he smiled, and held his thumb up in the air, as if proud of saving the ball before it was hit and damaged by a car.

"He was lucky these cobblestone streets slowed me down. Otherwise, you'd spend the night alone while I slept in jail for running over that kid."

"We're the lucky ones . . . Oh, here's Recreo Street. Turn right."

Eduardo followed Nikki's instructions and turned the car onto Recreo.

"Damn kid. I nearly ran over him, even though it was his fault."

"Careful. Don't smash a future soccer star lurking around the corner. Next, we'll drive past the block containing the bullring. To get around the one-way streets, turn left on Huertas and take another left on Barranca. We'll circle three sides of the block hiding the historic bullring behind all these brown and yellow colonial walls."

Eduardo turned corners at each of the streets Nikki indicated.

"Wish we could have a peek at the municipal bullring," he said. "It's a multicultural venue for concerts and weddings, though they hold rodeos there every year. Hey, that's an idea. We could get *married* there."

"I'd rather get married in a nice little church," Nikki said. She was very focused on her mission, and right now that mission meant finding and talking to the Italian woman. Wedding plans would have to wait. Nikki studied the map on her phone. "The restaurant is on Montes de Oca, a short diagonal street, a block away from the bullring. Turn right on Montes," she said.

"How can anyone have a restaurant on such a steep hill?" Eduardo asked. "Man, I don't know if this Jetta has enough horsepower to get us up there."

"We're almost there."

"There's no street parking," Eduardo said, exasperated.

"Drop me off at the ristorante, and you can double back to the parking garage on Recreo. It's almost four o'clock. So after parking, you can catch up with me."

"You need to interview the woman by yourself," Eduardo said as he turned the steering wheel and the car bumped over the cobblestones while he slowed the speed even more. "You're the private eye. I'll park and then walk to the church, the one with those pink limestone spires we've been watching since we arrived here. Maybe it'd be a good wedding chapel for us."

"I think they're granite spires, but who knows? I'll walk to the church when I finish," Nikki said.

"Send me a text as you leave the ristorante. Then we'll find our bed and breakfast through this maze of medieval streets."

"Medieval is a misnomer—" Nikki said.

"Okay, it's a Spanish colonial town dating from the sixteenth century," Eduardo said, interrupting Nikki. "But this spot was inhabited by local Indians before the Spanish arrived. Look over there. The ristorante is on your left, that building with the burnt-ochre and orange exterior. You may now descend from your carriage, Madam Medieval Private Eye."

Eduardo stayed until Nikki walked through the double-wide set of carved wooden doors, large enough for a horse-drawn carriage, each door hanging from large metal hinges embedded in an elaborately sculptured limestone arch.

A tall, attractive, European woman with short, stylish, chestnut-colored hair stood inside the archway. She wore a casual, neutral-colored dress with interwoven hazel-blue and pale-green paisleys and greeted Nikki with a concerned smile.

"Ms. García?" she asked. Her Mediterranean accent weighed heavily in her voice, which sounded pleasant yet hesitant. "I'm Sofía Lombardi. Call me Sofía."

"It's nice to meet you, Sofía. And you can call me Nikki. Let's get on a first-name basis from the start." Nikki emitted a barely audible sigh as she admired the simple yet elegant courtyard. "Your ristorante is lovely. I had no idea from the rather austere exterior that the interior would be so richly decorated and beautiful."

Nikki's eyes took in the welcoming and tasteful design of the space. Exquisite French doors on the right side connected the covered patio to formal dining rooms. A terraced garden, lush with flowering plants, divided the informal patio restaurant from a charming bar area. The actual bar—a large, intricately carved wooden structure surrounded by six live jacaranda trees strategically placed to create a warm and harmonious atmosphere—gave the impression that it expected important people to arrive at any moment. A terra-cotta tile floor brought the final touch to the large enclosure. In the middle of it all, a busboy made his way around a table, laying out silverware on the patio tables for the evening's dinner guests. Overhead, an opaque roof of either glass or plastic overlaid on narrow steel beams allowed sunlight to brighten the entire patio.

Nikki started to comment again on the beauty of the interior space but stopped when she glanced at her hostess. Sofía's eyes watered, and she appeared on the verge of breaking down. Nikki touched Sofía's arm to comfort her.

"We will find your daughter," Nikki said, making an effort to sound reassuring. "Can we go to a private room and talk?"

Sofía pointed toward a doorway on the left side of the patio.

"My living quarters."

Nikki followed her into a small parlor. Two tall windows with wrought-iron bars and thin white lace curtains faced the street. The window sills were accented with heavier brocade draperies hanging on each side, creating a contrast with the delicate lace. An upright piano pushed into a corner of the room competed for wall space with framed photographs of a child with long, curly, golden hair, two large Impressionist-style landscapes, and a set of six framed oil paintings, either by a primitive painter or a child artist. A stone mantel over the fireplace displayed several stand-up picture frames showing photos of the same child at various ages.

"Is this your daughter?"

Sofía, trying to keep her emotions from spilling over, nodded.

"I understand your anguish," Nikki said, "and I'm sorry you're going through this nightmare. To help us find her, I must ask you several questions."

Sofía nodded again. "Ask whatever you need," she said, choking as she held back the tears.

"First, we need to know the situation of her abduction. Where and when she was taken. What she was doing, and if anyone witnessed it. We'll also need a couple of recent photos of her."

"Every Tuesday I purchase the bulk of the week's fruit, vegetables, and fish for the ristorante at the Tianguis del Martes. They are open on Tuesdays, as their name implies, and again on Sundays, though I never go on Sunday. They have the freshest produce. I pay for my purchases, and the vendors arrange delivery. Yesterday morning, I took Bibi to the market with me, like I always do. It's early. When I finish ordering my produce, we take a taxi and I drop her off at school."

Her voice trailed off to a mere whisper. Tears tumbled out of her eyes and streamed down her rosy cheeks, like rain drops falling down a rose petal. She dried her tears with a tissue and wiped her nose.

"But yesterday, she disappeared before I could take her to school."

"What were you doing when she disappeared?" Nikki asked.

"Bibiana, that's my daughter's name. It means 'alive or lively' in Latin. Yeah, Bibi, she's so full of energy, so her name is very appropriate. I was standing at the fish market, holding Bibi's hand. I let go to check the freshness of the fish and shrimp the vendor was showing me. I placed my order, paid him, received my change, and reached down automatically to take Bibi's hand again, but she was not there."

Sofía began weeping again and took a few steps to the carved wood antique side table near the door where the two women had entered the parlor. She drew several tissues from a box on the marble tabletop.

"It happened in an instant, while I was distracted. I called Bibi's name, but she was gone. Just like that. Yeah, just like that." Sofía snapped her fingers to accentuate the swiftness of her daughter's disappearance. Working to maintain her composure, she walked to the fireplace, took two pictures off the mantel, and gave them to Nikki. Then she sat on the piano bench, placed her head between her hands, and started crying—heavy, convulsing sobs this time.

"I know how difficult this is, especially since she is so young. Who do you suspect may have taken Bibi?" Nikki asked.

She anticipated the tissues were not going to be sufficient to mop up Sofía's tears, so Nikki walked to the side table to get a fresh supply.

"My husband and mother-in-law. I mean, my ex-husband and his mother," Sofía said. She took the tissues Nikki handed her.

"How do you know they did it?"

"They have threatened many times to take Bibi away. My former mother-in-law has all the money in the world. She was never happy Paolo married me. Yeah, from the time Bibi was born, she wanted to take her away. Yeah, she always tried to take her."

"Take her away as a baby? Why?"

"She wanted to give me a nanny to take care of my daughter, my own daughter, as if I could not care for her myself. The old woman wanted to raise Bibi the way she had raised her own son. Yeah, now she wants her granddaughter back in Italy for half the year. Can you imagine what that would do for Bibi's schooling?"

"Did you see anyone take Bibi at the market?" Nikki asked.

"If I'd seen them, I would have my daughter with me instead of you. Yeah, my daughter would be here."

Sofía looked up to the ceiling, as if she were trying to restrain her emotions and trying to be polite, despite Nikki's interrogation of a difficult situation. The more nervous Sofía became, the more she used the word "yeah," which her Italian accent made softer than the German pronunciation.

"I understand," Nikki said, "but I need to know the sequence of events so we can work on getting Bibi back. What did you do at the market when Bibi went missing?"

Nikki wanted to reach out and touch Sofía and tell her it would all be okay, but she felt compelled to keep it on a strictly professional basis.

"I called for her. I shouted her name out. Yeah, shouted her name. Bibi was nowhere. I raced to a couple of stalls and asked people if they had seen her. My fish vendor, I buy from him every week, he called a woman from another stall to tend to his shop to help. He checked the men's bathroom. People were concerned for her and concerned for me. Several female shoppers helped, and a few vendors left their vegetable stands to search for her. One checked the women's bathroom. We double-checked the street. Nothing. Bibi simply vanished."

"Did Bibi have friends she may have gone off with?"

"She's not with any of her friends. I called them all. I talked to the school."

"Is there any reason Bibi would want to hide from you?"

Sofía's semblance changed, and she looked at Nikki with an expression of anger.

"It's my ex-husband who took her, I tell you. In Italy, he managed twice to grab her at school. Yeah. He took her twice. I had to go through the courts to get her back. That's when I decided to move here, and he'd been quiet until last week when a lawyer in Mexico City contacted me."

"What did the lawyer say?"

"He wanted to work out a custody deal where Bibi would be in Italy for six months of the year and six months with me. I declined to split custody with him, so he filed a case at the courts here in San Miguel to get full custody. If they ever get Bibi, they will hire a nanny to raise my child."

Sofía started sobbing again. Nikki touched Sofía's arm in a sympathetic gesture and allowed her to cry for a bit.

"Have you thought of a random kidnapping for ransom?" Nikki asked, interrupting Sofía's show of emotion.

As Nikki waited for Sofía's response, her hand went to her neck in an absentminded movement. Her fingers wrapped around the world tree necklace for a few seconds.

Sofía stopped crying long enough to look Nikki straight in the eye.

"If I thought it was a kidnapping for ransom, I would not have called your firm. A negotiator from my insurance company would be here," Sofía said.

"No ransom requests?"

"None. And no requests will be made. Yeah. It's my ex and his mother. Why won't you believe me?" Sofía asked, biting her lip in despair.

"I do believe you, but it's my job to explore all the possibilities, simply because horrible things happen to kids these days. I want to rule out any wrongdoing by organized crime. Do you have a picture of your ex-husband?"

Sofía stood up and lifted the seat of the piano bench. She took out a photo album, closed the seat, and sat down again.

"Photos of my wedding. These are the only ones of Paolo I have not burned. This album I was saving. Yeah. Saving it for Bibi." Sofía took two pictures out, hesitated as she looked at one and put it back in the plastic sleeve, turned the page of the album, and took a different one out. "He's a handsome man, but he's a playboy," she said. "And a terrible father. This one also shows Paolo's mother, Chiara. And Paolo's cousin, Matteo. He's another bad one. He carries out all of Chiara's caprices."

"Caprices?"

"Yeah. All her whims. Whatever that evil woman wants."

"Can you give me the contact data for Paolo's attorney in Mexico City?" Nikki asked.

Sofía got up and walked into the adjoining room, waving for Nikki to follow her.

"This is the dining room of my house, but if I ever have guests, they eat at the restaurant, so I keep it as my office."

She walked to a desk and scribbled on a piece of paper.

"Have you talked with him since Bibi went missing?" Nikki asked.

"Oh, yes, and I was very upset. He denied knowing anything about it." She handed the slip of paper with the contact data to Nikki. "Héctor Sánchez is reputed to be a real son of a bitch lawyer who works for the very rich. He told me, if Bibi is missing, I need to file a denuncia with the authorities as it's against the law for me not to report the crime."

"Have you reported it?"

"No, and I'm not going to."

"Why not?" Nikki asked.

"The police are too corrupt, that's why. If you call Sánchez, do it early, before he goes to the courts. He's the only attorney in this country who is in his office by seven a.m. Yeah, call very early."

Nikki put the contact data in her purse and pulled out a business card, which only stated her name and email. She borrowed Sofía's pen to jot down the number to her burner phone before handing the card to Sofía.

"If anything comes up, please call me," Nikki said. "I'll be in touch with you as I need additional information or I have news to give you. I'll be in San Miguel tomorrow morning to check a few things out while I'm here. I know this is a terrible time for you. Let me assure you, we will do everything possible to find Bibi."

"You can't begin to imagine what this is like."

"Yes, I can," Nikki said. "I lost my only child, my son, when he was thirteen. He was three years older than Bibi is now. Believe me, I know how you feel, and I promise you, I will do whatever it takes to get her back."

"How long did it take you to get your son back?"

Nikki looked at Sofía, shook her head slightly, and sighed heavily.

"I didn't get him back. My son was not abducted. He died in a tragic accident that could have been avoided. To this day, I have nightmares over it."

"I'm sorry," Sofía said. "I'm so consumed by Bibi's disappearance, I feel as if I'm the only mother who has ever suffered." She used the crumpled up tissues to wipe her nose one more time.

"That's understandable," Nikki said. "When your own child is gone, your universe falls apart. It takes a lot of fortitude to get through it. As far as Bibi is concerned, I mean what I've said. We will do everything possible to get her back safely."

"Please find my daughter," Sofía's pleaded. She reached for Nikki's hands, holding them for a few seconds while she composed herself.

As Nikki turned to leave, she noticed more framed paintings on medium-sized canvases. Two of them depicted cuddly puppies, a third one showed a cat eating from a dish on a Mexican tile floor, and the other three were portraits—a European queen, perhaps, judging from a tiara on her head, and another looked like Benito Juárez, the first indigenous Mexican president. The last one was a thin-faced, balding man, but what hair he had left was long, stringy, and gray. Nikki reached back in her memory to her grandmother's stories about Mexican history. Then she remembered. That was Miguel Hidalgo, famous as the activist priest who rang the church bells declaring independence from Spain. Nikki took her time to appreciate the paintings and noticed Bibi's name in block letters on the lower right-hand side.

"Your daughter painted these?"

"She did. A framed set of eight is hanging in the ristorante and another set of six in the parlor. The ones in the ristorante all portray famous Mexicans. Yeah. From Frida Kahlo to Benito Juárez, similar to the Juárez painting here."

"She's certainly talented. And she's mastered a wide range of subject matter."

"Bibi's taken quite a liking to Miguel Hidalgo, the father of Mexico, the activist priest born in this state. He declared Mexico's independence at a nearby town called Dolores Hidalgo. Then she also likes Benito Juárez, Mexico's first Indian president. He came from the Zapotec tribe in the state of Oaxaca. Maybe her sense of compassion makes her admire the story of an impoverished Indian who attended law school and fought in the war for independence. Bibi loves how Juárez rose from poverty to become president of this nation."

"That's admirable," Nikki said.

"Bibi admires both Hidalgo and Juárez. At the other end of the spectrum, she likes Marie Antoinette. On a trip to Europe last year, when we flew over so she could see Paolo, I took her to Versailles. She fell in love with the palace and its history. Yeah. She loved the history. But she also loves animals, especially puppies."

"She seems talented, far beyond her age. A female Picasso?"

"Her teacher says Bibi is quite gifted. I hope someday . . ." Sofía's voice lowered until it approached a whisper.

"Take care of yourself, and I'll pray for Bibi."

"I had not prayed in years, but I've done a lot of it in the past two days," Sofía said.

CHAPTER 3

San Miguel de Allende—Wednesday afternoon, day one after abduction

Nikki walked up behind Eduardo and put her arms around him. He turned and slipped her into his embrace and kissed her passionately. After a few seconds, Nikki caught her breath.

"Hey, hold it. We're in a church."

"So what? I shouldn't kiss you because we're inside a church? The day we get married, I'm going to kiss you passionately in front of the altar," Eduardo said.

"That will be a totally different situation because the priest will have married us by then."

"Are you being silly or what?" Eduardo asked. Then his face became more serious. "How did your meeting go with the Italian woman?"

"I'll tell you more over dinner. Her name is Sofía Lombardi. Nice lady, but an absolute wreck, as you might imagine. She's convinced her ex-husband and former mother-in-law conspired in Bibi's disappearance, but I'm not so sure. The child is a talented painter for a ten-year-old. I saw her work."

"What does my investigator princess want to do next?" Eduardo asked, taking Nikki's hand.

"I'd like to walk to the spot where the Tuesday Market takes place. It won't be open, but I'd like to get the lay of the land over there."

"Walk? Close enough to walk, is it?"

"Just a few blocks from here, according to the walking map. And it's such a beautiful afternoon."

"Over these cobblestone streets," Eduardo said, "it seems more like an obstacle course set out over crooked alleyways. How about catching a cab?"

"We can get a soccer ball and play as we go," Nikki teased as she kept her eyes on the cobblestones to make sure she was placing her feet so she wouldn't take a tumble.

"That kid probably lost his two front teeth by falling as he played soccer on these impossible streets."

"Are you complaining? You can stay behind at the church if you prefer."

"Next time I'm in church it'll be because we're getting married," Eduardo said. His eyes smiled as he touched Nikki's arm.

Nikki reached out to grab his hand and pull him in close to her for a kiss.

"You're so wonderful, but so sarcastic. I'm glad you love the quaintness of this place, especially the cobblestone streets."

"Look who is being sarcastic now," he said.

The streets, bordered with old homes, radiated away from the main square. Most of the homes had been converted to small businesses. Yet, very shortly, Nikki and Eduardo were walking in a residential area where colorful houses lined the street continuously along each city block. Solid walls rose straight up against the sidewalk, almost in a buttress-like fashion—typical construction in Spanish colonial towns of Central and Southern Mexico. Owners of a few of those big, rambling houses had turned them into bed and breakfast places. A few ranked as top-rated boutique hotels.

Nikki stopped and studied the colorful architecture. She pointed to the top of a house where large, single stock, bearded cacti loomed over the top of the roof, like sentries waiting to bounce on intruders.

"I would not want to get caught up in one of them," Eduardo said.

He laughed and took advantage of the pause in their walk to flag a taxi over. They had walked uphill on cobblestones for three blocks, and the street ahead looked steeper yet.

The driver seemed perplexed why people wanted to visit the empty site of the Tuesday Market, but he parked at the José María Correa Téllez

Municipal Stadium, locally known as the Capi Correa, named after San Miguel's legendary athlete turned sports announcer. Nikki and Eduardo stepped out of the car. Across the street, the vacant market venue extended for two city blocks.

The location—a huge, dual-level lot with concrete slabs that were crumbling along the edges—stood about a mile and a half from the center of town. Hard-packed dirt surrounded each concrete slab, suggesting the huge crowds attending the market flowed over from the cement floor to the bare ground. Bathrooms bordered the east side of the lower lot, with concrete walkways connecting them to the vacant lot.

Nikki stopped and studied the empty premises.

"Looks pretty desolate," Eduardo said. "It's mostly empty space, like two football fields, maybe more. Are you sure about this?"

Eduardo took his phone out to snap a few pictures of the area. Nikki followed him as he moved closer to the bathrooms to take photos. The little building had a six-foot wrought-iron fence that completely enclosed both the men's and women's bathroom doors, with turnstiles to enter and exit.

"Sofía said they put tents up. That building across the street," Nikki said, pointing at an old, brown-stuccoed structure with locked storefronts, "must be part of the market, probably where the finer goods are located. We may have to return next Tuesday when the market is functioning. There's not much to see right now."

A wrinkled old woman—perhaps an Indian woman from one of the tribes whose ancestors dated back to the pre-Colombian era, a woman who appeared by the clothes she wore not to have assimilated into modern Mexico, a woman with a visible limp—hobbled up to them, leaning on her cane.

"¿Les puedo ofrecer un tour?" the old woman asked.

"Tour? How much?" Eduardo asked, speaking to her in Spanish.

"You're not serious, I hope. There's nothing here," Nikki said. "We'll come back next Tuesday."

Anxious to find their B&B, Nikki looked forward to taking a bath and relaxing. She studied the woman as Eduardo bartered with her. The woman wore a tattered embroidered Indian blouse that hung loosely over a full-length skirt that dragged in the dirt. She looked and smelled as if she had not bathed in over a month, and she appeared to be carrying her meager possessions in a bag. Eduardo and the old woman haggled in Spanish over a price until they reached an agreement.

"Twenty pesos for a tour of an empty market?" Nikki asked, sounding annoyed and irritable. "She's a bag lady, what can she possibly tell us?"

"Don't insult her, Nikki. Why don't you stay back as I investigate? I've never had a tour guide like this before, so I'm going for the adventure."

Both Eduardo and the old woman started to walk away.

"Wait for me," Nikki said, grudgingly following them. "I'll come along."

"I've been offering tours for several years," the old lady said in rapid-fire Spanish, "and you're my first customer." She grinned a toothless smile at Eduardo.

"You see. You're wasting your time, my darling," Nikki said.

Nikki lagged behind as the tour began, thinking for several minutes about different possibilities a crowded market offered for abducting a child. Eduardo and the old woman carried on a conversation until he called Nikki to catch up with them.

"You have to hear what she just told me," Eduardo said with urgency in his voice. "Please tell la señora about what things you see happen in the market," he said to the woman in Spanish.

She responded in her rapid colloquial Spanish.

"I was telling the señor that life in San Miguel plays out in this mercado. You hear gossip you would not imagine, like who is sleeping around on her husband or which government officials take bribes. Or you see things, like children being kidnapped."

"Kidnapped children?" Nikki asked, continuing the conversation in Spanish. Her voice went up by two octaves. "What do you mean by *kidnapped* children?"

"Just that, mi doña," the old woman said as she curtsied to Nikki, as if Nikki were royalty. "I've told the police many times that, every full moon, a man comes here to buy food for the children he has stolen. He also brings young men with him sometimes. But the police don't believe Juana la Marihuana. Or maybe the man has bribed the police."

"Eduardo, she's speaking gibberish," Nikki said in English, "calling me 'my lady.' Is she trying to pander to me? Pay her and let's go find our bed and breakfast."

"No, wait," he said. "I want to ask her more questions."

"Then ask her if she also hears wild coyotes howling at that full moon every month," Nikki said, looking impatient.

"Ah, coyotes, sí, sí, the man, he is a coyote," the old lady said. She put her bag on the ground and leaned heavily on her cane. She shook her head as she continued in Spanish. "I think he takes people across the border into the United States. That's why he comes here to get food during the full moon."

"What does a full moon have to do with it?" Eduardo asked.

"He drives them to the border and smuggles them at night into the States under the new moon when the night is darkest. That way they won't get caught by the migra."

"Yeah, the full moon, the new moon," Nikki said in English. "She's full of shit. She apparently doesn't know immigration uses night vision goggles. And she does not know the border is more patrolled and protected than ever. We'll come back on Tuesday to investigate what I want to know when the crowds are here."

Eduardo took money out to pay his eccentric guide.

"El coyote, he took the little girl with the golden curls," the old lady said.

Nikki stopped dead in her tracks and turned around. "What did you say about the little girl with the golden curls?"

"That man, the human trafficker, stole her on Tuesday."

"How do you know?" Nikki asked.

"Juana la Marihuana saw him take her," Juana said as she patted her chest with her empty hand. "He offered her a puppy. That's why she followed him."

"Why didn't you stop him or yell or something?" Nikki demanded.

"I did speak up, but no one listened. They all think I'm a loca because I smoke marihuana. If they heard me, they pushed me aside, and they ran about like chickens chasing loose kernels of corn, looking for the child all around the market. But by then, the man was gone. And he took Ricitos with him."

"How many times have you seen Ricitos at the market?" Nikki asked.

"Many times. Her mother brings Ricitos before school. They always stop at the fish stand right there on the street side," Juana said, pointing at a spot in the upper portion of the empty lot. "Her mother owns a restaurant. A big, fancy restaurant, where Juana la Marihuana is not welcome." Juana made an ugly face, emphasizing her breathing and fanning her nose, as if there were a bad odor in the air.

"What makes you think you're not welcome?" Nikki asked.

"Just look at me, señora. I'm poor. I'm a beggar." Again Juana made the gesture, as if a rancid odor filled the air. "I went begging there once, and la Italiana told me to stay away, that she didn't want me scaring her dinner guests off. La Italiana would rather throw food out than give a mouthful to a beggar like me."

Juana's expression changed. She smiled broadly, her eyes glistened, and she stood up straighter.

"But Ricitos is beautiful, like a little angel. Ricitos always smiled and waved at me. She's not at all like her mother. And like all kids, she probably loves puppies and kittens, but that Italian woman is too germ conscious to let her have one."

"Why do you think that man wanted to abduct Ricitos?" Nikki asked.

"To sell her," Juana said. "He will get much money for her." She rolled her thumb against her index and middle fingers to emphasize the big bucks he'd get for her.

"Hey, Nikki," Eduardo said, interrupting Nikki's interrogation of Juana while staring at his smart phone. "I know this sounds preposterous, but I've just checked the phases of the moon. Guess what. Tuesday happened to be full moon."

"Juana, can you give me specifics on how the man snatched her?" Nikki asked, making a mental note of Eduardo's comment to deal with later. "Where did he seize her? What did he do to keep her from crying when he took her?"

"Too many questions, mi doña." Juana curtsied to Nikki again. "Let's take one at a time. He took her from the fish stand at the middle of the market over there by the street." She pointed with her cane toward the location, as if a tent with a fish vendor actually stood on the empty lot.

"Her mother was busy buying fish for her restaurant and let go of the child's hand. The coyote moved in quickly. He had a puppy and kneeled down by Ricitos, and he handed the little dog to the girl. He remained kneeled down on one leg to talk to Ricitos. He pointed to his parked truck. She went with him without making a fuss."

"Why didn't *you* make a fuss if you knew he kidnapped children?" Nikki asked.

"I did. First, I told the attendant in the stall where I stood. She dismissed my warning. Next, I raised my cane in the air and shook it plenty as I yelled. It happened, mi doña, as I stood right there under a vegetable tent where chilies are sold. Ten different types of chilies from all over Mexico that stand sells. I was a couple of tents away from the fish stand. I told them a coyote took her away. No one, not a single soul, paid attention to me. The attendant at the vegetable stand told me to leave, and he threw three or four potatoes at me, so I left."

"You left?" Nikki asked. "Why?"

"The previous time I'd made a fuss, that time in front of her restaurant, la Italiana called the police on me and I spent the night in jail. There are bedbugs in the jail, you know, so I didn't want to go there again. But the newspaper had my picture in the paper that time."

The old woman sashayed a bit and rolled her eyes sideways to look at Nikki, as if to pose the way the newspaper photo may have shown her. Then she lifted her long skirt thigh-high and leaned over to scratch her right leg from her ankle up to the top of her calf. Her dusty feet, wearing a skimpy, worn-out set of sandals, had long brown toenails whose tips curled under. She proceeded to lift her skirt up to her waist, displaying short, loose, dark-gray pantaloons that may have been white at one time. With a twist of her wrist, she pulled out a pouch from the top of the pantaloons and then dropped the skirt back over her legs.

"That man comes here to buy food," Juana said. "Eggs, sacks of beans and sacks of rice, packages of corn tortillas, and bread. And lots of bottled water. Sometimes he brings a child with him, but he looks around carefully when he does. They are young, like twelve or thirteen, but most times he brings a young man, different ones at different times, about age fifteen or sixteen, or maybe one in his early twenties."

She opened the pouch, reached into a pocket in her skirt, retrieved a small packet of papers from which she withdrew one piece, and then placed the packet back in her pocket. She dropped the cane on the ground next to her bag.

"Those facts alone cannot confirm he's a coyote," Nikki said. By now she listened intently, while trying to ignore Juana's unseemly antics.

"No," Juana said, "but I think he works as a coyote. Like I've told you, he's always here at full moon, giving him time to drive to the border by the time there is very little moonlight. I've watched a couple of very young children he's brought with him, and they looked scared. He's a kidnapper of young girls. I've seen him at this market with little girls. None as pretty as Ricitos, though. He'll get many dollars for her." Juana rubbed her thumb and middle fingers together again as she said "muchos dólares."

"Couldn't those other children be his?" Nikki asked.

"Only if he has several the same ages and a lot of them," Juana said. Rolling a joint with the weed she'd pulled from the pouch, she licked one edge of the paper and sealed it.

"What if he's a school teacher?" Nikki asked. "And he brings different kids each time to experience the market?"

"No, mi doña, don't be naïve. He's not a teacher." Juana curtsied to Nikki again and then took a matchbook from another pocket in her skirt and lit up the joint. She took a few puffs to get it started and offered it to Nikki.

"No, thank you. Enjoy your cigarette. Smoking makes me sick, so I stay away from it."

Juana took a big draw on the joint, and when she exhaled, she blew the smoke straight at Nikki's face.

"It will take away all your physical pains and even help with the emotional ones too," Juana said.

Nikki turned her head and breathed slowly to control her annoyance.

"What was the color of his truck?" Eduardo asked in Spanish, and then he switched to English to address Nikki. "I'd continue questioning her. She may have good info."

"I've seen different trucks," Juana said. "I remember one that is brown with orange details on the side, sort of like a flame running along the sides of it. Another one is dark-gray. That's the one he drove here last Tuesday. It's only one color, but the license plate is from Sinaloa. You know, there's a big cartel there. Maybe that's why he kidnaps children. To sell to the cartel."

"Do you remember the number on the license plate?" Nikki asked as her interest in the interrogation revived.

"VGM 56 something, but it said Sinaloa at the bottom," Juana said.

"Take a note of that, please, Eduardo," Nikki said. Turning her attention back to Juana, she got another big puff of smoke in her face and coughed.

"I'm the one smoking, and you're the one coughing," Juana said. She threw her head back and laughed a full, rich laugh. Her teeth, what teeth she still had, were as dark-brown as her toenails.

"I told you, I get sick if I smoke," Nikki said. "Can you tell me the make or brand of the truck?"

"No, mi doña, I'm not sure." She saluted Nikki instead of curtsying this time. "Maybe a Ford. It was a big truck. I don't know much about cars. I know the colors and whether they are clean or not. That truck was plenty dirty."

"New or old?" Eduardo asked. He already had his mobile phone out and typed in a note on the make and color of the vehicle, as well as the partial tag number.

"Under all that dirt, it looked very old, but I don't know. Maybe it was new. Who knows?" Juana said, nodding her head. "But narcos use old trucks for certain jobs to avoid catching the eye. Pobrecita la Ricitos de Oro, if they kidnapped her," Juana said. "What a terrible fate awaits her if they did."

"I agree. Poor little girl with golden curls," Nikki said. "That's why I need for you to remember everything that might help us find her before that human trafficker sells her for top dollar, as you said."

"I've told you all I know," Juana said.

"Can you give us an address where you live?" Eduardo asked. "In case we need to speak with you again."

"I live very, very far away," Juana said. She took her gaze away from Eduardo and looked aside as she spoke. "So far away, you can't get there. But I come here almost every day. Maybe I fly on a broom because a woman has to eat, after all. You'll find me around here. Especially on Tuesdays. I come here where I hear all the gossip. I go to the zócalo. It's the Jardín in the center of town. That's where I get money from the turistas."

Eduardo took out a fifty peso bill and told her to keep the change.

"Gracias, patrón," Juana said. She offered Eduardo a draw on her joint.

"Gracias," he said. Eduardo tried to look natural as he took a light puff before handing it back to Juana.

"Mi doña, I noticed your necklace." Juana barely curtsied this time. "That's a good luck omen, a very good omen. It's a tree of life, and it will help you find Ricitos." Juana threw her hand-rolled cigarette butt on the ground, picked up her bag and cane, and turned to take her leave. "I'll be at the Jardín tomorrow. If you need me, you know where to find me."

⌇⌇⌇

"What did you make of all that?" Eduardo asked. They were bouncing along the cobblestones in the taxi taking them back toward the parking garage on Recreo.

"Hard to tell. She's a weirdo," Nikki said. "Yet some info, like the license plate, sounded promising. Also, she described the fish vendor situation exactly as Sofía did. The only difference is Sofía did not mention Juana at all. On the narcos, Juana seems to know quite a bit about them, like knowing the license tags come from a state with big cartels, and that cartels use old trucks on occasions when they want to avoid being conspicuous."

"It's uncanny that she described the incident the way Sofía told you. Means she most likely saw it," Eduardo said. "Why don't you call Sofía and talk it over with her? Confirm Juana was there at the time."

"Maybe I should go in person since the parking garage is close to the ristorante," Nikki said, "and I'd like for you to come with me this time to meet Sofía. I'm also going to call Floyd so he can check out the license plate."

Nikki dialed Floyd's number as their taxi continued bouncing across the cobblestones.

"Hi, Floyd," Nikki said. "Yes, we're in San Miguel, and I'm on the case with Eduardo acting as my assistant. I'll send you a report tonight, but I need you to check out a tag from the state of Sinaloa. Two or more digits are missing at the end, but see what you can find. It might help."

Eduardo held up his mobile phone so Nikki could read the partial tag numbers and the truck's details to Floyd.

"The eyewitness, who may not be credible, said it was a dark-gray truck, maybe a Ford, but she wasn't sure." She gave Floyd the details, paused to listen, and then said goodbye.

As they paid their driver, he recommended a nearby food court for dinner.

"It's on Relox, called Dôce 18. Nice place."

The driver pointed toward Relox Street as they stepped out of the taxi to the loud beat of mariachi music near the Jardín in front of the church of San Miguel Arcángel, also called La Parroquia by the townspeople. The trumpets were especially shrill, overpowering the string instruments, but the animated singing voices of people rose above the horns in a heavenly fashion. Eduardo opened the camera on his phone and took a photo of a rotund balloon vendor completely encircled by children of various ages. They watched as a boy started crying, his high-pitched screams even louder than the music, when he let go of the string and a gust of wind scooped his balloon high up into the air. A woman in heels, probably the child's mother, moved toward the balloon man to purchase another one for the screaming child. Nikki smiled.

"I can remember my grandmother bringing me here. The environment has not changed much. It's just as noisy as it was then. The musicians, people hanging out in the Jardín, the beggars, and the balloon vendors—the center of town has not changed."

"Do you remember the hat vendors?" Eduardo asked as he snapped a photo of a young man strolling by with a four-foot stack of hats on top of his head, trying to sell his wares. He wore clean but faded blue jeans and a well-worn blue sweatshirt with Walt Whitman's name in white letters across the front. "I wonder if that guy even knows who Walt Whitman was."

Nikki shrugged her shoulders.

"Shall we check out the driver's recommendation for dinner?" Eduardo asked.

They started walking toward Relox Street. The din of music, people talking, cars driving by, and children screaming all melded into a cacophony of sound.

"I don't know how much I want to inform Floyd at this point about our eyewitness. Floyd may feel I'm wasting my time on such a questionable person. I'll decide after we speak to Sofía again." She raised her voice enough for Eduardo to hear her over the deafening noise of the street.

"Also, if it's a drug cartel vehicle, they use stolen plates and change them frequently, but it's good he's checking it out anyway."

Suddenly, the music changed. A lone snare drum started beating out a machine-gun-like roll of ra-ta-tas, followed by noise from the trombones, trumpets, and tubas, and eventually joined by more horns.

"That piece is called 'La Diana,'" Nikki said, describing the music, "and is often used for announcing the arrival of special people. Though, according to my grandmother, its origin was on the battlefield when insurgents followed Pancho Villa in the Mexican Revolution. It was meant to notify troops to start the attack against federal forces."

"Look, Nikki. The music's announcing that wedding party over there. The bride is getting out of the car right this minute. Shall we join them and have a double wedding?"

Eduardo turned away and walked toward the balloon vendor. He selected a big, red, heart-shaped one and paid the man. Then he returned to Nikki, holding the balloon by a string, kneeled on the cobblestones, looked up at her and said, "Will you marry me this very minute?"

"What's your hurry?" Nikki asked, laughing. "You're a Quixote without a windmill. I'm already wearing the engagement ring you gave me, you silly man."

Nikki laughed again as Eduardo stood up, and joy filled her face as she gazed at the bride across the street. She moved closer to Eduardo, put her arms around his shoulders, and kissed him.

"Yes, I want to marry you," she said, "but I don't want to share my wedding day with anyone but you. Let's enjoy a few prenuptial honeymoons before we tie the knot."

"Prenuptial honeymoons? You mean like this one? Don't you remember? We're supposed to be in the Yucatán sharing a romantic vacation, not sharing joints with a bag lady on a dusty, empty lot in San Miguel. But, hey, I'm happy to enjoy several mini-moons before we marry, as long as we enjoy a full-blown postnuptial honeymoon. At least three weeks."

"Mini-moons? What are you talking about?" Nikki asked. Then she laughed. "You and the crazy Marihuana lady are always talking about the moon."

"A mini-moon is a very short honeymoon," Eduardo said. "So short it evaporates into the air almost before you savor it. Like in the Yucatán."

Nikki moved closer to Eduardo, and he put his arm around her. She noticed most women in the square wore rebozos or light sweaters as the air was cooling down, yet the evening was very pleasant.

"Like the Yucatán?" Nikki asked. "We'll make up for that tonight."

"I need more than one night to make up for that," Eduardo said, smiling.

They arrived at the entrance to Dôce 18. A bakery offering pastries and a jewelry shop were at the entrance to the mid-block mall. As they entered the building, they could see what appeared to be the food court at the rear. Just past a coffee shop, a beer bar emanating energy, with noisy and jubilant drinkers sitting on plush red sofas, was across the hall from a wine bar. Spotlights of red and purple light colored the thick limestone doorways on both establishments. Nikki peeked inside the wine bar to take a closer look at a large table in the center of the room seating eight people. The guests sat around a unique wood tabletop made from a six-inch swath cut from a huge tree. The highly varnished wood still maintained the organic shape of the original tree, and the rings in the wood were clearly visible. The varnished tabletop reflected the light emitting from the spotlight, bathing the doorways in red and purple. The wine enthusiasts invited Nikki and Eduardo to join them, but Nikki declined the friendly group, telling them she could not afford to relax with a glass of wine before completing her workday.

CHAPTER 4

San Miguel de Allende—Wednesday evening, day one after abduction

Nikki introduced Eduardo to Sofía, who ushered them into her private living quarters. Eduardo busied himself, studying the twenty or so photographs showing Bibi at different ages and in various environments—inside, outside, on ski slopes, and in a swimming pool. He also studied Bibi's oil paintings, especially the one of Benito Juárez, while Nikki spoke with Sofía.

"I came back to ask you a few questions, even though I realize your ristorante is full right now so I'll be quick. What can you tell me about a woman who hangs out at the Tuesday Market? She calls herself Juana la Marihuana."

"She's a nutcase," Sofía said. "You can't believe anything she says. I get upset whenever I think about that hag. Rumors say she came from a good family, attended a private school, and then became a narco's girlfriend, a capo in the Sinaloa cartel, but he threw her out when she acquired a serious drug habit. Narcos live by double standards. Yeah, they sell drugs, but they don't want it in their family or close allies. That rumor has been around for years, before I arrived here. Why do you ask?"

"I checked out the location of the market. Juana was there, and she talked with us. Since she was the only person around, I asked her if she'd seen anything unusual last Tuesday. She mentioned she'd seen Bibi with you the morning of the abduction."

"That horrible woman would be capable of stealing and selling my child to get money for her habit. I took pity on her when I first opened the ristorante, and we'd give her leftover food at the back door. Yeah, then she started begging for money outside my main entrance. Customers complained, so I told her not to ever set foot near my ristorante again."

"You asked her to leave?" Nikki asked.

"I did, yeah. She became angry, and one Sunday evening, she defecated on the hood of a BMW belonging to one of my best customers. I called the mayor. He sent two policemen, who booked her. San Miguel is a small place. Word gets around. Even the local newspaper printed up a story about the incident. It developed into an awful situation and terrible publicity for my ristorante. Yeah, terrible. That old witch lives on about ten acres outside of town, so she's not as poor as she appears."

"Do you think Bibi might go somewhere with her?" Nikki asked.

"No way. Bibi's teachers and I have instructed her never to go near strangers or talk with them. Bibi would not go away with that witch and not anyone else, for that matter. Unless it was someone she knew, like her father. Or a friend from school. I don't understand where this is going," Sofía said. She looked annoyed with the questioning. "You're not taking Juana seriously, are you?"

"If Juana saw Bibi go off with a man, would you believe that?" Nikki asked.

"She made an accusation like that when Bibi disappeared. And yes, I believe Bibi's father did walk away with her, and that's the man the crazy woman saw." Sofía's voice became louder, and she appeared to be getting agitated.

"I have to check out all the leads," Nikki said in a soft voice, trying to have a calming effect on Sofía.

"But why didn't that witch stop the man from taking Bibi? She may have even helped him by distracting the crowd with her accusations, yeah. She's used that ploy at the market before when she's encouraged some homeless kid to steal. She's a bad woman, I tell you."

"We wondered if she was credible when she told us about seeing a man take Bibi. I also wondered why you did not mention Juana when we spoke earlier," Nikki said.

"I'd ignore that drug addict if I were you," Sofía said, her words and attitude emphatic in her advice. "Now, if you don't mind, I don't want to lose my composure. If I start crying, it takes me hours to get control of myself again. And I still have to pay the bills, including your fee. Yeah, even if it's hard right now, I still have my ristorante to run."

Sofía's jaw tightened. She tilted her head up and focused her eyes high on the wall in front of her, as if there were a bug there to watch.

"Were the police present at the market when Bibi went missing?" Nikki asked.

"No. And you know I did not call them. In Mexico, the police are so corrupt, you don't want them involved. They will come in your home and steal from you as they write up the report." She looked as if she were on the verge of tears.

"Does Bibi love dogs?"

"Adores them. Why?" Sofía looked surprised.

"That's how the kidnapper lured her away at the market, according to Juana. That's all for now," Nikki said. "I'll be calling Paolo's attorney in Mexico City tomorrow."

"A dog? Yeah, that makes sense. Bibi's father would use a ploy like that to take her from me before she had a chance to say something to me. That fucking ex-husband of mine would—"

"Your daughter's art is very good," Eduardo said, interrupting. "I can't believe a ten-year-old painted them. She handles oils very well, but she's obviously very creative too. The expression on this man's face is incredible."

"Thank you. That's a portrait of Benito Juárez," Sofía said. "Many people consider him the Abraham Lincoln of Mexico. Yeah, Bibi loves that man who became president of Mexico, despite being born in poverty, who went on to become a lawyer." She reached out and touched the portrait, as if she were caressing her daughter's face. As the three of them returned to the courtyard, she stopped and turned to Nikki. "Please find my daughter. Talking to Juana is not going to help, trust me."

"Man, she sounded upset," Eduardo said. "Angry and cold-hearted. Not at all what I expected from your earlier description of a devastated mother."

Eduardo and Nikki held hands as they headed for the parking garage. It was getting late. A room at a bed and breakfast awaited them, the place Floyd had reserved for them.

"I understand her anger," Nikki said. "When I lost my Robbie, I went through phases of denial, total heartbreak with plenty of crying, and then the anger set in. Of course, this is not a good comparison because my son died. Yet Sofía in many ways is suffering through all those phases, even if her daughter is still alive. I pray the child is alive. All of this brings back so many memories."

"Are you sure you want to continue on this job if it reminds you so much of losing Robbie?" Eduardo asked.

"The job in Colombia reminded me of Robbie much more. Fortunately, you were there, and you helped me get through a lot of my lingering grief over losing him, though I will always miss him." She stopped and pulled on Eduardo's hand so he'd stop walking. She looked at him with faintly glistening eyes, as if her thoughts brought painful memories. "You took a load off my suffering, which I'll always be grateful for." She hugged him, and then they continued walking.

Nikki glanced down the steep street. In the late evening light, long shadows stretched across the cobblestones. Two boys, tossing a soccer ball back and forth as if it were a basketball, broke up the drab shadows.

"I guess children have to play in the streets in this town," she said. "Changing the subject, what did you think of Sofía's attitude on Juana?"

"She overreacted about Juana. Since Sofía experienced open conflict with that woman, I guess her attitude is understandable. She also thinks Juana may have helped the kidnapper get away." He put his arm around Nikki's shoulders. "Moving on to better thoughts. Do you realize work is over for today and we now have the rest of the evening to ourselves?"

"Yes, but first I need to write a report to Floyd."

"Oh, no. That means no mini-moon tonight," Eduardo said, looking a bit downcast. He opened the car door for her.

"Hell, yes, we will enjoy a mini-moon . . . after I write my report," Nikki said. She inched in close to Eduardo to give him a kiss before she got in the car.

"Let's order a bottle of champagne," he said.

"Floyd said he'd ordered a bottle for us. The B&B will deliver it to our room."

At the B&B, once they received the luggage, Nikki settled down at the large desk in their suite and opened her laptop. She typed a detailed email to Floyd, repeating the license plate data and providing the information she had already obtained on the kidnapping. She also told Floyd how much better she felt having Eduardo with her for the investigation. *It reminds me*, she wrote, *of how he helped with the job in Colombia.*

The doorbell rang.

"Our champagne is here," Eduardo called to her. "Can you hurry on that report?"

"I've submitted it to Floyd, and I'm signing off the computer right now."

Nikki opened her suitcase and pulled out a sexy nightgown. She undressed quickly, dropped her clothes on the floor, and pushed them aside with the big toe of her right foot. Eduardo popped the cork on the champagne, poured chilled bubbly into glass flutes that came on the tray, and placed the bottle back into the ice bucket before turning to face Nikki. He walked toward her, carrying a glass in each hand. She slithered into her silky, see-through gown.

"Careful," he said, "you might make me drop the champagne."

"That's exactly what I'm trying to do."

CHAPTER 5

San Miguel de Allende—Thursday morning, day two after abduction

Nikki held the burner phone close to her ear. It was seven a.m. She'd called Héctor Sánchez's office, and the receptionist had placed her on hold while she checked if Mr. Sánchez would take her call. An incoming call buzzed in Nikki's ear. When she saw it was Floyd, she ignored it. She'd call him back on her secure phone after she talked with the attorney.

Waiting for a voice to return to the phone, Nikki stood in the semi-dark room. They'd enjoyed champagne and lovemaking last night, so she had not noticed much in their suite. She'd turned on a dim light so she could see enough to dial Sánchez, but thinking daylight would let her better appreciate the room Floyd had reserved for them, she pulled heavy curtains open and revealed sliding doors to a private balcony. She let out an audible sigh of delight as her eyes settled on the magical sight before her. The neo-gothic façade of San Miguel church—its pink granite and limestone bell towers added in the late 1800s by an architect reported to have been inspired by drawings of famous European churches—dominated the scene. The towers were close enough to appreciate the carved details. Stepping out onto the balcony, Nikki's gaze swept the view and landed on the patio below. Light and shadows danced with the movement of the lavender-colored blossoms of jacaranda trees as the breeze swept through the branches. Shadows even waltzed on the brick walkways. Nikki turned her attention to the interior of their suite as she stepped back inside. The decoration was pure San Miguel, with religious icons on the walls and furnishings which evoked a rustic feel and emanated an overall bucolic atmosphere that was also balanced with the comfort expected by well-traveled guests.

"Héctor Sánchez a sus órdenes," a masculine voice said, interrupting her delight at exploring the decorative details in the suite. His deep baritone voice sounded classy and charismatic.

Nikki returned to the balcony and immediately focused on business and forgot, at least momentarily, the beauty of the panorama from their terrace.

"I'm Nikki García. I've been engaged to locate Bibiana Lombardi. I understand you represent Paolo Lombardi, the child's father. The reason for my call is to see what you know about her whereabouts."

"You tell me. Her father hired me to gain joint custody because he feels his ex-wife is not capable of giving his daughter the attention she needs. You know the mother owns an upscale restaurant in San Miguel. Running a business like that takes a lot of time, and the child is often left alone in the private living quarters, or she spends time in the kitchen with the chef and kitchen help. That is not the kind of atmosphere for a ten-year-old, especially a girl. The day after I filed suit in the San Miguel courts, the child disappeared. Mr. Lombardi believes it's a tactical maneuver by his former wife to stall the case."

"I can assure you, it's not Sofía's ploy to detract from the case," Nikki said. "We believe the child was either abducted by her father or, worse yet, taken by organized crime. I ask for your cooperation in what is potentially a devastating case."

"I'll speak with my client," Sánchez said. "Give me your contact data in case I need to call you. In the meantime, you might counsel your client to report the crime. She is breaking Mexican law by not filing a denuncia on the abduction of her child. The only way the authorities can legally work on a case is to have the crime reported to them."

"Mrs. Lombardi is not going to file a denuncia," Nikki said. "Why involve the authorities if the father took the child?"

"I can tell you without a doubt, the father did not take Bibi," Sánchez said.

Nikki provided Sánchez with the number to her burner phone. She never traveled without disposable phones. As she walked back into the suite and placed the phone down, her skin tingled from excitement, a feeling she loved. She also felt relieved the man took her call. At least she'd made contact with him.

"He's as sly as a fox," she said out loud.

"Who is sly as a fox?" Eduardo asked. He had awakened and heard Nikki talking on the phone.

"Paolo Lombardi's attorney in Mexico City."

Eduardo got out of bed and walked up behind her. He put his arms around her waist and kissed her neck.

"You're working early this morning, my beautiful workaholic."

"The early investigator gets the job done," she said as she moved her upper body in closer contact to Eduardo. Then she turned around to look at him.

"Is that like the early bird gets the worm?" Eduardo asked as he gazed into her eyes and then kissed her.

"Why don't you shower and shave while I continue working," she suggested.

As Eduardo moved toward the bathroom, Nikki pinched his butt.

"Whoa," Eduardo said, startled. "I hope you won't pinch the Italian bambino snatcher like that. I understand Italian men do such things to beautiful women on the street in Italy but women, not wanting to be left out of the game, will pinch a good-looking man too."

"You're handsome. That's why I pinched you. To see if you're real."

Eduardo walked to the bathroom and stood by the door to look back at Nikki. He smiled and then winked at her suggestively. Nikki waved him on and dialed Floyd on her secure phone on speaker mode.

"Hey, Floyd, you're up early. When you called, I was talking to the Mexican attorney who filed the custody suit against Sofía Lombardi. He was firm on the fact that he knew nothing about the abduction, even blamed it on Sofía as a stall tactic. But he could be lying. I couldn't read him well, so you may have to visit him in Mexico City, eyeball to eyeball, when you fly in."

Floyd agreed to follow up with Sánchez in Mexico City and told her the report she'd sent him the night before sounded distressing.

"We may have organized crime involved, not a simple custody case, which changes our whole approach. We need to rethink our strategy, real pronto." Floyd's voice over the speaker phone sounded loud and clear.

"That's my fear, although Sofía is convinced her ex took the child," Nikki said. "Our eyewitness may not be the most credible person, sort of a gypsy type, but I do believe there's truth in what she told us."

Floyd asked Nikki if she was ready to take the information on the Sinaloa license plate.

Nikki sat down at the desk and grabbed a pen. "Ready."

Floyd proceeded to give her the details on four Sinaloa vehicles fitting the dark-gray truck and tag description:

VGM 56-10—Subaru, dark-gray, registered to Ana Valdez
VGM 56-17—Chevrolet, dark-gray, brand-new, registered last week to Raul Pérez
VGM 56-57—Ford, dark-gray, registered to Juana Beltrán García
VGM 56-83—Ford, dark-gray, registered to Juan José Cervantes

When Floyd finished giving Nikki the information on the tags, he informed her he also had addresses for each vehicle. He would email those to her later. Then he asked her if she had any thoughts on the tag data.

"I'd rule out the Subaru immediately since the witness described a big truck. I'd leave the new truck out too. The two Fords fit the description—the one registered to García and the one to Cervantes."

Nikki absentmindedly drew squares and rectangles on the paper pad where she'd written down the information as she listened to Floyd. Then she scribbled the name Juana Beltrán García on the pad. The call of a rooster startled her. He sounded very close, too close, as if he were just below the balcony. She walked to the sliding doors and closed them.

"My eyewitness's name is Juana," Nikki said, "but I did not get her surname."

"You need her full name as it might come in handy for the investigation," Floyd's voice said over the speaker. "The García woman from Sinaloa might be related to you."

"Related to me? Not a chance. García in this country is like Smith in the U.S."

"Now I have a question for you," Floyd's voice said over the phone. "Do you want to stay on the case, even though it may involve drugs and human traffickers out of Sinaloa? Those are hardened criminals, not the easy case I'd promised you."

"Absolutely, yes, I'll stay," Nikki said. "Besides, I have Eduardo with me. I feel much safer with him here."

Floyd asked Nikki to get Eduardo on the speaker phone so the three of them could talk. Nikki called out to Eduardo, who walked from the bathroom to join in the conversation. Floyd set the tone in the discussion and explained the case could involve human traffickers. He asked Eduardo to join forces with Nikki and him. He explained he needed another private investigator on this job.

"In case you don't remember," Eduardo said, "I'm a medical doctor. I'm also starting to consult at the orphanages the Barefoot Kids foundation has in Medellín. I don't know this type of work. I don't want to endanger anybody for my lack of knowledge."

Floyd reminded Eduardo that his help had saved his and Nikki's asses when they did the job in Colombia.

"Floyd and I would not be alive today if you had not orchestrated the plan to dig us out of that trouble," Nikki said, chiming in to convince Eduardo.

"Thanks, Floyd, but I didn't do anything you wouldn't have done yourself," Eduardo said.

He stood close to the desk with a towel tied around his waist. The white of the towel contrasted with his tanned body, a remnant of relaxing by the pool at the Miami Beach condo he and Nikki shared after he'd followed Nikki to the Sunshine State when she left her previous employer and joined Floyd's firm.

"No reason to be so modest of your accomplishments," Floyd said, his voice coming through loudly over the speaker, "but I'm looking for someone to help us with the case in Mexico now that we know it's far more complex and dangerous than we originally anticipated. You and Nikki are already there. I'll fly in as soon as I can. My question to you is the following: Will you join us as a private investigator for this case?"

"You can't be serious, Floyd," Eduardo said. "I don't have any experience, except with the military in Colombia, but that was a long time ago. You'd be better off hiring a qualified private investigator here in Mexico."

Floyd explained to Eduardo that P.I.s are not available in Mexico. He elaborated on the topic by saying Security Source was hired out of Miami to handle the Lombardi missing child case precisely because investigators don't exist in Mexico, except for a few retired Federales, federal police, who hire themselves out as "security advisors" to follow an unfaithful wife or husband and take compromising pictures. Floyd continued his explanation that some of the Federales are also hardened criminals. They either join the cartels and narcos, or accept bribes and avoid enforcing the law. These Federales are well trained in combat situations and intelligence gathering. Often they've been trained by the U.S. military or other U.S. facilities before they join the cartels. But they want the money the drug lords pay them. In addition, the cartels have low-level killers, called "sicarios." Floyd painted a dangerous picture.

"Sounds similar to what happened in Colombia," Eduardo said.

"Now back to working with us," Floyd said over the speaker. "You have an innate ability to know what to do and how to do it. Granted, doing investigative work in Mexico is more complex due to Mexican laws, but you've got what it takes to do this type of work."

"Don't you have someone in your Miami office you could send here?" Eduardo asked.

Floyd did not answer Eduardo directly. All he asked Eduardo to do was to think about it. He added he did not need an answer from him right now. Then his voice boomed over the speaker, as if he were trying to make his final point.

"Nikki has extensive training and experience in the field. She and I will do the hardcore work, but we can use your help."

"Look, Floyd," Eduardo said, "on second thought, maybe I should not turn this opportunity down. What I've learned by living around Nikki is that her work is her life. If I want to see this beautiful woman, I'll have to join forces with you. But keep in mind, I'll need a lot of on-the-job training. Nor am I saying I'm giving up my medical career. This is only for the duration of my sabbatical."

"Good," Floyd said over the phone. "We'll talk more about the work when I get there."

Nikki turned the phone off and placed it on the desk as she turned to face Eduardo. She threw her arms around him, then backed up a little and smiled.

"Working together, that calls for a celebration."

"At seven thirty a.m. it's too early for champagne," Eduardo said. "What does my romantic workaholic suggest?"

"Mimosas. We have leftover champagne from last night, and there's orange juice in the mini-fridge. I've always thought the best way to start a day is with a mimosa." She removed the towel around Eduardo's waist. "No underwear?" She shrugged her right shoulder, turned her eyes down slightly, and then looked up, teasing him with flirtatious eyes. "Maybe we don't need mimosas after all."

Eduardo reached his hand through the slit in Nikki's terrycloth robe. "What, no underwear either?"

Eduardo started kissing her as he undressed her. They both laughed and collapsed on the bed with a heap of terrycloth enveloping them like wrapping paper, which they tore off with the speed of kids opening birthday gifts.

CHAPTER 6

San Miguel de Allende—Thursday morning, day two after abduction

Nikki knew that narcos operations and the gangs who work with them were disciplined in a fashion similar to the military. They train the same, starting with both physical and medical evaluations, boot camp preparation, and seven or eight months of advanced training in firearms, explosives, and combat. Like the military, the narco armies have foot soldiers and career officers going all the way up to generals. The training instills a code of honor in them—to leave no fellow soldier behind and to obey their commander and to die for him if necessary. Same as the military.

She also knew that Fort Benning in the state of Georgia had trained Mexican soldiers on behalf of the Mexican government to combat drug trafficking organizations. Too many of these men turn and join the cartels when they complete their training. Not only do the cartels pay them more money, they also take care of their families if they die. The drug lords do more for them than the Mexican government ever could. In exchange, the cartels require two primary qualities: absolute loyalty and obedience.

Nikki had dozed in Eduardo's arms but now lay fully awake, thinking about the Lombardi case. To find a kidnapped child in Mexico promised to test both her and Eduardo to their limits. Nikki moved as unspoken anxiety arose in her conscious mind. She got out of bed for the second time and headed for the shower.

Eduardo stirred when he realized she had left. He joined her, his second shower in less than two hours. They took time to scrub each other's backs, and they nudged one another under the showerhead, each vying to wash the soap off under the meager dribble of water coming out of the nozzle.

"Breakfast time," Nikki announced as she toweled herself dry. "Then we'll visit the Jardín to find Juana. If we get there around eleven a.m., Juana might arrive by that time, but if she's not, we can go to the market place. I want to have a look at the bathrooms and get a sense if the kidnapper used the bathrooms to hide Bibi before making off with her."

"I don't think the bathrooms would have been used to hide the child temporarily. I took photos, and the bathrooms are very small, which provides too much of a chance for witnesses to have seen the kidnapper with her," Eduardo said, speaking loud enough for Nikki to hear him over the sound of water running down a poorly designed drain. He turned the water off, got out of the shower, toweled himself, and put his clothes on. "Besides, don't you remember the turnstiles at the bathrooms? There's no way anyone would use those bathrooms as an escape route."

"You're right," Nikki said as she finished dressing. "The kidnapper probably left the market as soon as possible. I would like to scour a block in each direction of the market. You never know what you might discover, so maybe we can go there later."

Eduardo carried a backpack with water, trail mix, and tissues for use in bathrooms devoid of paper. Over his neck, a camera hung from a sturdy cord. They strolled like tourists, gaping at the Spanish colonial Baroque and Neoclassical architecture, snapping photos of picturesque views of the narrow, winding streets. Occasionally, they moved aside when they heard a car engine coming up along the pedestrian streets. As hotel guests, Nikki and Eduardo had entrusted their rental to valet parking. In San Miguel, it was easier to take a taxi or walk.

Nikki and Eduardo stopped twice to admire antique carved wooden doors, doors that complemented the cobblestone streets. They plodded along toward the zócalo in the center of town. Walking down a steep cobblestone path, Nikki stepped around a sleeping dog that lay sprawled out in the shade of a jacaranda tree. Flies buzzed the dog's head, and his eyelid fluttered involuntarily when a fly landed on it.

Residential buildings, as well as those converted to commercial endeavors, manifested their uniqueness through the paint of their exterior walls, which were often done in clashing colors—bright yellows, burnt ochers, pinks, orange browns, cerulean blues, forest greens, and rust reds—all from vegetable dyes approved by the township committee to keep San Miguel authentic to its colonial roots.

Open doorways let Nikki and Eduardo glimpse perfectly tended patios otherwise hidden behind those impenetrable street walls, some homes with televisions blaring or the crying of very young children not yet in school. Open doorways held another hidden surprise for passing pedestrians, sharing the sweet aroma of honeysuckle growing in the courtyards. The rich odor of seasonings or pungent garlic emanated from interior patios of buildings converted to restaurants. Framed menus exhibited on stands near open doors or through windows attested to the many ethnic or international cuisines that had evolved in San Miguel to cater to foreigners now making this quaint and friendly town their home.

Five blocks beyond the Jardín, Nikki pointed at Juana trudging along, hunched over like a tired donkey, leaning heavily on her cane with each step. A shabby, pint-sized dog followed her—perhaps a Pomsky, a Pomeranian-Husky cross—its hair so matted and dirty it was almost impossible to distinguish it from a mutt.

"We're in for good luck," Eduardo said. "I was afraid she would have disappeared, never to be seen again."

"Buenos días," Juana said. She stopped and leaned on her cane as Nikki and Eduardo approached her. "Se levantaron temprano."

"Early?" Eduardo asked. He covered his eyes with his hands as he leaned his head back and spotted the sun high overhead. "It's almost noon."

"That's early for an old woman like me," Juana continued in Spanish. "This body doesn't move well in the morning. Not until after the fourth cup of coffee. I spike my coffee with mezcal to lubricate the old bones." Juana cocked her head to one side, took her hand to her neck, and rubbed it. Then, with a big, semi-toothless smile, she looked at Eduardo in a flirtatious manner as she scratched her left hip. "Mi chulo, you might try it sometime."

The Pomsky, looking as tired as his owner, had stretched out near Juana's feet.

Eduardo ignored her comment. "We want to ask you a few more questions," he told her in Spanish with a glance at the dog, which by now had its body curled up to scratch its mangy belly.

"Who wants to know? Both of you, or just you?" Juana asked. Her breath smelled of stale alcohol, like the day after a big binge.

"Well, both of us," he said. "Why?"

"You can ask me all you want, but that one there," she said, pointing at Nikki with her cane, "needs to pay me if she wants to pump me for more information."

Nikki started to speak, but Eduardo continued talking, ignoring Nikki's interruption.

"Pay you?" Eduardo asked. "Why is that?"

Juana looked at him, turned to look at Nikki, and then returned her gaze to Eduardo. "Well, for one, la doña didn't share my joint yesterday, afraid of what she might catch from me, I guess. Then she treated me with impatience and arrogance. Plus, I figure she's getting well paid to find Ricitos, so why shouldn't I participate in the wealth?"

"If I pose the questions, the information comes free?"

Juana looked at Eduardo for several seconds before answering. She cleared her throat and scratched her right armpit, almost in unison with the Pomsky, who had turned over and, with his hind leg now reaching up to his head, clawed behind one of his ears with vigor. Juana turned her head down to eye the canine. She took her left foot out of the dirty old sandal she wore and poked him.

"Enough of that, Fígaro. Stop."

The pup stood up, shook the dust off his skinny little body, whimpered, and looked up at Juana.

"Fígaro? From *Barber of Seville*? That's my favorite opera," Nikki said in amazement.

Juana ignored Nikki's remark. Instead, she observed Eduardo again for a few seconds.

"Free, yes, but I need two hundred grams of marihuana. So I'll trade you answers for that amount of mota."

Nikki looked at Fígaro. The pup was now licking Juana's toes, which were sticking out from under her long skirt.

"How about if I give you the money and you buy your own mota?" Eduardo asked. "And I'll throw in a little more so you can buy food for Fígaro so he won't eat your toes."

Juana threw her head back and laughed heartily. "What do you want to know?"

"For starters, we didn't get your full name."

"Bah, you already know that one," Juana said. She made an outward motion with her hand, as if she were annoyed with the question. "I'm Juana la Marihuana."

"I mean your full Christian name," Eduardo said.

"When you get as old as me, you tend to forget things you don't need. I suppose I had a regular name a long time ago, but now I'm Juana la Marihuana. You can even check the newspaper article on me. That's what they called me."

She rummaged through the pockets of her long skirt, eventually pulling out a wrinkled and yellowed newspaper clipping. She handed it to Eduardo.

"You see, this makes me official. It's more official than a birth certificate." Juana held her head and shoulders a little higher as she spoke.

"Maybe two hundred grams of marihuana will jog your memory about your full name?" Eduardo asked.

"Maybe," she said with a smile. "You never know till you try."

"You mentioned you'd charge la señora Nikki for answering her questions. So you must have information to share with us. If it's good, maybe I can convince Ms. Nikki to pay you."

"I want four hundred pesos," Juana said.

"How about that, Nikki? Are you willing to pay four hundred?" Eduardo asked. He spoke in English with Nikki to keep the negotiations sounding formal.

"Tell her yes, but the data has to be solid."

After Eduardo translated, Juana started talking. "Last night, I looked up at the night sky and saw the barefoot print embedded on the surface of the moon."

"Barefoot print on the moon?" Eduardo asked.

"Some people see a man on the moon. Some see a rabbit. I see the image of a barefoot print. The toes are at the top. One is very long, but a couple of toes are missing. Now, two days after the full moon, you can see it's a waning moon, but it still gives off a lot of light."

"And what does that . . . ?" Eduardo's voice, sounding perplexed, trailed off, not knowing what to ask.

"At this phase, my guess is Ricitos is now held at one of the abandoned silver mines near the town of Zacatecas. And will be held there for five days or a bit more."

"An abandoned silver mine?" Nikki sighed as she observed Juana. *This woman is out of her mind*, she thought.

"What I'm trying to tell you," Juana said, "is they will round up the next group in that area. They will stay there until the moon wanes, but the coyote needs a place to keep his victims. Each phase of the moon is about seven days, so from full moon to new moon is roughly fourteen days. He will need to be at the border at least two days before the new moon to get organized and get them across."

"This all sounds complicated. How do you know this?" Eduardo asked.

"An old woman knows things. There's a saying that the devil knows more because he's old than because he's the devil," Juana said.

"You're not that old . . ."

"You have no idea, mi chulo, how old I am. But I can tell you, one time the coyote came here with a young man who was talkative. I spoke with that chavo while the coyote paid for his purchases. As the chavo loaded sacks of beans, I stood behind the truck where the coyote couldn't see me and I asked the boy where they were going. He said Zacatecas, to a mine, a long-ago abandoned silver mine, before moving north to the border two or three days before the new moon."

"It won't be easy to find an abandoned silver mine without knowing exactly where to look," Eduardo said.

"That's another negotiation." Juana looked down at Fígaro, who had finally given up licking Juana's toes or scratching himself and had fallen asleep.

"Hey, wait a minute," Eduardo said. "Don't change the rules in the middle of the game."

COYOTE ZONE

"For an additional two hundred pesos, I'll tell you everything I know." Juana glanced down at Fígaro and whispered, as if to avoid waking him up from his canine slumber. "You see, I have another mouth to feed, my closest friend, the only one in the male species who never abandoned me."

Eduardo turned to Nikki, who nodded her okay.

"El chavo confided the coyote goes to market in the town of Zacatecas, near the cathedral, about two blocks away. He goes there before they leave for Chihuahua, to buy more water and other provisions he needs to replenish."

"That's all you know? That's not enough to find Ricitos with," Nikki said. She spoke in a smooth, slow tone, as if trying not to sound aggressive.

"It's more information than you had before," Juana said. She scratched her armpit again and laughed.

Her laugh sounds like a cackle, which fits with Sofía's description when she called Juana a witch, Nikki thought.

"You previously had the whole of Northern Mexico to search. Now you know where to go. You know the route the coyote uses, the old Pan-American Highway."

"That's not solid information," Eduardo said. "That's just a guess."

"The chavo snitched on the coyote, I tell you. When the coyote saw him talking to me, he raised hell. I quickly intervened and told the coyote, 'If this chavo doesn't have money to give to a poor old beggar woman like me, then you should share a bag of beans with me.' The coyote dismissed the whole incident and stopped harassing the young man. He didn't give me no beans either."

Juana leaned on her cane, as if she experienced pain and was holding herself up. It must have passed quickly for she soon stood up a little taller without leaning on the cane.

"What other info do you need to tell us?" Eduardo asked.

"If you go to that market, you'll see the coyote in that old gray truck or the brown one with the orange-colored flame I told you about. The chavo mentioned a woman called Petra. That's where the coyote buys bulk food in the market, from Petra's taniche. The chavo whispered that Petra also gets children for him. If they use the old Pan-American Highway, that means they cross in Juárez or thereabouts. That's it, mi chulo. My brain is

51

empty now. Go find la Bonita, mi Ricitos de Oro. And bring her back so I can see her."

"Find the pretty one, my little girl of the golden curls?" Eduardo said, repeating her words. "It'd help if you gave us more info to find her."

"I told you, it's all I know. Now pay up." Juana stuck her hand out, preparing to receive the payment for her work.

"I'll give you more if you will allow me the pleasure of driving you and Mr. Fígaro back to your home," Eduardo said.

"I've told you, Juana lives far away, too far for tourists to go. It's a poor neighborhood. It would scare you. And as for that one," she said as she pointed her cane at Nikki again, "la doña, she'd be afraid of getting tuberculosis or dysentery at my place."

"If it's so far, that's all the more reason for me to take you," Eduardo said.

"Juana has her bodyguard. Fígaro is the best bodyguard I've ever had." Juana stooped over and picked Fígaro up. "Besides, we're not ready to return home yet."

Nikki pulled out six hundred eighty pesos and handed it to Juana. "The extra eighty is for Fígaro's dog food."

"Did you hear that, Fígaro?" Juana asked. "Maybe la doña isn't so bad after all. Even if she doesn't like me, she's our friend now because she's taking care of my precious little pedigree."

CHAPTER 7

San Miguel de Allende—Thursday afternoon, day two after abduction

"Man, she likes you," Nikki said, "flirting with you and calling you 'mi chulo.' I'm sure she means it in an endearing way, such as my sweetie or my little rascal, but it can be crude too, like in *my pimp*."

Eduardo took Nikki's arm and brought her around to him in a twirling dance step.

"You're just jealous," he said. He smiled and looked into Nikki's eyes. "Jealous that she flirts with me. Jealous that she finds me attractive."

"Oh, yeah, I'm dying of jealousy," Nikki said. She made an ugly face, stuck her tongue out, crossed her eyes, and shook her hands in the air like a clown.

Eduardo touched her chin and laughed. "I love it when you look so glamorous. Now, on a serious note, my gorgeous clown, don't you think it's sort of strange Juana doesn't want us to know her full name or where she lives?"

"I also noticed she's pretty well educated," Nikki said. "The designer dog's name is taken from an opera character."

Eduardo laughed. "Designer dog? That's no designer dog. He's a mutt."

"I'll tell you, under all those fleas and dirt, he's a designer pup. People pay big bucks for them," Nikki said and then changed the subject. "She seems pretty confident about those routes taken by the coyote."

"Almost as if she's pushing us to investigate abandoned caves and ignore other possibilities."

"Like maybe she arranged the whole abduction herself."

"God, do you realize we're finishing off each other's sentences? And we're not even married yet."

Nikki looked at Eduardo and smiled. "Let's keep it more adventurous than that. I can think of exciting things, but we'll need to wait until we're back at our B&B."

"Can't wait," Eduardo said. He leaned in and kissed her lightly on the lips. "But before we create excitement, I think we should follow Juana home."

"Good idea," Nikki said. "Let's cross the street and get a cup of coffee while we watch what she does."

Eduardo looked at the building Nikki was pointing out. It was an enticing coffee shop at the corner of Recreo and Correo, with a storefront that bulged out a little into the street with two large windows, each one containing small panes of thick, undulating transparent glass. Each strategically placed window offered good views—one looking toward the street leading to where Juana was standing against a wall, and the other with a straight line of sight of the street heading into the center of town. Even though the location was fairly close to the Jardín, parking was allowed and cars lined the street. A pickup truck tried to move into a spot vacated by a compact car where both Nikki and Eduardo waited to jaywalk to the other side.

"Don't think he's going to get in that small space," Nikki said.

"Look again," Eduardo said as he took Nikki's hand. "These people can park in the tiniest places. It's almost as if cars and trucks shrink-wrap themselves into the spaces."

After witnessing just such a magical parking job, Nikki and Eduardo crossed the narrow street and stepped inside the coffee shop. Ambient music filled the air, and the aroma of coffee, cinnamon, and freshly baked bread added to the appeal of the place. An area a couple of steps lower, set up with tables, was available for patrons to stay and enjoy the offerings.

"I'll watch Juana and Fígaro while you get coffee for us," Eduardo said.

He put his arm around Nikki's waist and touched his lips to hers before she walked to the counter to place their order. He picked a table where he could see Juana through the window, standing less than half a block away, without being seen himself. He watched the Indian woman's slender figure grow thinner and taller or shorter and fatter as the undulating glass distorted her body, like a child jumping in front of a carnival fun mirror. Juana leaned against the corner of an orange and brown building, moving slightly away from the wall only to approach passing tourists or residents in obvious panhandling attempts.

Nikki placed two napkins, two cappuccinos, and two turkey jalapeño sandwiches on croissant rolls—heaped tall with lettuce, tomatoes, and fried cilantro—down on the bistro-type table.

"We might as well have an early lunch," she said as she sat on a high upholstered bench. "Watch the jalapeño peppers, my sweet. They might prove too hot for your delicate Colombian palate."

"Did you catch what Juana said about the barefoot print on the moon?" Eduardo asked.

"Yeah. Curious she should see the moon that way. Her use of the word barefoot reminded me of the time you took me to Barefoot Park in Medellín, with all those kids playing in the fountains, getting soaking wet. Such a nice memory." Nikki's hand went to her neckline to touch the world tree pendant—a nervous, absentminded habit she had fallen into since she started wearing the necklace.

"Barefoot Park," he said, smiling as he looked into Nikki's eyes. "That does bring back a lot of memories."

Eduardo glanced out the window, yet always kept alert on his immediate surroundings too. Juana was in clear view, and he watched as she pulled her skirt up to retrieve something. After she had let the skirt down again, he realized she was talking on a mobile phone.

"That woman carries everything she needs in the interior pockets of her skirt. She's a real magician. She's pulled a phone out and is using it. Can you imagine that? Maybe you should use long skirts like that."

"And dirty pantaloons," Nikki added with a devilish smile. "Now that would turn you on."

The thought brought a disgusting expression to Eduardo's face, and Nikki laughed. Eduardo placed his hand on Nikki's arm and spoke in a soft voice.

"Don't look now, but there's a guy, about fortyish, thin, and wearing lightly tinted glasses with wire-frames. He may be following us."

"Following us? We've just started this job. How can ... ?"

"He's working on a laptop at a table against the far wall. He came in after we did."

Eduardo took the top croissant section off his sandwich, removed the slices of jalapeño, and replaced the top back before eating it.

"Keep an eye on him." Nikki took a bite of her sandwich and licked her fingers. "Boy, is this jalapeño spicy."

"Let's strategize a bit. I'm thinking you should be ready to follow Juana if she moves from here," Eduardo said as he chowed down on the lettuce, tomato, turkey sandwich. "This sandwich is delicious." He sipped the cappuccino and moved in closer to Nikki. "If she leaves, you'll trace her steps, and I'll see what this guy does."

Nikki cleaned her fingers with a napkin, turned, and gazed out the window in Juana's direction.

"Look outside," Nikki said, keeping her voice low. "Juana seems engaged in an altercation."

Eduardo looked through the window and saw Juana taking menacing jabs with her cane at an older man. She had the top of the cane in his face, inches from his nose. He kept backing away from her, trying to keep from getting hit by holding his arms up like a boxer in a defensive stance. As he walked backward and relinquished a few feet, she thrust forward to cover every bit of ground he gave.

Eduardo put his cup on the table and stood, ready to go outside and protect Juana.

"Where are you going?" Nikki asked.

"Outside."

"No, you're not. Juana has made the guy walk away," Nikki said softly but firmly. "Don't make a scene in here. Besides, she's capable of taking care of herself. Let's watch. If she leaves, then I'll follow her. But what about the fellow watching us? What do we do about him?"

"We'll follow our strategy, or play it by ear as we need to," Eduardo said. "I'll see what he does."

"But if I lose track of Juana, I'll come back here," Nikki said. She finished the last bite of her sandwich and started drinking her coffee.

"That's the plan," Eduardo said, "but we need to flush him out and see if he is following us or if I'm just paranoid."

COYOTE ZONE

Eduardo turned his gaze away from Nikki and looked out the window to check on Juana. She sat on the high sidewalk, talking on a mobile phone again, her cane resting against the edge of the sidewalk. As she spoke, her arms flayed around. Then she stood, grabbed the edge of her long skirt, and brought it up to tuck the phone away again in one of her many pockets or pouches. She picked up her cane, smoothed her hair with one hand, and started walking with Fígaro trotting along at her side.

"She's coming this way," Eduardo whispered. "Follow her, Nikki, and I'll wait to see what this guy does. I'll either catch up with you or I'll text you. And take a look at the guy on your way out."

Nikki waited until Juana walked past the coffee shop before she stood up. She swept the room with her eyes to get a glance at their possible tail. Next, she hit the street to follow Juana.

Eduardo got up and ambled over to the dessert counter. One of the attendants immediately came to help him.

"Are these desserts for decorative purposes only?" Eduardo asked. He kept the man with the wire-frame glasses in the periphery of his vision.

"Oh, no," she laughed. "They are to be eaten. We have churros, the fried doughnut-type bread, dusted with cinnamon and powdered sugar. Churros are eaten by dipping them in a cup of heavy hot chocolate syrup. They're my favorite. We also have coconut flan, tres leches cake, margarita cake, and wedding cookies, which have lots of chopped almonds." She pointed at each variety through the glass countertop as she spoke.

Eduardo noticed the man with the wire-frame glasses used his mobile phone to make a quick call.

"Today there is also sopaipilla cheesecake, avocado-lime cheesecake, and sweet empanadas, all handmade here." She looked up at Eduardo with a smile. "What can I serve you?"

"I'll take a dozen wedding cookies," Eduardo said. "To go."

While Eduardo waited for the attendant to get the order ready, the man with the wire-frame glasses went back to working on his laptop. As Eduardo waited to pay for the cookies, he heard a ruckus outside, with people running and yelling. He forgot the sack of goodies and hurried outside.

Right before Eduardo stepped off the curve, a nondescript, light-beige-yellow Honda Accord bounced by at a hefty clip over the stone-laid street and turned at the first corner past the coffee shop. Two lanky teenage boys ran toward a group gathering about a block away.

"¡Llamen una ambulancia!" a voice in the crowd yelled. "Call an ambulance!"

Two or three people were helping a woman get up off the sidewalk.

"My God, it's Nikki," Eduardo cried out loud. He sprinted as fast as his feet could maneuver the cobblestones. As he got closer, he saw another person on the ground. His heart rate accelerated.

Nikki saw him approach and moved into his embrace.

"I'm okay, I'm okay." She repeated it twice more. "But I'm worried about Juana. She's not responding. That gentleman called an ambulance," Nikki said, pointing to a well-dressed older man with gray hair.

Eduardo, with Nikki in his arms, turned his head and looked down. He saw Juana's thin body, crumpled up like a rag doll, sprawled lifeless on the cobblestones. Her face was contorted out of shape, and her mouth was open, typical of someone who had died. Fígaro was licking her hand.

"She saved my life. Juana saved my life." Nikki's voice was shaking. "But I'm afraid she's dead."

Eduardo released Nikki, squatted down next to Juana, and examined her. He searched for a pulse in her neck and then noticed a severe wound to the left side of her head. He turned her head slightly to get a better look. Blood matted her dark tangled hair and pooled in the spaces between the cobblestones under her head.

Eduardo stood up and put his right arm around Nikki.

"You're right. She's gone. What happened?" Eduardo asked. He sounded alarmed, yet he tried to control his tone of voice.

"That crazy driver in the Honda ran over her. He didn't even stop. He was parked on the street and pulled out. Then the driver charged Juana and me. Juana shoved me to the other side of her, literally throwing me on top of the sidewalk right before he hit her. I don't know how she managed to throw me like that."

Eduardo took Nikki's hand. It was sweaty and shaky. He found the pulse at her wrist and checked it against his watch. Then he looked in her eyes and asked her to watch his finger as he moved it up, down, to the right, and to the left. Next, he felt her forehead.

"Tell me how you feel," he asked.

"I'm okay, I told you. It's Juana who—"

"Thank God it was Juana and not you. Why were the two of you walking together? I thought you were going to follow her?"

"When I stepped out of the coffee shop, she was panhandling a bit south of the shop. She saw me and asked if she could walk with me. I didn't want to be rude, so we walked together and talked for a few minutes as we went down the street until that driver . . . until that car hit her."

Nikki's entire body started shaking. Eduardo hugged her closer to him.

"We need to get you to the hospital and have you checked out."

"Yes, we'll go to the hospital after the ambulance comes for Juana," Nikki said. "You should also return to the coffee shop and see if that guy is still there. I'll stay here while you check the café."

"I'm not leaving you alone. Not now."

The older gentleman standing close by overheard Nikki and Eduardo.

"Besides getting the ambulance, I've also called the police. They'll show up to take a report and talk to eyewitnesses. If you two want to get to the emergency room, I can tell the police to catch up with you there."

"Thanks, but no, we'll stay put until the police arrive," Nikki said. She left Eduardo's embrace and moved closer to Juana, bent down, and searched for a pulse. She looked up at Eduardo and said, "Nothing. There's no pulse. You're right. She's no longer with us. I wonder if she knew she was saving my life at the risk of losing hers."

Nikki reached out to pick up Fígaro, who by now had lain down beside Juana.

"Now that she's dead, we have to take care of Fígaro," Nikki said.

The dog whimpered but allowed Nikki to take him into her arms without a fuss. With Fígaro firmly in her hold, she stood and clutched the pup close to her chest, not caring if he was covered in fleas.

"It's only now beginning to sink in," she said. "It was deliberate." She took a hand up to her neck. "Man, my neck really hurts."

Eduardo stepped behind her to check her cervical vertebrae as he gently massaged her neck and shoulders. In a minute or two, he realized her necklace was gone. He looked on the ground to check for it, but he didn't see it. He kept working on Nikki's neck and shoulders.

"Were you wearing your world tree necklace?"

"Yes. I haven't taken it off since you gave it to me. I'm not going to take it off. Juana told me it was a good omen."

"But you don't have it on now," Eduardo said.

Nikki reached a hand up to feel for it. The necklace was gone.

"It's lost. Oh, my God, we need to find it. It must have fallen off when Juana pushed me away from the oncoming car. I know it's superstitious, but we need good luck."

Nikki started looking on the ground to see if she could spot it. Her eyes dashed back and forth, but she saw nothing.

Eduardo walked around a bit, looking for it. He stepped up to the narrow sidewalk, and as he searched for it on the concrete, his eyes fell on a shiny object reflecting the bright sunlight. He bent over to pick it up.

"My world tree. Oh, thank you, my love," Nikki said when she saw him find it. "It's strange, but it makes me feel so much better."

As Eduardo tried to fasten the silver chain around Nikki's neck, he realized the clasp was broken.

"I'll fix it back at the hotel," he said as he placed it in his shirt pocket.

"If only we could fix Juana and bring her back to life. I can't believe all of this happened."

There was not much else to say, so Eduardo held her until the siren of an ambulance sounded and flashing lights came around the corner. It had taken twenty minutes or so for the first responders to arrive on the scene.

"Even if Juana had not died instantly, she would not have survived such a long wait," Nikki said as the paramedics climbed out of the ambulance.

Eduardo took his mobile phone out. "I'm going to call Floyd to tell him what's happened."

CHAPTER 8

Mexico City—Thursday afternoon, day two after abduction

Wishing he could get a cup of coffee to overcome the late-morning drowsiness he was feeling after his flight in from Miami, Floyd sat on a white leather sofa in the sleek law offices of Héctor Sánchez, located in the upscale district of Santa Fe on Mexico City's west side.

Prior to the 1960s, Santa Fe had been used as a sand mining operation. When the sand deposits became too costly to exploit, Santa Fe became a garbage dump. After another dozen years, the city closed the landfill to reclaim the land for the city's need for prime real estate. Megatons of good dirt were trucked in, large equipment was used to compact the soil, and the city opened the area to developers, who descended like vultures on roadkill. A new Santa Fe emerged. The advent of the North American Free Trade Agreement (NAFTA) in 1994 brought an unprecedented flow of money into the country, further transforming Santa Fe into the city's ultra-modern-style business center, with steel and glass skyscrapers, high-rise luxury condo buildings, and one of the largest shopping malls in Latin America.

A voice caused Floyd to turn toward the open reception area. The young woman, sitting behind a marble-top counter, made an appointment for a client over the phone. Floyd noticed the stone used for the counter matched the marble floor. He also noticed four attractive young women working in front of computer screens. The one on the phone finished her conversation and walked over to him.

"May I bring you a cup of coffee?" she asked.

"How about a cappuccino?" Floyd asked, not expecting even a successful law firm such as this one to offer a full range of coffee options.

"I'll prepare it, and María will take it to Mr. Sánchez's office for your meeting."

Five minutes later, another young woman, this one in a white tailored suit, emerged from a hallway and escorted Floyd back down the same hallway. The marble floor of the reception area gave way to thick, white, sculptured carpeting. The woman's attire made her fade into the lily-white of the walls and floor. Only her red lips, red nails, black hair, and false eyelashes contrasted with the minimalist décor of the offices.

They walked past a conference room and several individual offices—a few with open doors but most with closed doors. She led him to a corner office with the same white carpeting as the hallway.

"Mr. Sánchez, this is Floyd Webber." After the introduction, she disappeared into the hallway, closing the door as she left.

A tall man in his early forties rose from behind a desk to greet Floyd.

"Good morning. I'm Héctor. Let's sit at the table." His arm made a sweeping motion toward a round table in the room. "Coffee is already served. María brought you a cappuccino."

As both men took a seat, Floyd glanced toward the street through a floor-to-ceiling glass wall. He saw a large shopping center on the other side of the wide avenue. A huge flag flew at the top of the entrance to the mall, wind currents whipping the giant emblem into various contortions of green, white, and red, as if an unseen bull fighter snapped the tricolor cape to taunt an angry bull.

"So you want to talk about the Lombardi girl."

"Yes," Floyd said. "She's been missing since Tuesday. We have reason to believe she's been kidnapped. I want to know what information you have about it."

"Look, the child went missing one day after I filed a custody suit at the courts in San Miguel. The child's mother has a stormy marital and divorce history with the father. We have reason to believe the mother is faking her daughter's disappearance to prevent my client from obtaining joint custody."

The attorney took a cigarette from a red leather case lying on the table. A matching leather-covered lighter and a glass ashtray sat at the center of the table, and he pulled both toward him.

"Do you mind if I smoke?" Héctor asked.

"Go ahead. I'm a smoker too. Returning to our business at hand, if your assumption is wrong and the child has fallen into criminal hands, we're losing precious time to recover her."

"The coincidence is too great, and my client said, while the mother was still living in Italy, she pulled shenanigans such as this to prevent him from seeing his daughter. Also, why hasn't the mother filed a missing person report with the police?"

"You know perfectly well people here are afraid to bring the police in. You're an attorney. You know how corrupt the police are. They don't solve problems, they create them."

"Under Mexican law, it's illegal not to report it. She'll be considered an accomplice to the crime if the child has been kidnapped." He pushed the cigarette case and lighter closer to Floyd. "Help yourself."

Floyd ignored the cigarettes. "Fuck Mexican law. Why did a car try to run down my agent in San Miguel?" His voice got louder, his face became flushed, and he focused on Héctor so intently his eyelids and face wrinkled to the point he looked like a barn owl searching its surroundings.

"Run down your agent? You mean that woman who called me?"

"Her name is Nikki García," Floyd said. He grabbed the cigarette case and squeezed it till the top popped open. He dropped it with a thump on the table near the cigarette lighter.

"If someone tried to run over her, I had nothing to do with it. What the hell do you think I am? A goddamned ambulance chaser running people down to find customers? This is a serious law firm, not some fly-by-night operation."

"Then forget about client privilege and share with me what you know about the Lombardi girl," Floyd said. "We have a divorced couple's kid missing, and each parent is accusing the other of kidnapping her. We're not talking a custody case. We are dealing with the child's abduction. You and I need to talk before her body turns up dead somewhere."

"When I spoke to my client this morning, he said he'd fly in from Italy on Monday. He's extremely worried."

"Not till Monday? And he's a worried father, you say?" Floyd asked, his aggravation growing as the seconds ticked by. "He sounds like a very concerned father all right."

"All I can tell you is he's not responsible for her disappearance. If the mother has hidden Bibi, then we'll fight for complete custody."

"Look, Héctor, if Sofía hid her daughter, I would not be on this case," Floyd said, his voice angry and sarcastic. He gulped down the remaining cappuccino in his cup and stood to leave. "Excellent coffee. If only you were as interested in saving a missing child as you are in a good cup of coffee."

"Come back any time you need a coffee break. I imported that espresso-cappuccino machine directly from Italy. From the Lombardi factory in Milan. That's how I met Paolo Lombardi, the missing child's father."

"If I don't find out who tried to run over my agent this afternoon and who kidnapped that child, you bet I'll be back," Floyd said, walking out of the office without saying goodbye.

<hr />

The phone rang one, two, three, four, five times. Héctor Sánchez tapped his fingers impatiently on his desk. Six rings, then seven. Finally, a voice answered.

"Arturo, I want you in my office today. When you arrive, ask to see your daughter, as usual."

Héctor clicked the off button, stood up, and paced back and forth in front of the glass wall of his office.

Two hours later, María's father greeted her at the law office. Arturo Béjar, a former judicial agent in the federal police force, always paid his respects to Héctor Sánchez when he called on his daughter at work. On this occasion, Arturo handed her a large envelope and told her to handle it with complete discretion and take it anonymously to the hotel whose address appeared on it. He also gave her a small envelope with cash. He would text instructions for the cash later, he explained to her. María placed the two items into an empty manila folder she was carrying as she escorted her father down the white carpeted hallway to Héctor's office.

The visits didn't go unnoticed by her coworkers. It was obvious to María's colleagues that she adored her father, yet the staff suspected Arturo's meetings with the senior partner of the firm were not mere friendly social discourses but most probably business dealings with a sinister twist.

María kept to herself at the office. She figured others kept their distance from her either due to her father's relationship with the boss or due to her family's humble origins. Her father had been born in the very spot of Santa Fe where Sánchez's office building stood, but Arturo had been born in a one-room shack when the area housed the city's main garbage dump. He had been one of the lucky ones, though, and got out. He was smart, had graduated from high school at age sixteen, and managed to attend Mexico City's National Autonomous University on government grants, despite the cutbacks in educational programs under the newly installed president at that time—Miguel de la Madrid.

De la Madrid had inherited a country in complete economic collapse and had turned to the International Monetary Fund for a rescue package. Negotiations to receive financial aid outlined an austerity program de la Madrid was forced to implement. The program affected all areas of the economy, including higher education for the peasant class. The young Arturo had an uncle in the federal police agency who arranged for his nephew's scholarship by calling on a few of his contacts. Upon graduation, his uncle also arranged employment for him with the federal police.

When Arturo had left the federal agency three years before, he told his daughter he'd done it to open his own consulting business. He wanted to earn enough money to purchase one of those luxury condos in the glittery, new Santa Fe. His dream, he told his daughter, was to return to his roots but in the swanky style his birthplace had become.

It was common knowledge that attorneys in Latin America who cater to the wealthy often hire people to grease the wheels and improve the outcome of their cases, and Héctor Sánchez worked exclusively for the rich in Mexico City. Office gossip buzzed with intrigue that Sánchez had hired María as a cover for bringing her father to his law firm for consultations without raising suspicions.

What Sánchez had achieved, however, was the exact opposite.

As soon as María closed the door to Mr. Sánchez's office, Héctor deliberately lowered the volume of his voice.

"Arturo, I instructed you to follow her, not to kill her. What the hell were you thinking?"

Héctor's manner was controlled but demanding. Despite the air conditioning, beads of sweat on his forehead glistened in the light coming in from the glass wall in his office.

"I told Joaquín to follow the Americana. But a crazy puta, a street person called la Marihuana, was walking with the gringa, and the old woman stepped into Joaquín's oncoming car. It was an accident, but Joaquín could not stop. Otherwise la Americana would recognize him later. He had no choice but to leave the scene so he would not be implicated. It's unfortunate the Marihuana died, but don't be concerned, she was just a pothead."

"If that's the case, why was he driving down the street so fast? It's hard to drive fast in San Miguel. Get rid of Joaquín and get yourself a better asset," Héctor said. "I don't want anything to happen to that woman. I've hired you to find out where the child is. So do your goddamned work and call me when you know the child's location. When you find her, she cannot be harmed. Do you understand me?"

"Si, patrón." Arturo nervously adjusted his wire-frame glasses.

"Don't 'yes, boss' me. Your assignment is to find out what the Americans are doing and report it back to me."

"Consider it done, jefe."

"How long has Joaquín been working for you?"

"Three days."

"And where did you get him?"

"Estrada, my old boss from the federal police, recommended him. He knows him through a Colombian friend of his."

"Why didn't Estrada hire him?"

"He's a foreign national, waiting to get his permanent visa."

"A foreigner?"

"Colombian."

"I don't want problems, and Colombians can be problems. Get rid of him."

"Yes, patrón."

"Is there anything else you need to tell me?" Héctor asked.

"Since I'm here, I'd like to discuss something with you." The former federal agent lowered his eyes, focusing them on the portion of Héctor's diamond-studded Rolex watch peeking out from under the monogram of his white starched cuff.

"I'm listening."

"It's about the money. I need an advance to pay my people. Several months ago you promised me an increase, and I have not seen it yet."

"When we wrap this case up, you'll have plenty to pay your hired guns. You'll get a big bonus. If the outcome is right."

Sánchez stood and bid Arturo farewell.

CHAPTER 9

Zacatecas—Thursday, late afternoon, day two after abduction

Fígaro barked when Floyd tried to pick him up. The pup crouched behind Nikki's chair in an apparent need for protection.

"You feisty little opera mutt," Floyd said, "don't you dare leave your fleas here when you go back to your room. That's an order."

"Don't worry, Floyd. We stopped to purchase a powder that kills fleas and everything else that crawls on dogs," Nikki said. "Eduardo dusted it all over Fígaro. But if you find fleas on yourself, we still have plenty of it to sprinkle on you."

"Flea powder me? Like hell you will. Being an investigator gets more dangerous all the time," Floyd said. His voice sounded purposely sarcastic as he laughed with an equally sarcastic laugh. He wiped his hand on his pants leg, an unconscious reaction likely caused by the thought of fleas.

The three investigators sat in overstuffed accent chairs around a low coffee table in Floyd's room at the Quinta Real hotel in Zacatecas. Floyd flew in from Mexico City after his meeting with the attorney. He'd rented a truck at the airport in Zacatecas. Nikki and Eduardo drove in from San Miguel after the terrible ordeal of Juana's death. They'd all converged at the Quinta late in the afternoon.

Floyd got up to close the glass door that opened onto the balcony of his spacious suite, which overlooked a large, enclosed, oval-shaped patio on the ground floor that transformed the former bullfight arena into a stunning space with stone walkways and greenery, a space where the luxury hotel combined its amenities with history. The seventeenth-century San Pedro bullring was surrounded by Baroque pillars and stone arches. An old aqueduct that had delivered water into the town four centuries earlier was incorporated into the towering wall visible behind the newer construction of hotel suites. The architecture for the former box seats, which would have been reserved for dignitaries, jutted out like a grandstand in all its majesty, awaiting the next political dignitary, movie star, or other entertainment royalty. It stood as a sentry, guarding the presidential suite tucked behind it—a suite used by well-heeled bridegrooms spending their wedding nights behind its stuccoed walls in the historic confines of the most commanding view of the arena.

"We need to determine if the driver was aiming for Nikki, for Juana, or for both of them," Floyd said. He took one more sweeping glance at the arena through the balcony door and returned to his seat. "What do you think, Nikki? Were you the target? Or were you simply an unlucky bystander?"

"From Juana's actions, she must have thought I was the target. You can't imagine what strength that thin little woman had. She grabbed my arm and threw me like a boomerang onto the sidewalk." Nikki looked down at the carpeting and saw Fígaro stretched out near her feet. "Poor little guy." She scratched Fígaro's head, and he turned over so she could scratch his belly, which she complied with for about a minute. "Juana definitely saved my life."

"Let's consider the reasons it happened," Floyd said. "Do you think they may have been out to kill Juana because she knew too much and had talked to you? Do they know you're working for Sofía Lombardi? Were they aiming to kill both of you?" Each question sounded increasingly rhetorical.

"If it's related to our case, how did they find out about our investigation?" Eduardo asked. "Besides us, only Sofía and Héctor Sánchez know about our operation."

"I have no doubt it's connected to the Lombardi case," Floyd said.

"Who else but the attorney could leak it?" Nikki asked. "And if Sofía needed to get rid of Juana, she would not have had her killed in front of me. The taxi driver who took us from the Tuesday Market to the town's central plaza may have overhead my conversation with you, Floyd, where

I stated a few facts about the Sinaloa license plates. Also, he could have seen us talking with Juana at the market before we jumped in his cab."

"Never give out sensitive data in front of others unless it's in code," Floyd said.

"Yeah, I know, it was stupid of me, but do you seriously think a random taxi driver could have given that info to someone trying to harm us?" Without waiting for an answer, she walked to the bathroom to wash her hands and get rid of any flea powder she picked up when she scratched Fígaro.

The doorbell rang. Floyd walked over, checked through the peephole, and opened the door. He stood in the doorway and looked to both sides of the hall. Then he waved his hand to allow a uniformed hotel employee into the suite. The bellman pushed a food cart right up to the coffee table. He took dishes, food trays, and napkins with flatware rolled up inside from the cart and put them on the coffee table. He also placed glasses, a bucket of ice, and soft drinks on the low table. Floyd, still standing by the open door, handed him a cash tip and signed the tab before the young man pushed the cart into the hallway.

"We don't know if they planned to get me later," Eduardo said, continuing Nikki's thought. "An older gentleman who called the ambulance told us the Honda did not have license plates, only a temporary tag in the rear window, but he stated it was falling off so the paper was curled over and he couldn't read it..."

Eduardo stopped in mid-sentence. His face turned red and reflected a series of emotions, like the face of a cartoon character going from normal to pensive to inquisitive to surprise.

"That old man," he said. "He must have been part of the crime. He stood there to make certain it went according to plan."

"Hey, you're right," Floyd said. "To control the scene and gather information on both of you."

He removed the covers from the food trays and handed them to Nikki, who was returning from the bathroom, and she placed the lids on a newspaper on top of a chest of drawers. Floyd handed a plate, napkin, and flatware to Eduardo and then did the same for Nikki.

"A little snack," Floyd said, motioning to the spread. "I missed lunch."

"Can you believe no one took a video?" Nikki said as she sat down and placed an empty plate on the coffee table. "In the U.S., the incident would be all over the internet by now."

The aroma of chili, oregano, and onions melded into a bouquet of appetizing scents. Floyd served himself three gorditas. Even Fígaro raised his head, sniffed, and looked around.

"I'm convinced it was not an accidental hit-and-run," Eduardo said. "This driver was out to kill. And I'm sure Nikki was his target. When I arrived at the scene, I focused on making sure Nikki did not go into a state of shock. I can't believe I failed to see that critical piece of evidence, the old man, the one who called the ambulance..."

Eduardo stopped in mid-sentence again. He served himself two sopes—small, thick corn tortillas filled with refried beans, chicken strips, onion, tomato chunks, and spices, topped with sour cream and guacamole.

"Let me backtrack a little," Eduardo said. He put his plate of food on the coffee table, and his focus seemed to center on the information he'd processed in the last couple of minutes. "When Nikki left the coffee shop, a guy I suspected of tailing us made a very quick call from his mobile phone. Within two minutes, more or less, I heard the commotion outside, and I left in a hurry to see what was going on."

"We can assume he tailed you both and that call notified the driver about Nikki leaving the café," Floyd said. "That confirms to me Nikki was the target."

"Let me complete my thought," Eduardo said. "Earlier, I did not get a good look at a man on the street, an older man that Juana had an altercation with. He was standing with his back to us. Nikki and I watched from inside the café. But I'm sure he's the same man who called the ambulance and the police, the one who controlled the scene. He formed part of the setup. So maybe Juana was the target."

"God, that *was* the same guy. How did we miss it?" Nikki asked. She felt as if she might be sick and need the bathroom again.

"My meeting at noon today with Héctor Sánchez, the attorney for Mexico City's rich and famous, didn't help at all," Floyd said. "I questioned him about the attempt on Nikki, and I had the impression he did not even know about it. Changing the subject, I've been in touch with a contact in

Mexico City, Fernando, who works at Gobernación. That's equivalent to our Homeland Security. So where do we go from here?"

"What can your contact do for us?" Eduardo asked.

"He can provide information. He can order a group of Federales, a few federal police he can trust, to help us with the investigation. Of course, we'd need to give him a solid lead, and we'd need to step aside once they get involved. We can't coordinate with them. It'd be against the law to work side by side with them."

"That's understandable," Eduardo said.

Floyd took a bite of a gordita, a small but thick tortilla hollowed out and filled with green chile, beans, ground beef, and cheese.

"Man, these are good." He wiped his hands on a colorful green, white, and red napkin as he savored his food.

"I'd say Eduardo and I stake out the market place," Nikki said. "Juana told me a woman called Petra runs a store there that sells boxes of bottled water and sacks of beans to the coyote. All we need is a day or two to find out if Juana gave us solid info."

"So you do feel Juana was trustworthy enough for us to follow her indications?" Floyd asked, helping himself to another gordita, the spicy filling overflowing onto the plate. He also took a sope, which he demolished in two hungry bites.

"Nikki and I talked at length about that issue," Eduardo said. "We came back to the same point every time."

"And that is ... ?" Floyd asked. He used his fork to pick up chunks of food that had fallen off the sopes and gorditas onto his plate. "I can't stop eating these little tacos, they taste really good."

"We don't have any other leads," Nikki said, answering his question. "Juana was an eyewitness to the kidnapping, but we don't know if she was trustworthy or not. Despite being a street person, presumably even hooked on drugs, she made perfect sense when she talked. And yes, she made strange comments about the moon and so forth, but that's how she tracked time."

"Are you sure she saw the kidnapping?" Floyd asked.

"Yes. I confirmed it with Sofía," Nikki said. She picked up her plate and served herself a sope for the first time. Fígaro jumped up and placed his front paws on her leg. "Oh, no you don't. There's no begging for food in this family." Nikki took his paws off her leg and pointed her finger toward the floor as he continued to look up at her, his mouth salivating. "Sit, Fígaro."

And the Pomsky obeyed.

Floyd raised his eyebrows. "Looks like your mutt has some training. Now, getting back to your plan. You and Eduardo stake out the market, and you sit there and wait for the coyote to arrive. Then what?"

"I'll dress like a peasant woman with old-style peasant clothes from Walmart or Soriana. I'll add the stuff I asked you to bring to complete my attire. I'll pretend to be looking for a coyote to get me into the U.S.," Nikki said.

"Is that why you're wearing that weird necklace, so you fit in with the local indigenous population?" Floyd asked.

"Hey, it's the world tree. Eduardo bought it from a local vendor in Palenque." Nikki took her hand to her neckline and felt the pendant. "Juana told me it's a good luck charm and will help me find the child with the golden curls. I lost it when Juana whipped me out of the way, right before the car hit her. Eduardo found it before we left the scene of the accident, and he fixed the clasp as I drove on the way here."

"Give me a break," Floyd said. "You now have a dog and you've become superstitious. What's next?"

"Whatever it takes to find Bibi," Nikki said. "My dog is a Pomsky and has a name—Fígaro."

"Is Pomsky what you call a mutt these days?"

"Don't be funny, Floyd. A Pomsky is a designer dog."

"Looks like a mutt to me," Floyd said. "At best, he looks like a baby wolf."

Nikki sighed and shook her head.

"Getting back to our planning," Eduardo said. "I'll dress like a homeless drunk to keep an eye on Nikki while she's in the market."

"Then the two of you find the coyote. So what am I supposed to do?" Floyd asked. He snapped open the top on a Coca-Cola can, poured it into a glass, and added ice.

"You can take care of Fígaro and sing to him," Eduardo said. Then he broke into song. "'Hey, Fígaro! I'm here. Fígaro here, Fígaro there, Fígaro up, Fígaro down,' and I don't remember the rest."

Eduardo and Nikki laughed while Floyd kept his hands over his ears to show a lack of appreciation for Eduardo's baritone voice.

"Floyd here, Floyd there, ready to save us, you'll back us up," Nikki sang, trying to emulate Rosina's mezzo-soprano voice—the heroine from the *Barber of Seville*. "Back us up, back us up, day and night, back us up, search for us, search for us from a helicopter."

"Why don't you sing Falstaff's part? I like him better," Floyd said. "Don't forget, he's a character in this opera too."

"No, Floyd," Nikki said, correcting him. "Falstaff is a comic character created by Verdi in the opera by the same name, *Falstaff*. Fígaro is in *Barber of Seville* by Rossini."

"Enough of that, let's get serious."

"I am serious," Nikki said. "Hire a helicopter to locate where he's keeping the kids."

"And I get out of the chopper in my shining white armor with my beautiful white stallion, arrest the villain, and release the captives," Floyd said. "Nikki, I don't want to rain on your parade, but that's not a feasible plan."

"I mean that I'll go underground with the coyote so you can locate where he's keeping the kids. I'll wear a GPS locator chip, like I did in Colombia. You coordinate with your contact in Mexico City. Between all of you, you can locate me and figure out how to set us free."

"Don't fantasize, Nikki. How can Fernando, my contact in Gobernación, and I set you free before you're seriously hurt or dead? Don't even think of going underground."

"Me? Fantasizing? I almost got killed earlier today. Remember? I'm cognizant of the serious situation we're in. I'm only simplifying as we brainstorm. But let me ask you, Floyd, do you have a better plan?"

"Wish I did," Floyd said pensively. His eyes seemed to focus beyond the glass door leading to the balcony. "But I'm not putting you in such a dangerous position that we live to regret it. Women trekking and crossing the border with coyotes are subject to getting raped or even killed."

"Younger women risk that, but if you brought me the mask I requested, I won't look young or even middle-aged, and no one would touch—"

"We should investigate more before we pursue the option you and Eduardo are presenting," Floyd said, interrupting Nikki. "I'm going to San Miguel tomorrow to gather information. See what I come up with, and we'll devise a plan. Fernando will also get the police report on the car accident and other intel for me."

"What is there to investigate in San Miguel?" Eduardo asked. "And how much time will we lose in locating the coyote here and miss our opportunity to get the child back?"

"Eduardo makes a good point," Nikki said. "By the way, Floyd, you *did* bring the masks and stuff I asked you for when we spoke over the phone? I hope you brought good items, to make both Eduardo and me look convincing as peasants. Also, you did bring GPS locator chips, like we used on the job in Medellín, didn't you?"

"Yep, but it's a chip you can place in the sole of old-looking tennis shoes. Before I left Miami, Charlotte prepared the shoes for you. She even made small holes at the toes."

"Nikki has been using new training shoes with a chip to track her steps," Eduardo said.

"Yeah, Charlotte mentioned you had new shoes with a training device. That's where she got the idea to get a new pair and scuff them up. All you'll have to do is simply take out the training chip and replace it with one of the GPS chips I brought. And wait till you see the latest full-body mask used by undercover CIA agents. You'll love it. Even Eduardo won't recognize you."

"Even now, on mornings before I comb my hair, I look terrible and wonder if Eduardo knows who I am," Nikki said.

"That's not true," Eduardo said. "You always look gorgeous."

"Okay, lovebirds, besides the new mobile phones, secure and untraceable, with apps and powerful GPSs for us to track you, I brought a whole lot more," Floyd said, returning to the topic of their disguises and equipment.

"So we're ready to follow the kidnappers," Nikki said.

"We can buy a day or two before you take a drastic step, Nikki. I'm calling Fernando tonight to coordinate and see what info he's managed to get on the hit-and-run," Floyd said as he started stacking the dishes and gathering the flatware for room service to pick up.

"When you call him, I need a favor," Nikki said. "Ask him to provide a credible name of someone in Oaxaca who could serve as my contact to set me up with Petra."

"Who's Petra?" Floyd asked. "You've mentioned her twice."

"It's the name Juana gave us of a woman who sells food supplies and other provisions to the coyote and who might be coordinating people, even kids, from this area for the coyote to take into the U.S.," Eduardo said.

"My point is for you to ask Fernando for a contact," Nikki said. "It has to be a person who will not blow my cover. It could be an Indian woman from the Oaxaca Mountains where there's no phone service so Petra can't call her."

"Why Oaxaca?" Floyd asked.

"My parents grew up in Oaxaca before they moved to Minneapolis," Nikki said. "And my grandparents lived in the city of Oaxaca until they passed away. My brother and I spent the summers and holidays with them, and that's where we learned the Zapotec dialect. My grandmother's housekeeper was an indigenous woman from the mountains."

"And that makes you an expert?" Floyd asked.

"Makes me more of an expert than either one of you. My brother and I still speak it, and what's more, I can imitate the accent of the mountain tribe she came from, making me believable as my undercover self, but I'll need that contact as soon as possible."

"Okay. I'll follow up with Fernando," Floyd said. He stood up and took out his wallet. "By the way, here are a couple of Fernando's business cards with his mobile phone in case either one of you needs him in a pinch. I've already told him you might call him. If he doesn't answer, just leave your first name and phone number. I gave him both of your numbers. He'll get in touch as soon as he can. I recommend you memorize his number."

Floyd opened a large black suitcase and pulled out two white plastic garbage bags, which he handed to Nikki.

"Here's the stuff you asked for, including two nine millimeter Lugers. Fernando got them, one for each of you. They're completely illegal in Mexico and will get you in heaps of trouble with the law, if discovered. Fernando could get them registered under aliases, but we don't think that will help any. Nikki, you need to consider very carefully if you really want to carry one. Obviously, it's impossible to avoid detection in a frisking." He handed both guns to Eduardo.

"I'll think about it," Nikki said as she peeked in the bag. "Feels like my birthday."

"Then you'll like this lipstick for your birthday," Floyd said, handing Nikki a tube about three inches long and three-fourths of an inch thick. "It's the new stun gun female agents are using at the CIA. Unleashes four point five million volts. Zapping someone for three to five seconds will incapacitate a person's muscle system, making them lose voluntary muscle control. It also causes disorientation and mental confusion in the victim."

"Thanks. I like that. I've read about them," Nikki said as she inspected the case.

"Here are the instructions, but basically you'll take the top off," Floyd said as he took the case back from Nikki and demonstrated how to remove the top. "This button here will do it. You push it and *zap* goes the jolt, disabling an attacker. You can't zap yourself if you simply pay attention to your actions. At the opposite end, you have a small toggle, like a hinged switch. It will disable the whole device so the attacker can't turn it on you if he wrestles it away."

"I'll practice using it," she said. "Eduardo, pretend to be my attacker." Making a fist, she punched his arm in a playful manner.

"How about I try it on you instead?" he asked. He smiled at Nikki, his eyes spilling over with his love for her.

"Okay, lovebirds, here are the spy phones I've told you about," Floyd said as he opened a small bag and took out two small, plastic mobile phones.

"Spy phones," Nikki said as she pushed strands of her hair behind her ear. "I like that too. Let me see them."

"Not very fancy. They look like cheap phones for kids, but in reality they contain the highest powered code possible short of the NSA's code currently inserted in android phones to collect data. These act like a short-circuit TV system. Charlotte will monitor them from our Miami office, but they are internal to us and not connected to national security systems in any way."

"Do they have long-length batteries?" Nikki asked.

"Of course, and let me explain that, even when the phones are turned off, the cameras and microphones are on. Even though they are synched to our command center in Miami, they are currently off-line. Charlotte can turn them on, but as soon as you need them, any one of us can call Charlotte. She'll monitor them, with help from two assistants. They'll work in shifts. Let me show you how you can turn them on remotely too."

"Wait a minute," Eduardo said. "You mean you can spy on us twenty-four-seven?"

"Yes."

"Well, I don't like that. It's an invasion to our privacy," Eduardo said, his facial expression showing deep displeasure.

"I understand," Floyd said. "But Nikki's been talking about going underground, and the only way I know to make sure she gets out alive is to listen in. But if you don't want them, then don't go on this mission."

"For privacy," Nikki said, "can we put them in a different room and wrap them in a towel so photos and conversations are not transmitted? Can we do that at least for the periods when Eduardo and I want our privacy?"

"Hell, yes, you can do that. But be aware that, anytime you block the spy software, we will not see or hear people or circumstances that may endanger your lives."

"I want to make sure I understand," Eduardo said. "You, Charlotte, Nikki, or I can turn the mikes and video on? But even when we turn them off, they are still on?"

"That's right, once they're on-line," Floyd said. "You can turn individual phones on and off. They need to be turned on for you to be able to use them like a normal phone. But let me tell you, the NSA has you on its radar anyway. You for your travels to Colombia, and since Eduardo is a Colombian national, he may be tailed electronically too. They'll collect data but won't access it unless they need to, but you'd be surprised how much info the U.S. government has stored away on people."

"Yeah, I know. I'm fully aware of the social network graphing the NSA conducts," Nikki said. "First, it started a pilot program in 2010, but after that, it continued to monitor people, even if the only justification was that an American citizen had contact with an ice cream street vendor in England or a bozo salesman in Turkey."

"Bozo?" Eduardo asked.

"Oh, I'm exaggerating," Nikki said. "Bozo is a traditional alcoholic beverage in Turkey that dates back to the Ottoman Empire. It was sold for centuries by street vendors and a few still do in the old neighborhoods of Istanbul. But seriously now, I'd feel much safer if we did use these spy phones."

"Are you okay with that, Eduardo?" Floyd asked.

"If the lady says yes, then the answer is yes," Eduardo said, but he looked hesitant and not totally convinced.

"Why don't you two talk it over and tell me how you want to proceed with this type of surveillance. Your old secure mobile phones are still good, of course. But if Nikki can only carry one, it'll have to be the spy phone. Regular phone calls can be made from the spy phone, but only if you absolutely must use it."

"And we'd probably have to erase any trace of calls we make," Nikki said.

"That's right. Once you get back to your room, go through the other items you requested and make sure I brought everything you need. I even included a flashlight, a compass, and a small tool box for Eduardo. When we get together for dinner tonight, you can give me your final answer on the spy phones."

"We can answer the spy phone issue right now. We will use them," Eduardo said.

"Good," Floyd said. "We'll finish our planning over dinner. I'll drive to San Miguel tomorrow and pay a visit to Sofía."

Nikki handed the goody bags to Eduardo, and she picked Fígaro up.

"We need to get a leash for him."

Floyd opened the door to the hallway, glanced down both sides of the hall, then he looked at his watch.

"It's almost five. Let's meet at the Plaza Restaurant here in the hotel at six for a real dinner."

"Are they even open at that time?" Nikki asked.

"Yeah, I checked. The crowd hits about eight p.m. so we should have the restaurant to ourselves."

Nikki carried Fígaro as she and Eduardo walked to their own suite down the hall. Eduardo opened the door, stood in the doorway, and placed the two bags inside the room. Then he turned and picked Nikki up in his arms. Fígaro looked as if he owned the place as he peered down from his high perch in Nikki's arms while Eduardo swept them both across the threshold and kicked the door closed behind them. Eduardo's face burst into a big smile as he put Nikki down. He kissed her and then gazed at her.

"We can enjoy a mini-moon before going to dinner."

Nikki smiled and backed away a little as she put Fígaro on the floor. Then she stood up and inched her fingers seductively across Eduardo's torso until her arms embraced him. She looked up at him and smiled.

"You're amazing. You could've been an opera star."

"Oh sure," Eduardo said, laughing as if he enjoyed the compliment.

In a tender touch, he caressed Nikki's ear and smoothed a couple of loose strands of the shiny, dark hair dropping over her forehead. Then he held her chin in his hand and looked into her eyes.

"I love you," he whispered in a voice that was both caring and adoring.

He embraced her and brought his lips to hers, kissing her slowly at first, then more intensely, and finally with complete passion and abandon.

Nikki responded, expressing her own passion. Slowly she pulled away just enough to reach the buttons on his shirt to undo them, in a sexy and seductive manner, as she slipped his shirt off and held it like a bullfighter might hold a cape. She taunted him with it. Next, she untied his belt as she swayed side to side, rubbing sensually against him, and tossed it onto the bed. She took the shirt, still in her hands, and brushed it against his body in a teasing move before dropping it on the floor. Then she looked up at him, her face beaming with both love and triumph.

Eduardo picked Nikki up in his arms again and laid her on the bed, adjusting a pillow under her head. He took his shoes and socks off and climbed onto the foot of the bed, where he proceeded to remove Nikki's sandals, tossing them on the floor, one by one, with a bang.

Fígaro barked. He stood up and ran around the room like a wild dog, barking the whole time, but he finally calmed down and lay by the door, his ears perked up and listening attentively to every sound, like a watch-man guarding the whole room.

Eduardo started pulling Nikki's pants off, and the bed rocked up and down as he struggled to remove them. Then he stretched his body on the bed next to her and glided an arm around her. They both laughed with joy.

As their laughter became louder, Fígaro growled and started howling. He attempted to jump on the bed, but when his short legs prevented him from climbing up, he clawed the side of the bed in an obvious effort to protect Nikki. She spoke to Fígaro, trying to quiet him down, but he wouldn't stop his commotion. Eduardo sat straight up in bed. Their newly adopted pet kept barking, as if defending Nikki or trying to warn her of eminent danger.

"Sit," Nikki commanded.

Fígaro stopped barking and lowered his hind legs into a sitting position, keeping his eyes on Eduardo the whole time.

"Don't look at me that way, Fígaro," Eduardo said. "I promised Nikki a mini-moon, and now you're spoiling our romantic rendezvous. We won't have amorous interludes once our spyware is listening to us, so give us a break." Eduardo reached down, picked Fígaro up, and looked the pup straight in the eyes. "You and I have to talk, man to man."

Fígaro turned his head away, as if the canine knew he was in trouble and wanted to avoid making eye contact with Eduardo.

Floyd was waiting for them as Nikki and Eduardo walked into the Plaza Restaurant. Nikki looked around her in amazement at the décor of the place as the maître d'—who wore a white shirt, black pants, and a red sash around his waist in appropriate bullfighting fashion—showed them to their seats. The restaurant, set on three tiers with expansive windows boasting splendid views of the converted bullring and panoramic vistas of the aqueduct from every single table, also featured high ceilings with gigantic solid wood beams. Artwork hung on walls at the rear of the highest tier.

Floyd placed a copy of the latest edition of the *Reforma* newspaper on top of a white plate set on a red charger at Nikki's seat. She looked at the photo of the accident without picking the newspaper up.

"God, this picture is certainly graphic."

Nikki doubled the paper in half and handed it to Eduardo. He shook his head and set it aside.

A waiter arrived carrying a pitcher of water. After filling the glasses, he placed the pitcher in the center of the table. They waited to talk until he took everyone's order and returned to the kitchen.

"It's strange," Floyd said. "I can't find any mention of eyewitness accounts in the *Reforma* article or on-line either. Wouldn't the newspaper interview that older gentleman you mentioned? Reporters often quote a witness's testimony, especially in a hit-and-run incident."

"That older gentleman, who seemed like a Good Samaritan, would not want to call attention to himself," Eduardo said.

"You're on to something, the way you say he controlled the scene," Floyd said. "Any chance he followed you up here?"

"Good God," Nikki said. "If he tailed us, then I can't be seen on the streets here in Zacatecas with Fígaro, especially if I'm in disguise. I can't risk blowing my cover. What a shame. That little guy and I are really bonding."

"I'll take care of him," Floyd said. He paused, looked around the room, and came back with another comment. "Man, I can't believe I said I'd take that fleabag."

"I'm all for keeping him in Floyd's room," Eduardo said. "That will give us—"

Nikki shot Eduardo a killer look.

"Fine, I'll keep him in my suite for tonight to see how it goes, but I'm not adopting him," Floyd said. "You guys can feed and walk him twice a day. If he behaves himself tonight, I'll help with him as needed. Back to work issues. Fernando found out Juana had a roommate, a woman. He got the address for me, so I'll stop by tomorrow to interrogate her while I'm in San Miguel. Hey, what if I take Fígaro with me and return him?"

"No way," Nikki said, her voice emphatic. "He's *my* dog now, and if you don't believe me, just ask *him*."

"He's definitely Nikki's dog," Eduardo said. "You can't believe how he protects her when—"

"You can help us out if we need it over the next few days," Nikki said, interrupting, "but don't call him a fleabag."

"Okay, okay. Forget I said it," Floyd said. "He is a cute dog. He's growing on me, so don't take offense when I tease about his fleas. Before I leave for San Miguel tomorrow morning, I'll drop him off at your room."

"Thanks. We'll bring you his water bowl for tonight," Eduardo said.

"Changing the subject," Floyd said, "Fernando gave me the name of Ramona Tafoya, someone he knows in Oaxaca. Be careful, since you never know if she is a double agent, but Fernando has always had good results with her. But don't go underground, Nikki. I'm concerned Juana may have been more involved in the Lombardi kidnapping than you might think. You and Eduardo get the lay of the land here tomorrow. I'll work in San Miguel, and we'll reconvene tomorrow evening in my suite."

"I won't take unnecessary risks," Nikki said, "but I need the freedom to make the call if and when I go underground. Trust me."

"I do trust you, Nikki, but do you know how bad drug and human traffickers are?" Floyd asked. "There are only three of us, and kidnapping gangs often work for the narcos, who are paramilitary organizations with superbly trained narco-armies."

"You've said that before, and I'm fully aware of the dangers. I'll be careful, but I will determine if I go underground. If something happens to me, I don't want either one of you to feel guilty. I'm doing this type of work because I want to."

"If that's the case, Nikki, then you'll need about ten thousand dollars on you," Floyd said. "Coyotes used to charge about two thousand for a simple 'meet me at a specified location on the border and I'll walk you across the river.' But with the extra border protection and surveillance these days, they are charging triple or quadruple that amount. Now they even use transports and coordinate with corrupt border officials on the U.S. side. But I still urge you not to go underground until we investigate a little more."

"The money pouch you brought me will come in handy," Nikki said. "I'll put that pouch in my bra with my riches inside."

"It might make you look lopsided," Eduardo said, smiling.

Nikki kicked him under the table.

Floyd ignored the comment. "I'll get you ten thousand in small bills and take it to you when I return Fígaro tomorrow morning. You should carry most of it in your stockings." He scribbled out a name and number on a slip of paper and handed it to Nikki. "Both of you should memorize this number, just in case you need help on the U.S. side. It belongs to Jim Acosta, a border patrol officer. He's responsible for Texas."

The three of them discussed their options, talked about a plan, backup plans, and last-resort plans, including the rules for using the spy phones. Then they ordered dessert. Nikki asked for flan, Eduardo decided on tres leches cake, and Floyd requested a triple chocolate mousse.

After dessert, their server, accompanied by the maître d', arrived at the table with three very small shot glasses on a display dish covered with a cushioned red satin cloth, like one might find in an expensive jewelry case. Propped up at the back of the dish, a miniature matador sword had been thrust through the cushioned satin to evoke the atmosphere of the art of bullfighting. The maître d' carried a miniature oak barrel adapted to display an elegant bottle of tequila.

"To complete your dining experience," the maître d' said, "we are offering you very special tequila, Barrique de Ponciano Porfidio, one of the finest tequilas on the market."

Nikki admired the abstract sunburst on the bottle, which also sported a decorative, hand-blown glass cactus immersed in the rich amber liquid of aged tequila.

"The bottle is handmade," the maître d' said, "and it is a work of fine art, just like the tequila itself."

"To complement the original artwork exhibited on the walls," Nikki said.

"Not to mention the exquisite architecture of this historical landmark," Eduardo added.

The maître d' proceeded to pour a small amount into each shot glass, and the server passed one to Nikki, then Floyd, and finally to Eduardo.

"Salud, dinero, y amor," the maître d' said. "Health, money, and love."

Floyd held his glass up for the toast and said in accented Spanish, "Y tiempo para disfrutarlos."

"And time to enjoy them," Nikki and Eduardo said in unison as they raised their shot glasses and joined in the toast.

Nikki and Eduardo returned to their suite after delivering Fígaro to Floyd's room. They unloaded the bag containing the spy paraphernalia Floyd had given them earlier in the day, spread it out on the bed, and inspected everything—the 9 mm Lugers, masks so lifelike that no one would ever suspect they were masks, wigs for both of them, and of course, GPS chips, one for each of them, in plastic cases. Eduardo took the new phones and placed them on the desk. He tested a set of binoculars by looking at Nikki.

"This baby is powerful," he said. "So powerful I can see your heart, Nikki." He slipped behind a heavy curtain covering the window to test them by looking out onto the street.

"You're silly."

Nikki was engrossed with an item she had not requested, a carpetbag made from fabric that looked a hundred years old. *It can add a practical touch to my disguise,* she thought. A few other non-requested goods also looked promising, like duct tape, special socks for carrying bundles of money, and a thin money pouch she could insert into a bra cup. It also had a string for hanging it around her neck.

"This carpetbag is perfect for carrying a change of clothes. I need to buy a peasant-style Oaxacan outfit," Nikki said. She ran her hand inside the bag and felt the bottom of it. "You know, there's an extra thickness at the bottom where I can cut the fabric and stitch in a secret compartment for my spy phone."

Eduardo came out from behind the curtain and, with the binoculars, playfully pretended to be looking for Nikki around the room.

"I've just found the most beautiful woman in my room," he said as he went up close to her and peered into the field glasses.

"Silly man, come here and give me a kiss."

She put her arms around him, and he kissed her on the lips. He looked at her and smiled.

"Floyd is right about waiting to go underground until after he's checked out more details in San Miguel tomorrow," he said. "I don't want you taking unnecessary risks."

"I'll go underground when the opportunity presents itself, but only if it seems like that's the right decision."

Nikki pulled away from him and opened her suitcase, where she retrieved a travel sewing kit. She sat on the chair in front of the desk, opened her sewing kit, and removed a small pair of scissors, thread, and a needle to work on the carpetbag. But instead of working on the bag, she put it aside and examined the box containing the GPS chip. She stood up and returned to the bed, sat down on it, and picked up the tennis shoes Charlotte had sent with Floyd. Taking out the insoles, she found a hole in the removable lining of the left shoe and tried to insert the GPS chip, but found the chip was too big to fit in the hole. She took the lining back to the desk, placed it on the desktop with the locator chip on top of the hole, and used a pen to draw a circle around it. Next, she used scissors to make the hole bigger and slipped the chip in, where it fit snugly this time. She returned the lining to the shoe, which she then covered with the insole, and tried the shoe on her foot.

She glanced at Eduardo, who by now was sitting on a loveseat examining the spy phones, as she walked around the room.

"Do the spy shoes fit?" he asked, looking up from his task.

"Perfectly. And you're working on the spy phones. Speaking of phones, an open line on a cell is a good idea in our line of work so someone can hear what's going on. But mistakes can happen, like a story I heard of a man who got caught being unfaithful to his wife because he accidentally hit his home phone number when he took his girlfriend to a motel." She returned to the desk and sat down, threaded the needle, and knotted the two ends of the thread. "The spy phone is much better. You can't hit the wrong button. It simply transmits *everything* to the people monitoring it."

Eduardo looked pensive. "In the case of the man, it may have been a Freudian slip, but the wife was better off without him."

Nikki looked up from her sewing. "Hey, love, can you make a run to Walmart for me? It should be open until midnight, but check with the concierge. I don't think the wig Floyd brought will work. It can fall off too easily. Coloring my hair or, better yet, removing the color from my own hair will create more convincing gray. I'd hate for a wig to fall off at the wrong moment and expose my true identity."

"I'll also check with the concierge on my way out about the location for Walmart," Eduardo said. He picked up the keys to the rental car from the dresser.

"I'll need powdered bleach and an activator from the hair coloring part of the health and beauty section. Then you can also get me—"

"Not so fast, Nikki, let me write all this down." He grabbed a notepad from the table.

"Okay, I'll need an activator or developer for the powdered bleach. If there's no activator in the hair products area, then hydrogen peroxide from the pharmacy will work just as well, so get me a liter of that. And buy a plastic highlighting cap kit. The kit should contain a cap to go on my head with a tool that resembles a crochet needle."

"Do you need any plastic gloves?"

"Good idea, yes. Oh, and bring a plastic bowl with a brush. Everything is in the hair aisle, except for the peroxide. And get a cheap peasant blouse and long skirt from the clothing section. And brown shoe polish and laundry bleach to make the new clothes look old."

"Got it."

Eduardo stepped over to give Nikki a kiss before he left on his errands.

"I've been thinking about the name I'll use if I go underground. It's Nita Zapote. It's a common name in Oaxaca. You'll have to get used to calling me Nita."

Eduardo stepped back, placed his hand over his chin, and studied Nikki for a few seconds.

"Hmmm. I guess you'll look like a Nita after you get in full disguise. As soon as we finish the prep work for our new identities, I want us to relax." Eduardo smiled. His eyes smiled even more than his lips whenever he looked at Nikki.

"Don't be gone long," she said.

She turned the carpetbag inside out and started cutting the top layers of fabric that formed the reinforced bottom of the bag. Eduardo walked to the door and stopped to glance at Nikki, still smiling.

"I love you, Nita Zapote. And guess what?"

"We don't have Fígaro to interrupt us tonight," Nikki said with a smile of her own. "But Floyd will bring him back to us first thing tomorrow, so hurry back."

CHAPTER 10

San Miguel de Allende—Friday morning, day three after abduction

Floyd sat on a high stool at the elaborate wood-carved bar in Sofía's restaurant. She stood behind the bar, half facing a large, shiny, steel coffee machine with brass knobs, where she frothed milk to combine with espresso for a cappuccino.

"Is that a Lombardi machine?" Floyd asked.

Sofía turned to face him, almost spilling the milk. "How did you know?"

"Sánchez, the attorney in Mexico City, has a very similar one."

"That can't be a coincidence," she said. She spooned the froth into the cup already half-full of espresso. "Cinnamon?"

"Yes, thanks."

Sofía dusted the spice over the thick foam, used the handle of a spoon to create a design of a woman's face with long flowing hair, placed two biscotti on the saucer, and served the cup to Floyd.

"Paolo, my ex, and the attorney must know each other. The attorney led me to believe he didn't know the Lombardi family."

"Sánchez said he imported a machine from Italy a couple of years ago. He purchased it from Paolo, and that's why they know each other," Floyd said as he looked at the intricate design Sofía had made on the surface of foam. "You're quite the cappuccino artist. A good cappuccino is just what I need after my drive in from Zacatecas this morning."

"You must be hungry. Yeah. Would you like breakfast?" Sofía asked.

"No, I'm fine. When we get your daughter back, you can invite all of us for dinner." Floyd looked around the restaurant, trying to fill the pause in their conversation. "You do know how to cook, don't you?"

"Of course. I grew up in the business in Northern Italy. My father was a top-rated chef in Milan and owned his own place. He taught me to bus tables, wash dishes, make purchases, manage inventory, wait tables, tend bar, and I eventually became head sous-chef, according to him, not because of nepotism but due to my own abilities. Before I married, I managed the entire operation."

"Marriage spoils everything, doesn't it?" Floyd asked, still attempting to fill awkward silences before questioning Sofía about her missing child.

"It should not. Yeah. Paolo's mother, Chiara, spoiled everything. My work fell below the tolerable social threshold for the Lombardi family. She interfered in my marriage constantly by using her nephew, Matteo, a good-for-nothing who buttered up his aunt to get money from her. She raised Matteo. That guy intervened in our marriage to the point I gave up my restaurant, even though I loved it. Yeah. I gave up my career. Yeah, after Bibi was born. That's when the pressure was on. But it only got worse."

Sofía breathed heavily, and her eyes grew misty. Then suddenly her shoulders slumped forward and an onslaught of tears came forth, followed by heavy sobs. She placed her head on the counter, her upper back rising and falling in unison with her crying.

Floyd put his hand on her shoulder. "We're working to get Bibi back. Please be patient." He noticed how tight the muscles in her shoulder felt through the violet-colored crepe blouse she wore.

"Why does Paolo have to make me suffer so much?" she asked when she looked up. Tears ran down her face. Her eyes had looked bloodshot, even before she started crying. Now they appeared red.

"We don't think Paolo has Bibi, so I need to ask you a few questions."

"If he does not have her, why did he call me last night?"

"He called you? What did he say?" Floyd asked without attempting to hide his surprise.

"Nothing. Twice he called. Yeah, twice, but never spoke." She took a paper towel from under the bar and wiped her tears.

"Going back to what I was saying, we think Bibi was kidnapped. If they ask for ransom, it should be forthcoming in the next day or two given the three days they've had her. I'll need to be involved in the negotiations."

"And what if they never call for ransom?"

"In that case, it's far more serious."

"I pray that's not the case," she said, her face turning pale from fear. "I've been too afraid to think about that."

"Can you give me the number Paolo called you from last night?"

Sofía picked up a phone from under the bar and searched through the previous night's incoming calls. She took a business card from a brass holder on the bar, wrote the number down, and handed it to Floyd. He stared at the number for a couple of seconds.

"Where is this area code from?" he asked.

"Thirty-nine is the country code for Italy. It's not his usual number, but he's probably changed mobile phones."

"So you're not certain it's his number?"

"Technically, no, but who else could be calling from Italy? Yeah. Who else?"

Sofía wiped the counter in front of Floyd's cup with a fresh paper towel and threw it in a trash can under the bar.

"I'm going to call this number, but I also need his old cell phone or office numbers to make sure I can reach him," Floyd said. "On another topic, I know you spoke with Nikki and Eduardo about Juana, the bag lady."

"You know she was hit by a car yesterday? Yeah. She died."

"Yes. It's too bad because she gave us information we might be able to use, and she could have given us more," Floyd said. He dunked one of the almond biscotti in the cappuccino and took a bite.

"I'm surprised you'd believe anything that old woman said. Nikki knows how I felt about her."

"Does Bibi participate on-line in social media?" Floyd asked.

"All kids do. Why?"

"That old woman mentioned a man approached your daughter in the market with a dog, maybe a puppy. Check her social media accounts and see if you find anything unusual, an unknown person who may have friended her to learn more about her."

"That's scary, but I don't think so. Yeah. I'll see on the computer what I can find. I cannot check her cell phone. It was with her when she disappeared, but she never called me."

"A kidnapper would take a phone away from her. And destroy it. Try to check her chats on her computer. See if she revealed personal information, name, address, school, etcetera. Call me if you find anything."

"I saved the newspaper with the article on Juana's hit-and-run. Do you want it?"

"No, thanks, I read it this morning, plus I read about the accident on the internet. Listen, Sofía, if you get additional phone calls that sound unusual, call Nikki or me immediately. That also includes details catching your eye inside or outside the restaurant or anyone hanging around here, including any employee who is acting differently. Little details like that often help a lot. Now, if you will give me Paolo's other phone numbers, I'll get on my way."

Floyd took the card where Sofía wrote Paolo's numbers and walked to his car. He called Charlotte at his Miami office before he turned the engine on, gave her the Italian phone number, and asked her to get the scoop on it.

Floyd knocked on the door for a second time. He heard shuffling as a squeaky peephole opened in the door.

"¿Que quiere?" a woman's congested voice asked.

"Unas preguntas," Floyd said in broken Spanish.

"Questions on what?" the voice asked in accented but understandable English. "Who are you?"

"My name's Floyd Webber. I want to ask about Juana. She spoke with a friend of mine, Nikki García."

"Juana's dead. Go away."

"It'd be helpful if you'd open the door," Floyd said. "I want to figure out if she was murdered."

Floyd stood there in dead silence for a second before he heard deadbolts turning. The door opened slowly. A short, stocky woman dressed in black with a Muslim head scarf covering her stood in front of him. One end of the shawl was arranged to sweep across the bottom portion of her head, covering her mouth and most of her nose as the cloth came to rest over her opposite shoulder. He noticed her eyes had scars on both lids, and a large scar cut straight across her left eyebrow and as far up her forehead as the scarf allowed it to be seen. That eye looked oozy and infected and moved out of unison with the right eye, appearing to be blind.

"Juana told me about Nikki and also the man who accompanied her. You must be that man," the woman said. "Come in."

Floyd stepped inside a hallway without denying that Juana had met him. From where he stood at the entrance, he noticed a spacious room to his right with a living room or parlor filling half the space, and he guessed the other half consisted of a dining room.

The woman closed the door and bolted it.

"My name is Josefina," she said as she motioned for Floyd to follow her.

He stepped into the living room, noticing a cathedral ceiling covering the span of the large room. He also saw that the other portion of the room was the dining area he'd anticipated. The ceiling over the dining room rose well above the ceiling of the parlor, creating a room-length, horizontal clerestory window that allowed natural light in, casting a soft, yet eerie, glow over the living area. A tan-colored sectional sofa filled the center of the parlor, and the long portion of the sofa faced a wood-burning fireplace with a mantel over it. A television hung on the wall about twelve inches above the mantel. He noticed no decorative items, except for a very realistic-looking stuffed black bird mounted on a dry tree branch with a thick wooden base, placed on the far edge of the mantle.

A desiccated bird is a fitting artifact to have in the house of an eccentric woman called Juana la Marihuana, Floyd thought.

Magazines were scattered over a glass-top coffee table in front of the sofa. The room, while not luxurious, appeared comfortable. Although it was not dirty, it did not sparkle with cleanliness either.

"You look perplexed," the woman said. "Are you surprised because I lived with Juana? Or is it my attire?" She coughed, paused, and looked closely at her visitor. "Maybe the house is too nice for a beggar?"

"The house is very nice," Floyd said.

From where he stood, Floyd took time to look around. Through the windows in the dining room, he noticed two fair-sized greenhouses at the rear of the backyard. Flapping wings and a screaming cry brought his attention back into the room.

"What the fuck…?" Floyd said as he jumped and instinctively covered his face with his hands for protection as the bird flapped its wings close to him.

The crow on the mantle had come to life and had flown down and landed near Floyd's feet. The bird made a sound—not cawing, not squawking, not like a human voice either, but somewhere in the realm of speech. By the third time Floyd heard it, he was certain the crow was trying to talk.

"I thought that was a stuffed bird," Floyd said.

"That's Juana's crow. She nursed him and kept him alive after she found him in the backyard when he fell out of his nest. He was a fuzzy little white guy, but look at his shiny black feathers now. You'd think—"

An ear-deafening screech filled the room. "Fígaro! Fígaro! Fígaro!"

"That's the crow calling for Juana. He learned to speak a few words, just like a parrot would. He calls Juana by the dog's name. We figured he associated Juana calling for the pup as the name he should use for his human mother. Whenever he called out the dog's name, Juana went running to see what her feathered child needed. It's so sad. He's been moving from room to room, calling her."

"I didn't know crows could talk," Floyd said. "You're sure he is calling Juana and not the dog?"

"Absolutely certain he's calling Juana," she said. "Whenever Sebastián, that's the crow, was outside and he was ready to come indoors to get his meals, he called 'Fígaro' and Juana would come running. Juana clipped his wings to make sure he'd never go back into the wild. He uses them like sails to sputter from a high place to the ground, but he can't really fly. Since he does not know how to forage for food or defend himself, he'd die if he went back into the wild. Her two pets, Sebastián and Fígaro, were like children to her."

"Nikki has Fígaro. I'll return him to you—" Floyd said.

The woman held her hands out in a negative gesture. "No, no, tell your friend to keep him. Sebastián and the dog do not like each other. With the state of my health, I'm better off with the bird. Fígaro gets fleas. Sebastián's easier to take care of."

Floyd glanced down at the crow. The bird looked like a black porcelain raven on the floor, now standing next to Josefina.

"Let me show you," Josefina said.

She took three steps away from the crow, and he stepped in behind her like a miniature soldier, his shiny black feathers matching Josefina's dark attire. The two of them appeared to be marching to silent drums. She turned a light switch to brighten the space and walked around the sofa past the coffee table. Sebastián followed her steps. She stopped abruptly. So did the bird. They both stood in front of Floyd again, the bird a miniature version of the woman in black.

"Juana trained him, like she also trained Fígaro. So you can see, it's not your normal—How would you North Americans say it?—*bag lady's* house. Juana and I pooled our money and built it."

"It's a nice house with a very different atmosphere," Floyd said, "especially with the crow as mascot."

"Cleaning up bird shit is easier than getting rid of Fígaro's fleas. We had the whole house fumigated twice for those damn fleas," she said, scratching her left arm as she spoke.

Floyd scratched his head in an unconscious reaction to the woman's talk of fleas. His eyes focused on various aspects of the room, observing details.

"Maybe I should turn to begging for a living," he said when he realized Josefina caught him studying the house. "You live comfortably."

"The money, my part of it, came from a settlement I got from my boyfriend when he dumped me. He had me beaten and had acid thrown on my face. I thought I'd die in the hospital, and then Juana, a friend from my school days, heard what happened to me. She went to Mexico City and brought me to San Miguel to live with her. She hired a lawyer, who got a settlement for me for the injuries I suffered."

Josefina stopped talking and looked at Floyd.

"I'd like to ask about Juana," Floyd said.

"I can't believe she's dead," Josefina said in a quivering voice as she made the sign of the cross. "Que en paz descanse."

"Yes, may she rest in peace," Floyd said as he thought about the unexpected gesture the Muslim woman had made. "I'm sorry to ask at a time like this, but I need to know a few things. Tell me, what was Juana's surname?"

"García."

"Her birth name?" Floyd asked.

"Yes."

"I understand her husband is in the Sinaloa cartel," Floyd said.

"Well, they never married, but yes, they had a common-law marriage. That was a long time ago. She lived with a capo."

"I also understand she was a drug addict."

"Not by choice. She caught her husband cheating on her. She confronted him and the woman. They were in a pickup, and Juana stood in front of it yelling at them, demanding the woman get out. Raimundo, Rai for short, that sorry bastard, ran her down and crushed her pelvis."

"It's amazing she could walk after that," Floyd said.

"To this day she lives, well, she's gone now, but she lived in terrible back pain from that accident. Juana turned to illegal drugs for the pain, drugs she could get through her husband's supply, and got hooked on them for five years, but when she brought me here, she felt the responsibility of taking care of me. She got off hard drugs, cold-turkey, and that was a dreadful time for her, so she started smoking marihuana." On the verge of tears, she turned away and coughed again.

"Are those greenhouses out there where Juana grew her weed?" Floyd asked, looking out the back windows.

"No, that's for my flowers." She coughed again. "I grow flowers and sell them to a buyer from Mexico City."

"What's Rai's last name?" Floyd asked.

"Beltrán."

"Beltrán?" Floyd asked. "Like in the big drug cartel family?"

"Yes, kind of, so don't mess with him. He's very corrupt. He's a distant cousin of Chapo Guzmán. That's the same Chapo from the Sinaloa cartel, who's incarcerated in the U.S. now. He's also related to the Beltrán-Leyva cartel gang, so he's not as big a capo as he could have been. You see, El Chapo never completely trusted him."

"Any chance Beltrán had Juana killed?"

"I'd like to say no, but I don't know for sure. He's left her completely alone. In fact, he'd have nothing to do with her when she contacted him after they split. But they had not been in contact for about nineteen years. After all that time, what motivation could Beltrán have?"

"That Juana identified the kidnapper of the Lombardi child to my colleague as a possible member of the Sinaloa cartel," Floyd said.

"Juana left Rai so long ago, she could not know if the cartel was involved, not that she would have known back then either. She told me the Lombardi child's kidnapper drove a truck with Sinaloa license plates. She found it a curious coincidence. Besides, how would anyone know she told your colleague of her suspicion?"

"I don't know," Floyd said. "I was hoping you could tell me."

"I'm afraid not."

"But I do know the kidnapper's truck was registered to a Juana García in Sinaloa," Floyd said.

Josefina jerked her head in a startled reaction. Her scarf fell over her shoulders, and Floyd saw her scared and acid-burned skin. She turned her face, pale and white, away and covered it with her hand as she readjusted the shawl with her other hand.

"That can't be true," Josefina said. She coughed as she continued arranging the shawl over her head and face, leaving only her eyes and the bridge of her nose uncovered. She flipped the end of the shawl back over her shoulder.

"That's the name on the registration from the license plates Juana gave to Nikki," he said. "I think it also included Beltrán—"

"Fígaro! Fígaro!" the crow interrupted.

Josefina bent over and placed her hand next to the crow. He hopped on, and Juana took her hand to her shoulder, where Sebastián walked off and settled.

"This is why I'd rather keep the crow over the dog. Just look at him. Isn't he cute?" she said, turning her shoulder at an angle where Floyd could admire the bird.

"Don't change the subject on me, Josefina."

"Maybe Rai uses Juana's name. He can bribe his way to anything. But it might be another Juana García, totally unrelated to my Juana. García is a common surname." Josefina looked away as she spoke.

"There's something you're not telling me."

"What you said made me think."

"About what?"

"A child. Juana's child."

"Juana has a child?" Floyd asked.

"Yes, a long time ago. A daughter. When she left Rai, he took the child away, claiming Juana was unfit because of her drug addiction."

"Had Juana seen her child recently?"

"No. The daughter died when she was about five or six years old. Juana never saw the girl after she split with Rai. He never allowed it."

"What was the daughter's name?"

"Juana, the same as the mother, though she called her daughter Ana."

"Did Juana say anything to you about being afraid or someone following her before her accident?"

"No, nothing of the sort. You know, I did not think about it until now that you're asking, but she received two phone calls where she stepped outside the house to talk. I figured it had to do with her supply of marihuana, but she'd never needed privacy before. But I did hear her call the man's name—Antonio Enríquez."

"When did the calls take place?"

"Both happened the morning she was killed. About ten and again around ten thirty. Then she left the house and I did not see her again until police called me to identify her."

"Do you have her phone available?"

"Her phone? You mean her mobile phone?"

"Yes."

"The police must have it. At least, they should. They did not return it. And I did not think of asking for it. Wait, Juana did call me again about half an hour or so before the time the police calculated she was killed."

"What did she say?" Floyd asked.

"That you and your friend gave us money to feed Fígaro."

"Is that all?"

Josefina nodded. As Josefina moved her head, the crow mimicked her movement. Then he cocked his head and, from the side closest to Floyd, the crow's black eye stared at the investigator in an almost human-like manner.

"When the Lombardi girl was kidnapped," Floyd said, "Juana said she tried to tell the mother about the man who took the child, but Mrs. Lombardi paid no attention. Did Juana mention this to you?" He stared back at the crow, who was still eyeing him.

"Yes. The Italian would not listen."

"Why do you think that was?" Floyd asked.

"Bad blood between Juana and the Italian woman."

"Bad blood? Explain yourself."

"Because of me."

"You? Why you?" Floyd asked.

"When I was young, I fell in love with a married man, a prominent attorney in Mexico City. He set me up in a condo and promised to leave his wife, the usual song and dance men give to stupid women like me. I became pregnant, and he sent a couple of thugs to kill me. I was an easy target. They caught me outside the condo, carrying two bags of groceries."

"He knew you were pregnant?"

"Oh, yes. That's why he wanted me killed. The thugs stabbed me twice in the stomach, once under the rib cage, and slashed me across the face. They threw acid on me, ruining my left eye. A neighbor drove up during the attack, spooking my assailants, and they took off. Later, in the hospital, I lost the baby."

"I guess I don't get it. What does your life story have to do with Juana's and Sofía Lombardi's bad relationship? Can you get to the point?"

"Patience, I'm getting there. Sofía had been providing leftover food to Juana. Then, one day, Juana stood across the street from the restaurant's main entrance. She recognized a man who pulled up in a BMW and got out with his wife. Juana wanted revenge, so she waited until they entered the restaurant. She got on the hood of the BMW and used it like a toilet for what the man had done to me years before."

Floyd kept a straight face.

Josefina laughed, at first a muffled laugh, deep in her throat, then it evolved into a cackling that turned into a boisterous laugh. When she stopped laughing, she added, "Juana was very proud of shitting on that shiny, black luxury car. You see, he was my former boyfriend, the one who wanted me killed."

"Tell me about Beltrán," Floyd said, ignoring Josefina's last comment.

"He's not a kingpin, but Beltrán was with Guzmán when the Tijuana cartel opened fire on a fancy Mercury Grand Marquis in Guadalajara, thinking they'd found Guzmán."

"Yeah, I remember the incident," Floyd said. "Wasn't that when they killed the Catholic cardinal?"

"That's right," she said. "How did you know?"

"It was all over the news at the time."

"The capo was in a Buick sedan, crouching in the backseat, afraid to even breathe, parked three cars away from the slain cardinal. He knew they meant those bullets for his skin, not the cardinal's. Beltrán helped Guzmán get to a safe house near the airport." Josefina coughed again.

"I'm no expert on the Mexican drug cartels, but I thought Guzmán killed off a bunch of the Beltrán-Leyva cartel," Floyd said.

"Yes, that occurred later. The Beltrán-Leyva brothers worked for Guzmán, but when their oldest brother, Alfredo, was arrested, the other brothers blamed their boss for the arrest. That's when the split happened between Guzmán and the Beltrán-Leyva gang. These were Rai's relatives too. Guzmán believed Rai was loyal to him, but the paranoid capo kept Rai at a distance after that."

"You do know my friend Nikki was with Juana at the time the driver killed her?" Floyd said, changing the subject.

"With Juana? No, I didn't know. Is she okay?" Josefina took the edge of the shawl flowing down her chest and wiped her oozing bad eye.

"Yes, she's fine. Can you give me Juana's phone number and the house phone?"

"Of course."

She rattled them off, and Floyd made a note of the numbers in his cell phone.

"I'm curious. Are you Muslim?" Floyd asked.

"People think that. They don't see me without my shawl, as you did a few minutes ago. I dress like this because of my face. But people stayed away from Juana and me. They considered us beneath them, too low-class for their refined palates." Juana coughed.

"When is the funeral?" Floyd asked.

"No funeral. I'm getting Juana's ashes tomorrow. I'll bury them in the backyard. I've ordered a tall headstone in the shape of a cross, and I'll encircle it with cannabis plants. She would like that."

"Cannabis around the tombstone?" Floyd repeated. He did not know whether to laugh or not, so he kept a straight face.

Sebastián called out for Fígaro, flapped his wings, and flew off Josefina's shoulder. He landed near the front door, screeching Fígaro's name. Josefina followed him and opened the peephole.

"Did you hear the footsteps?" she whispered. "I think he heard them and he thought it was Juana." She lifted Sebastián into her arms as he called out for Fígaro three more times. She closed the peephole and returned to the living room where Floyd was still standing.

"If you had to guess where the Lombardi child is, where would that be?" Floyd asked.

"I'd say what Juana already told you. The coyote has her somewhere on the route to Juárez. Juana thought they'd be hiding in caves in Zacatecas until the moon wanes."

Sebastián took flight again, landing on the coffee table. Josefina followed him with her eyes, taking in every movement the bird made.

"Que mierda, mira lo que hiciste," Josefina said. Her voice moved up the scale to higher pitches as she spoke. "Shit, look at the mess you've made. Now I have to clean up after you."

Floyd glanced at the coffee table and saw Sebastián's deposit on the shiny glass top. Josefina walked to the kitchen, returned with paper towels, and proceeded to clean up the bird's droppings.

"One last question," Floyd said. "Did Juana kidnap the Lombardi child?"

"Now you're the one who's shitting," she said.

"Me? Shitting?" Floyd asked, moving his hand to his chest, looking stunned.

"Yes, you're shitting—on Juana's good name. So that's what you think of her? Well, listen here, mister gringo good-for-nothing. No way would Juana ever do a dirty trick like that. Juana was a good woman. Despite her appearance and eccentric personality, she had a heart of gold. Besides, she loved Ricitos de Oro, as she called the child."

CHAPTER 11

San Miguel de Allende—Friday, day three after abduction

As he drove to San Miguel, Arturo thought about the meeting he'd had the day before with Héctor Sánchez in Mexico City. He considered Héctor a highfalutin son of a bitch, who paid Arturo to perform his dirty work. If the lawyer did not come through with better pay, Arturo was already working to branch out to bigger and more profitable activity.

Arturo had called his recent hire, the Colombian, to meet him for coffee in his favorite dive, Paco's Cantina, on the hill overlooking San Miguel, two blocks from the Plaza Real del Conde shopping center. He parked his black pickup in the parking lot, and as he walked to the meeting place, he saw Joaquín's army-green-colored Jeep parked along the side street. Ranchera music, folk ballads about narcos, could be heard coming from Paco's a block away. When he entered the cantina, he saw Joaquín sitting in a booth with a beer in front of him, carrying on an animated conversation with a waitress. Arturo recognized her as one of the topless girls who worked the night crowd, now doing her duty as a daytime waitress. Or maybe she was the owner's woman. As Arturo walked up, the shapely young woman with the low-cut blouse asked him for his order.

"Bring me a cup of coffee, black, and a burrito with beef birria," Arturo said as he eased into the empty side of the booth.

As soon as the waitress walked away, he looked at Joaquín and shook his head.

"Pendejo, you fucked up," Arturo said. "I have a buyer for the kid. Camorra, in Italy. Big bucks they're willing to pay for that little Italian princess. I need to snatch her from the kidnapper, not be making excuses to Sánchez for your stupidity of killing the Marihuana. I've bribed the police to cover up your dumbass fumbling of this job."

"Camorra?" Joaquín asked as he took a swig of beer. With total disinterest, he added, "Never heard of them."

"Camorra is one of Italy's largest mafias. We have business opportunities I want to pursue with them. They come from a real nice place. Naples. I went there a month ago. They took me to a motherfucking expensive whore house. You would not believe the women. They were all shit-in-your-pants gorgeous."

"So we're nothing better than bajadores, stealing little putas from the coyotes and supplying them to those malditos from Camorra for the U.S. market. Why not go direct to New York?" Joaquín asked.

"I have ties to Italy, not the U.S."

"So what else besides little virgins does Camorra deal in?"

"Shit man, esos pendejos," Arturo said, "they're into fucking everything. Sex rings, gun trafficking, drugs, porn, extortion and usury, counterfeiting and money laundering. Those hijos de puta are tough. Got their start in the same place where so many gangs start—in jail. Several sons of bitches agreed..."

The loud music had stopped. Arturo turned to catch the waitress's attention and saw she was on her way to his booth.

"Oye, chula, don't stop the rancheras."

"But this customer wants to watch the soccer game on TV," she answered, motioning with her head toward a man sitting at the bar wearing a cowboy hat as she set a cup of steaming coffee on the table in front of Arturo.

"Let him watch the game in silence, but turn that music back on, mi linda. Give him another beer and add it to my check."

She walked behind the bar, winked at the customer watching the soccer game, handed him another Corona, told him it was from the man with the glasses, and turned the music up again.

Arturo, his jaw clenched, put two teaspoons of sugar into the coffee and returned his gaze to Joaquín.

"Several of those hijos de puta agreed to reunite after they got out of prison. They offered protection services, same as the narco-protectors started doing here during Felipe Calderón's presidency, when he cracked down on narcos and his government forces killed or incarcerated the Beltrán-Leyva gang and murdered Nazario from La Familia in Guadalajara. Protection services, the world's second oldest profession," Arturo said, laughing. He took a sip of coffee and burned his tongue. He stopped laughing.

"If they're Italian, why are we getting a little golfa for them? Can't they get enough chavas in their own country?" Joaquín asked.

"Camorra is sending children from various countries, especially little girls, to the Middle East, mostly Bahrain, Abu Dhabi, and Qatar. They like the güeritas. Seems like they want their virgins to be little blonde girls."

"Not many güeritas up for grabs around here," Joaquín said. He drank more beer, put the bottle down, and looked intently at Arturo. "There's more you're not telling me."

"That's not the only business venture they're opening up. They want into Latin American cocaine—direct access to it. The other Italian crime syndicate, called 'Ndràngheta, from the Calabrian area in Southern Italy, has controlled that market for several years. 'Ndràngheta controls the flow of drugs, money laundering, and human trafficking from South America into the European market."

"We're small fry. Sounds too fucking dangerous to get between two mafias," Joaquín said.

"It's a great fucking opportunity for us to break into the big leagues. Just like the Mexican cartels, the Italian ones have a working understanding of their respective territories, yet each group tests their rival's control over their territory, like the Sinaloa syndicate and the Zetas did a few years ago. Fucking Italian Camorra now feels there's enough room for both of them. And that's where I need your experience in drug trafficking."

"Estás loco, buey. You sure you want this alliance?" Joaquín looked at his boss with contempt and finished the Corona he'd been drinking. "What is it you're not telling me?"

"Why in fucking hell did you kill the Marihuana?" Arturo asked. "I told you to follow the gringa, not try to kill anyone."

"That Indian woman was a nothing. You told me to make it easy to take the girl from the kidnapper," Joaquín said. "I was working on where they're keeping her, and the gringa got in the way. If that Marihuana had not saved her, I'd have killed her and I'd make no apologies to you. That way, those Americanos would not get the girl before we put our fucking hands on her."

"You'd better *not* kill the gringa. So where's the gringa now?"

The waitress arrived with the barbecued birria for Arturo.

"Get me another Corona and make it fucking cold," Joaquín said. "I don't like hot beer. I like a woman with a big, fat, fucking, hot ass, and a beer as cold as a frigging iceberg." He slurred the words, as if to emphasize his thought, and slapped her on the butt before she walked away.

The server looked over her shoulder and smiled at Joaquín, but he ignored her.

Arturo adjusted the wire-frames of his glasses while waiting for Joaquín to answer his question. He added another teaspoon of sugar to his coffee, stirred it, took a sip, and added one more teaspoon.

"She and that man she's with went to Zacatecas," Joaquín finally said. "Then we lost her trail."

"Lost her?" Arturo's voice and the look on his face were in complete disbelief. Once again he adjusted the wire-frames of his lightly tinted glasses. "All you had to do, buey, was track her." He shook his head. "Que pendejada."

"Stop calling me an asshole."

"Answer me," Arturo said.

"I had to stop and fill the tank with gas. That's when we lost their trail. The Yaqui stayed in Zacatecas to locate them. That old man will hunt them down. He told me his good Yaqui blood was meant for tracking wild animals, so he'll find those pendejos Americanos and the little puta too."

"Don't even think of killing the foreigners. Let the kidnapper take care of them if they get in his way, but not you," Arturo said. "That's an order." Joaquín gave his boss a slight nod. "If they lead us to the kidnapper, that's fine. That's one way to find the girl. But don't depend entirely on them to find her. I want that kid. In virgin condition. Do you hear me?" Arturo cut the rolled-up flour tortilla that contained the barbecue beef. Then he took the knife and clutched it in his right hand until his knuckles were white.

COYOTE ZONE

He leaned across the table and stabbed the knife in the air three times in front of Joaquín's eyes as he spoke. "They will fuck you if you mess up. Camorra does not appreciate broken promises."

"They don't even know me," Joaquín said, shrugging his shoulders slightly, as if to show his lack of interest.

"If you botch this one, you can expect an introduction. A fucking introduction that will hurt," Arturo said in a low but menacing tone.

"Screw Camorra," Joaquín said.

"I was going to take you on my next trip to meet them. If for no other reason than to see you shit in your pants when you saw those gorgeous putas," Arturo said. "Don't forget, I did you a favor giving you a job."

"You're doing Cristóbal Arenas a favor, not me, in hiring me. Watch what you say. Arenas is big-time. For a few putas, I might consider going to Italy with you if—"

"Héctor Sánchez doesn't like the way you handled things," Arturo said, interrupting. "If you fuck up, he'll have you deported back to Colombia."

Arturo ate his birria in silence. Then he stood up, walked to the bathroom, and dialed his daughter, María, at the attorney's office.

"I need a favor from you. Arrange two tickets to Italy. To Naples. I'll text you the details, including names and dates, but delete my text after you order the tickets. Get the expensive tickets, in case I need to change dates or airports. Go to the travel agency your office uses and pay with the cash I gave you."

CHAPTER 12

Zacatecas—Friday, day three after abduction

A wrinkled old woman with unevenly cropped gray hair hobbled down the central aisle of a crowded, covered market two blocks from the cathedral in the picturesque and historic town center of Zacatecas. She carried a large carpetbag over her shoulder. A middle-aged man, wearing dirty clothes and sporting a ponytail, came from the opposite direction. He made eye contact with her for a split second and brushed her shoulder as they crossed paths. His body odor overwhelmed her nostrils as he walked by, and his foul scent lingered in the air. She adjusted her bag, as if that action might remove the impression of the smelly old man.

Nikki, still adjusting to her persona as Nita Zapote, entered a clothing store. She looked out to observe people in the market to make certain not a single one was following her. She also checked if anyone appeared to follow Eduardo in the central hall. Convinced they were both safe, she turned her attention to a long peasant skirt and blouse hanging on a rack. She took the items off the hangers, held them up against her body for size, and handed them to the attendant.

"The dressing room is behind the curtain," the attendant said. "This is Oaxacan cotton and it will shrink."

"Don't need to fit them. They're fine."

Nikki handed pesos to the attendant and smiled as she placed her new outfit in the carpetbag. She felt her personality slipping into the world of a Zapotec woman, and it made her feel good. Dangerous times might be ahead, but right at that moment, she enjoyed the exciting tingle of adrenalin rushing through her body.

Nikki returned to the crowded central corridor. She could no longer see Eduardo but knew he'd be out there checking on her. She mixed in with the crowd and walked until she reached a small food court at the far end of the building. She sat down on a bench at a long table—European style, where various people sat together, whether they knew each other or not—and put her bag between her feet. Most of the patrons sitting at the table were picking at a late breakfast, but a few of them were already eating an early lunch as they all participated in lively conversation and watched the crowd.

Four tall, robust-yet-attractive women waited tables. The server who came over to take her order had a deep voice, and she listened as the waitress offered the day's specials. She selected chilaquiles, a regional specialty of corn tortilla chips smothered in green chile salsa topped with chunks of grilled chicken and sour cream. As the attendant filled a cup of coffee, Nikki noticed the server's big, masculine hands. The older woman studied the younger one, looked around at the rest of the wait staff, and returned her gaze to her server. She looked for an Adam's apple and upon seeing it realized the entire staff was composed of transvestites.

When breakfast was placed in front of her, Nikki dug her fork into it and stuffed her mouth. She chewed with her mouth open and talked to her server in Spanish, all at the same time.

"Ay, ay, ay, this is delicious. To think a cook can take a few ingredients and make such a spicy and tasty dish. Hey, listen, mi linda, can you tell me where I can find a woman called Petra?" She spoke with the soft, melodic, sing-song Spanish typical of the Oaxacan Zapotec indigenous people.

"Are you trying to get to the other side?" the server asked in Spanish.

"Yes, I need to get to the U.S. to see my daughter. She lives there," Nikki said. She continued wolfing the food, as if she had not eaten in days.

"Petra has a taniche down the street. The rent here got too expensive. Go out the main entrance to Tacuba Street and turn slightly left, cross over at the traffic light, and take Aguascalientes Street to number three hundred six. Tell her Adelita sent you. It's Friday morning, so Petra should be there today. You need to have American dollars to pay for the services.

They say the coyotes are charging more these days. It's getting harder to get people across the frontera."

Nikki nodded her thanks, and the server moved on to the next table.

Once she finished eating, Nikki paid the bill, picked up her carpetbag, and headed to the exit. On her way out, Eduardo brushed up against her again. He certainly looked and smelled the part of a street person with an alcohol problem.

"The older man from the hit-and-run is here at the market," he whispered. "I don't think he's spotted us."

She looked away from the gray-haired, ponytailed Eduardo to adjust the bag on her shoulder, to avoid being seen speaking with him.

"Good to know. I'm headed to Petra's at three hundred six Aguascalientes Street," she said barely loud enough for him to hear her.

After Nikki crossed the street, she checked her reflection in the window of a store, studying it intently. She smoothed her hair to make sure it covered the almost imperceptible edges of her mask. Yesterday afternoon she was Nikki García, age thirty-eight, with long, black hair and no wrinkles. This morning she had awakened and slipped into a full-body mask. Her reflection showed a hard-lived sixty-eight-or-so-year-old woman with short-cropped gray hair. She was dressed in peasant clothing Eduardo had purchased at Walmart, which she had stained and torn to make them appear worn. In her new identity of Nita Zapote, she felt satisfied she looked authentic.

Nikki continued walking on to number three hundred six, where she entered a small taniche. Once inside, she found a long, narrow room with floor-to-ceiling shelves along the walls holding all types of bulk food: piloncillo—the hard, brown, conical shaped molasses—dried chile pods, and gallon-sized cans of lard. Three large mixing bowl type containers of dry shrimp sat on top of a counter where an old-style mechanical cash register dominated the space. A few strategically placed copies of the perennial Latin American comic book character Mafalda, sort of a Lucy-type cartoon without a Charlie Brown, were set next to the cash register, providing an impulse item few people could resist as they paid their bills. Nine wooden barrels—each about three and a half feet high, held together by three iron bands wrapped around the barrel at the top, bottom, and center—were lined up in the main aisle. The barrels offered a selection of pinto beans, black beans, and rice. Two barrels were sealed, and a spigot low on the barrel indicated they contained liquid, probably homemade pulque since the floor was bleached underneath the small faucets. A young teenage girl chewed gum behind the counter.

Nikki said hello to the woman. "I'm looking for Petra," she said in Spanish with the distinct intonations her character required.

"She'll be back shortly."

Nikki moved casually toward the rear of the store to see what products a taniche carried. School supplies—mainly notebooks, pens, pencils, cheap solar calculators, crayons, bundles of blank newsprint, backpacks, and lunch boxes—occupied two shelves along the back wall. As she looked at the poor quality of the school supplies, she heard someone crying. It seemed like a child weeping. An adult's brassy voice jarred with the wailing sound. The voices were muffled to the point of being incoherent. On the back wall, an open doorway led down four steps to a dingy and dirty hallway with boxes littering the way, a perfect hiding place for rats and cockroaches. The crying seemed to emanate from a room off the hallway.

"Is Petra your mother?" Nikki asked. She was getting jittery and attempted idle conversation to calm her nerves rather than for any real reason to converse.

"No, she's my aunt," the girl replied, looking out the window, clearly bored.

"Adelita at the market sent me to see her," Nikki said. She felt a nervous gnawing in her stomach, so she engaged the girl in more conversation. Maybe she could also learn a fact or two.

"You want to cross the border?" the girl asked.

"Yes."

"In that case, you don't need to see Petra. Take a bus to Juárez, at the border with Texas. Once you're in Juárez, go to the Aguila Azul hotel on Avenida Insurgentes. It's way out on Insurgentes at the outskirts of town. Tell the receptionist, an old man, that you're there to see Goyo." The girl chewed gum with her mouth open.

"What's Goyo's last name?" Nikki asked.

"He's just known as Goyo. He'll get you across the river."

"That's it? Get to the border city of Juárez, go to the Aguila Azul hotel, and ask for Goyo?"

"I forgot to mention to have your money ready," the girl said.

"How much?" Nikki asked.

"I thought Adelita told you. It used to be two thousand dollars. Goyo only accepts dollars, but the price is a lot more now. Ask Goyo." The girl blew a bubble with her gum. It popped, and she used her tongue to draw the gum back in her mouth.

"I still need to speak with Petra," Nikki said.

"Who needs to speak with me?" a brusque voice asked from the hallway.

Nikki's pulse rate shot up. She turned and saw a short, rotund woman, almost as wide as she was tall, walking up the steps into the shop from the dingy hall. Petra's powerful presence reflected resentment and bitterness, perhaps even cruelty.

"Me."

"I can see that. Who are you?" Petra asked.

"I'm Nita Zapote."

"From Oaxaca, I gather."

"How can you tell?" Nikki asked.

"Well, I hear it in your voice. So, what are you after?" Petra gave the woman inside her store a hard look. Disgust showed on her face, and she looked as if she could not be bothered with an uneducated peasant who wanted to talk with her.

"I need to get to the border. Ramona Tafoya from Oaxaca recommended you and—"

"Take a bus."

"Yes, I know that, but I've made it all the way here by myself, so I was thinking I'd get a ride with a coyote and work for him."

"No coyote will hire you. They like young girls, not old hags like you."

"But I can cook—"

The door opened, and two men walked in off the street, interrupting the gray-haired Nikki in mid-sentence. One of them, his long sideburns sporting more hair than the top of his head, wore a light jacket. He appeared to be in his late-forties. He had a rugged countenance with a thin mustache and the shadow of a three-day beard growing on his face. A scar ran below his right eye and across his broken nose, making his piercing black eyes even more intimidating. The skin around his right eye, especially on the lid, had a visible twitch. The other man was young, maybe twenty at most, very short, and thin. He wore jeans and a washed-out, wine-colored Notre Dame sweatshirt.

"Goyo. I didn't expect you till next week," Petra said, grinning wide, showing tobacco-stained teeth. "How are you?"

Nikki focused on steadying her legs when she heard the man's name. She wanted to turn her head away, as if to study the beans in the barrel she was standing by, but her neck muscles froze, and she stared straight ahead at the man who walked toward Petra.

"It's fierce out there. Work gets me down, you know? With the new controls on the border, business is tough. You have to find new ways to get the pollos across. If you turn your back, the competition steals your business. As soon as my son graduates, I'll retire from this shitty business."

"You're the best there is, Goyo," Petra said, her voice both respectful and flirtatious.

"Do you have my provisions?"

"Your order is ready, as usual," she said. "A man came looking for you yesterday."

"What did he look like?"

"A foreigner, maybe in his forties. Very nice clothes. He had an accent. Said he wanted to talk to you about a business venture."

"Who is the old lady?" Goyo inquired as he looked down the aisle at the old woman standing by the barrel of beans at the back of the room.

Nikki had composed herself by now. She leaned on one of the barrels of beans and ran her fingers through the kernels, as if to inspect their quality. She could watch Petra and Goyo from the periphery of her vision.

"That old woman wants to go with you to the U.S. Says she'll cook for you on the way. She's a Zapotec Indian from Oaxaca," Petra said.

Goyo glanced at the gray-haired woman again as she filled a small paper bag with beans. Nikki tried to appear as if she did not hear the conversation about her.

"Don't need a cook. I need a strong-armed man who knows how to shoot cuernos de chivo," he said.

"I told her you would not want her. When you go around back to load up, I have something else for you," Petra said and winked at him.

Goyo looked down the aisle again at the old woman, who hadn't moved.

"Oye, old one, meet me in Juárez at the Aguila Azul hotel. Ask for Goyo. I'll be there in six or seven days. Be prepared to pay American dollars."

"Yes, but if I make the trip with you—"

"Didn't you hear me tell Petra I don't need you? If you want to cross the border, meet me at the Aguila Azul." Goyo turned his attention to Petra without waiting for an answer from the old woman. "Add four extra cases of water."

Nikki emptied the beans from the bag back into the barrel, folded the paper bag, and placed it back in a wire holder. She hobbled to the front door and left the taniche. As soon as she was outside, she limped along faster and turned the corner into an alley behind Petra's tiny neighborhood grocery. She looked down the alley, spotted two garbage dumpsters, and hobbled toward them, hiding behind one. Then she reached in her carpetbag, retrieved her spy phone, and dialed Eduardo's number.

"Yes?"

"Notify Charlotte or Floyd to turn on the spyware on my phone to catch important conversation," she whispered.

"It's already on. I arranged it with Charlotte this morning."

"I think I've found the coyote. His first name is Goyo, like the painter Goya, but with an O at the end. Don't have his last name."

"Nikki, please don't go underground. Not yet."

"Remember, my name is Nita. This may be the only chance we have. The coyote arrived early, at least a couple of days, to pick up his provisions. I doubt he's going to return here for more supplies, so he may be preparing to leave Zacatecas. I have to go. Bye."

"I've asked you not to do this."

Eduardo's voice sounded angry and commanding, but Nikki barely heard his request. She put the phone in her pocket and lifted the lid on the dumpster closest to her. It was only a third full. She looked around and spotted a wooden crate near the garbage container and repositioned it, hoisting herself over the top and into the dumpster. The putrid odor nearly overwhelmed her. Adjusting her body to a hump-shouldered stance, she took a tissue from her bag, tore off a couple of pieces, and rolled them up, stuffing a piece in each nostril. She checked the spy phone to make sure she'd turned it off, and holding the phone, she admired how cheap it appeared, despite the state-of-the-art electronics it contained. Placing the phone in the secret compartment of her carpetbag gave Nikki the secure feeling Charlotte at the Miami control center would be monitoring her activity. Closing the lid on the dumpster made the putrid odor even worse to bear.

A battered, gray pickup rolled into the alley. From her hiding spot, only her eyes peeked out as she used her head to push the lid slightly open and focused on the license plate. The tag number made Nikki's heart beat out of her chest and sweat break out on her forehead. It must be the same truck that Juana had seen.

The scrapheap of the kidnapper's pickup stopped short of the dumpsters. Flies buzzed Nikki's head, and one landed on her nose. At first, she let it walk around on her face until it got to the tear duct in her eye. Only then she used a hand to brush the pesky insect away, taking care not to make any noise. After a couple seconds, more flies buzzed around her face, and a few landed on her again. She hunkered down even more when she heard Goyo and his assistant loading the truck and Petra's voice confirming the items Goyo had requested. She held each breath, as if that would alleviate the fear she felt. Despite her makeshift nose plugs, the overwhelming odor of the garbage nearly asphyxiated her. She wanted to cough but managed to suppress the urge.

Petra, Goyo, and his assistant all returned inside the store. Everything fell silent, except the flies.

Nikki breathed again.

With no one else in the alley, she seized the opportunity to open the lid of the dumpster. She hoisted herself out and hid behind the smelly container and removed the nose plugs. No sooner had she done that when a door from the back side of the store swung open, hitting the wall. A child came down a couple of steps into the alley. She was crying, and Petra's voice commanded her to climb in the truck. Goyo yelled at the child to shut up.

"I want to see my mother," the child wailed in Spanish.

"She left you with me to send you to a better life," Petra said. "The man asked you to shut up, so you'd better mind him before he hurts you."

The child cried louder.

"Shut up, I told you." Goyo knocked the child to the ground with a punch to her chin. "Or I *will* send you to a better life."

At this point, Nikki hobbled out from behind the dumpster. "Goyo, take me with you and I'll—"

Goyo spun around, pulled a gun from a holster hanging from his belt, and pointed it at Nikki. She raised her arms in the air and took two steps back. Fear made beads of sweat roll down her back, despite the cool temperature.

"I'm offering to take care of her," Nikki said, still holding her arms up.

"Where the fuck did you come from?" His voice was harsh, and his penetrating eyes stared Nikki down. His right eyelid twitched to the point of a severe spasm that spread to the entire right side of his face.

"I walked into the alley to check the dumpster, hoping to salvage something to sell. I need my money for crossing the border. Let me come along with you, and I'll keep this child from bothering you."

The girl, about eleven or twelve, got up off the ground and stopped crying. Her eyes looked swollen, and her chin had a red spot from the punch she'd received. Nikki knew a nasty bruise would appear later. Despite her appearance, her long, black hair framed an oval-shaped face, setting off big brown eyes and high cheek bones. She was a pretty child.

"That might not be a bad idea," Petra said.

Goyo looked at Petra and clamped his jaw so hard his face stopped twitching.

"Are you telling me how to run my business?" he growled.

He grabbed the girl's arm and pushed her toward the truck, and she started crying again.

"Never," Petra said. "But this might be a way to keep this bratty child from spoiling everything. She's an unruly one. I can tell you. Her mother dropped her off three days ago, and she's done nothing but cry. She won't eat—"

The girl started sobbing and yelling for her mother. Goyo grabbed her throat and pressed it hard until she gasped for air and turned red. Nikki's heart pounded, but she knew she would risk both of their lives if she intervened.

"Yeah, or I can sedate her," Goyo said, dropping the girl to the ground.

"Do what you want. But remember . . . that other one. I am merely suggesting . . ." Petra said.

"You won't get much money for a dead child," Nikki said.

She turned and started to walk away, hoping she hadn't gone too far in her comment.

"Where do you know that woman from?" Goyo asked.

"Ramona Tafoya in Oaxaca sent her," Petra said. "She's sent people to me before."

"Can you trust Ramona?" he asked.

Petra nodded.

"Why are you headed for the U.S.?" Goyo asked, raising his voice to make sure Nikki heard him.

Nikki stopped and looked back. She swallowed hard before speaking. She knew it was safer not to go underground, but she remembered the pictures of Bibi—a beautiful, carefree child, who was now in the hands of these kidnappers, rapists, and murderers.

"My daughter lives there. She's going to have her first baby," Nikki said.

"Here's the deal," Goyo said. "I'll take you along, but you have to pay me an extra thousand for the transportation from here to the border, plus the eight thousand for crossing you."

"Why so much?" Nikki asked.

"It's harder to cross the border now. I take people over the border in a vehicle, so it costs more. If you can't control this one or the other ones, I'll get rid of you. Do you understand me?" Goyo said before he spat on the ground.

Nikki started walking toward Goyo. As she got closer, she protested the extra thousand. She felt her voice tremble and she cleared her throat, trying to negotiate a reasonable deal for a woman like her false persona, who would not have much, but she didn't want to push it either.

Goyo stood firm on the price.

Avoiding eye contact with him, Nikki's focused her eyes on the front of the pickup, up the hood, and on toward the windshield. She studied the wreck of a pickup the coyote drove, and she noticed something unusual on the windshield—an untarnished Notre Dame decal, with its distinctive blue and gold initials, the N mounted over the D.

How odd, Nikki thought, *for a pickup in Mexico to have a Notre Dame decal. The vehicle is probably stolen. And if they kidnapped the owner, that explains the sweatshirt Goyo's assistant is wearing.*

"What's your name?" Goyo asked.

Goyo's harsh voice startled her, and she realized her whole body flinched in response. She hoped he hadn't noticed. She turned to face him.

"Nita Zapote," she squeaked. She cleared her voice again and realized she was becoming overwhelmed by the danger she'd negotiated herself into. All she could hear now was the crying of the young girl.

Goyo walked to Nikki, grabbed her by the arm, and shoved her against his truck. He did a body search, feeling up and down her thighs, arms, and torso. He removed the carpetbag from her shoulders and dumped the contents on the hood of the pickup. Her clothes, an old comb, a couple of tissues, and the lipstick tube tumbled out. With one hand, he crushed the empty bag, as if to check for a gun or knife. Nikki watched as the lipstick case concealing a Taser, the only defense equipment she had, rolled from the hood onto the ground.

"Where's your money?" he asked, throwing the carpetbag on the hood.

"In my socks." Nikki gulped as she said the words. She stooped over to pick up the lipstick zapper. As she rose up again, she slid it in the pocket of her skirt and then placed her other personal belongings back in her bag.

"Give me the nine thousand now," he said in a stern voice.

Nikki bent down and picked up the hemline of her long skirt. Her socks went all the way to her knees, and each one bulged with her hidden cash. She reached first into one sock, removed the money, counted the ones, fives, tens, and twenties, and handed them to Goyo. Then she reached down to the other leg and removed another bundle of very used bills, all in small denominations, to complete the count.

Goyo pocketed the cash.

The girl kept crying, and it rubbed on Nikki's nerves. She had to get the child under control before Goyo decided to pull the gun again and kill them both. She stepped over and put her hand on the child's shoulder, an action that served to steady the tremor in her arm.

"And your name is . . . ?"

"Florencia," she said as she continued sobbing.

"We're going on a trip, Florencia. We're going to see new things, and we're going to experience things most people don't have a chance to do. Some of it will be good."

"I want to go back to my mother," the girl said. Her voice whimpered, but she was quieting down. Tears streaked her face.

"Florencia, come help me pick out a few things to buy." Nikki turned to Petra and, trying to steady her voice, said, "Petra, let me purchase a couple of items before we leave."

"I want to get going," Goyo said. "I thought you didn't have any money. Get whatever you need out of the dumpsters."

"I'll be quick. I'm going to get chucherías. Trinkets and sweets don't cost much."

She took the girl by the hand and walked toward the taniche's rear door in the alley. Petra looked at Goyo with a surprised expression on her face and then followed the two into the store.

Goyo spat on the ground. "Asshole women. They're all the same."

Once inside, Nikki hurriedly grabbed four packets of crayons, the wax kind and the chalk type as well. She took masking tape and a bundle of blank newsprint sheets off a shelf. Before she paid Petra, she added a *Mafalda* comic book and a bag of hard candy. She asked Florencia to help her carry the crayons and the masking tape while she carried the rest.

The three of them walked back outside. Goyo told Nikki and the girl to get in the truck and ordered his assistant to jump on the back.

"No, Florencia and I will ride in the back of the truck. She doesn't need to distract you while you're driving."

"If you try to escape, I'll kill you both," he said, his voice quiet yet venomous.

Even though Nikki and Florencia had already seen the weapon, he pulled open the left side of his jacket to let them see the gun in the holster hanging from his belt.

"You won't have to kill anyone," Nikki said. Her voice sounded more controlled now. "I need to get across the border."

Nikki heaved her goods and carpetbag over the tailgate of the pick-up. They made a loud banging sound as they landed on the truck bed. Florencia screamed and threw herself to the ground until she realized the noise had not come from Goyo's pistol. She got up, dusted herself off, and moved closer to Nikki. Goyo laughed—not a friendly laugh, but a mean-spirited, vicious one. It activated the involuntary twitch around his eye.

Nikki ignored the whole incident as she carefully placed a foot on the rear fender and used her arms to pull herself up by the tailgate to climb in. She extended her arms out to bring Florencia up. They both sat between the boxes of supplies Goyo and his assistant had loaded. Nikki sat on the passenger side, next to the truck's side panel, where she could rest her arm. Florencia sat next to her but closer to the middle.

Goyo drove out of the alley onto Aguascalientes Street toward Tacuba. Eduardo sat on the sidewalk at that intersection—his upper body propped up against the wall, his legs stretched out in front of him on the concrete. His breath smelled of the same cheap rum that was in a bottle next to his right hip. An earpiece positioned in his right ear, covered by a dirty straw hat, was connected to a mobile spy phone hidden in his rear pocket. He watched the truck go by. His face showed an expression of grief, yet passersby, whether driving or walking, took no particular notice of him except to avoid looking at a homeless drunk. The woman on the back of the truck hung her arm over the side and moved her hand in a gesture only he would recognize.

When the pickup turned the corner out of sight, Eduardo stood up. He picked up his rum bottle and pushed the hat down securely on his head. He looked around to make sure no one was watching, and he walked as fast as he could to the hotel, where he would enter through the stairwell from the underground parking. He would change clothes in the suite, re-turn to the garage, and retrieve his rental car.

Goyo drove on through the historical center of Zacatecas, a UNESCO World Heritage Site. He followed the main road through town—a narrow street, which had been laid out in the sixteenth century by the early Spanish settlers. During the silver boom years, the rest of the city had been built up on both sides of the big ravine running through the rugged terrain. Early Spanish settlers exploited the abundant silver mines surrounding the town, a few becoming immensely wealthy.

As soon as Goyo drove away from the center of town, Nikki pulled the *Mafalda* comic book out of the bundle she'd purchased and handed it to Florencia.

"I loved Mafalda when I was your age. Look at the pictures and then tell me how you think Mafalda would behave if she were on this trip with us."

Florencia did not look convinced, but she took the comic book and started leafing through it. The wind flapped the pages back and forth, making the book come alive like a primitive video cartoon. Soon Florencia laughed at the wind-animated cartoons.

Nikki reached into her carpetbag's secret compartment to feel the slick, plastic spy phone. She confirmed Florencia looked engaged with *Mafalda*, and she also made sure she was not in range of the rearview mirror or being watched by the assistant sitting in the cab. Retrieving the phone, she held it inside the carpetbag at an angle where she could see what she was doing. She deleted the only number she'd dialed. Deleting it left her phone totally clean except for a few numbers that came with the software that she could not erase. One was a special number that would ring at Security Source in Miami, which would be answered in Spanish by Charlotte or her assistants. Only an expert could tell the phone had powerful capabilities, and only if the expert examined it thoroughly. She slid it back into the secret compartment she had sewn into the carpetbag the night before.

Goyo, sitting straight up behind the steering wheel, drove with fierce determination on his face without uttering a word, even after they'd left the city and traveled over a dusty dirt road across the desert.

CHAPTER 13

San Miguel de Allende—Friday afternoon, day three after abduction

"Hi, Charlotte, any news for me?" Floyd was driving. He signaled a right turn, looked for a place to park, saw a small lot ahead, and steered the rental into it.

Charlotte's voice over the phone told him the phone number he'd asked her to investigate was from Italy—a cheap burner phone, not traceable to a specific owner.

"Did you have Jack trace it?" he asked.

"Yep," Charlotte's answer came into Floyd's ear, "and Jack got recent history of incoming and outgoing calls through last night. Not a lot of activity, but what's interesting is the calls are made to Mexico. Activity increased in the last three days, with San Miguel and Mexico City being the area codes used. Jack also informed me the phone is roaming in Mexico."

A parking attendant approached as Floyd opened the window and handed him a twenty peso bill. Floyd followed the attendant's signals to park the vehicle in an empty space.

"Have you sent me the list?" Floyd asked.

Charlotte informed him she'd traced one number—the Ristorante Italiano—where two short calls had been dialed yesterday. She'd email the list immediately.

"Tell Jack to get a daily update on that phone until I tell you to stop," Floyd said. "Thanks for the good work, Charlotte."

Charlotte asked Floyd to wait. She informed him Eduardo had called and asked her to activate the mike and camera on Nikki's spy phone.

"Anything of interest?" he asked.

She reported to him the camera wasn't sending images, but from the recordings they'd captured, Nikki seemed to be in crowded spaces. From the various voices, all speaking Spanish, they could not discern any particular danger for Nikki, though they were still trying to identify the unfamiliar voices they were hearing.

Floyd thanked her again as he hung up, put his phone on the passenger seat, reached around to the backseat, grabbed his tablet, opened it, and logged in to access his encrypted email account. He looked over the phone numbers Charlotte had sent him. He was always good at remembering numbers. He could remember phone numbers for years once he'd used them a couple of times. On the ones Charlotte sent him, he'd need to double-check against his notes to make certain, but he recognized Juana's telephone number as one of those called. He studied the list and another number popped out at him: Héctor Sánchez, the attorney in Mexico City. And Sofía's ristorante twice, as Charlotte had informed him.

He was closing out of his encrypted email when his phone rang. It was Sofía. She was crying. In between her sobs, Floyd was able to discern she'd had a phone call. From the kidnappers. They had her daughter.

"Sofía, do you know who called you?" Floyd asked.

Floyd gripped the phone as he heard her say they'd asked for two million dollars.

"I would pay it if I had that kind of money," she said. Her sobbing continued over the phone, making her voice difficult to understand.

"Sofía, please give me the number that called you. It's important so I can work on it."

Floyd heard her say the phone I.D. showed only that it was a private number.

"Did you speak with Bibi?" Floyd asked.

He listened intently as Sofía told him they'd threatened to kill Bibi if she didn't pay.

"They won't kill her," Floyd said, trying to reassure Sofía. "They need your daughter. Breathe in slowly and be calm. I'll be right over."

Floyd turned the phone off, started the engine on his rental truck, and headed toward Sofía's restaurant. He dialed Nikki's secure cell.

No answer.

Floyd feared she'd gone underground when Charlotte informed him about monitoring the transmissions captured in Miami. He dialed Eduardo next. When Eduardo answered on the third ring, Floyd lost his usual cool and spurted gibberish about Nikki. When Floyd realized Eduardo did not understand what he was saying, he slowed down.

"Eduardo, if it's not too late, tell Nikki she can't go underground because now I know—"

When Floyd heard Eduardo's response, the words sprang with a bang into his ears and ricocheted in his brain.

"It's too late, Floyd. She's already made the plunge into the coyote's den."

"You should have stopped her!" Floyd yelled into the phone. "I told her last night—"

"Shit, Floyd, don't you think I tried."

He explained that Nikki had driven past him about forty minutes earlier. He was driving the rental car, lagging behind a dark-gray pickup, following Nikki's GPS signal. Nikki was sitting in the back of the coyote's vehicle, right next to a child, maybe a teenager, dark complexion and black hair, so definitely not the Lombardi girl. Eduardo reminded Floyd that Nikki was determined to get Sofía's child back.

"Sofía received a call asking for ransom," Floyd said. "I don't think that coyote Nikki has gone off with took Sofía's daughter."

Fear gripped Eduardo. He could not respond. He pulled off the road, stopped the car, and barely made it out before he threw up.

CHAPTER 14

San Miguel de Allende—Friday afternoon, day three after abduction

When Floyd arrived at Sofía's place, he found parking on the street, a feat he considered close to a miracle in this town. He entered through the covered patio of the ristorante. Sofía was standing near the carved wood bar, talking to a man. She waved her hand for Floyd to join them, and he could feel the somber atmosphere between the two people as he stepped toward them.

"Paolo Lombardi, Bibi's father. He arrived from Turin this morning," she said as she introduced Floyd.

Sofía looked as if she had aged ten years in the few hours since Floyd had spoken to her earlier that day. Her face was puffy, her eyelids were swollen, the whites of her eyes were bloodshot, and her hair was a sloppy, uncombed disarray. Lines appeared on her forehead where none had shown before.

Floyd extended his hand to Paolo. The Italian man was dressed in a wrinkled, light-weight, tailored yet casual suit. He wore an equally wrinkled Tommy Bahama-style linen shirt that coordinated with his sporty, tan-colored suit. The top two buttons of his shirt were unbuttoned, and his hair was disheveled. Yet he exhibited that sexy appeal that turns women's eyes.

"I wanted to meet the man heading up the investigation to find my daughter," Paolo said. He spoke English with an elegant British accent. "You know Sofía received a call requesting a two million dollar ransom?"

Floyd could see Paolo had been raised and educated with a Roman silver spoon in his mouth, whereas Sofía was far earthier in her style. He understood why a mother-in-law with aristocratic taste had not been fond of her daughter-in-law.

"Yes," Floyd said. "The reason I'm here. I want to bring in a negotiator from my office in Miami—"

"Whatever it costs," Paolo said, interrupting as he ran his fingers through his rumpled hair in a fashion reminiscent of playboys at a beach party. "I'm prepared to pay what they're asking, the full ransom. I only want assurances she will be returned unharmed."

"First, we need to speak with the child so we can confirm she's alive and well," Floyd said.

"We have no way of contacting them," Sofía said.

"That's correct. That's the way they operate," Floyd said. "Second, we don't agree to pay the full ransom—"

"I'll pay whatever they want. We want Bibi back," Paolo said. As he interrupted Floyd, he took out a handkerchief and wiped the sweat on his forehead. "Before I left Italy, I signed preauthorization forms for wire transfers. For large amounts."

"Understand, it's in their best interest to keep Bibi alive," Floyd said. "What we need to do is ensure they *return her alive*. And for that reason, I want to bring in my negotiator. We do not pay until we receive assurances she will be released unharmed."

"Bring your negotiator," Paolo said. "I'll pay for him." He looked at Sofía briefly and returned his gaze to Floyd.

"I'm bringing in two people, not one."

"I said, whatever it takes," Paolo said.

"So there will be three of us here. My electronics expert will track incoming phone calls to try to locate the kidnappers' location. Between the negotiator and me, someone will always be here to talk to the kidnappers," Floyd said. He turned to Sofía. "Can three of us camp out here?"

"Of course." Sofía looked as if she wanted to explode into tears but managed to maintain a semblance of composure.

"It's best to keep the police out," Floyd said. "You don't want this hitting the news. This is Mexico, and we don't need to complicate matters. My biggest concern is your restaurant staff."

"They've worked with me a long time and they are very loyal," Sofía said. "Like family."

"Yet they must be speculating about what's going on. And people talk," Floyd said. "If they know about the ransom request, instruct them to keep quiet about whatever they know. Bibi's life could depend on it."

"No, the request came right before Paolo arrived at my door. So I called you, yeah, and told Paolo, that's all," Sofía said.

"Three men staying on the premises will look suspicious," Paolo said. "Maybe I should also camp out here starting tomorrow, otherwise the staff will suspect the worst with Floyd and his helpers hanging around. I'm Bibi's father. It makes sense I'd be staying here with three strangers around."

"Sounds like a plan to me if it's okay with Sofía," Floyd said.

"Anything, anything to get my daughter back. Yeah, anything," she said. She clamped her lips together in an obvious attempt to keep from crying.

"Better yet, Sofía, to keep the staff from learning too much, give them all a vacation and close the restaurant," Floyd said.

"That doesn't make sense, they will know—"

"Then maybe it's a better idea to tell them I'm here because you and I are getting back together," Paolo said, interrupting her.

"Well, they all know I've badmouthed you for years so I don't know..."

"Let's consider the idea, Sofía," Floyd said. "I think it might work."

"And what do I say about Bibi? They know I suspect Paolo of taking her, and he didn't bring her with him," Sofía said. She looked at Floyd and started crying again.

"True," Paolo said. "Tell them I took her to Italy and my mother is taking care of her. That explanation gives them the idea we will use our time together to work out our problems and see if we can reconcile."

"That's not a bad idea," Floyd said. "The least said to them, the better. They will still gossip, but they won't know exactly what's going on. Will you play the game, Sofía?"

"I guess it's worth a try, yeah." She sighed heavily. "Let's do it."

"Then close the restaurant until we get Bibi back," Paolo said.

Floyd excused himself and moved a few feet away from Paolo and Sofía. He called Charlotte to make arrangements to have Timothy Ramos, his expert negotiator in kidnapping cases, fly into León, Guanajuato, that day and then take an airport limo to San Miguel. Floyd also arranged to have his telephone consultant, Jack Levy, arrive through the Querétaro airport and also take a limo to San Miguel.

"Tell Timothy to contact Jack. We'll need telephone monitoring equipment. We can't wait to get import approvals, so they need to bring it with them. They need to separate the equipment into two parts, each one of them can bring in one part. Tell them to list it as sales demo instruments on their customs declaration. It's important they travel separately and through separate airports. Can't risk customs officials finding surveillance instruments that should not be brought into the country. They would confiscate them."

When Floyd finished his phone call, he rejoined Paolo and Sofía.

"Let me explain that Timothy and I will use a lot of psychology in the negotiations with the kidnapper. We'll need a room that is totally quiet. Jack will try to track the location of their phone. I cannot afford to have anyone talking or making noise. The danger is too great."

"You can use my bedroom for operations, and I'll move into Bibi's room. Whatever you need, you'll get. It's my daughter's life," she said, looking at Floyd with imploring eyes.

"I'm in need of rest," Paolo said, rubbing his eyes. "I haven't slept for two days. Now that you're here, Floyd, I'll walk back to my hotel down the hill. The Sierra Nevada. Sofía knows where it is. I'll bring my luggage up here tomorrow."

"I'll walk with you, Paolo, if you don't mind," Floyd said.

Once outside, Floyd thought about the questions he had for Paolo. He wanted to pose them in a way to avoid sounding like an interrogator. Both men stared at the ground for every step they took on the steep cobblestone street to avoid slipping or twisting an ankle.

"I was wondering if you don't mind sharing what you told Sofía when you called her yesterday."

"Yesterday?" Paolo asked. "I did not speak to her yesterday, only today after I arrived this morning. I wasn't sure how she'd react to my flying in after all the problems between us, so I waited until I landed."

"You're sure you did not call her yesterday?" Floyd repeated.

"Yes. Why do you ask?"

"Sofía received two phone calls yesterday from an Italian phone."

"Calls from Italy?" Paolo asked. With a surprised expression, he stopped and looked at Floyd. "Could have been Chiara. That's my mother, but she does not communicate with Sofía. Doesn't Sofía know who called?"

"No, the caller hung up both times."

"What's the number?" Paolo asked.

Floyd said it out loud.

"No, that's not Chiara. Don't recognize it at all. Can't you investigate it?" Paolo asked.

"I have my expert doing just that," Floyd said. "We know it's a disposable phone, but I thought I'd ask to save time if it had been you." Floyd flagged down a taxi. "My knees can't take walking down this hill."

They crammed into the small car. In no time, the driver stopped in front of the upscale Sierra Nevada. Two guards opened an iron gate and welcomed Paolo. Both Floyd and Paolo stepped into a patio full of flowering bougainvillea. Paolo led the way to the second patio, a larger space with jacaranda trees exploding with purple flowers, where he had rented the presidential suite.

"Has Héctor Sánchez, your attorney, given you any information I should know?" Floyd asked.

"No. He doesn't even know I'm in Mexico. He thinks I'm flying in two days from now. I thought I'd him call later, after I get some sleep. Now, if you don't need me, I'd like to rest, but call me if I can help."

Paolo walked up the stairs leading to the presidential suite. Floyd hailed a cab for the ride up the winding street back to Sofía's restaurant.

Floyd found Sofía inside, standing next to the bar. He gave her an inquisitive look.

"What changed his mind? He's so cooperative."

"Paolo said he flew to Miami and then to León once he realized Bibi really was kidnapped. He told me he hasn't even notified his attorney that he's here. Yeah, now he's worried." Sofía's voice sounded strained, and her Italian accent seemed stronger than ever.

"At least he's helping. Can you show me where I'll be staying?" Floyd asked.

Sofía took him to the living quarters and showed him her bedroom.

"Why don't we use your daughter's room?"

"I'd prefer you use this one," Sofía said. "It's bigger, contains a phone extension for the land line, the same line as in the restaurant, and has both a table and a desk. It has its own bathroom, whereas Bibi's room has a hallway bath."

Sofía opened the closet and shoved her own clothes to one side, selecting a teal-green blouse and black pants and folding them over her arm.

"I've already let my staff go on vacation. I'm going to the kitchen to make sure they are all prepared to leave the premises, and I'll return shortly to clean out cosmetics and other personal stuff from here and the bathroom so you can use it more comfortably. We'll put in inflatable beds for your two consultants. You can use that old roll-top desk."

Floyd wasn't really listening. He was leaning against the frame of the doorway, analyzing the next steps to take. He had to figure out the lay of the land in Sofía's property. He needed to inspect the whole building and examine the streets behind and to the other side of her property.

"Sofía, you need to give me a tour of the whole interior and exterior of your property. Then I'll go outside to see exactly where you're located and what major thoroughfares you have close by."

"Thoroughfares, like in major streets? In San Miguel, they don't exist. But the street that takes you to the highway to Querétaro is one short block away. Yeah, my street dead-ends into it. The whole property is walled in. Within the confines of the walls, my valet uses empty space on the east end of my property as a parking lot. He accesses it through a large gate in the alleyway. The alley also dead-ends into the street taking you to Querétaro. You can park your truck in my valet parking. I'll give you a key for the gate."

"And what is the name of the alley," Floyd asked.

"Calle del Ciudadano Garza. A pompous name for a short alleyway. Callejón de la Garza for short. Or just Garza."

CHAPTER 15

Zacatecas—Friday afternoon, day three after abduction

Wind howled and whipped around Nikki. She bounced along next to a large box on the bed of Goyo's dilapidated pickup as he drove over the poorly marked desert road. She was having second thoughts about going undercover, but it was too late. Her soul felt as conflicted as the gusts of wind that periodically showered the back of the pickup with tiny grains of sand. As the wind whistled through the rock formations of the Zacatecan landscape, it made her think of sayings she'd heard from her grandmother about the devil making himself evident in whirlwinds as he rustled up evil.

The devil is on the loose here for sure, especially in the demonic hearts of coyotes who have stolen innocent children, Nikki thought.

Her stomach churned in anxiety over the mission she'd embarked on, but trying to escape now would only get her and Florencia killed. And Bibi would be lost forever. She also thought of Eduardo, how she'd disappointed him when she accepted this job. She had ruined their vacation and was regretting it. It had been about an hour since she'd parted from Eduardo, but she missed him terribly.

In the future, she told herself, *I'll have to balance my need to work in this line of business with my love for Eduardo and our lives together.*

She was so accustomed to being single, making all the decisions, and working all the time. It was an adjustment now to consider another person's feelings, but it was a wonderful adjustment. She just hadn't made the full transition yet.

Research she'd done on her laptop during the flight from the Yucatán to Querétaro popped up in her mind. At the time, she did not think it was useful, but she'd done it out of curiosity to learn about kidnappings in Mexico. She rehashed in her mind the portion on human trafficking to get a better grip on the situation she now confronted.

Human trafficking the world over exploited girls in particular for sexual purposes. She knew the unspeakable consequences for young women. She also knew trafficking happened primarily from poor and oppressed neighborhoods to rich neighborhoods, or from poor countries to richer ones where the markets existed. But it spilled over more and more into all neighborhoods, regardless of socio-economic conditions. She mulled over in her mind that, in every economic issue, two sides coexisted side by side, each dependent on the other.

It is no different in sex trafficking, she thought. *The first is the demand side, which represents the buyer of sex services, and the second is obviously the supply side, which is there since demand is present. The exploitation of children and teenagers comes from transactions between traffickers, who provide customers with underage individuals. These customers demand a variety of sexual services, from pornography to the most depraved sexual abuse, even murder at times. A horribly, dirty business, the worst type.*

Another gust of wind made the skin of her face and arms sting as the tiny grains of sand pelted her face and body mask.

While the pickup bumped along the hilly desert road, Nikki continued mulling over the research the United Nations had conducted in 2012, the last year facts were available. She'd read that the UN calculated the global human trafficking industry, if it can be called that, at thirty-two billion U.S. dollars annually. Eighty percent of that number was attributed to sex slavery of one form or another. Most victims found themselves in situations where escape from their captors was life-threatening. Abduction, deceit, and coercion were tactics used to obtain, recruit, transfer, and maintain control over enslaved individuals. Nikki felt even more depressed about the task she was undertaking, but she had to save the Lombardi child from that awful destiny. And hopefully save Florencia too. She couldn't anticipate how many children Goyo was responsible for stealing. But saving all of them, she realized, might put her whole operation at risk.

A chilling thought.

COYOTE ZONE

Goyo drove his gray junk heap off the dirt road and bumped along a path that appeared to only recently have been cut through the desert terrain by a few tire tracks. He drove right up to a steep mountainside with rocky outcroppings and steered straight into the mouth of a cave. Then he stopped the truck.

Nikki, her back toward the cabin of the pickup, looked around from the bed of the truck. Both surprise and fear mounted in her as she realized they'd gone from the bright sunlight outside to the interior of the dark cave. She squinted to adjust her eyes to the barely visible surroundings. Glancing back to where they had entered this dungeon, she noticed a large cave opening where light entered, but it quickly dissolved into a murky blackness that enveloped the space.

Everything Juana told us has panned out to be true. The coyote is using a cave in Zacatecas to hold his hostages. Fear made her stomach churn. *Was Juana in on this deal and that's why they killed her?*

Nikki detected the odor of bat guano, which pervaded the stale air, and she heard a motor rumbling. Then she saw another vehicle, a large transport truck, parked inside the cave. Shivers ran down her spine. She figured it was a refrigerated intermodal shipment container, called a "reefer" in the industry. People could be transported in a truck like that. A secret compartment, behind a refrigerated area where meat or fruit could be loaded, would conceal the real commodity being driven across the border. In the low light, the truck appeared to be in good condition, not like the junk heap Goyo drove. Her prior employer in Minneapolis was a worldwide conglomerate, which owned a division that manufactured freight trucks similar to that one. Nikki knew her heavy trucks and transporters. Large trucks like that one crossed the border into the U.S. carrying perishables, construction materials, petroleum, or other products. They had to abide by highway and transport regulations, including emission controls that had been established by the North American Free Trade Agreement. Goyo's pickup would never pass, but the refrigerated transport truck would clear easily.

That's how they get children into the U.S. With the extra border security these days, they do not walk them across, but instead drive them in the reefer.

The sound of the motor continued to hum. Reefers rumbled in rounds of low, continuous tones, but the noise she heard was too high-pitched for the reefer. Nikki looked around to find the source but could not figure it out.

A man, toting an automatic weapon, came out of the darkness, like a person emerging from black fog, and approached the pickup.

"How are you, jefe?" the man asked in Spanish.

"I'm fine, Bernardo," Goyo said, continuing in Spanish as he and his assistant got out of the pickup.

The assistant motioned to Nikki and Florencia to get out of the back. Nikki grabbed her carpetbag and the package of goods from Petra's store. Then she put all of it, including the newsprint bundle, into her bag.

"Everything is quiet on this front," Bernardo said. Then he saw Nikki and Florencia. "Who the fuck is this?"

"A woman who is going to cook for us. Her name is Nita," Goyo said.

Bernardo shook his head. "Why did you bring this old woman? Don't you know, Goyo, a bad apple ruins the barrel?"

"I have my reasons," Goyo said.

Goyo turned to face Nikki and gave instructions.

"Follow Bernardo. He will take you to the kids. He'll show you where you'll cook and where you'll sleep tonight."

Bernardo mumbled under his breath as he walked off. "This old hag is not even good enough to serve as a whore."

Nikki hobbled off behind Bernardo. She held Florencia's hand and de-tected trembling, and for a moment she was unsure whether it was her hand or Florencia's that was shaking. She brought Florencia a little closer to her and put her arm around the girl's shoulder.

The sound of the motor Nikki had heard when they entered the cave seemed to come from the extreme right side, near the cave's entrance. Her eyes had adjusted, and she looked back and saw sand bags piled in a heap about three feet high by three feet in length. She guessed they surrounded a small gasoline-operated electric generator. The acrid odor of bat guano prevented the fumes from being detected.

Bernardo used a flashlight to light their way as he took them farther into the bowels of the cave. As they walked, dim light could be seen ahead. Bernardo made a right turn. Nikki and Florencia followed, and with each step they took, the light glowed a bit brighter. After a few more steps, they turned slightly and came upon a room of sorts. The light came from a single bulb hanging from the end of an electrical cord that had been looped over a natural ledge formed in the cave wall. The light cast long shadows on the rock wall on the opposite side of the room.

In the shadowy light, Nikki stared at several kids, mostly girls, in a type of improvised kitchen with a gas stove, refrigerator, portable sink, a standard forty-four gallon water dispenser on a metal stand often used in Mexico, and two large wood tables with long benches. Wooden crates and cardboard boxes stacked haphazardly against the rock wall of the cave gave the space a disorganized atmosphere. Three children sat at the tables, one stood at the sink, three were sitting on crates, and another two sat cross-legged on the floor. They all glared at Nikki. She broke the silence.

"What have we here?"

No one answered, and no one moved—frozen, as if they were characters in a science fiction movie.

Bernardo looked at the old woman and back at the kids.

"Nita is here to do the pinche cooking for all of you. Angela, you'll help her and show her where the provisions are kept."

He ignored mentioning Florencia, who was holding Nikki's hand again.

Nikki's eyes darted from child to child, trying to identify Bibi. She noticed three children were boys. Angela, she reasoned, had to be the taller girl at the sink, who appeared older than the others, maybe fourteen or fifteen.

One of the cross-legged children on the floor had curly hair and sat close to the wall of rock, left of the refrigerator. She appeared to be around twelve years of age. The child did not look up, but she held a short stick in her hand and poked absentmindedly at the dirt, as if she were digging in a sandpit. The ground underneath this child looked less compressed than the more trafficked areas, where people's feet had worn the earth into a hardened dirt floor. Nikki studied her but after a few seconds realized it could not be Bibi.

Nikki searched desperately for Bibi's curly, light-colored hair. None of the girls looked like the child in Sofía's pictures. Did Juana purposely steer her and Eduardo in the wrong direction? She felt a spasm in her gut, grimaced, and took her hand to her stomach.

"Do you have any questions?" Bernardo asked.

"About dinner. What time is the meal?" Nikki asked, her voice cracking.

The atmosphere felt heavy and dense, weighted down with the odor of bat guano. The stale air was enough to sicken anyone.

"Supper is early, between seven and seven thirty," Bernardo said. "Now hand over your pinche purse."

Bernardo did not wait for her to hand it to him. He yanked it off her shoulder and emptied the contents on the table closest to him, spilling crayons and loose change on the ground. He took the change of clothes Nikki had packed, laid them out across the planks in the table, and ran his fingers over them. He pressed his hands against the blank newsprint and left it on the bench. Then he threw the carpetbag on the floor.

Nikki picked her bag up off the ground, dusted it, and placed it on a bench. She folded her clothes and returned them to the bag. Going to her hands and knees, she gathered the scattered crayons and coins. She arranged the crayons in the cardboard boxes and placed them, along with the change, in her bag. Then she put her hand on the bench, as an old woman would, to help herself stand up.

"Now, I'll show you where you'll sleep," Bernardo said.

His gaze moved slightly down to study Florencia for a couple of seconds, and he reached for the book she held tightly against her chest. She held it so tight that he had to wrestle it away from her.

"So you think you're tough? Well, I'll find out later how much of a fighter you really are," he said, laughing in a sinister way. He turned the book over and looked at the cover. "Aha, I see. *Mafalda*. Where the hell did you get this? Can you even fucking read?"

Nikki reached for Florencia's hand. "I gave it to her."

Bernardo raised the butt of his AK-47 and hit Nikki across her left cheek. She lost her balance and stepped back in an effort to regain her equilibrium. Florencia, standing next to Nikki, helped to steady her.

"Let the damn girl answer the question," Bernardo said.

Florencia moved in slightly closer to Nikki.

"I'll read to you tonight." He laughed in a diabolic manner. "Now let me show you where you'll sleep."

Nikki rubbed her check to lessen the pain without letting go of Florencia's hand. As Bernardo walked away, Nikki limped behind him, pulling

Florencia along with her, knowing he would hit her again if they did not follow him. He backtracked to the area where they'd made the right-hand turn for the kitchen, but instead of returning to the entrance, he headed deeper into the cave. With the flashlight turned on again, he walked close to the cave wall. Then he stopped and put the flashlight on the ground. The light beamed straight up toward the roof of the cave.

Nikki took in Bernardo's features, features she'd never forget. She also scrutinized the area but started coughing. She'd been so fully focused on taking in details that her brain took twenty or thirty seconds to detect what her olfactory receptors already perceived. A foul odor. A *very* foul odor. It filled the area to such a degree that it overpowered the bat guano.

Bernardo retrieved a matchbook from his shirt pocket. He took a match out, struck it on the sole of his shoe, and used it to light a Coleman gas lamp on the cave floor. The lamp was placed near a large metal box. As the Coleman lamp flickered before it emitted a steady light, Nikki could see two makeshift metal boxes and realized they were construction-type portable toilets, except that these appeared to be permanent fixtures built on site. The stench was so overpowering, she figured the putrid contents were not removed frequently enough, if ever.

"I hope this is not the bedroom," Nikki said, coughing again.

Bernardo snorted. "Nothing but shit here, puta. The sleeping is farther down. But you'll get used to the smell. They all do." He bent over to pick the flashlight up.

"I'm surprised your match didn't cause an explosion on the fumes in here," Nikki said.

"Shut up." Bernardo held his automatic weapon up, but he did not touch her this time. His voice was vicious as he continued. "Unless you want me to beat you into submission, do as I ask." He spat on the ground. "Follow me."

Bernardo turned, flicked the flashlight toward the ground, and cast light along the cave's contour to illuminate the physical layout of the cave. Then he walked on, leaving the Coleman lamp behind. The lamp emitted a haunting, amber glow in the darkness.

Nikki followed, pulling Florencia along. Their shuffling feet on the ground sounded eerily magnified. Not quite an echo, yet their footsteps caused an auditory sensation in her ears.

Effects from the enclosure of a cave, she thought. *It feels like I've been buried alive.*

Bernardo stopped a few feet away and beamed the flashlight from side to side to shine light on bundles of differing heights and sizes set out in a makeshift pattern on the cave floor, filling the space ahead of them. The bundles, Nikki realized, were beds and bedrolls. The stomach-wrenching odor of human feces lingered in the air.

"You'll get that bed," Bernardo said, shining the flashlight on a ramshackle cot. "Being an old puta brings its privileges." He laughed in a macabre manner.

The low ceiling in this part of the cave was confining, and Nikki felt clammy, despite the cool humidity of the environment. She took a deep breath in, trying to calm her nerves. The odor she inhaled made her want to puke, and her stomach hurt. But the physical reaction of a sick stomach had occurred as soon as she realized she'd made a huge miscalculation.

Bibi was not there.

Nikki did not know how she was going to get out of the mess she'd immersed herself in. She tried to analyze her situation, but she was at a loss as to what to do. She'd need to think of something to get out alive from the trap she'd willingly walked into, but she also knew she was wasting precious time to find Sofía's daughter.

Besides, can I walk away from all the children in this cave who are in a desperate situation, children who do not have parents with enough money to save them from a horrible fate?

Even as Nikki wondered, she knew the answer. She didn't want to leave them in this helpless position.

But how can I save them all? What about Bibi? That's the child I'm supposed to save.

Bernardo picked up a rock and threw it with force against a large overhanging stalactite. Bats, thousands of them that had been hanging from stalactites and the surrounding cave roof, flew by, first in panicked bunches of a few hundred and then in thousands. The chamber filled with noise as the bats blasted past in chaotic disarray, emitting high-frequency sounds. Nikki and Florencia ducked, yet a couple of them hit her as they flew past. Obviously, being surprised and stirred up unexpectedly created confusion among the colony, leading to total pandemonium. Outside the cave, a bat would never hit another object, but being frightened off their perches inside a cave caused disorientation, which, in turn, made them ignore their internal radar.

Bernardo laughed hysterically. Then he walked in front of Nikki, put his face right up into hers, and yelled, "If you don't work out as a cook for us, I'll lock you in a box with these flying animals."

Nikki simply stared back at him in the dim light, and as he moved away, she wiped the minuscule drops of spit off her mask that Bernardo's screaming had deposited on her.

In about a minute, the bats started settling back into their hanging colony and the cave became quiet again. Her thoughts went from Bernardo's nasty outbreak back to the features of the cavern. That's when Nikki heard the sound of dripping water, a few drops at a time. She wondered if there were any live stalactites, the rock buildup formed by minerals precipitating out of the water solution filtering through the limestone caves. She doubted it since she reasoned people had been using these caves with reckless disregard—they would have killed the process by abusing the environment. But water was filtering into the cave somewhere.

Can I get these children out alive? she thought as she listened to the melodic spatter of water drops.

CHAPTER 16

San Miguel de Allende—Friday evening, day three after abduction

Floyd paced back and forth in his makeshift operations room. He stopped at the roll-top desk to take a bite of a smoked salmon and tomato sandwich, topped off with thin slices of mozzarella cheese, which Sofía had brought him. He washed it down with a gulp of black coffee. Then he sat down in the ergonomic chair in front of the desk and picked up his phone to dial Eduardo.

"Where are you now?" Floyd asked.

Eduardo reported he was about to enter the garage at the Zacatecas hotel after following the kidnapper's pickup truck until the guy turned off onto a secondary road. After that, Eduardo couldn't follow him anymore without the coyote knowing he was being tracked.

"Are you sure he didn't know he had a tail?" Floyd asked.

Eduardo explained he had followed the GPS signal. The terrain was so hilly, he had not even seen the coyote's vehicle for much of the time, although he had seen where the guy turned off. At that point, he'd stopped the car to climb a hill and watch the pickup's path with binoculars.

"Are you sure he didn't see you?" Floyd asked.

Floyd listened as Eduardo told him he was positive he had not been detected by the coyote. And he added that, since he knew where the truck went, it'd be easy to pick up Nikki's GPS signal when they searched that night, after dark. They could locate the cave the guy used.

"Not tonight," Floyd said as he took another bite of the salmon sandwich. "I'm stuck in San Miguel until I get new assets in from Miami. I need to stay here in case the kidnappers call to discuss ransom."

Eduardo offered to go alone. "I can't leave her out there alone with a coyote if—"

"Stay put. Nikki knows how to handle things. You'd endanger her more by going out there on your own. We will find her tomorrow. With kidnappers calling Sofía for ransom, I can't leave until both Timothy and Jack arrive. Sofía cannot handle this situation on her own. My guys will get in late tonight."

"But Nikki needs us."

"I told you, Nikki can take care of herself for tonight," Floyd said.

"Earlier you were upset because she'd gone underground."

"Look, Eduardo, I need Nikki helping us, not chasing a trafficker who doesn't have Bibi. I need to interview Josefina again. That's la Marihuana's friend. That woman is holding back useful information on the kidnappers, but I can't leave Sofía's house. You can help by going out to talk to Josefina. Come straight to Sofía's place, and I'll give you all the details once you get here."

Eduardo sounded angry and exasperated when he asked Floyd if he'd forgotten about Nikki's safety.

"Sounds like you're pretty upset with me," Floyd said. "Think strategy. Think about the best approach to this case. That means we'll search for Nikki tomorrow. She has the experience and training to take care of herself. Besides, Jack's an expert in electronic surveillance and communications. With his knowledge, we can tail our suspects in digital format and apply the technology to locate and save Nikki."

From the conversation, it was clear to Eduardo that Floyd was dismissing the danger Nikki faced. Eduardo would have time to ponder their conversation on the hour-and-a-half drive from Zacatecas to San Miguel to interview Juana's friend.

And Eduardo was thinking—okay, wondering—if Nikki had misled him when he'd met her in Medellín. Much as he loved her, Floyd's remark about Nikki's ability to take care of herself still made him wonder if Nikki had indeed worked for the CIA, despite her denials.

Had she been a CIA agent when she had worked on the investigation in Colombia?

CHAPTER 17

Zacatecas—Friday evening, day three after abduction

Bernardo's harsh voice commanded Nikki and Florencia to return to the kitchen. Florencia, standing next to Nikki and still holding her hand, trembled every time Bernardo spoke. Despite the unpleasantness, Nikki kept hearing the drops of water filtering into the cave. She found it amazing that little droplets could make themselves be heard in such a dank and dark environment. She also wondered if the source of the water might provide some route for escape.

As Bernardo started walking toward the kitchen, Nikki and Florencia followed. Nikki had hoped she could locate the pool where the droplets were falling, but soon the sound of the dripping water dissipated.

The bang of a metal door, which was followed by waves of echoes reverberating throughout the cave, brought Nikki back to the present. In the dim light, two small figures emerged from the area of the foul-smelling toilets. The Coleman lamp Bernardo had left near the outhouses provided so little light that he shined the flashlight in the direction of the primitive outhouses.

The light shone on two girls.

The smaller one had blonde, curly hair. Nikki started shaking.

Bibi? she thought. *Is that child Bibi?*

Nikki's pulse rose, and her heart started pumping so hard, the sound of her own heartbeat was deafening in her ears. Her immediate impulse was to leave Florencia standing alone with Bernardo and rush over to hug the curly haired child, embrace her and assure her she would soon be home, safe in her mother's arms. But Nikki had to remain rooted to the ground, motionless. She could not endanger them all.

I'm thankful for the shadowy light, which keeps my emotions hidden, she thought.

The two children headed slowly toward the kitchen area. In the dark cavern—its uneven ground littered with rocks, sporadic mounds of bat guano, and other debris—the girls stumbled along past periodic wisps of light, which bounced their silhouettes on the cave wall like primitive Asian shadow puppets twisted around by a cruel puppeteer. The girls were holding hands, probably to steady their fear as much as their balance.

"Come on, you bitch, move," Bernardo said, thrusting the tip of the AK-47 into Nikki's jawline. "Get back to the kitchen and cook. Take this puta chava with you. In case you think of escaping, don't even consider it. We'll hunt you down like an animal, torture you, and cut your fingernails out. You'd beg for fucking mercy."

He pushed Nikki away by thrusting the barrel of his automatic into her jaw even harder. She did not respond but merely shuffled away from Bernardo's threatening weapon. Taking Florencia's hand, Nikki guided the two of them toward the wall of the cave to use it like a guardrail to avoid falling. They trudged along like phantoms, following Bibi and the other child.

Bernardo started whistling a lively tune as he headed toward the front of the cave. Soon he turned to singing, moving the flashlight in step with the rhythm of his song, the sound of his voice echoing throughout the chamber.

When they arrived at the hole called a kitchen, Nikki wanted to speak with Bibi, wanted to confirm without a doubt she was Bibi, but she decided not to single the child out and create problems. She also wanted to make sure none of the men were guarding them so closely that they could detect her intentions. She listened for chatter between the kids, but she only heard voices coming from the front of the cave, obviously Goyo and his men. As intently as she tried, she could not distinguish their conversation. The echo made it difficult to decipher their words.

Angela still stood at the makeshift sink, washing dishes. Nikki, considering she would need someone to help her from within the group, walked right up to Angela.

"Can I help you?" she asked Angela in Spanish. The girl barely turned to acknowledge Nikki.

She was a tall, thin girl, her slender body making her appear taller than she really was. On her neck, a tattoo message stated "Soy del Animal Chavero." The words looked like finely chiseled, antique, Gothic block letters, done in black ink framed by small red roses and green leaves.

"Your tattoo ...?" Nikki asked.

"A present," Angela whispered. "The pimp who handled me. He put his name on me." She stole a glance at Nikki, as if afraid to say too much.

"You've worked as a prostitute?" Nikki asked as she positioned herself where she could carry on a conversation with Angela, yet observe most of the kids. Looking at the curly haired one, Nikki felt pretty certain the child was Bibi.

Angela's eyes, filled with tears, locked with Nikki's for a second. Then she looked away, embarrassed.

"Sí, seño. They all put their names on their girls, like they were the masters and we were the slaves."

Considered them chattel, Nikki thought. *So unfortunate and so true.*

"So why are you crossing again?" Nikki asked.

Angela turned to face her, as if the young girl was struggling for an answer. "My bad luck."

"I'm crossing the border for the first time," Nikki said, "so I don't know much about this. Can you explain the process?"

Angela gazed at Nikki and seemed to study her for a few seconds.

"What do you want to know?"

"I thought you could tell me about your experiences crossing the border."

Angela stopped washing dishes and looked at the ground.

"I crossed once before, but I got away and came back to my hometown. I'd only been there one week when my step-father sold me to Goyo. This time, Goyo will sell me directly into prostitution. He told me that."

Nikki looked at the lanky girl. "Do you think escape ...?"

"Goyo paid for me, seño. He owns me now. He'd have my mother killed if I escaped. My mother's husband is an old drunk. He sold me to get money for mezcal."

"Then he's sold you twice?"

Angela shook her head. "The first time I crossed the border, I did it on my own, seño."

"Just call me Nita. So you decided to cross on your own?"

"Well, it was my mother who took all the money she had and paid Goyo. I was going to get work as a hotel housekeeper in New Mexico. A friend of my mother's from our hometown does that in Albuquerque, so she had arranged for me to be hired where she worked, but Goyo's group got assaulted by bajadores, men who took us by force. They kidnapped all of us."

"Bajadores?" Nikki's attention was distracted as she saw Bibi put her head down on the table where she sat at one of the long benches.

"Yes. Goyo took us to the U.S. side through tunnels. I guess we went under the Rio Grande. We were walking in the dark when those bajadores caught us. It was very dark. We walked for an hour, maybe, after we left the tunnels."

"So what did they do to you?"

"They took me to Houston. To a dirty cantina in a run-down, rough, and dangerous area. Gun's Point, the local gringos called it. Earned its name for gang shootings. I kept dreaming of escaping. Tall, beautiful buildings of steel and glass stood a few blocks away. A different world, maybe a kilometer up the road, but they'd kill me if I escaped."

"Are you sure they were bajadores, or is it possible they were Goyo's partners waiting on the other side?" Nikki asked.

Angela shrugged her shoulders and returned to the dishwashing. "Never thought about it. When the men attacked us, they pulled out guns, loaded us into a covered truck, and drove us to Houston. Others in the group said they were bajadores."

"How did you know you were being taken to Houston?"

"It took two days. We made several stops. A man would open the panel door and look the pollos over. Pollos, that's us, the illegals. Guess we're like chicks seeking protection from a parent figure, in this case from the coyote. They stopped several times. He'd choose one or two men, and they'd get them out, and they'd be left behind. On the second day, when the door was open, I saw a green sign that said 'Houston—50 miles.'"

"You couldn't escape? Didn't they stop to let any of you use a bathroom?"

"No, we used buckets."

"What happened after you got to Houston?"

"I was the last one in the truck, and they dropped me at the cantina, where I joined a dozen other girls already working there. The owner was a miserly old woman, who showed us no pity. Not even when we had our periods. Her son put his name on me, and he collected the money for my work."

Angela moved a couple of large pots into the sink and started to scrub one of them.

"We'll talk more in a minute and we'll start cooking, but let me get these kids interested in drawing," Nikki said.

She limped her way to the table where Bibi was sitting and placed a hand on her shoulder. She leaned over and put her face very close to the girl's. Bibi did not react.

"Can you draw something for me?"

Bibi turned and stared at the strange woman.

"I can't."

"Why not?"

"I don't have my paints here. Or canvas."

"What if I give you some paper and crayons?" Nikki asked.

A faint smile touched the girl's lips. She looked at the old woman with inquisitive eyes, and then her gaze settled on the necklace around the woman's neck.

"It represents the world tree. It's a good luck charm," Nikki said when she noticed the child staring at the necklace.

Bibi touched it for a few seconds. Nikki unclasped the necklace and put it around Bibi's neck.

"It will bring you good luck," she said as she stepped away to retrieve the carpetbag still sitting on the opposite bench.

Bibi's fingers touched her new pendant as she watched Nikki.

Nikki dug into the bag to retrieve crayon boxes and turned them upside down, spilling the various colors one by one on the table. She tore two sheets of the newsprint from the roll and placed them in front of Bibi. Then Nikki turned to a couple of children close by and told them to grab paper and join in.

COYOTE ZONE

The child who'd been to the portable outhouses with Bibi approached. She looked timid as she asked if she could also participate. At that point, Nikki said anyone in the room could engage in the coloring activity but to keep their voices low if they spoke. Each person had to do his or her own drawing, and the subject matter could be an eagle, the symbol of Mexico, or a portrait of Benito Juárez, one of the heroes of Mexico.

Nikki made sure each child had paper and access to crayons. Once they were settled at spots around the tables, she walked back to Angela. Nikki picked up a cloth so dirty and grungy, it was stiff. She used it to dry one of the pots Angela had stacked on the side of the sink.

"You were telling me about the pimp who tattooed you," Nikki said.

"All I could think about was escaping from him and his puta mother. My stupidity was going back home. My stepfather beats my mother, and I wanted to see her, make sure she was okay. Stupid mistake."

Angela's voice was monotone—it displayed no feelings, yet Nikki detected a huge reservoir of emotion held in check, waiting to erupt and overflow.

"Are there no guards watching us here?" Nikki asked.

"They stand at the mouth of the cave. Sometimes back here too. You can't get out. They have guns, and they'd kill us if we try to escape."

"Can't you talk Goyo into letting you go to the hotel in New Mexico? You can tell him you'll pay him over time for your liberty."

Angela sighed and looked at Nikki. "Coyotes do not negotiate, except to their benefit."

"Were you doing the cooking for the whole group?" Nikki asked.

"Yes, usually beans and rice. There are enough leftover beans for tonight in the fridge, but we need to make more rice. We need to cook beans for tomorrow."

"What about water?" Nikki asked, gesturing toward the forty-four gallon container. "Is that water supply for drinking, cooking, and washing dishes?"

"There's a little spring, by the cave wall behind the sleeping area and the outhouses. That's where we pull water for dishwashing. We use those two buckets on the floor," Angela said, pointing down to the side of the makeshift sink.

Water from a spring within the cave by the outhouses, Nikki thought. *It'll be a miracle if we don't all die of dysentery.*

The children, spread out around the two tables, were busy drawing, except for one boy about ten years old, who stood sulking against the wall of the cave near the refrigerator. Nikki walked closer to the tables and, like a school teacher, gazed at the newsprint pages laid out in front of each child.

Suddenly, the silence was broken by the sound of gunshots. Nikki saw one small boy hide under the table. The other children, afraid to move, froze in place. As she braced for more gunshots, she could not tell if it had been only one shot that kept echoing through the chamber or more than one. Of one thing she was certain. It had been a pistol and not an automatic weapon.

As the echo subsided, three of the children resumed work on their drawings. The whole cave seemed to have gone silent. Even Angela had stopped working.

Nikki knelt by the table and coaxed the little guy out from under it. She reached out and patted his back as his little body trembled.

"It's all okay," Nikki said. "We're all going to be okay."

He crawled out, threw his arms around her neck, and nestled his head on her shoulder. She spent two or three minutes talking to him in a calm voice. The time allowed her to determine if the kids were in any immediate danger. Slowly, she disengaged his arms and led him back to where he had been drawing. She handed him a crayon and spoke softly as she encouraged him to apply more pressure to the crayon.

"You're making a wonderful picture. Now, see how pretty that color is looking. If you push harder on the crayon, it will make the color darker."

Nikki looked at the work of the other children. A few pages of newsprint depicted mere outlines, while others were cartoonish sketches. One older boy's work displayed a sort of cubist rendition of an eagle as opposed to the otherwise primitive interpretations of either an eagle or a portrait of Juárez.

Save for one. The one that seemed drawn by a professional artist. Nikki moved toward it and stood behind that young artist. She let out a sigh of relief.

Thank God. This is indeed Bibi.

Nikki heard voices and realized men were approaching. She tried to move away from the table, but Goyo and Bernardo were there before she could move. Goyo stepped right up and surveyed the layout on the tables.

"What the fucking shit is going on?"

In the shadowy light, Nikki saw the twitch in Goyo's eyelid spread out to his right cheek, like a full-blown facial spasm.

Probably an anxiety neurosis, she thought as she smelled alcohol on his breath.

"I'm keeping the kids occupied so they don't bother you," Nikki said in a calm voice.

She noticed Goyo still wore the pistol in the belt around his waist. Bernardo carried the automatic weapon.

Goyo grabbed the portrait Bibi was working on, looked at it, and said, "What a piece of crap."

He crumpled the sheet into the size of a baseball and tossed it, as if it were a basketball, into an empty cardboard box near the stove. He noticed Angela. A diabolical smirk crossed his face, and his right eye started twitching to the point it seemed closed rather than open.

"You, come with me."

Angela's shoulders slumped, and she looked down as she started walking toward Goyo.

"While Angela and I are occupied," Goyo said as he pointed a finger at Bernardo, "you stay and make sure this evil bitch cooks dinner for us instead of wasting time. And pick up these pinche papers. Throw them away. When I get back, I'll stand guard for you. Think about who you want tonight."

"Have monstrous fun, Goyo. For my turn, I'll try the new girl, Florencia."

Nikki's stomach clenched and tears sprang to her eyes as she watched Angela follow Goyo from the room. There was nothing she could do to save either girl.

CHAPTER 18

San Miguel de Allende—Friday evening, day three after abduction

"She's dead," Eduardo said into the phone in hushed tones, as if afraid to be overheard. He stared at the ground near the entrance to the larger of the two greenhouses that edged up to the fence along the perimeter of Josefina's backyard.

"Dead?" Floyd asked, horrified. "My God . . ."

Eduardo hesitated momentarily while thinking about Floyd's reaction. Then he realized he had blurted his findings without preparing him. He had not intended to scare Floyd or, worse yet, have him think Nikki might have been killed.

"Josefina is dead," Eduardo said quickly.

A sigh of relief rushed over the phone, and Eduardo apologized for springing Josefina's death on him without being clear who had been killed.

"Tension set in my neck as soon as you mentioned a dead person," Floyd said. "I don't know what I was thinking, but moments before I answered your call, I had Nikki on my mind."

Eduardo, feeling guilty for the chord of fear he'd struck in Floyd, apologized again as he walked toward the house.

"Looks like the killer bashed her head in pretty badly and dragged her body into the larger greenhouse. I'm looking at marks in the dirt where he pulled her across the yard, so I'm assuming it was only one killer. Otherwise, they would have carried her. I found blood on the concrete slab by the back door of the house."

Floyd asked if the body displayed any gunshot wounds.

"None that I can see. My guess is, whoever murdered her, did it by the house and then hid the body in the greenhouse. I have not found the murder weapon, but I'll look again. From the head wounds, it looks as if she was bludgeoned to death."

"Have you searched inside the house?" Floyd's question sounded overly loud in Eduardo's earpiece.

"I'm headed that way. I wanted to tell you of my findings first before going into the house. I'm at the back door now."

"Before you enter, you should know the woman has—"

Eduardo heard the warning too late. A squawking object hurtled toward his face as he stepped inside. He ducked and threw his arms up over his head.

"Holy shit!" Eduardo yelled as his mobile phone went flying like a fumbled football. A black bird, obviously a crow, landed on the floor in front of him. It let out an eardrum-shattering screech. Keeping his eyes on the bird, Eduardo grabbed the phone off the floor and spoke into it to make sure the connection with Floyd was still open.

"So you've met Sebastián," Floyd said. "I tried to warn you about him."

"Why the hell would someone have an uncaged crow inside their home?"

Floyd told Eduardo that Sebastián is not an ordinary bird, that he protects the house.

"That he does. He scared the hell out of me," Eduardo said.

"I'd forgotten about him or I would have told you sooner. Juana was his mother. She found him abandoned after he'd fallen out of a nest, and she hand-fed him and raised him. He thought Juana's name was Fígaro."

Almost on cue, Sebastián cried out again. Eduardo realized the crow was calling for Fígaro.

"Sounds like he's calling for the dog," Eduardo said.

"The bird's evidently been missing her, and he sounds pretty upset. After you finish looking for evidence, why don't you take Sebastián back to Zacatecas with you?"

"Take a bird in the car with me? Shit, Floyd, are you nuts? I'm going to turn him loose in the yard."

Eduardo did not want to hear what Floyd said next. "His wings are clipped, so he can't fly much. He doesn't know how to hunt since Juana always fed him. Nikki would not want that bird to die. That's exactly what will happen if you turn him loose outside."

"Okay, okay, I'll bring him with me."

Eduardo sighed as he walked to the front of the living room. He crept up to the large window overlooking the street to make sure no one was lurking out there.

Floyd's next instruction was for Eduardo to complete his search in the house and, once he was ready to get out of there, to call again to indicate what else he'd found. After that, Floyd would call Fernando in Mexico City and have him report Josefina's death anonymously to the police. Floyd's advice to Eduardo was to scrub his fingerprints from every surface before he left. It might erase other evidence, but that couldn't be helped.

"What about Nikki?" Eduardo asked.

As he expected, Floyd said they'd find her tomorrow, like they'd agreed. Floyd would meet him in Zacatecas.

"I'll call you after I wrap up the search," Eduardo said.

Not seeing anything unusual in the living room, he returned to the kitchen, where he opened drawers until he found a paper bag. He punched holes in it with the tip of a paring knife he found in the sink. He didn't want the stupid feathered fowl to suffocate. He'd catch the crow and put him into the bag until he could get a cage. Certainly the hotel would not approve of a loose bird in a suite already containing a dog. A pooch was tolerated. But a bird? Housekeeping at the Quinta Real would report him to management and they'd ask him to leave, and Eduardo did not want to get evicted. He'd stop by Walmart and buy a damn bird cage. He was on edge, and he realized it.

He examined the rest of the house. The bathroom was well-used. The porcelain sink had stains so yellow they turned brown as they streaked downward toward the drain. The bathtub showed the same streaking on the porcelain under the faucets, and he realized the water must have a lot of minerals to leave such dirty and permanent discoloration. Towels hanging on a rack, extra rolls of bath tissue on the lid of the toilet tank, and the toilet itself, with the usual long-handled scrubbing brush half hidden between the toilet and the wall, all appeared normal, except for a clothes washer hooked up between the toilet and the bathtub. He broke off a piece of bath tissue and used it to raise the lid of the washer. Damp clothes were inside. He picked up a piece to check for mildew, but it smelled fresh and must have been washed earlier that day, before Josefina was attacked.

He moved on to the first bedroom. It was a small room, with windows along two walls, one facing the street and the other looking out to the side of the house. A queen-sized bed, unmade, with a patchwork quilt draping over the edge and spilling onto the floor, took up most of the space along a windowless wall. On top of the bed, a plastic laundry basket containing wooden clothespins, the old-fashioned type Eduardo had not seen in years, looked ready to be taken outside to air-dry the freshly washed clothes that were still waiting in the washer. Realizing he could use them in his bird trap plan, to keep the bag closed with the crow inside, he picked up a clothespin and clipped it to the front of his shirt, along the crease where the buttons were sewn onto the shirt. He took two more and pinned each one next to a button.

On the other windowless wall were a closed door and a bureau. He moved toward the door and opened it, expecting to see a bathroom. Instead, it opened into a closet jammed full of clothes, books, shoes, and boxes stacked in rows of twos and threes, wherever there was space. He closed the door and peered at the bureau. A large, gold-gilded frame, looking out of place in a room with modest furnishings, hung on the wall behind the bureau.

As Eduardo examined it, he saw the frame contained a collage of photos of the same child—some pictured by herself, and in others she was either in the arms of a thin woman or the child was holding hands with the same woman. All the photos were black-and-white. Then he noticed a discolored newspaper clipping that was as brownish and yellowed as the porcelain in the bathroom. Upon reading the article, he realized it spoke of the premature death of a child, Juana Beltrán García. He studied the photos and connected the dots. The thin woman was a young Juana, and the child was her daughter. As Eduardo read the article, he learned the little girl had died at age five.

With his mobile phone, Eduardo snapped several photos of the collage and newspaper obituary. He went back to the closet door, removed a white handkerchief from his pocket, and cleaned the door knob.

Walking into the hall again, he entered the adjacent room, expecting to find a second bedroom. Instead, it was a small library with built-in shelves. The two women must have shared the one bedroom. On the wall opposite the built-in bookcase, a small coffee table with a lamp on it and two easy chairs on each side were set against the wall. The lamp was lit, and an old-style yellow notepad next to the lamp had writing on it. A twenty-four inch television sat on one of the bookcase shelves. He moved to the shelves next to the TV and examined twelve brown leather-bound books with gold trim. He pulled one out and saw *The Complete Works of William Shakespeare* embossed in gold lettering. As he pulled other books out, all hard covers, he noticed titles like Melville's *Moby Dick* and Tolstoy's *Anna Karenina* and *War and Peace*, titles that surprised him given Juana's vagabond appearance.

Maybe Josefina was the literary person in this household, he thought as he opened the cover of *Anna Karenina*, but he discovered Juana García written in beautiful cursive penmanship across the top of the title page. He quickly opened a second book, *War and Peace*, and found her signature again. And the same for the Shakespeare volumes. He snapped a couple of pictures of her handwriting. The book covers showed substantial wear, and the pages had notes in the margins in the same handwriting as Juana's signature. This collection did not constitute an artefact to make the owner feel she could boast of being well-read without having opened a single book. No, these books really had been used and cherished.

Nothing much stands out in this one bedroom/one bath house, as a realtor would describe it, he thought, *other than the person who had inhabited it was as mysterious and complicated as the great books she had apparently treasured.*

Turning to leave the room, the yellow pad caught Eduardo's eye again. Only the top page had writing. In Juana's handwriting was a single sentence: "Antonio Enríquez, he threatens to turn me over if I don't cooperate." Below that was a crudely drawn diagram, maybe depicting a town square or possibly just a doodle. He used his phone to take a picture of the page.

As he walked back into the hall, Eduardo stopped in the bathroom to get a towel. Returning to the library, he used the towel to wipe his fingerprints before proceeding toward the kitchen.

It's time to catch Sebastián. Can't believe I'm doing this.

Using the towel to open drawers and kitchen cabinets, he searched for birdseed but didn't find any and made a mental note to purchase a bag of it at Walmart.

He spotted Sebastián sitting on a perch on the living room mantle next to a large television hanging from the wall above it. He approached slowly and quickly threw the frayed towel over the bird. The perch fell off the mantle, banging loudly on the ground, as the towel pulled the bird to the floor. Eduardo lunged for the towel to catch a stunned Sebastián before the bird had time to react. Holding the towel to the floor with his knees, Eduardo's hands grabbed the squirming bundle under it. Using his elbow to hold the towel down, with his free hand, Eduardo eased the shopping bag to the edge of the towel and moved the agitated bundle toward the open bag.

That's when Sebastián pecked angrily at him through the thin towel. And drew blood.

Eduardo almost lost control of the wiggling bird, which managed to get free of the towel and flapped his wings, trying to get away. Eduardo grabbed Sebastián's legs with one hand while thrusting the surprised crow into the bag with his other hand. He folded the top of the paper, took the clothes pins, one at a time, from his shirt, and pinned the top of the bag closed. Only then Eduardo wiped his bleeding finger on the towel. He checked the floor to make certain he was not leaving his own blood stains behind.

Before leaving, Eduardo took his handkerchief and scrubbed all the surfaces he'd touched, and he double-checked that none of the blood from his finger was on any surface. Holding Sebastián's bag in one hand and the towel he'd used to catch Sebastián under the other arm, he returned outside to search for a murder weapon. When he did not find any, he snapped several photos of Josefina—full body, close-ups, and the bloody head wound. In his final action before leaving the place, he used his handkerchief to clean the remaining surfaces he'd touched outdoors.

Carrying the crow in the brown paper bag, Eduardo walked to his car. Vigilant to any possibility of being watched or followed, he opened the car door and got in on the driver's side. He reached across the console, placed the bag and towel on the floor on the passenger side, and snapped his seat belt on. After pushing the ignition button, he shifted into drive and pulled away from the house that had been owned by Juana la Marihuana and her friend Josefina.

"Hey, Sebastián," Eduardo said, "I'll introduce you to Nikki tomorrow."

When he realized he'd talked to the bird, Eduardo thought he might be losing it until he remembered what Nikki told him when he teased her about talking to Fígaro. *It's okay to talk to an animal, as long as you don't hear them talking back.*

Then Sebastián screeched, "Fígaro, Fígaro, Fígaro!"

Oh my God, Eduardo thought, *the crazy bird's talking back to me.*

CHAPTER 19

Zacatecas—Friday, close to midnight, day three after abduction

The cave echoed a wounded sound—a frightened, lonely sound, a whimper seeking comfort, yet it was a comfort that could not come. The mournful murmur repeated over and over, like the moaning of an injured animal.

Nikki could not sleep. Not because the cot was hard and uncomfortable. Nor did the cave's dankness and fetid odor keep her awake. Neither was it the discomfort of being fully clothed, nor the chafing from the shoes she wore and the full-body mask that prevented her from sleeping. It was Florencia's whimpering. Whimpering that was interrupted periodically with sneezing. The poor little thing she had traveled with and tried to protect. Bernardo had come for her during the night, and Nikki had been helpless to stop it. Clearly, whatever plans they had for the child did not include keeping her virginity intact. Nikki dared not go to her until she heard snoring from Goyo and Bernardo. She figured Goyo's young assistant was standing guard.

I can handle him, she thought. *He'll be at the cave entrance.*

She eased off the cot, took the light blanket with her, followed the sound of whimpering, and placing one foot ahead of the other in the pitch-black cavern, she inched along to avoid falling, her feet maneuvering around bundles of sleeping children, until she arrived at Florencia's side. She sat down and spoke softly to the child, but Florencia continued weeping, not conscious of the woman's presence.

Nikki placed her hand on the girl's forehead. It felt hot and sweaty.
"Can I help you?"

The weeping stopped. She felt Florencia move, as if she'd raised herself onto her elbows. The girl's arms slid around Nikki's shoulders.

"It hurts," she whispered in her ear.

Nikki cradled Florencia's head against her chest as she dabbed the child's wet face with the edge of the blanket.

"Can you tell me more?"

"They hurt me. They told me to keep quiet or they'd kill me. Then they stuffed a towel in my mouth and tied a cord around my head to hold it in place so I couldn't yell."

"Bernardo?"

"Yes, and the other one too." She started whimpering again. "It hurts a lot, like they cut me open." Then Florencia sneezed.

"Goyo?" Nikki felt a thousand bats gnawing at her stomach again.

"No, the other guy, the young one."

"The assistant," Nikki said. She felt Florencia's head nod in agreement. *Those dirty bastards, raping a child.* "I'll be back. Stay still so you don't wake them up. I'm going to get a wet cloth to clean you up."

She took the small blanket from Florencia's bed and placed it over her shoulder with the other one.

Shuffling toward the small water hole in total darkness, still using her feet to feel for the torsos and limbs of the sleeping kids, those blanket-covered bundles strewn haphazardly on the cave floor like piles of garbage, she sidestepped them to avoid falling. The darkness tested Nikki's skills to maneuver the cave, but thinking of all those children strengthened her resolve to do what she could to rescue them. She could hear gurgling water and focused her full attention on that sound as she moved along until she stubbed her toes on a broken stalagmite. She suppressed the urge to scream, but the pain made her stop.

I hope it's not broken, she thought as she rubbed her big toe through the tennis shoe.

As she stood quietly, waiting for the pain to subside, Nikki heard the sound of water droplets becoming more distinct. She got down on her hands and knees and slowly crawled toward the pool.

This is surreal, she thought.

It felt as if sounds, aided by the tactile feel of the ground on her hands, returned her eyesight so she could move in the darkness. For the first time in her life, she realized how people who have lost their vision rely on auditory clues and the sense of touch. She also realized she longed to be with Eduardo, to be in his arms, to make love to him. But right now, she had more urgent needs—to keep herself alive and rescue the kids.

Her fingers felt moist ground. She crawled closer and felt the water of the pond. Taking one of the blankets from around her neck, she dipped about half of it into the water and wrung it out to prevent it from dripping all the way back. Then she dipped a corner of the second blanket into the pool. As she stood to edge her way back to Florencia, she heard the girl sneeze twice more. When she arrived at the side of the low-whimpering bundle, Nikki knelt and touched her hand on the girl's forehead.

"I'm going to place the edge of a cloth on your forehead to cool you down." Her voice was barely a whisper.

Nikki lifted Florencia's head to tuck the blanket under it, leaving the moist corner free, which she draped over the girl's forehead.

"Now, I'm going to hand you a blanket soaked in water so you can clean yourself where they hurt you."

After that painful process was done, Nikki stayed with Florencia until the young girl fell asleep. Crawling back to her own miserable cot she thought, *I must save them. I was not able to save my son, but in his memory, I will do all I can to save the ones here.*

State of Zacatecas—Saturday morning before dawn, day four after abduction

Bernardo hit Nikki on the side of her hip with his flashlight. Startled awake, she sat up in the cot for an instant before getting out of bed and taking a defensive stance.

"You move quick for an old puta. But don't worry, all I want from you is breakfast."

He shined the flashlight in her eyes, making Nikki squint. She had no idea what time it was. She made a show of rubbing her eyes, but she was really checking to make sure the mask was still in place around them. Fortunately, it was as high-quality a disguise as she had been promised.

"Angela is up and already in the kitchen. Get your ass over there. Cooking's *your* fucking job, not hers."

As Nikki walked to the kitchen, she could smell coffee, and she needed a cup badly after not sleeping for most of the night. Her first instinct, as she approached Angela near the stove, was to reach for a cup.

"Coffee is only for the men," Angela warned in a low voice.

"Says who?"

"Goyo. And I wouldn't cross him this early in the morning. Maybe later, if there's any left, you can sneak a cup."

Angela had already placed paper plates, individual water bottles, three coffee mugs, and plastic utensils on the tables. She had laid out two egg cartons, a package of corn tortillas in a plastic bag, and a big ceramic container full of cooked pinto beans on a low, wobbly, makeshift table leaning against the stove.

"So eggs for breakfast gives us a break from the usual rice and beans for lunch and dinner," Nikki said as she started breaking eggs into a bowl. She added lard into a large frying pan, picked up eight corn tortillas, and tore them into shreds before dropping them into the hot grease. "Instead of scrambled eggs, I'm going to fix migas, eggs with fried tortilla pieces."

Ignoring Nikki's comment, Angela removed another frying pan from the cabinet under the sink and added four heaping tablespoons of pork lard from the square tin container Nikki had left open. She joined the older woman at the stove to melt the lard before she added the pinto beans to prepare refried beans.

As the tortilla pieces sizzled to a crisp, golden color, Nikki's mouth started watering.

It's as if life has gone to the most basic Zen quality, she thought. *I'm in a dangerous situation, where I don't know if I will come out alive, but my taste buds are reacting to the immediate stimulus occurring in the present moment.*

She beat the eggs with a fork, added salt, and poured the mixture over the shredded corn tortillas, tilting the pan to get the eggs to spread evenly over the crisp tortilla bits.

COYOTE ZONE

Migas were a childhood favorite for Nikki. She had always cooked them for Robbie as he was growing up, before his untimely death. Her heart still ached for her son. But then her memories went further back to the times when her parents had taken her to Spain. She had been about ten years old the first time and fifteen on the second trip.

That condo complex where we stayed twice at my Aunt Carmen's place was out of this world, pure fantasy, she thought. *I always wanted to return, but then my parents died in that car accident, so it never happened. I'd planned to take Robbie and explore the Gaudí architecture, but that never happened either. Maybe Eduardo and I can visit Barcelona . . . if I get out of this alive.*

Nikki was brought out of her daydreaming when she realized Angela was watching the final preparation of the migas. The girl, standing next to Nikki at the stove, saw the migas were ready to be served, so she turned the heat off on the beans she was preparing.

"You really know how to cook. I'll spoon out the migas to everyone," Angela said as she moved closer to Nikki and grabbed the pan. You can get the cheese from the refrigerator. Goyo always wants quesadillas for himself and the other two men."

Angela served the eggs on the paper plates she'd set out on the tables earlier that morning. Bernardo had rounded up the kids, who appeared to be half-asleep. Quietly, they sat down and devoured the eggs put in front of them, save for two—Bibi, who picked at her food, and Florencia, who was not even in the area.

How strange, with so many children, that none of them are rowdy, Nikki thought as she cut slices of cheese. *But if they get rowdy, they know Goyo could hurt them. Or worse.*

Angela retrieved a jar of Tabasco sauce from the makeshift cabinet under the sink and placed it at the end of the table where Goyo and his henchmen were now sitting. She returned to the stove and carried the pan of beans to serve everyone while Nikki was busy grilling cheese quesadillas on a dirty, greasy, stovetop cast-iron grill.

Nikki served the pungent-smelling quesadillas to the three men. When those seated at the table finished eating, the two women ate their breakfast. Then they cleaned up the kitchen together. Most of the kids remained seated, either staring into space straight ahead or looking absentmindedly

159

at the top of the table, a couple of them doodling on the table with their fingers. When two boys got up to use the portable bathrooms, the assistant walked with them. Bernardo stayed behind, guarding those who remained in the kitchen. Nikki wanted to check on Florencia but hesitated, knowing it could cause problems with Bernardo.

"Pack up the food. Goyo is ready to move out," Bernardo announced as soon as the kitchen was clean.

Nikki started walking past him, limping as usual. He shoved his automatic rifle into her waist.

"And where do you think you're going, stupid old hag?"

"To use the bathroom and to pick up my bag. It's back at the cot," she said, although checking on Florencia remained the most pressing reason for her to return to the sleeping area.

"I'll follow you." Bernardo moved the AK-47, its barrel resting against his shoulder, as he stepped menacingly in right behind her.

Though she couldn't see his face, Nikki could feel his negative energy spreading across her back, like an ocean wave hitting the beach. She walked steadily ahead with Bernardo a foot or so behind her. Enough electrical lights, hanging from outcroppings of rocks along the wall, were lit, making Nikki's path toward the bathroom seem like a hallway in a dungeon. But at least it was not pitch-black. She entered one of the fowl smelling compartments, pulled up her skirt, and opened the discreet flap on her body mask that allowed her to use the bathroom. She had done so sparingly after going underground as she had deliberately diminished her water and food intake.

After she had finished that nasty task, she headed for the bed area with Bernardo right behind her. Florencia was sleeping. Nikki touched the girl's forehead with the back of her hand and discovered the child was burning up with fever.

"Get up," Bernardo said, pushing his foot aggressively into Florencia's ribcage.

The girl's eyes opened. "I can't," she mumbled as she recoiled from Bernardo's foot digging into her side.

"She's sick. She needs to be carried," Nikki said.

"If she can't get up, she'll be left behind."

Nikki squatted down to help Florencia get up, but the feverish child could not stand of her own volition. Nikki tucked her arm under the girl's armpit to help her stand.

"Now take one step at a time..."

"If the little puta can't walk, she'll stay here," Bernardo said.

"No, I will help her."

Bernardo stuck the muzzle of the AK-47 into Nikki's stomach again.

"She either walks on her own or she stays behind." He repositioned the barrel of the weapon, pointing it squarely at Florencia. "We don't deal with the sick. Can you walk or not?" he asked in a cruel, demanding voice.

Without moving her head, Florencia turned her eyes to look at him, tears rolling down her face. "I can't," she said in a whisper that sounded more like a whimper.

"Come on," he said as his nostrils flared and his eyes squinted in anger. "For the last time, start walking toward the truck."

Florencia fell. Nikki, still holding the girl's arm, kneeled down to help her. Then a fire burst of bullets sounded. Nikki collapsed, throwing her hands over her head for a split second, thinking Bernardo had shot her. After hitting the ground, she realized it was Florencia who'd been shot.

Nikki sat halfway up, staring at Bernardo in total disbelief. She was so shocked, she couldn't speak. Her eyelids blinked with fierce velocity, the only movement her body seemed capable of performing.

"We don't mess around," he said. "Now go. Get that fucking ass of yours moving before I blow your head off too."

Nikki struggled on her feet. Uneasy, she lost her balance but managed to stand up. "You miserable—"

Bernardo grabbed her by the collar before she could say any more.

Terrified, Nikki went for his eyes, ready to dig her nails into them and blind him. Instead, Bernardo raised his elbow forcefully, shoving her away, still clutching her collar with his free hand as he pushed her. With the force of his grip, he ripped several buttons off. Her blouse split open, and he saw the money pouch dangling from her bra. It had become dislodged during the struggle. He reached for it and yanked it off. As he did so, the lipstick case Floyd had brought her tumbled from her bra, where she had hidden it, onto the ground. Nikki froze as it hit the cave floor.

Bernardo opened the pouch, saw the cash, and stuffed the pouch in his pants pocket.

"I'll keep this," he said with a vigorous laugh. "Those breasts of yours carry a lot of shit." Bernardo bent over to pick up the lipstick case. "You keep the lipstick. Your old, wrinkled puta face needs all the help it can get," he said as he threw the little case to her.

Unable to breathe until she saw the lipstick in the air, she reacted quickly to catch it and placed it back into her bra to secure it.

"Let's get your bag," Bernardo said.

Nikki, now realizing she had blood splattered over her clothes, looked down at Florencia's dead body, which was bloody and curled up in a fetal position on the ground.

Why couldn't I stop this bastard from killing her? Nikki's body shivered.

She wiped a tear from her cheek and rubbed it between her fingers, as if it were a raindrop. It felt thick. She glanced at her thumb and forefinger and discovered it was blood. She rubbed her finger against her already blood-stained clothes.

I have to do what Bernardo commands, or I'll be killed too.

Goyo and his assistant came running up, responding to the gunfire.

"She was sick and couldn't walk," Bernardo said, pointing to Florencia's body on the ground.

Goyo spat on the ground next to the dead girl. "She's better off. I knew this little puta would not work. She was just a waste of our time. Plus, I would hardly have broken even on her." Goyo turned toward his assistant and barked orders to the young man. "Get a shovel from the truck and start digging a hole outside. Make it on the slope where the afternoon shadows fall. The dirt is softer on that side. Pick a spot behind shrubs, so it's hidden. The hole needs to be big enough so we can bury the other dead sons of bitches too. When you finish digging, call me and I'll help you carry the little puta's corpse."

Goyo turned and stared at Nikki. His eye twitched in rapid-fire sequence. He took a pack of cigarettes from his shirt pocket, removed one very slowly, and put it in his mouth as he pulled a lighter from his shirt pocket, staring at Nikki the entire time.

"You didn't do your job." Goyo lit the cigarette and walked away.

COYOTE ZONE

Totally helpless, Nikki started limping toward the cot she'd slept on. As soon as she turned in that direction, Bernardo stepped in right behind her, his AK-47 pointed at her back. She staggered toward the sleeping area, depressed, with her head and shoulders unconsciously stooping forward. Nikki picked up her carpetbag from the ground near the cot, and the weight of the bag felt enormous, as if the burden of her situation had descended into it.

"Change into clean clothes," Bernardo ordered.

Nikki placed the bag on the cot and took the spare clothes from it. As annoying as it was, she was immensely grateful for the full-body mask that made her look old and wrinkly all over. She pulled off her torn, blood-stained blouse and dropped it on the cot. Then she turned her back to Bernardo as she took her dirty skirt off and slipped into the spare blouse and long skirt she'd purchased at the market.

As she changed, Bernardo leaned his AK-47 against the cot. He picked up her bag, emptied the contents, and sifted through them. Leaving the contents on the cot, he yelled for the young assistant's help. Whatever he was searching for in her personal belongings, he had apparently not found, but he continued to hold the bag.

Nikki, fully changed into fresh clothes, turned to see her belongings spread out on the sleeper and Bernardo holding her empty bag. Empty, except for Nikki's phone in the secret compartment. She panicked silently for the third time that dreadful morning.

I'm doomed if he finds that phone.

Her eyes focused on the AK-47 as she considered making a move for it.

"You like my big gun?" Bernardo asked, picking up the automatic rifle and pointing it at Nikki. "If you were younger, I'd give you a piece of my other gun." His hand made a lewd gesture at his crotch as he erupted into peals of laughter.

Approaching footsteps echoed in the chamber. The young assistant came into view, a shovel over his shoulder. Bernardo called out to him to hurry, his voice echoing loudly, drowning out the footsteps.

"Pick up her dirty clothes and throw them in here," he said, holding the bag open for the young man to drop the clothes in. "Throw this bag in the grave with the girl."

163

A single shot rang out and reverberated throughout the cave. Bernardo and the young assistant ran toward the front. Nikki stood, shaking, unable to get her feet to move her forward. Her pulse raced and her heart pumped so loudly, she wanted to rip her chest open.

Not another child, she prayed. *Please, God, not another child.*

CHAPTER 20

Zacatecas—Saturday morning, day four after abduction

"Fígaro! Fígaro! Hambre."

The Pomsky, who'd slept curled up at the foot of Eduardo's bed, started barking. The bird continued its deafening cry.

Eduardo woke up with a jolt. He sprang from the bed, grabbing the gun under his pillow in the same movement. He looked around the dimly lit room but did not see anything out of order.

What did that damned crow screech? Eduardo thought as he glanced at Sebastián's cage, trying to figure out the words Sebastián had used. *It sounded like the word "hombre," but fortunately, I don't see a man in here.*

Nor did Eduardo sense any immediate danger at all. He put the 9 mm Luger back under the pillow and rubbed his aching head with both hands before checking his watch. It was five fifteen in the morning.

Eduardo had not slept well, and though he hated to admit it, the unusual wake-up call was exactly what he needed. As he headed toward the bathroom, Sebastián let out another ear-popping caw, followed by the word he had learned to call Juana.

"Hambre, hambre. Fígaro, Fígaro."

Sebastián is hungry. Now how did that bird learn to communicate that way? At that point, Eduardo reasoned it through and guessed Juana had taught the crow to say "hambre" when he begged for food, and she had obviously rewarded the bird by feeding him. *Very clever,* he thought. *I wonder what other surprises Sebastián has in store that his mistress taught him.*

Eduardo's head pounded as he walked to the desk, grabbed the birdseed he'd purchased at Walmart the night before, and poured a small amount into a tin container that came with the cage. He retrieved a second container from the cage and refilled it with water. Sebastián had either walked on it during the night or otherwise dumped it over on the newspaper Eduardo had placed at the bottom of the cage to catch droppings. As he closed the cage door, the crow cocked his head and looked at Eduardo.

"Fígaro." Sebastián now cooed like a dove rather than cawing like a crow. He buried his beak in the birdseed and then brought his beak back up above his head to swallow his food.

How about that? He's thanking me for his meal, Eduardo thought as he stared into the cage. "When I find Nikki and bring her back here, you can't be a starving bird. She'd be furious with me."

Man, I can't believe I'm talking to this damn bird again. This is ironic. I used to serve as mentor to orphaned children in Colombia, and now I'm tending to an orphaned dog and bird in Mexico.

After he used the bathroom, Eduardo dressed and put on a jacket. He knew Floyd would be following up in San Miguel with the ransom demand and making sure Timothy, the negotiator from Miami, was organized and capable of handling the kidnappers. After that, he, Floyd, and that other guy from Miami could start their search for Nikki.

Eduardo did not want to wait any longer to start the search. But before he could leave, he had to arrange for someone to feed Sebastián. He grabbed the phone, dialed housekeeping, and requested the housekeeper come to his room immediately. When the woman arrived, he asked her to step inside.

"I need someone to take care of my pet bird until I get back. I could be gone three or four days, even longer. I'll continue to pay for the room during my absence. Can I pay you to take good care of him, feed him, and make sure he always has water?" he asked, showing her the supply of birdseed.

The woman hesitated. "What about the dog?"

"He's going with me," Eduardo said as he took a hundred dollar bill from his pocket. "I'll double this when I get back, but you must take good care of Sebastián. He's not just any old crow. He can talk."

She took the hundred dollars, smiled, and promised she'd take good care of her charge. Eduardo thanked her and closed the door behind her as she left.

Looking at his watch again, Eduardo knew Floyd would not leave San Miguel until the kidnappers called. But in Eduardo's experience years ago with the Revolutionary Armed Forces of Colombia, known as the FARC, kidnapping negotiations had taken not days but weeks to come to an agreement with the kidnappers. A few times, it even took years, like in the case when the FARC abducted Íngrid Betancourt, a case which took over six years to resolve. He rubbed his head again.

As he looked around the room, Eduardo decided he'd at least locate Nikki and the group she had gone underground with, regardless of whether they were the ones holding Bibi or not. He started organizing the purchases he'd made at Walmart the night before: an ice chest, food, drinks, water, and a dog muzzle. He took the cooler to the bathroom and drained the water that had accumulated in it overnight from the ice he'd placed in it before going to bed. He returned it to the dresser, opened the small fridge, and took all the soft drinks and water bottles from it. One by one, he pushed the drinks into the ice inside the chest. A bag containing fruit, chips, and sandwiches he'd prepared were packed next. A bag of baloney and the dog muzzle were the last items he threw in the cooler before he closed the lid. He returned to the side of the bed, took the gun from under the pillow, tucked it in his belt, and made sure his jacket kept it hidden.

If Juana had given him accurate information, the kidnappers would be staying another couple of days in the Zacatecas area. Had it not been for the two mascots, Fígaro and Sebastián, he would have spent the night in the car off the road near the turnoff where he saw Goyo's truck leave the highway, though he admitted to himself that staying at the hotel had turned out to be more comfortable than spending the night in the car.

He put his backpack on, grabbed the leash off the desk, and snapped it on Fígaro's collar. As he pulled the handle on the ice chest to roll it toward the door, the dog wagged his tail with excitement.

Eduardo pulled off the highway and drove on the dirt road Goyo had taken the day before. As soon as he was about five hundred meters from the highway, far enough that he could not be seen by passing traffic, he stopped and placed the muzzle on Fígaro. He did not need a barking dog giving away their location. He knew the risk of bringing Fígaro along, but since he was only going to stake out a point of observation, he considered the risk and had decided to bring the Pomsky. What would it have cost him to bribe the housekeeper to care for the crow and the dog? Also, for some strange reason he could not explain to himself, Eduardo felt more comfortable with the Pomsky along.

Standing outside the stopped vehicle, Eduardo examined the road. Fresh tire tracks showed up in places where loose dirt allowed a faint impression to be imbedded in the soft soil. Judging from the size of the imprint, he knew they were from a large cargo-type vehicle. For the tracks to appear so fresh, he figured the truck had traveled by within the last couple of hours. Using the camera on his mobile phone, he took three photos of the tire treads.

Since he had already stopped, he opened the car door to take Fígaro on a short walk. Glancing at his watch, he saw it was six thirty. The cool morning air was crisp yet pleasant.

Perfect weather, he thought, *for a dog with a Husky bloodline.*

After they returned to the car, Eduardo followed the tracks for another half-hour as he drove slowly over hilly, semi-arid terrain with sparse shrub vegetation. Orange-red clusters of ocotillo flowers stood atop the plant's wand-like branches and painted bright colored highlights on the otherwise yellow-ochre hills. Nopal cactus made occasional appearances and probably hid more small reptiles among its leaves and roots than any other desert plant. Sword-shaped yucca leaves surrounded the panicles of creamy, yellow-white blossoms spraying up from the center of the species, while tender, young grass sprouted on the slopes containing more soil than rocks.

Not that Eduardo was enjoying the vegetation. He constantly scanned the area for people, cars, or trucks. Or any other signs of humans. He could see, though, that he was getting closer to the mountain range.

At times, the tracks were hardly visible. He stopped again, took his binoculars, and scanned the area. What looked like two abandoned mines, with timber planks closing off the entrances, were located high up on rocky ledges.

That's where the tracks are going to take me, he thought.

As he moved the binoculars down vertically and swept the area, searching for roads leading to the mines or at least to areas of access where trucks might be parked, an unusually big cave came into focus in his line of vision. It was considerably to the right of the bluffs where the mine entrances had caught his attention. He could tell it would probably be accessible by truck right up to the mouth of the cave.

That's the location, not the boarded up, abandoned mines, he confirmed to himself.

The tracks became even harder to follow as the terrain became rockier, and he had to take it slower until he came to a stream running down a gully where the truck had obviously crossed. Eduardo drove up the gully about a quarter mile until he reached an embankment that narrowed the path. He parked the car as close to the embankment as he could. Satisfied the rental was hidden from the line of sight where the truck had left tracks on both sides of the stream, he got out and popped the ice chest open, unsealed the package of baloney, and rolled up five slices for Fígaro. He put these into a plastic bag, took a sandwich for himself, two bottles of water, an apple, the flashlight, and stuffed all these items into his backpack. He reached under the seat of the car, where he'd hidden the Luger, and placed it in his belt again.

He held onto the leash as he and Fígaro started walking up the embankment. Eduardo moved away from the cave in a circle-type approach to avoid being discovered by a guard. This tactic meant they could reach the cave from the side instead of straight on and avoid being detected. Eduardo walked fast, and Fígaro kept up the same pace. Checking for guards until he could no longer see the cave opening from the route he'd chosen, he figured he could listen for voices or other noise if he could get close enough to the cave's entrance.

His one concern, judging from the freshness of the tire tracks, was the truck had moved out of the area instead of going in. After twenty minutes of walking, he headed up the side of the mountain toward a spot of shrubs and short trees not too far from the cave. The vegetation would provide a hiding place, if necessary.

They were getting close to the area of vegetation when suddenly Fígaro tugged on the leash. For such a small dog, his movement was strong and determined. The muzzle kept him from barking, but he was making a whining sound. In an effort to keep him quiet, Eduardo picked the pup up in his arms. He walked about fifteen steps, and his mobile phone vibrated in his pants pocket. Holding Fígaro with one arm, he retrieved the phone. When he looked at the screen, he realized it had picked up Nikki's GPS signal. It made Eduardo shudder. He rubbed Fígaro's head and whispered to him to be quiet. Remembering the time Juana told Fígaro to "sit" and the canine had obeyed, Eduardo put the Pomsky on the ground and whispered the command to sit in the dog's ear. Fígaro obeyed, sitting on his hind legs while looking to the right, toward an outcropping of rocks near the area of vegetation. A few guayule shrubs were growing near the outcropping. He commanded Fígaro to heel, and Eduardo was not surprised when the pup followed. But the pup pulled toward the shrubs and kept looking in that direction, wagging his tail and moving his snout close to the ground, as if trying to sniff the environment. Figuring Fígaro needed to mark his territory, Eduardo led him to the guayules.

Fígaro, uninterested in watering the shrubs, stretched out as far as he could on his leash and started sniffing the ground behind a guayule. He pawed at the dirt, whined, and continued to sniff.

Eduardo's phone continued to vibrate. Focused on the signal from his phone, he tied Fígaro's leash around the trunk of a guayule surrounded by low shrubs and left the dog. He wanted to sneak up on the cave without Fígaro making noise and forewarning the coyote of their presence. He also wanted to confirm the coyote and his victims were there before he returned to the car to stake out an observation post.

Crouching in as close as he could toward the mountain, Eduardo walked slowly for another five minutes to the mouth of the cave. It was eerily silent. *Could they all be asleep? Maybe Nikki has been left inside, alone or with a few of the children. Maybe the truck left, taking some of the kids.*

Once he stood so close to the cave, he felt a strong urge to sneak in and see if Nikki or anyone else was left in there. Not hearing noise from within, he drew his gun and eased himself inside, hugging the wall of the cave with every step. When he felt secure he would not be detected against sunlight filtering in from the outside, he stopped to let his eyes adjust. It was dark. So dark, he could not see anything. He listened for noise but heard nothing. Besides feeling apprehensive, he became sensitive to the dank, cold, musty air. He turned the flashlight on and saw a motionless, bulky mound. As he inched closer, he could see the mound was made up of either large bags of cement or sacks filled with sand. As he got right up to it, he realized they were large sand bags forming a barrier to hide a small electric generator. The generator was shut down. He touched it, and it was cold.

Shining the flashlight on the ground to see where he was stepping, he saw the same tread of tire tracks that led him there. He also saw the imprints of boots and others that looked like tennis shoes. He shined the light to investigate the footprints, and he found a lot of smaller shoe prints—tennis shoes and sandals—which were clearly evident. The prints then stopped abruptly. Crouching down, he noticed impressions where a plank or loading board may have been placed.

They loaded the kids into the truck and took them away earlier today or last night, he thought.

As he flashed the light ahead of him, he saw a pickup truck, and his gut felt a quivering stab of pain. It was the pickup where he'd last seen Nikki as it drove past him on the street.

He walked up cautiously and tried to open the door on the driver's side, but it was locked. Using the flashlight to look through the windows, he saw nothing out of the ordinary, but he walked around to the other side to see if that door was open. It was not.

Knowing the cave was probably devoid of people, he flashed the light ahead of him in an attempt to see the back of the cave, but the space proved too big for him to see much. He took the light down to the ground and noticed electrical cables that led toward the inner chamber. He followed them with a feeling of dread overcoming him, knowing that, if the kidnappers had been there, and it certainly looked like a well-planned hideaway, they were long gone. Hesitant whether he should return outside or continue investigating the cave, he decided to walk farther into the cave.

He came upon another chamber where the flashlight illuminated a refrigerator. Panning the light from one side to the other, he saw a well-equipped kitchen with a stove, tables, and benches. The smell of cooked food still lingered in the air. Walking to the fridge, he opened the door and found it cold inside, despite the fact the electric generator was turned off, confirming his gut feeling that the kidnappers had left a few hours before. He shined the light around and saw several boxes. One contained paper plates and cups, along with plastic utensils. All garbage. He approached the next open box, looked inside, and found crumpled paper. Figuring it was packing material, he thought it might contain a clue of what the box had contained. He took it all out and walked to the table, where he laid the flashlight on the bench, facing up to provide needed light. Then he laid the papers on the table to stretch them out.

Instead of wrapping material, he discovered drawings. Children's drawings. About the fifth one he pressed out made him stop and examine it closely. It was a portrait of Benito Juárez, exactly like the one he'd seen hanging in Sofía's house, that she'd described as the Abraham Lincoln of Mexico.

Do they have Bibi after all?

He folded the drawing, put it by the flashlight, and quickly looked through the other newsprint drawings to see if any more of them looked like Bibi's work. The other ones appeared to be line drawings or more crude renditions of birds, perhaps eagles, or portraits, presumably of Benito Juárez. Unlike the one he'd folded to take with him, the rest did not look like the work of Sofía's daughter.

He took his backpack off, slipped Bibi's drawing in a side pocket, and decided to take a sample of the eagle drawings too. Every single eagle was done in blue, so he picked one and stuffed it into the side pocket, along with the portrait he attributed to Bibi. After putting his backpack on, he counted the drawings and concluded once more that none of them had clues he should take with him. Picking the primitive art up and crumpling it again, he put it all back in the box where he'd found it.

He took his flashlight to investigate the rest of the cave. Moving along the uneven ground, he smelled the distinct odor of bat guano. But as he continued toward the back of the cave, he noticed a much stronger fetid odor. He flashed the light around and saw the makeshift outhouses. He ventured on to investigate but suddenly stubbed his toes. Almost falling, he managed to regain his balance before hitting the ground. He expected a broken calcite formation to be the obstacle that had tripped him, yet instead his flashlight revealed the low frame of an old cot, one of several old army cots laid out ahead of him. Crayons were scattered on the one he'd inadvertently hit. Four open crayon boxes were also lying on the dirty old cot. He shifted the light up and down and saw the back of the cave, and he took a few more steps to the rear of the chamber to ensure he was not missing important clues. Convinced nothing else merited his attention, he turned around and headed toward the front again.

As he approached the mouth of the cave, the renewed vibrating of his mobile phone made his heart almost stop beating. He had been so involved investigating the cave that he'd forgotten about the app on his phone picking up Nikki's GPS signal. Inside the cave, it had stopped vibrating, but once he was near the opening, the signal started up again. He turned the flashlight off and reached his hand around to put it in the side pocket of his backpack before he started running.

Outside, Eduardo cupped his hands to protect his eyes from the bright sunlight and continued running to the guayule tree. Despite being tied, Fígaro had managed to dig a small hole in an area of soft dirt that looked freshly moved. It had to be a shallow grave. His heart pounded as he fell to his knees and started removing the earth with both hands. His mouth went dry, and he broke out in a sweat from his feverous exertions.

His hand hit something. Clearing the dirt around the object, he discovered Nikki's carpetbag. Pulling it out of the ground, he dumped the contents. They were Nikki's clothes, the clothes she'd been wearing when she went underground. He picked them up and clutched them to his chest, cursing and crying at the same time. Did this mean she was dead? He stood up and kicked the dirt where he'd been digging. Fígaro inched in close to Eduardo and whimpered.

Still clutching Nikki's clothes, Eduardo leaned over, picked up a stone, and flung it with full force at an outcropping of sedimentary rocks that formed a ledge about thirty feet away. It bounced off the ledge, hit the ground, and rolled a short distance, stopping in the shade of a small oak. Eduardo threw a tight-fisted arm into the air and screamed in rage, though it came out as a hoarse growl, almost like a frog croaking. He took the clothes into both hands, clutching them tightly into his chest again. Then he went to his knees, put his head on the ground, let go of the clothes, and pounded the earth with his fists, sobbing like a child.

Nikki's words, spoken to him two nights ago as they made love in the hotel in Zacatecas, kept rattling over and over again in his brain.

I've lost almost every person I've ever loved—my parents, my son, my grandparents. I'm afraid to love you unconditionally with total abandon. I'm afraid to lose you, and I'd rather die than go through losing a loved one again.

As he dried his tears, Eduardo noticed the rip in the blouse. He examined it more closely and saw the blood stains for the first time. He stared at the stains as he felt all the energy drain from his body.

If only I could have stopped her from going on this absurd investigation, he thought as he gently folded the skirt and blouse.

With reverential silence, he put the clothes back in Nikki's carpetbag and searched it for the secret compartment she had sewn into the bottom. He felt a thickness in the lining.

Nikki's secure cell phone. That's why I was picking up the signal, he thought as he retrieved it from its hiding place.

He input a code to block the signal from continuing to make his own phone vibrate. Then he tucked it in his backpack before laying the carpetbag on the ground to continue his digging. He knew the GPS chip in her shoe would activate a signal on his phone, and he was relieved when it didn't vibrate again.

She can't be buried here, or I'd be picking up the signal from her shoe, he reasoned to calm himself. *I'm thankful she's wearing another chip in her tennis shoe, so hopefully we can find her soon.* But he was still nervous.

Figaro sniffed the bag and swept his nose back and forth over the ground. He put his belly on the soft soil and used his front paws in an attempt to pull off the muzzle covering his nose and mouth.

Eduardo continued removing dirt, a laborious task since he was using his hands, and the tip of a shoe came into view. As he scraped dirt away, a full boot became visible, and then a leg wearing jeans. Eduardo's mind raced with thoughts. He pulled the body by the leg and uncovered the complete torso of a man. The body had a bullet wound in the chest. Working quickly to get dirt off the face, he stopped short when he saw the head of the corpse. The man's throat had been slit wide open, but what made

Eduardo's heart skip was the person's face. He recognized the older man from the scene of the accident where Juana was killed, the same man they saw at the market in Zacatecas the day before.

I thought this guy was part of the kidnapper's group.

He stopped and wiped the sweat off his forehead, studying the fresh dirt covering the makeshift grave site and noticing for the first time how extensive it was. He went down on his hands and knees again, digging until he felt a stiff bundle.

Oh my God, another body.

Working as quickly as he could, he removed sufficient dirt to find the corpse of another man, probably in his mid-thirties. Eduardo did not recognize him. He pulled the body out, turned it over, and studied it. The cadaver had one bullet hole in the middle of his forehead. Checking the pockets for identification, he found none. Both bodies had been stripped of all personal items they may have carried with them—wallet, watch, sunglasses, keys, money, or rings. He took photos of the two cadavers: full body, torso, and close-ups of their faces.

Exhausted, Eduardo stopped to look around. His eyes searched past the guayule shrubs and followed the contour of the cliffs, checking the valley and taking the time to slowly scan the whole landscape below to make sure he was not being watched. He glanced at Fígaro, who was pulling on his leash again and still sniffing the ground.

Don't tell me you've found another body, he thought as he watched the pup.

With trepidation, Eduardo looked the grave area over to locate any further bulging areas. He noticed one just out of reach from where Fígaro was sniffing, lodged between two scrubby bushes. Using his hands to make short, brush-like strokes, like an archeologist uncovering an antique ceramic vessel, he removed enough soil around the protrusion to reveal another bundle.

Eduardo went numb and sat down next to the grave as tears sprung to his eyes. As he suspected, it was a third body. A child. Buried face down. A corpse with long, black hair. He turned the small body over. He didn't know her name, but he had seen her with Nikki as the pickup sped away from the market.

He dropped his face into his dirt-covered hands and let the tears flow.

CHAPTER 21

San Miguel de Allende—Saturday, early morning, day four after abduction

Sofía tried to pray, but her mind wouldn't stay with it. She turned over in the twin bed, the bed that belonged to Bibi. It squeaked as she opened her eyes. Light splashed on the wall above the window, like impressionist brushstrokes. The unevenness of the plaster created a faint painterly pattern of light and dark spots, a pattern which Bibi had often pointed out to her mother when Sofía came in to open the curtains every morning. Regret filled Sofía as she observed the play of light, regret that she had not taken the time to enjoy these little moments with her daughter. Tears flooded her eyes.

The phone rang, and Sofía jumped from the bed. The tears that had welled up cascaded down her face as she threw on a bathrobe over her pajamas. As she rushed to the door, it swung open, the bright light of the adjoining room blinding her. She charged past Floyd, who had opened the door and now stood like a sentry, keeping it open. Her eyes still adjusting to the brightness, she squinted at the phone sitting on top of the night stand and saw the same words, *Private Caller*, lighting up the Caller I.D. The ringing phone made Sofía shiver with dread, yet it was the lifeline to her daughter. She focused on Timothy, who would tell her when to pick up.

Jack Levy and Timothy Ramos were placing headphones over their ears, and Timothy signaled Sofía they were ready for her to answer. Floyd moved away from the door while adjusting his own set of headphones.

Dio mio, aiutami, Sofía thought, trying to calm her nerves as she picked up the phone.

"Let me speak with my daughter," she said in heavily accented Spanish as her voice cracked, but she managed to keep her composure.

Timothy gave Sofía a thumbs-up signal.

"When we get your money, you can speak with her," the voice answered in Spanish over the phone.

Sofía swallowed hard. "I won't pay until I speak with her." She'd practiced saying this over and over with Timothy late last night after he arrived from Miami.

"When you transfer the money to me, you can speak with her," the voice said.

"I'm not paying anything until I know she's alive," Sofía said, using a standard negotiating phrase she had learned from her tutoring session with Timothy.

"Give me a ten percent deposit and you can speak with her after I've confirmed the transfer," the voice demanded as everyone in Sofía's room listened.

Timothy held up all ten fingers.

Sofía proceeded with the instructions. "I don't have that much money. I'll give you ten thousand dollars."

"If you want her alive . . ."

If you want her alive rang so loudly in her ears, Sofía was willing to offer them the two million dollars in ransom Paolo had agreed to pay to get it over with and get their daughter back. But having the three men in the room with her made her realize she needed to follow their advice if she was ever to see Bibi again. They had been very specific in their meeting with her the night before.

". . . you must give us one hundred fifty thousand dollars," Sofía heard the man conclude.

Timothy flashed the five fingers of his right hand three times.

"I can give you fifteen thousand."

Sweat broke out on Sofía's forehead.

"Look, woman, if you want to talk with your Bibiana, you must give me one hundred thousand."

Sofía looked at Timothy, who signaled fifty thousand. She offered that amount over the phone.

"You're wearing me out. Do you want to see your daughter alive?"

Timothy passed a note to Sofía.

> *Your final offer is $75,000. You don't have more.*
> *Ask for his bank info.*

As Timothy handed the note to her, Sofía stiffened. The kidnapper had warned her against getting anyone else involved if she wanted her daughter back. Timothy approaching her put her on the verge of breaking down.

I have to hold up, she told herself, trying to fully regain her composure. *I have to do this negotiation. Otherwise, they'll kill Bibi.*

"I'll transfer seventy-five thousand today. It's all I have. Give me the bank account where I can deposit the money for you." Sofía bit her lip so hard as she muttered the words that she drew blood.

Silence.

Sofía sat on the edge of her own bed, where either Floyd or one of his guys had slept. Her disheveled appearance seemed to match the state of her emotions as she waited for a response. Following instructions she'd learned from Floyd's expert, she repeated her request for a bank account.

"Seems like you don't care to speak with her. But I'll show you my goodwill. Send me the money to the Swiss Bank in Cayman Islands, account number 584675." The voice followed up with a nine-digit bank routing number.

Sofía's hand shook as she wrote every detail on a pad next to the phone.

The voice repeated instructions he'd already stated in the past phone call—no games, no police, and no negotiators. Then he stated to send the transfer in U.S. dollars. He would call and let Sofía speak to her daughter after he confirmed the receipt of the money.

Jack sat in front of a monitor, focused on trying to locate the caller. He'd rigged his usual state-of-the-art equipment by uploading a detailed map of Mexico from a portable navigation system. Not the perfect setup he would have wanted, it was spotty and sluggish and worked in bits and starts, but it was the only tool he had to track the caller. With the make-shift equipment, it would take him longer to decode and find a location.

Timothy handed Sofía a note.

> *Confirm bank data with him. Keep him on as long*
> *as you can.*

After swallowing hard, Sofía stood up with the notepad in her hand and repeated the bank account and routing numbers in a slow and methodical voice. Then she heard a click and the dial tone. Sobbing, she collapsed on the bed.

Floyd took the phone from her hand, confirmed the line was off, and returned it to its cradle.

"We have his location," Jack said. "The guy is down the street. It's a slow-moving signal."

"You come with me," Floyd motioned to Timothy. "Jack will tell us where he's headed. Sofía, you start the wire-transfer process."

Jack gave a voice command to his phone equipment to start a conference call with Floyd and Timothy. Floyd took his headphones off, Timothy followed suit, and both men popped their mobile phone earpieces in. They bolted out the bedroom, sprinted through the covered patio, ran through the kitchen into the outdoor yard, and headed for the exit leading to the alley.

Jack then reminded Sofía it was Saturday, and the banks only had personnel available till noon. He instructed her to make the transfer immediately since it would be sent to a different time zone in the Caymans. Sofía stood up, took the landline phone from the cradle, speed-dialed her banker, and initiated the transfer of seventy-five thousand in U.S. dollars to the Cayman Islands.

CHAPTER 22

San Miguel de Allende—Saturday, early morning, day four after abduction

"Suspect's headed south," Jack's voice informed both men through their mobile earpieces. "He was either driving or walking very slowly along the side street, about half a block away."

Both men ran down the alley where it dead-ended into the side street. As they approached the corner, they saw a man in a black checkered shirt and a black cowboy hat get into a black Subaru pickup.

"Tim, stay on him. I'm doubling back to get my truck. Be ready to jump in as I drive by," Floyd said.

Floyd fast-hoofed it back to his rental, maneuvering the cobblestones as best he could. As he entered Sofía's yard and approached his vehicle, he pressed the unlock button, opened the door, and climbed in, cursing that the truck was parked inside a yard behind a tall wall. As he turned the vehicle into the alley, he noticed two teenage boys playing soccer. The kids got out of the way, and he turned south and then turned onto Montes de Oca, the street with the entrance to Sofía's restaurant. He saw Timothy standing in the middle of the street. A block beyond where Timothy stood, the Subaru turned a corner out of sight onto the road dead-ending into the roundabout and the highway to Querétaro.

"I've totally lost the signal," Jack's voice blasted from Floyd's earpiece. "I don't have the proper equipment to pick up his phone now that it's turned off. I thought I'd trace his number easily and then hack in through SS-7 to get complete access to his activity, but it's going to take another call."

Floyd gunned the engine and bumped over the uneven cobblestones, then hit the brakes to slow down, allowing Timothy enough time to jump in as the truck continued rolling.

"Damned son of a bitch," Floyd said. "Did you get his tag?"

"The car did not have a license plate. I'll bet he's heading out of the city, on the road to Querétaro."

"Are you sure?"

"About the road to Querétaro? I'm damn sure," Timothy said. "I studied the maps on the flight yesterday."

"No, I mean the license plate."

"The car had a sticker in the back window that I couldn't read. I snapped a photo, but the sticker is curled up and you can't read it."

"A temporary sticker all curled up?"

"Yeah, that's why I couldn't read it."

"That's got to be the same guy who killed Juana. He's got a black Subaru today. The guy who killed Juana had a yellow-beige Honda, but it can't be a coincidence. Not two vehicles with tags taped to their back windows. Temporary tags that are curled up so they can't be read."

Floyd continued driving as fast as he could while he followed the street signs toward Querétaro.

"I've got binos in my bag under your legs. Take them out and see if you can spot him ahead of us."

Looking through the binoculars, Timothy adjusted the vision on them. Floyd was approaching the roundabout and the wide boulevard. He slowed down for a yield sign and came to a complete stop while waiting to enter the heavier flow of traffic on the boulevard.

"There's a black truck ahead," Timothy said, still adjusting the binoculars. "Looks like a Subaru. Let me find . . . yeah, it's a Subaru. I don't see any police cars. Can you go faster?"

Floyd eased into the left lane to give Tim more visibility of the traffic ahead so he would not lose sight of the truck. They were forced to stop at a red light when they hit an intersection with another busy street. As soon as the light turned green, they drove for two more blocks, Timothy indicating the truck was still ahead.

"Okay, tell me quick. Which way? Both show arrows to Querétaro."

"Take highway one eleven," Timothy said. "The Subaru turned that way. If he's trying to get away, he can get lost in the big city, so either way, he's probably headed for Querétaro or Mexico City."

Floyd pulled onto Highway 111. Traffic was moderately heavy, and the black truck had managed to get considerably ahead of them, primarily due to the traffic light that had held Floyd and Timothy back for a minute or more, but Floyd sped up until they were passing every vehicle on the road.

As they approached the top of a hill, Floyd slowed down. He kept the speedometer at one hundred thirty kilometers, which was over the speed limit but the maximum he dared to drive to avoid getting stopped if the police were waiting on the other side of the hill.

With the binoculars glued to his eyes, Timothy held the Subaru in sight. Once he updated Floyd that no police cars were visible, Floyd floored the gas petal. He passed three cars in succession and then weaved to the right lane to get around a slower-moving truck pulling a horse trailer that was taking up the left lane. He continued weaving from one lane to another until he could see the Subaru a few cars ahead.

"Man, I never expected it to be this easy," Floyd said as he lifted his right hand off the steering wheel and stretched his arm toward the windshield as he tightened and released muscles in his neck. "Now we just have to follow him."

"I hate to tell you, it's not him," Timothy said. "That truck has a license plate."

Floyd drove on to verify the guy hadn't had time to remove the sticker and uncover a license plate. As they got closer to the Subaru, Timothy noticed two people in the cabin. Floyd passed the car slowly while Timothy took a good look.

"Shit, Floyd. It's two women."

"Hell, I should've known it couldn't be this easy. I'm turning back at the next exit. We need to rescue Nikki, and you need to get back and help Sofía when that guy calls back for the full ransom money."

Floyd slipped into the right lane, found an exit about two miles down the road, made a U-turn, and got back on the highway, heading toward San Miguel.

His phone rang. It was Jack.

"Hey, Floyd. Sofía got a call from the kidnapper confirming the money transfer. Paolo got here a few minutes ago. The bad news is the kidnapper told her he won't let her talk to her daughter. Says he saw two men running from the alley when he called earlier. He accused her of hiring people to help her, so now he's demanding the full amount of money to release Bibi or he will . . . He's threatening he'll kill the child. Paolo arrived, and he wants to pay the full ransom, and I'm saying—"

"At all costs, keep Sofía or Paolo from transferring money until Timothy and I get back," Floyd said.

He hung up and stepped harder on the gas pedal.

Floyd's phone rang again. This time it was Eduardo.

CHAPTER 23

San Miguel de Allende—Saturday morning, day four after abduction

Sofía was inconsolable and had closed herself up in Bibi's room. Floyd knocked on the door and asked her to join the rest of the group in the parlor. A few seconds later, Sofía entered the room, her appearance more disheveled than before to the point she was almost unrecognizable as the same woman Floyd had met one day earlier. She slouched onto the piano bench, her face swollen and red, her hair an uncombed mess, and she still wore her bathrobe.

Paolo nervously bounced his eyes from one side of the room to the other as he sat in a plush Louis XIV armchair next to the window, first staring briefly at every person in the room and then settling his sight outside, as if wishing himself to be out there and not inside in the stuffy, tense atmosphere of the room. Eventually, he looked at Sofía again.

Jack sat on a loveseat on the far wall, and Timothy leaned against the wall to one side of the loveseat. They all faced Floyd, who was standing by the antique side table near the doorway.

"The caller demanding ransom is not letting you talk to Bibi because he does not have her," Floyd said with authority and confidence.

"Oh my God . . ." Sofía said, her voice breaking into a hoarse whisper. She looked as if she was going to collapse.

"We believe Bibi is with the original person who kidnapped her, and we think he's taking her north of Zacatecas. We know she was in Zacatecas, in a cave there, last night."

"Are you sure my daughter is alive?" Paolo asked. He wiped his sweaty forehead with the back of his hand.

"We have reason to believe she is alive," Floyd said.

"You seem to think there's more than one kidnapper," Paolo said in a cautious voice.

"We don't know that," Floyd said, "but the picture that's emerging indicates the man calling Sofía does not have her in his possession. We will call his bluff before negotiating with him again. We want to make certain he lets us talk to Bibi before you pay him any further money."

Paolo looked at Sofía anxiously before returning his gaze toward Floyd.

"Unless you've already paid," Floyd said, reading Paolo's expression of disbelief.

"Sofía called me this morning," Paolo said, shifting in his chair to stare at Sofía. "She called me after she paid seventy-five thousand to the Cayman bank so the kidnapper would let her talk to Bibi. Then the two of you stupidly ran outside and were seen by the kidnapper and he demanded the full ransom."

Paolo stood up and shook an accusing finger at Floyd. "Your foolish behavior could have cost us our daughter's life. Sofía and I talked it over, and I called my banker at home in Milan to transfer the remaining amount—one million nine hundred and twenty-five thousand—to the Cayman Islands to get our daughter back." Paolo's face looked flushed and angry, and his elegant British accent did not fit his current demeanor.

"So that was half an hour ago?" Jack asked.

Paolo looked at his watch. "More like forty minutes, maybe less."

"Call your banker and stop that order for payment," Floyd said, checking his own watch. "And for God's sake, don't jeopardize Bibi's life by going to the kidnappers yourself. Fortunately, it's Saturday, so your bank in Italy may not transfer the money until Monday morning. With the seven hour time difference, that would be one a.m. in San Miguel."

"We want our daughter safely released," Paolo said, stuttering. "You are the one endangering her. I don't trust that you're doing the right things to get her—"

"You're the one endangering her. If that money happens to reach that scumbag demanding ransom, it's you who didn't allow us to negotiate her safe release." Floyd did everything he could to control his anger. *It won't*

help the situation to yell at Paolo, though I'd like to punch the hell out of him,
Floyd thought.

Paolo took his mobile phone from his pants pocket and speed-dialed a number. He put the phone to his ear, and after a few seconds, he rose and spoke in Italian as he walked toward the door.

"Ciao, Belinda, Paolo Lombardi here. May I speak to Stefano."

Sofía followed Paolo, but at the doorway, she held back and returned to the bench and plopped down on it, as if she could not carry the weight of her own body. She looked around the room, and then glanced at Floyd.

"He's calling the home of his banker friend in Italy. Belinda is Stefano's wife," Sofía said as she gestured with her hand toward the patio. "Yeah. Calling him at home since the bank is closed. Shouldn't the kidnapper be contacting us with instructions for releasing her?"

"Paolo will probably get the transfer stopped," Floyd said, "so the man who has been demanding ransom, let me call him the blackmailer, will not be calling unless the money already left Italy. In that case, he may not verify until Monday, depending if his bank accepts e-transfers on Sunday. My guess is that due to the weekend plus the time difference, that money has not been paid."

"I keep forgetting about the time difference," Sofía said. "But what if the man in Zacatecas who is holding Bibi is working with the caller? They will want the rest of the money in addition to my seventy-five thousand transfer, which was already received."

"Obviously, Paolo's trying to stop the transfer right now," Floyd said. "If the money was electronically transferred out of Paolo's account because of his insistence to pay it, it's gone. But that money should not have left Italy yet. As far as the bank in the Cayman Islands is concerned, only the account holder can verify transactions. But we're working on finding out who owns that account."

"When I get big checks at the restaurant," Sofía said, "I can call that bank and ask them if there are sufficient funds in the account for me to deposit the check."

"That's totally different," Floyd said. "Offshore bank accounts are intended for holding money anonymously or for transferring money in and out. Shell banks and unnamed accounts are prohibited on the islands, yet unlicensed operations function on the periphery all the time without government sanctioning. So it's hard to get access to private information."

"As the investigator you are," Paolo said, clearing his throat as he entered the room, "former CIA operative and whatever other credentials you have, why can't you get the name of the account owner and use that knowledge to find him and get Bibi released?"

"I've been explaining to Sofía that it's difficult to prove who owns offshore accounts. Proof of identity is required by law when accounts are opened, but as with other requirements, some Cayman banks overlook them. That investigation is started, but it takes time. We can't get answers right away."

"What did your banker tell you?" Jack asked.

"Stefano will stop the transfer." Paolo walked across the room.

"How do you know Bibi spent the night in Zacatecas?" Sofía asked as her gaze followed an exhausted-looking Paolo to the Louis XIV chair, where he sat down again.

"Eduardo's in Zacatecas. He found evidence she was there, and he's following her trail."

"And where's the woman?" Sofía asked.

"Nikki? She's working the case," Floyd said. "We'll find your daughter. Just be patient, and let me remind you not to take matters into your own hands. Consult with us before you take action. Now, if you'll allow me, I need to lay out plans for rescuing Bibi. If a phone call comes in, we'll need your help, Sofía. But right now I need to talk to Jack and Timothy alone."

Sofía and Paolo took the hint and left the room.

"While Timothy and I were driving back, Eduardo called me," Floyd said once they were out of earshot. "He discovered a cave with evidence the kidnapper held everyone there last night. He also found three dead bodies buried outside the cave. One was a young girl, maybe twelve years old. Definitely does not fit Bibi's description. Eduardo is pretty sure it was the girl he saw in the back of the pickup with Nikki when she went underground."

"And the other two?" Timothy asked.

"One was the man who witnessed the accident which killed Juana—the woman who gave us a lot of information on the coyote and knew that bastard trafficker used caves in Zacatecas to hold his victims. Eduardo did not know who the third body was, also a man. All identifying data they may have been carrying was missing."

"How do you know Sofía's daughter is still alive?" Jack asked.

"Don't know that for sure, but Eduardo found a drawing he claims is just like that portrait of Benito Juárez," Floyd said, pointing to the framed painting. "Eduardo is certain Nikki left it behind as a clue, and I agree."

"So what's our plan?" Timothy asked.

"First, I'll give Jack the photos Eduardo sent me of the dead people so he can run them through facial recognition software. See if we can get a hit on the two men. Then I'd say Jack and I meet up with Eduardo and we search for Nikki. I rented a helicopter yesterday through my contact Fernando. Comes with a pilot. You stay here, Timothy, so you can help Sofía and Paolo with any negotiations, if needed. But keep in mind, Sofía needs to hear Bibi's voice. Then call me."

"Give me a bit of time to build a drone," Jack said, getting up to retrieve his suitcase from the adjacent room.

"You're going to build a drone?" Floyd groaned as he looked at his watch. "You must be joking."

"A drone will help me locate Nikki."

"Look, we're losing precious time to find her," Floyd said. "I don't know if Fernando can arrange an extension on the chopper and pilot. I rented them for three days. The chopper's been on standby since yesterday. We're going to pick Eduardo up and then follow the old Pan-American Highway leading from Zacatecas to Juárez, the border town. Eduardo thinks they're in an eighteen-wheeler based on tire tracks he found at their hideout."

"Give me fifteen minutes to solder the wires. I can assemble the rest of it in the bird."

"Okay," Floyd said as he tried to calm down. "Take the time you need to do it right."

Jack started toward the other room, stopped, and faced Floyd. "By the way, I checked three stand-alone computers in this house while you and Tim were out chasing that guy. I found evidence on Bibi's laptop where she Googled the instructions to download Troll Line and Kik. Those are potentially dangerous apps for kids. Very dangerous. Users can post anonymously and bypass security since messages are not logged into phone history. If she Googled them on her laptop, I bet they're installed on her mobile phone. She probably has Snapchat too."

"Get your soldering done, and we'll talk about Bibi's social media apps on the way to the helicopter," Floyd said. "And I'll email you the photos for facial recognition too."

Jack walked to the other room to set up his soldering iron, while Timothy returned to the makeshift headquarters and sat down to tinker with the phone monitoring equipment. Floyd went to the patio to update Sofía on the decisions he'd made and to ask her to prepare sandwiches and provide bottled water to take with them.

CHAPTER 24

State of Durango, north of Zacatecas—Saturday, midday,
day four after abduction

"That's a Cessna down there," Santiago, the pilot, said in reasonably good English as he spoke into the headset of the internal communication system.

He pointed to a small clearing on flat terrain to the west side of the helicopter. He turned the single engine Eurocopter AS350 AStar, an improved six-seater version of the Airbus model originally known as a Squirrel, in a slow 180-degree pattern to give his passengers a better view of the plane he'd spotted.

"Could it belong to our kidnappers?" Eduardo asked, struggling to speak into the headset as wind whipped his face.

Eduardo crouched in the open door located on the right side of the helicopter and held an antenna out the door. Before the flight, the pilot had rigged a harness to a hook above the door on the inside of the AStar. The harness was around Eduardo, securing him inside the chopper. For double protection, Santiago had insisted on having an extension of the seatbelt wrapped around Eduardo's waist to keep him from falling out if the harness accidentally came loose.

"No, not too possible for kidnappers," Santiago said. "With those big, rear double doors, it's a Turbo 206, favorite of the cartels. It's abandoned. They do that. They have money to throw away, so they leave a plane behind when they don't need it anymore. The capos just buy a new one. But no one touches equipment like that for a while, just in case the capo returns."

COYOTE ZONE

The pilot had stored Eduardo's cooler in the back of the chopper and had also purchased a dog harness for Fígaro and attached it to a seat. The canine had squirmed and displayed his displeasure when Eduardo placed the muzzle back over his snout and deposited him into the harness. It did not take long, though, before Fígaro settled into the flight.

Eduardo pulled the antenna back inside for a few seconds so he could adjust the headset to a comfortable position. He leaned out again and aimed the antenna where Jack had shown him. He adjusted his legs so he could use them to balance against the banking maneuver the pilot was performing.

As the pilot flew by the Cessna for a closer look, Jack—who was sitting in the third row of seats at the rear of the chopper—checked the screen of his Toughbook, a rugged tablet computer he had placed on the seat beside him. Its top-grade security system and embedded wireless mobile broadband delivered connectivity, even in the most challenging environments. Though it did not demand a lot of energy, despite its powerful reach, it was supported by a bank of batteries stored in a roll-on case he'd secured under his seat. Jack had uploaded the photos of the two dead men into the facial recognition software. Despite the processing power contained in the Toughbook, it would require several hours to run the photos to try to find a match. The Toughbook made an excellent mobile command center, but its very portability made it slower than equipment used by government agencies.

The pilot hovered a short distance from the abandoned aircraft to give everyone a bird's-eye view through the rounded glass canopy enclosure at the front of the AS350.

Glancing at the Toughbook's screen to make certain he had not yet picked up a signal, Jack stopped working on the drone, setting it on his lap long enough to scan the landscape and locate the Cessna. Then he went back to work, connecting the various cables to the body of the drone.

When the pilot started circling the Cessna, Fígaro sensed the commotion in the cabin and tried to wiggle free. Despite the restraint that kept him in his seat, the pup managed to stand on his hind legs. He seemed to look out over the area where the Cessna was located, as if he'd understood that side contained an item of interest.

Jack, in the row behind the pup, watched Fígaro make one more attempt to wiggle out of his constraint. He reached around the seat and

191

rubbed the Pomsky's head through the harness straps, and the canine settled down again and fell asleep shortly after the pilot resumed his flight plan.

"I don't make serious miscalculations very often," Floyd said, looking over his shoulder as he spoke, "but I don't know what I was thinking when I allowed you to bring that dog with us."

"If I had not taken Fígaro with me this morning, I would not have found Nikki's carpetbag. Or those three dead bodies," Eduardo said, the wind distorting his voice over the ICS. "This dog's been trained."

"But he's not an Army trained K-9," Floyd said. "Big difference between an Army dog and a mutt that's been trained not to pee in a house."

"Fígaro, you need to earn your keep," Eduardo said. "Seems like Floyd's not crazy about you being here."

"I heard that," Floyd retorted in a harsh voice. "All I ask is that you keep him from messing up our investigation."

"The dog, he can stay with me at the helicopter," the pilot said in his accented English.

For the next forty-five minutes, Santiago flew a straightforward trip and followed the old Pan-American route, known in that area of Central Mexico as Highway 45. It provided the linking up of Highway 85, the original Pan-American route out of Mexico City, to the portion of the route called the El Paso spur, where the Mexican route crossed the border in Western Texas and became Interstate 25, which goes through Albuquerque where it is called the Pan-American Freeway.

The pilot deviated a few times when Floyd asked him to move away from the highway, either to check out a detail or to avoid overflying the paved roadway too much and raising suspicion in the traffic below.

The helicopter was well-suited for high-altitude performance in North Central Mexico, where the average altitude is seventy-three hundred feet above sea level. Soaring mountain ranges cutting through the central plateau offered considerably higher altitudes. The original Squirrel was a quiet chopper, specifically built for special use in areas with stringent noise requirements or where an element of surprise might be necessary. The AStar engineers had kept all those qualities, including reduced in-cabin noise, but the open door where Eduardo crouched down to operate the antenna created disturbances in the compartment.

They flew in silence. Jack continued tweaking the drone, knowing that, as soon as they landed, he would need it to help find Nikki's signal and possibly provide visuals of where she was located. He also periodically checked the Toughbook to see if he had a hit on the photos. He was busy verifying the final parameters he had input on his computer for the drone's remote control when suddenly the dashboard monitoring the GPS signal lit up with a pulsating arrow and two blinking lights. He cranked the audio up and listened to the very weak electronic chirping sound through an earpiece connected to the Toughbook.

"Hey, we have a signal," Jack said with total disbelief until the chirping came in again and his tone quickly changed to an excited, "Yes! Man, we have a signal."

Floyd turned to face Jack in the backseat and gave him a thumbs-up.

"Thank God," Eduardo said, breaking out in a cold sweat. "It must be coming from Nikki's shoes. I only pray she's alive."

The signal picked up by the tracking instruments started breaking up. In less than a minute, it had gone dead.

"Go back to where the signal was coming in." Jack barked the instructions to the pilot as he continued to adjust the calibration on his command center software to see if he could locate the signal again.

"We're approaching the Zone of Silence," the pilot said as he maneuvered the helicopter in a wide circle, returning the aircraft to the point where the signals were received. "Anomalies exist in sound waves here. That's the reason you cannot receive the signal. Radio waves, they come and go in this area."

Jack's equipment was completely silent.

"It's long been said that, here in this area, radio waves are not to be depended on," Santiago said, repeating his explanation. "Some say too much magnetism in the earth here. I say too much iron ore and rare earth from meteorites hitting here."

"Atmospheric conditions can affect cellular phones and GPS," Jack said, "which, as you know, use a range of radio bands in UHF and VHF, but you can usually see the conditions, and right now I can't see any weather that might cause interference in transmission or a limitation in range, so maybe it's an inversion."

"But that would only extend the range of the signal," the pilot said.

"My point exactly. We may not be close enough, and we picked up a signal that bounced over the normal horizon distance, like it hit skip zones, like a stone skipping along the surface of a lake. That can happen on clear, cloudless days with no wind. Just like today. Then a high pressure system forms and causes the inversion."

The pilot canvassed the area where the signal had been received. With each wide circle, Eduardo's white knuckles adjusted the antenna slightly, praying he'd pick up the GPS transmission points. Despite the cool air blowing on him, profuse perspiration in his armpits kept his shirt wet.

No signal.

The pilot leveled out and flew a straight line about twenty miles farther north.

The monitor lit up.

"We've got it again," Jack said. "Hey, man, keep the antenna steady."

"Ceballos is a town up ahead," the pilot said. "It's a dilapidated town on the verge of extinction. On the edge of the Zone of Silence. Signal could be coming from there."

"Make a big circle around the town," Floyd said. "Far enough out so the folks in the town can't hear or see us."

The signal was strongest on the northeast side of Ceballos. Jack used a hand signal with Floyd, who had shifted in his seating position to look back at him. Floyd then used his hand to point the pilot into a north-bound route, leaving the town way behind. After a while, Jack requested the pilot find a place to land.

Floyd searched the parched landscape and pointed toward the only grouping of trees he had seen in the scrubby desert, at the foot of a large hill. Santiago informed Eduardo it was time to bring the antenna in, close the door, and take a seat for landing.

"Circle around," Floyd said, "to make sure we don't spot people out here. And land as close as you can to that clump of trees." He pointed again to a cluster containing a couple of large cottonwood trees.

A cloud of dust obscured their sight for twelve seconds or so as the helicopter landed. When the dust settled, they were facing a beat-up, chocolate-colored pickup truck with extra-large tires, parked hidden under a very large cottonwood tree.

A dusty, dirty, wreck of a pickup, with two people sitting inside.

CHAPTER 25

Mapimí Zone of Silence—Saturday, early afternoon,
day four after abduction

Floyd and the pilot stared at the vehicle in front of them. "Did you see it?" Floyd asked in a flabbergasted voice.

"Only after we landed," Santiago said.

Eduardo unstrapped his seatbelt and struggled out of the harness. "I'll see who they are."

The pilot reached back and handed Eduardo a Smith & Wesson handgun, but he pushed the gun away.

"I've got one," Eduardo said as he turned to unlock and open the door. "You keep it, in case you need it."

"Hey, I'll borrow it," Jack said. "I don't have a gun."

Eduardo jumped to the ground, waved at the two unknown people, waited five seconds, and walked toward the pickup. As he approached, he could see a thin, gray-haired man behind the steering wheel, and a young woman with jet-black hair gathered into a ponytail sitting in the passenger seat.

"What's good today?" Eduardo asked in Spanish as he approached the driver's side, positioning himself so he could talk to the driver, but also where he could see the helicopter in the periphery of his vision.

"Whatever you tell me is good," the man said, answering in Spanish.

"So what are you doing here?" Eduardo asked, smiling in a friendly manner. He observed the pickup—the big tires in particular, which were oversized, but he could immediately see in his mind's eye the tread did not match the pattern of the tire tracks he'd photographed on the road to the cave that morning.

"It's a hot day. We're enjoying the shade under this tree," the man said.

"Do you live around here?" Eduardo asked, trying to elicit a concrete answer.

He glanced at the woman, noticing her stone-faced expression. She wore dangling gold earrings and a crisp emerald-green sweatshirt with a Ralph Lauren logo that fit her in a bulky manner.

"Not too far."

"Is the young lady your daughter?"

"No, no. A family friend."

"So what are you and this lovely lady doing out here, sitting in a truck in the middle of the day?" Eduardo asked.

His original friendly smile fading with each evasive answer, Eduardo casually observed the inside of the pickup for any unusual items or clues. Only a large rip in the upholstery in the seat behind the man's head caught his eye. A rosary hung from the rearview mirror—a trinket many vehicles, from taxi cabs to private cars, carry in Latin American countries.

"We had a couple of hours to kill, and we thought the shade here is very nice."

"Are you waiting for a shipment to be dropped off to you?" Eduardo asked, coming to the point.

"We don't deal in drugs, if that's what you're getting at," the man said. "But maybe you're looking to deliver drugs?"

Eduardo laughed, not a joyful laugh but one of disbelief. "No, sir, not at all."

Floyd and Jack were getting out of the helicopter. The pilot stayed inside with the Pomsky.

"Okay, so you are suspecting us of dealing in drugs," the young woman said in perfect English as she switched languages. "And we suspect everyone in airplanes and helicopters to be either dealers or Federales, so we have a standoff in the desert."

"You speak excellent English," Eduardo said. "Better than mine."

"I studied in the U.S. for several years, and now I'm home, putting my education to good use."

"I can see," Eduardo said, nodding his head slightly as he studied her. "So tell me, why do we have a standoff?"

Eduardo continued observing her features. *For some strange reason, she looks vaguely familiar,* he thought.

"You don't want to tell us who you are," she said, switching back to Spanish, "so we are not forthcoming about who we are either. Just following your lead."

"Excuse me. I'm Eduardo Duarte, and those are my fellow workers by the helicopter. We're performing routine work, checking equipment out here in the Durango desert, the Bolsón de Mapimí." He extended his hand to the man to shake in greeting. Then he looked at the woman and gave her a nod in acknowledgement.

"I'm Ana, and this is Father Abelardo."

"A priest? Well, what a nice surprise to meet a priest. Why don't you come over and meet my colleagues."

Ana and the priest descended from the pickup, and Eduardo noticed the bulkiness under both their shirts as he walked with them toward the chopper.

"These are Ana and Father Abelardo," Eduardo said, introducing them.

Jack shook hands with both of them as he muttered his name. Floyd looked them both over very carefully.

"A Catholic priest?" Floyd said. "This area must be mighty rough if priests run around wearing bullet-proof vests." Then he whistled in a high timbre, showing his amazement, while he shook hands with the man.

"Father Abelardo is different," Ana said. "He heads up a group of concerned citizens."

"And you're one of them, I presume," Floyd said as he eyed the green sweatshirt she wore over the obvious vest on her own torso as he shook hands with her. "I'm Floyd Webber."

"I'm Juana Beltrán García."

"Juana García?" Eduardo asked in an amazed voice. "I thought you'd said Ana."

"Legally, I'm Juana *Beltrán* García," she said, emphasizing the surname Beltrán. "My name is Juana, but my dad called me Ana as I was growing up, and it stuck as a nickname."

"But you did say Juana Beltrán García is your name?" Eduardo looked at her in a questioning manner.

"You speak with a Colombian accent, so you may not know that, in Mexico, we use compound surnames. The first surname is your father's, and the second one is your mother's. Though I lost my mother when I was five, and my father lost me—"

"Wait a minute," Eduardo said, glancing briefly at Floyd. "Could it be that your mother's name was Juana García? I can't believe this. Did you know your mother died recently? In San Miguel de Allende?"

"No, no, my mother died a long time ago. My dad raised me. Well, no, actually, Catholic boarding schools in the U.S. raised me."

Eduardo pulled his mobile phone out, tapped the photo icon, and scrolled through the pictures he'd taken. He enlarged the one he had snapped at la Marihuana's house. It showed a collage in a gold-gilded frame. As Eduardo moved in closer to the young woman, he showed her the picture.

"Is this you in the photographs in that gold frame?"

The young woman looked at the screen on his phone and then looked back at Eduardo. Her brow furrowed instantly into a deep frown, and her mouth formed a slight gape. She stared at the photo on the phone, very confused.

"I don't understand. Where did you get this photo?" she asked, an expression of total disbelief on her face.

"At the house of a woman, maybe your mother, by the name of Juana García. She lived there until she died earlier this week."

"No, it could not be my mother. This is a mistake. My mother died when I was five."

She turned to look at the priest, as if searching for an answer to a perplexing and troubling question.

Eduardo brought up another picture, one showing the yellowed newspaper clipping, and handed the phone to her.

"Maybe this will clarify a few things."

She read a few lines, taking her hand to her mouth.

"My God, look, Father. Take a look at this," she said. She moved closer to the priest to share the photo of the stained and yellowed newspaper obituary with him.

Ana and the priest stared intently at the picture while Ana scrolled it as they read. They both seemed to take in every word with trepidation, yet also with great interest.

"Where did you get this?" Father Abelardo asked.

"As I've said, at the home of Juana García. She was killed in the street by an auto on Thursday. We think she was murdered."

It was now the priest's turn to look surprised. He shook his head as he took a couple of steps back.

Everyone was silent.

Everyone except for the pilot, who was now climbing out of the helicopter with Fígaro in his arms.

"Perdón. I'm Santiago, the pilot," he said as he waved. "My puppy needs to use the bathroom, so excuse us and pretend we did not interrupt you."

"Are you saying the woman who had these photos lived in San Miguel?" the priest asked. He was now holding the mobile phone. "And her name was Juana García?"

"Yes, Father," Eduardo said.

Ana moved closer to the priest. "Do you think this was my mother?" Her voice faltered.

"It could be. But maybe it's all a coincidence."

"Do you think my father had this obituary forged when I was five years old to make her think I was dead?"

"It looks that way. Perhaps you can investigate—"

"That dirty bastard," she said. "He paid everyone off to get what he wanted. To think, he also gave me an obituary about my mother's death. He'd always told me she died when I was five and said he'd saved her obituary to show me when I was old enough to understand. It must have been forged too. Why, Father Abelardo? Why?" She looked perplexed, yet her eyes filled up with tears.

"He must have hated your mother a lot to keep her away from you that way. But he's a man full of hatred. You know that."

The three men looked uncomfortable as Ana and the priest continued their conversation, but Eduardo wore an expression that indicated the whole discovery was a fruitful one. He and Floyd glanced at each other from time to time as Ana's emotions swung from total disbelief to anger at her father back to disbelief. She choked up several times as she spoke with the priest.

"By any chance was your father Raimundo Beltrán?" Floyd asked.

Ana stared at Floyd, and her mouth fell open. The priest cleared his throat.

"How do you know that?" the priest asked.

"I interviewed Juana's close friend the day after Juana died," Floyd said. "Part of our work, what we're doing here, is linked to Juana's death. Before she died, Juana gave us very useful information on a kidnapping. Eduardo took those photographs at Juana's house. That's why he has them. Is there anything you should tell us?"

"My parents separated when I was very young. My father had custody of me. He said my mother died of an overdose when I was five. I was sent to boarding schools in the U.S. and Canada. And I also attended college in the U.S."

"You know your father is a capo?" Floyd asked.

"Yes," she said, clenching her teeth. "He came from extreme poverty but became rich in the cartel. He sent me to the best schools, and when I graduated, I realized I could not be complacent like the kids of other capos. Kids, like me, who attended the best Catholic universities, like Notre Dame and Holy Cross or the Sacro Cuore in Milan. After their good Catholic educations, they, and I mean mostly the guys, return to Mexico to join the family trade, though they may be attorneys or business school graduates, and forget how that extraordinary wealth is obtained."

"But not you?" Floyd asked.

"That's right. That's why I've joined Father Abelardo's group. I'm trying to help Father rehabilitate children we recover from the drug and human trafficking rings. We find their families and return them home again. We have a small orphanage."

"So what are you two doing out here?" Floyd asked.

"We're trying to track a fellow, a trafficker in underage children," the priest said. "He takes them across the border for prostitution and pornography. We know of him, know he's kidnapped children in this area. We even know his name. Yet, he is so elusive, we've never located—"

"What's his name?" Eduardo asked, interrupting.

"Goyo," the priest replied.

"Sounds like our man too," Floyd said.

Eduardo reached out to get his mobile phone back from the priest. He scrolled through to find the photos of the two dead men.

"Do you know either one?" he asked, holding the phone up for Ana and the priest to examine the pictures closely.

They both shook their heads. Eduardo showed them several shots: close-ups of their faces, three-quarters, and full body. Ana kept staring at one of the photos and shaking her head.

"This one," she said as she placed her finger on the younger man's image. "This one does not look Mexican. He's a foreigner, maybe a European."

Floyd grabbed the phone to see if he could detect what Ana was talking about.

"If you mean that his skin color is light, well, there are Mexicans with light complexions."

"Look at his clothes. Those are expensive. Cut differently. And he's not wearing jeans." She took the phone from Floyd's hand and enlarged the image. "The shirt is tailored. Not your usual guy doing the dirty work of a coyote."

"What do you think?" Floyd asked as he turned toward Eduardo.

"I think she's right," Eduardo said, stepping in closer to have another look.

Ana enlarged the photo even more and, together with Eduardo, studied the details of the shirt.

"See how beautifully finished the shirt is," she said. "I'd say it's not even an American shirt, but Italian made, like my father always buys, though it's hard to tell from the photo. And look at the monogram. It's MAL."

"Let me see," Floyd said as he took the phone. "Does that mean anything to you?"

"No," she said. "The fine stitching shows it's not a coyote who is wearing it."

Jack, who had been listening without participating in the conversation, borrowed the phone to have a look and handed it back to Floyd.

"So where do we go from here?" Floyd asked, turning to the priest.

"We've been trying to track this coyote, Goyo, out here. One of our people spotted a large container truck traveling up the Pan-American

Highway. He saw it south of Ceballos. He immediately phoned one of our volunteers, who lives north of Ceballos. He waited for the trailer, but he never saw it. We think it must have taken a dirt road a few miles north of Ceballos. Our first guy returned to the town to get a couple of people to go with him in his pickup to try to catch up with the truck, but there was no sign of it. It simply disappeared."

"Did they look for tracks in the dirt?" Eduardo asked.

"Oh, yes. The problem is the wind out here. Tracks don't last long."

"It's not windy today," Eduardo said.

"Not right now, but earlier this morning, there was a bit," the priest said. "But we could not canvass the whole area just looking for tracks. Lots of ranchers and miners use the various roads in this area, as well as local folks at smaller towns in outlying areas. A difficult task to find them when we don't know what tracks we're looking for."

"Okay, let's get organized," Floyd said, addressing the priest. "Will you go up with me in the helicopter to see if we can detect any suspicious activity or roads the truck may have used or hideouts?"

"I'll stay here with Ana," Eduardo said. "I can give free consulting on operating orphanages while you fly the area."

Floyd waved Santiago over, who had been walking Fígaro on a leash around the cottonwood trees near the priest's truck. Floyd and the priest headed toward the chopper as the pilot passed Fígaro off to Eduardo. The dog wagged his tail in appreciation to be with Eduardo again.

"Let's get over by the trees," he said, giving Fígaro instructions to heel.

"What do you know about orphanages?" Ana asked, proceeding toward the cottonwoods.

"I've set up orphanages in Colombia. For street children. In your case, you'll need more psychological help for children who've been through the abuse of kidnappers and human traffickers. We can talk about it while my colleagues do their search and rescue mission."

"That'd be great since we are just getting started on the orphanage idea," she said. "Mostly, we rescue the kids, then counselors work with them to regain self-confidence and their identity. Church volunteers locate the families, so we don't have them for very long. But that has changed. We have three right now, but we have not located the families. And it's sad, but sometimes the families don't really want them back."

COYOTE ZONE

They reached the trees, and they both turned to watch the helicopter take off. Eduardo frowned and squinted to avoid having sand get in his eyes. Fígaro crouched on the ground behind Eduardo's legs.

I'm more than happy to focus on orphanages and not go nuts over worry about Nikki, Eduardo thought. *Though I won't stop worrying until we find her.*

CHAPTER 26

Zone of Silence—Saturday, early afternoon, day four after abduction

Ana opened the passenger door to the pickup truck and took two bottles of water from a small cooler. She handed one to Eduardo. They could hear the helicopter in the distance as they continued talking. For thirty minutes, they had an animated conversation until the chopper approached and hovered in the air over the same spot where it had landed before. The noise obviously frightened Fígaro. The pup jumped up, placing his front paws on Eduardo's legs, and he kept pawing, as if begging to be picked up.

Eduardo returned his water bottle to Ana, picked the pup up, and tucked Fígaro's head into his right armpit to prevent the whirlwind of dust from getting into the dog's eyes. Eduardo and Ana watched as Santiago brought the chopper in for a slick landing, though the air turbulence from the rotating blades caused the same effect as in the first landing. As it raised blinding dust on the arid ground, Eduardo closed his eyes and silently prayed Floyd had discovered a clue, anything, that would prove they were on track to find Nikki.

Floyd jumped out of the helicopter as soon as the blades were no longer kicking up dust and called Eduardo to join him. Eduardo put Fígaro on the ground, handed the leash to Ana, and took one of the bottles of water from her.

"Did you find anything?" Eduardo asked as he approached Floyd. His throat was dry from nerves and dust, so he opened the water and took a slug.

"I'm going to call Paolo. During the flight, I realized the monogram may—"

"Did you locate the truck or anything giving us a clue where the kidnappers—?" Eduardo asked, so anxious to obtain answers he could hardly contain his emotions.

"No, but that monogram may be a clue. Think about it: MAL."

"Doesn't mean a thing to me," Eduardo said, drawing his response out as he thought about it.

"L for Lombardi. Didn't Paolo say he had a cousin named Matteo?"

"Are you thinking Sofía's accusation that Paolo kidnapped his own daughter is correct?" Eduardo asked.

"I don't know. It's worth some thought. Did he hire kidnappers who've now gone rogue on him?"

"Rogue? To get more money?" Eduardo asked, thinking out loud.

"That's usually the motivating factor."

"So you think Paolo orchestrated the whole scheme, and now it's backfired, so he sent his cousin to find Bibi, and the cousin got killed."

"Something like that. Plus, Paolo presents himself at Sofía's to get information from us once the kidnappers go rogue."

"That's a lot of assumptions based on a monogram," Eduardo said. He rubbed his chin as he thought about the possibility of Paolo being the culprit. "Besides, are you sure the monogram initials would be sequential and not with the L for the surname positioned in the middle?"

"At times the initials are sequential. Plus, the more I think about the guy's tailored clothes and European appearance, the more the whole puzzle starts coming together."

"Why don't you call Paolo and find out his cousin's full name?" Eduardo said.

"Good idea," Floyd said. "That's exactly what I'm going to do." He pulled his phone from his pants pocket and dialed.

Eduardo turned to face the chopper. The pilot was talking to the priest and Ana, who was still holding Fígaro's leash. Jack, whose Spanish was not totally fluent, had not joined the group but instead was kneeling on the ground, playing with the drone, preparing it for flight.

"Hello, Paolo. This is Floyd. How are things going there?" he spoke into the phone.

After Floyd listened to Paolo for a few seconds, he asked Paolo about his cousin Matteo's full name.

"Matteo Alfaro Lombardi," Floyd repeated out loud for Eduardo to hear him. "Okay, now I need to ask you a question. Does he wear fine, Italian-tailored monogram shirts?"

Again, after listening to Paolo for several seconds, Floyd resumed his questioning.

"Do you know where Matteo is at this point? Can you call him?"

Eduardo continued listening to Floyd's phone conversation as he watched Jack control the drone's aerial maneuvers. He had it flying up and then down at incredible velocities. He tested it by flying it up again to a certain altitude before proceeding with a slower forward-rolling motion. The final test seemed to be to circle the drone slowly, to scan the entire panorama.

I sure don't want to be hit by it, Eduardo thought as he took note of the incredible speed of the device.

"Call me back as soon as you've reached him. It's important," Floyd spoke into his phone. "And I think you told me he's very close to your mother. So if you cannot get ahold of him, call your mother to find out his whereabouts."

Instead of returning to the group, Floyd continued using his phone, making a second call.

"Hello, Timothy. Any news?"

Floyd observed the drone's cartwheels and gyrations as he listened to Timothy.

"Let me brief you on what's going on here," Floyd said. "I've asked Paolo to locate his cousin Matteo from Italy. My suspicion is, he won't locate him. When Paolo calls back, if he's unable to locate Matteo, I'll send Paolo a picture that could be his cousin. It's one of the dead bodies Eduardo discovered at the cave site this morning. Let me know ASAP if Paolo does anything unusual."

Floyd listened to Timothy's response.

"If Matteo is involved in the kidnapping," Floyd said, speaking into his phone again, "I'd have to believe Paolo is behind it. And that begs the question whether things have gone totally wrong in the kidnapping, and that's why Paolo is in San Miguel, trying to locate his hired kidnapper while pretending to be the concerned father."

As soon as Floyd finished his conversation, Eduardo pointed to the drone. Jack was manipulating it into short but lightning-speed aerobatic contortions. Both men stood amazed at the results of Jack's dexterity on the controls.

"Do you believe Paolo hired a kidnapper who now has decided to hold out for better money?" Eduardo asked.

"Maybe, maybe not. We have to consider it, though," Floyd said. "But looks can be deceiving. We have to analyze all the evidence and see what scenarios seem viable."

Floyd started walking toward Jack. Eduardo stepped in line and walked with him.

When Jack saw them approaching, he pulled the drone in and landed it with a softer touchdown than Santiago had performed with the chopper.

"I'm ready to scan the area with my miniature, unmanned, aerial vehicle," Jack said as Floyd and Eduardo walked up where he was kneeling. "But first, we have to baptize it."

"You mean, like give it a name?" Floyd asked, looking at his watch.

"That's exactly what I mean," Jack said as the other individuals, including the pilot, got closer to the group already around the drone. "Father, will you lead us in a baptismal ceremony?" Jack asked. "Can everyone suggest names?"

"Eye in the Sky," Floyd offered.

"Ordained Predator," Ana said.

The priest suggested Silent Spy.

"I like Detective Predator," Eduardo said.

"How about just plain Predator?" Santiago asked.

"If everyone is okay with Predator, that's my vote," Jack said. "Now, Father, I'll hold the drone in a pattern while you sprinkle him with a little of the water from the bottle Ana is holding."

Jack used the remote control to raise the drone about waist high and placed it into a hovering pattern as the priest drizzled a few drops on it, recited a short blessing, and finished by making the sign of the cross in the air over the small craft.

Floyd's phone rang. He moved away from the group to answer. "You can't locate your cousin? Have you asked your mother?"

Eduardo, standing near the priest and Ana, explained to them about Goyo using the phases of the moon to his advantage for crossing people at the border, but he kept one ear listening to Floyd.

"We found the body of a man, late-thirties or early-forties," Floyd said. "He was wearing an expensive shirt with the monogram I mentioned. I can forward a photo so you can confirm whether or not it is Matteo. Let me warn you, it's very graphic. And I trust you won't show it to Sofía. She's too upset to handle this. Call me back when you see the picture."

Floyd accessed his picture files and pulled up the foreigner's photos that Eduardo had forwarded to him that morning. All of them were ghastly, but he picked the three-quarter shot to text to Paolo and sent it.

In less than a minute, Floyd's phone rang again. He walked away to answer.

It was Timothy.

"Paolo's speaking in Italian? Outside?" Floyd asked, repeating what he'd heard Timothy tell him. "And he sounds angry, you say? He's probably talking to his cousin. Maybe the guy's not dead after all."

Floyd's usually calm demeanor looked concerned as he listened for a few more seconds before reminding Timothy to ask Paolo to call him to report back on the picture.

"I hate to do it right now, but if you think I need to fly to San Miguel, let me know. And don't let Paolo out of your sight," he said right before he pressed the button to end the call.

Floyd walked back to rejoin the group standing around the drone.

"Is that unarmed vehicle of yours ready to find our people?" Floyd asked.

"The Predator is ready to go," Jack said, "where no drone has gone before."

"Launch," Floyd said, "though I think your Star Trek lingo is lost on this group."

"May the Force be with you," Ana said, glancing at Floyd as the drone flew off. "I pray it finds Nikki and the children."

"Amen," Eduardo said as he watched Predator disappear. "All I care about at this point is finding them."

Jack monitored Predator's expedition on the Toughbook. Ten minutes ago when he prepared to launch the drone, he had placed the mobile command center on the hood of the priest's pickup. The entire group stood around the monitor, watching the live feed, when suddenly the monitor went blurry and then blank.

"What the hell . . . ?" Jack said.

"Is something wrong?" Floyd asked, leaning in closer to the monitor.

"Hell, yes. Looks like we've lost Predator," Jack said with a groan.

He played back the last thirty seconds of the video he'd been recording. Then he played it back again and slowed it down to analyze it. He stopped it in a frame showing what appeared to be Predator breaking apart. The next frame contained five pieces of scattered debris in the air.

"Predator has exploded," he announced, looking dejected.

"This area, I told you," the pilot said, "not good for radio signals, and not conducive for electronics of any kind."

"That has nothing to do with Predator going down," Jack said, his voice brusque and annoyed.

"Was it shot down?" Eduardo asked.

"That's a possibility," Floyd said. "Can you figure the coordinates where it went down? We can then check that location to see what we find."

"Yes," Jack said. "I'm working on that. Give me a minute."

Jack operated several windows on the monitor for a couple of minutes. Floyd fidgeted with his cell phone as he waited. Eduardo took Fígaro's leash back from Ana and knelt down to pat the Pomski, who rolled over to have his stomach scratched.

"Okay, here it is. The area we're in is called the Mapimí Silent Zone. Predator went down at 26.6909 degrees north 103.7456 degrees west."

"Let's fly over to that location," Floyd said.

Eduardo glanced up at Floyd as he continued to scratch Fígaro's belly.

"If Predator was shot down," Eduardo said. "I don't think that's a good idea. They could shoot the helicopter down. At the very least, we will give away our position. Instead, we should go in as close as possible by truck and then on foot." Eduardo turned to the priest and, with a sheepish grin, said, "If Father Abelardo will loan us his truck. Or I can walk there, and Jack can communicate with me using my phone."

"On foot in terrain with no foliage where we can't hide?" Floyd asked. "I don't think so."

"I did this when I tracked the FARC in Colombia," Eduardo said.

"You had a jungle environment where you could hide," Floyd said. "Plus, that was a long time ago."

"In a jungle, the bad guys can hide too. In a desert, we are all more visible. If you want, we can wait until dusk," Eduardo said.

"Let me round up some people first," Father Abelardo said. "We can provide a bit of backup."

"How long will that take you?" Eduardo asked.

"An hour or so."

Floyd's mobile phone interrupted the priest.

"Yes, Paolo. Did you locate your cousin?"

After listening for a few seconds, Floyd repeated part of Paolo's conversation so Eduardo could hear him.

"So that is Matteo's body in the photo. I'm sorry for your loss. That leaves a lot of questions, though, in need of answers."

Floyd shook his head as he listened again.

"Why was he in Mexico?" Floyd continued shaking his head and then spoke again. "You mean to tell me you didn't know he was here? Come on, Paolo, he's your cousin."

Eduardo stopped scratching Fígaro and stood up. He started pacing, first walking toward the helicopter, instructing Fígaro to heel, then abruptly turning back and returning to the group at the truck under the cottonwoods. He looked impatient, as if he wanted to grab the phone out of Floyd's hands and extract an immediate answer from Paolo. Eduardo's jaw was set tight, so tight he was grinding his teeth as he listened to Floyd's conversation.

"Was he tracking the kidnappers, or was he part of their team?" Floyd asked.

Floyd listened for a few brief moments, changing his phone from one ear to the other.

"If you don't know the answers, have you spoken to your mother about Matteo's actions?"

Floyd stopped asking questions and listened to Paolo for about three minutes, time that appeared to be driving Eduardo crazy. He wanted to move on with Nikki's rescue operation.

"Listen, Paolo, I'll go to San Miguel as soon as I can, but it's not going to happen today. I need to ask you if there is anything you know that you're not telling me about your daughter's kidnapping."

After turning off his phone, Floyd turned to face Jack, shaking his head.

"Paolo confirmed it is his cousin," Floyd said. "You can remove Matteo Lombardi's photo from the facial recognition software."

"I'm going to let it continue to run," Jack said, "in case he had a criminal record or other data that could help us understand the whole situation with Bibi's kidnapping."

"Good idea," Floyd said. "Now, let's focus on finding the reason for Predator blowing up. What are the odds that baby blew up on its own?"

"Like it overheated and exploded?" Jack asked. "None. There's not much reason for that to happen. It's not a hot-air balloon."

Father Abelardo changed the subject. "Ana and I will leave, round up a few men to help, and we'll be back."

They exchanged phone numbers with Eduardo and Floyd so they could be in contact.

As the old truck chugged away, raising a long trail of dust, Floyd asked Eduardo to walk with him.

"Can we trust the priest and that girl?" Floyd asked

"Why are you asking?"

"I've been thinking that it's such an incredible coincidence that the girl could be Juana's daughter, and that she's abandoned her father and all his money to help a priest rescue kids from human traffickers. It just seems so improbable. Maybe I'm too skeptical. And it worries me a little that we gave them too much information."

"You've heard the expression 'truth is stranger than fiction,'" Eduardo said. "Well, I think this is one of those situations. Ana seems way too genuine to be pretending to save children. Plus, she has solid plans for building an orphanage. While you were up in the helicopter, she shared information on how they've relocated stolen children through the church's organization. Sounded pretty real to me."

"I hope you're correct. We'll know when and if they return to help us."

⌒

Jack sat inside the parked helicopter, analyzing the breakup of the Predator—frame by frame, over and over again. Eduardo sat in the seat next to him, observing the data and periodically looking at his watch. As if to break the monotony, he glanced toward the large cottonwood and saw Floyd and the pilot sitting under the tree. Santiago was hand-feeding Fígaro. Shortly after the canine finished gulping his food, the pilot started stroking the pup's head. Fígaro lay down, rolled over, and enjoyed all the attention Santiago gave him.

"Why don't you back up the frames to what Predator sent before it exploded," Eduardo said, turning his attention to Jack.

"There's nothing there. I've gone over it thoroughly."

"Can you start the video up and let me see it anyway?" Eduardo asked.

Jack complied with the request. They watched the entire six and a half minutes of video.

"Let me look at it again," Eduardo said.

Jack returned the cursor to the beginning. It started where Predator took to the air. It picked up a partial view of the helicopter from the rear of the cabin, showing a blade of the main rotor, the tail boom, and all the way to the tail rotor. As the drone gained altitude, the mountain range was visible in the foreground, and as soon as Predator leveled off, its camera captured the ground below, as well as the terrain ahead of where it was flying.

"Stop there," Eduardo said, "and now enlarge that frame so I can see the ground."

Eduardo examined the picture on the Toughbook screen carefully, noticed nothing unusual, and asked Jack to do the same with the next frame, and the next, and the next.

"Keep it there, home in on the ground in the upper left-hand corner, and sharpen the image."

As soon as the image came into focus, Eduardo pulled the phone out of his pocket and searched for the photos he'd taken that morning when he'd traveled the road to the cave. He compared his photographs of truck tracks imprinted in the dirt road to the picture on the Toughbook's screen.

"Tire tracks. We've got a match," Eduardo said. He leaned out the chopper door, placed his right foot on the metal skid as he held on to the side of the cabin, and yelled, "Hey, Floyd, come over here and see this."

Santiago stayed under the cottonwood with Fígaro while the other three men sat in the chopper discussing Eduardo's findings.

"I'll go over and have a look to see where the tracks lead," Eduardo said, glancing down at his watch. "The priest has not returned with reinforcements. I'm not willing to waste any more time in finding Nikki."

"It's not just Nikki, but also the Lombardi child," Floyd said.

"In reality, when I say Nikki, it includes all the stolen children," Eduardo said as he put the phone into his pocket.

"The kidnapper is not alone," Floyd said. "We don't know how many people are with him, but we can assume he's well-armed and will put up a hell of a fight. And that's the reason for waiting on the priest. Or I'll call Fernando, and we can turn the case over to the Federales."

"Look, Floyd, no sense jumping the gun. I don't want the Federales ruining this operation. Let me walk over and have a look. It's not that far. I'll call if I find something or if I need help. After I scout the area, we can decide what to do."

"Okay, go ahead. But carry your phone where I can follow what's going on. And use your compass. The bullet-proof vests are on the floor of the chopper, behind the last seats."

Eduardo eased himself to the rear of the chopper and grabbed a vest resting on top of his cooler. He flipped it on and secured it. He opened the cooler, grabbed a bottle of water and one of Sofía's sandwiches and also took Fígaro's muzzle before jumping out of the chopper and heading toward the cottonwoods.

"You're not taking that dog with you!" Floyd yelled when he realized Eduardo planned on taking Fígaro.

"I'm not going without him!" Eduardo yelled back.

He took the leash from Santiago and picked the pup up in his arms.

Santiago joined the two men outside the helicopter and watched in silence as Eduardo walked away into the scrubby desert terrain.

CHAPTER 27

Mexico City—Saturday, early afternoon, day four after abduction

The ultra-modern, Roman-style bamboo blinds on the floor-to-ceiling windows in Héctor Sánchez's office rested at three-quarters mast to limit the strong afternoon sun from blinding his important guest. The sunlight still filtering into the room did nothing to alleviate the negative sentiment emanating from the occupants.

María, Héctor's assistant, carried a tray bearing two highly decorated porcelain demitasse cups on saucers to her boss's office. Hot espresso filled the cups within a centimeter of the gold-plated rims. Placing the tray on a side table, she proceeded to serve one cup at a time on the round office table, the guest of honor receiving the first one. Like an experienced barista, she laid a gold-plated demitasse spoon and a dainty, white napkin by each cup. María's solemn placement of a sugar bowl, in matching porcelain with miniature golden tongs, gave the coffee service a Japanese tea ceremony feel.

María tiptoed away in reverential silence and closed the door, but not before hearing Mr. Sánchez enlighten his guest that the espresso came from a Lombardi machine—Italy's best.

"Rinunciare al stronzate."

Héctor shuddered at the expression. *Forgo the bullshit*, he repeated mentally. He knew matters had gone woefully wrong in his work to locate the kidnappers. And now his strong-minded customer sat across from him, about to sip coffee so properly presented.

"Si chiama questo caffè espresso?" Her grimace showed repulsion as she tasted the Arabica infusion. She wiped the corners of her lips with the napkin in an affected manner. As she laid the napkin on the table, she pushed the cup and saucer away from her.

"Would you prefer a cappuccino?" Héctor asked with a solicitous air.

"Cappuccino is for breakfast only," she said in a blistering whisper as she checked her watch. "If your agency is incapable of preparing a decent espresso, how stupid was I to entrust Bibiana's well-being in your hands?"

"Signora Lombardi, I can explain—" Héctor said, words stumbling over his tongue, which felt so thick and dry he could hardly speak.

"Maybe then you can explain the death of my nephew, Matteo? He was like a son to me. Until yesterday, I did not even know he was in Mexico, let alone—"

"Matteo? Your nephew? Dead? I don't understand."

"Paolo called me earlier today from that provincial town where Sofía has her ristorante. I dare warn you, do not inform him I'm in Mexico," she admonished as her eyes bore straight through Héctor and her lips pursed up in disdain. "He thinks I'm in Milan."

"Paolo, here? I expected him tomorrow," Héctor said, stuttering.

"Regardless, Paolo called me with the terrible news of Matteo's death. Shot like a common criminal and shoved into a mass grave with gangsters."

"I'm so sorry."

"Your incompetency knows no bounds," she said. "I can't believe Matteo would do this to me. Though sad circumstances, I'm glad I'm here now. Maybe I can avoid any further damage to my family or the Lombardi name. Surely you know the Lombardi lineage goes back to medieval Europe. As for Matteo's remains, you must get them and ship them to me in Italy before the press gets hold of it and makes a scandal."

"I'll contact the authorities to issue required documents—"

"I've hired you to skip the authorities. After all, this is Mexico, isn't it? A little money accomplishes a lot."

"Signora Lombardi, you're informing me of an international incident. To avoid the authorities from intervening is unlawful," Héctor said, regaining his composure.

"The authorities did not intervene to keep my boy alive. It's for you to bribe corrupt officials, subvert the system, whatever you need to do, but I want Matteo's remains in Milan without making the news, without opening an investigation."

Beads of sweat broke out on Héctor's forehead, and he wiped it with the cloth napkin he had not yet used. He pushed his own espresso, untouched, to the middle of the table, adjusted the knot on his tie, cleared his throat, and then spoke in a controlled manner.

"When did Paolo arrive in Mexico?"

"Two days ago. He came to do what you can't do, get Bibiana back from the kidnappers. Thanks to you, my granddaughter is in the hands of God knows who. And now you're telling me you have to work through the authorities to return Matteo's remains to me? Matteo," she said as her voice broke, showing grief for the first time, "was like my very own son. I repeat, his remains will not be in any investigation. Capisci?"

"I'll see what I can do," Héctor said.

"One more request," she said. "I understand you have an employee by the name of Arturo Béjar."

"Arturo Béjar?" Héctor asked with dismay.

"Don't deny him. I know he works for you. He and Matteo met, and I want to see him here in your office. Tomorrow."

Chiara Lombardi stood.

"My chauffeur will drive you to your hotel," Héctor said, his voice faltering.

She looked at him straight in the eyes and laughed as her eyes turned ice cold.

"My hotel car and driver will take me. I don't want another international incident."

"As you wish, Signora. I'll see you to the door."

Héctor Sánchez returned to his desk as soon as he was sure she was out of the building, picked up the receiver, and dialed.

"Ciao, Paolo, this is Héctor Sánchez. I'm checking in to coordinate my driver to pick you up at the airport tomorrow."

More than protecting Paolo's mother, Sánchez wanted to see what excuse Paolo might give for avoiding his attorney after arriving in Mexico three days ahead of schedule without notice.

COYOTE ZONE

To Héctor's consternation, Paolo did not apologize. They spoke about the kidnapping. Héctor informed Paolo that his people continued to work on it, but they had not yet located the kidnappers.

"But I have my best assets on the job," he said in as positive a tone as he could muster. "I should have good news shortly."

After they hung up, Héctor picked up the control for the Roman blinds, opened them to a wider position, and walked to the wall of windows. Looking across the boulevard at the Mexican flag flying over the entrance to the huge Santa Fe shopping mall in his line of sight, his mind did not register the cityscape. Instead, Héctor scratched his chin as he analyzed why Paolo did not even mention Matteo, or Matteo's death, or why he did not inform his own attorney that he had already arrived in Mexico. Besides, Paolo sounded so formal and businesslike. Why wasn't he more expressive?

Paolo is Italian, after all. Italians are emotional, like all other Latins, he thought.

Héctor turned his thoughts to Arturo. He contemplated his options before calling his hired gun.

How did Arturo and Matteo meet? he wondered.

CHAPTER 28

*Mapimí Zone of Silence—Saturday, early afternoon,
day four after abduction*

Floyd, standing by the helicopter, followed Eduardo's actions from the screen of his phone. He watched as Eduardo put Fígaro on the ground and cleaned the sweat on his forehead with the back of his hand while he checked the app on his phone to verify his location. Floyd shook his head. Eduardo had been gone for over an hour, and Floyd had followed every sweaty step Eduardo took through the live feed transmitted from Eduardo's phone.

"What the hell is Eduardo doing?" he asked out loud.

Next, he saw Eduardo start to walk again, using the leash to keep the canine in step with him. As best as Floyd could discern from the patches of sky and terrain transmitted over the phone, the man and the dog found themselves engulfed in a deep gully formed by a natural break in the mountain range. Floyd also caught glimpses of cactuses growing in the chalky and sometimes sandy soil, and isolated slices of vegetation whipped past like passengers on a bullet train. The tedious task of watching Eduardo's live feed made Floyd dizzy, depending on the angle Eduardo positioned the phone as he walked.

Suddenly, Fígaro dropped his nose to the ground and rushed ahead of Eduardo, pulling on the leash with all the might the Pomsky could muster. As Eduardo slowed the pace of his walk, the dog continued smelling the ground. Floyd could tell he purposely held the phone to transmit Fígaro's actions.

COYOTE ZONE

Now Floyd saw Eduardo's face, as if he were pointing the camera at himself to take a selfie. A few seconds later, he received a text from Eduardo.

> Found tracks. Fígaro has picked up a scent.
> Send reinforcements so we can storm the place.

Floyd texted back.

> Jack and I are only reinforcements. Give me
> a call so we can plan our strategy.

Floyd pieced together enough information on his screen to detect Eduardo picking Fígaro up in his arms and walking, perhaps retracing his steps, to the opening of the canyon to find a secure spot to hide before making that phone call.

Floyd answered on the first ring.

Eduardo told him he was certain he was close to the coyote's den. He described how the tire tracks ran deep into the gorge and looked like they only traveled one way, making Eduardo assume the trailer was hidden at the end of the gorge.

"Then we must decide how to surprise them," Floyd said.

Both men agreed they would need to disarm the coyotes, but not knowing how many were involved, it might be difficult to overtake them.

"Santiago needs to stay at the helicopter so we can move Nikki and the girl as efficiently as possible, so that leaves you, Jack, and me. The priest has not returned, and that might be good, though it'd be nice to have his truck to move us in closer. I'll have Santiago drop us off, far enough from the gorge to avoid being spotted or heard. One last question. You are sure they are still hiding there?"

Satisfied with Eduardo's affirmative response, Floyd looked at his watch and spoke into his phone.

"Okay, man, we'll take off in five minutes."

Eduardo studied the canyon as he nervously entered it for the second time. He'd met the helicopter after it landed and handed Fígaro to the pilot, who would stay with the chopper. Floyd and Jack had descended to join Eduardo on the ground.

219

The men walked silently, guns drawn, like agents in an espionage movie stalking a criminal. Following their pre-agreed plan, the men parted. Floyd was on one side of the bright, sunlit ravine, while Jack covered the opposite side. Eduardo began walking down the center of the dry riverbed. The wind felt cool as it blew against him, evaporating the perspiration he had worked up only minutes before on top of the ravine.

As they penetrated deeper into the canyon, it suddenly came to an abrupt end, with walls facing them on three sides. Coming together, they stood and looked at each other with expressions of surprise and shock.

Before he spoke, Floyd studied the enclosing black rock walls for possible escape routes the truck may have taken.

"Shit. They're gone."

"It's like the trailer evaporated," Eduardo said. "How did they get that eighteen-wheeler out? There's no way to escape from here."

"They simply drove away," Floyd said.

"Impossible," Eduardo said. "There's only one set of tracks."

Floyd glanced at the ground, searching for the imprint of tires. "There ain't nothing here." He took a few paces and still found nothing.

"Will you cover me?" Eduardo asked in a whisper. "I'll go back and find where the tracks can be detected. We also need to keep our voices quiet. They're hiding here somewhere."

He studied the canyon before retracing his steps, but instead of watching for the coyote and his people, Eduardo now observed the ground, as if inspecting it for a lost object. He zigzagged along the floor of the ravine, his eyes covering each square inch, making note of every stone and every blade of grass. With sudden swiftness, he fell to his knees with such force that both Floyd and Jack leapt into position—ready to shoot the culprit for bringing Eduardo down—until both men saw Eduardo had identified an item of interest and was inspecting it up close in the sandy dirt. Both Floyd and Jack realized they were jittery and needed to steady their nerves.

Eduardo had found what he wanted—traces of tire treads.

He took several more steps and found plenty of tracks, as if the truck had turned around, but instead of leaving by the ravine, deep tire ruts approached the mountain. His eyes followed the path of ruts straight into the base of the mountain, as if it had parted to let the truck pass through. With haste, he returned to Floyd and Jack.

"I didn't see a cave," Eduardo said, whispering and out of breath from nervous expectation, "but that's the only thing that makes sense. They've covered the entrance. Like Moses parting the seas, those sons of bitches parted the mountainside. I saw where they've moved rocks to conceal their hideout. We need to go in. I'll go first, and you two follow me to provide protection."

Single file, they proceeded to the area Eduardo had discovered. He motioned with his hand for them to wait. With great care, he eased himself closer to several large rocks and then waved for Floyd and Jack to follow. As soon as they approached, he slipped between the boulders and the two men stuck right behind him, like wolves in a pack. They saw what appeared to be lean-to contraptions set against the side of the mountain. He used his hand to find out what they were and soon discovered sturdy wooden frames where plywood had been nailed to beams. Dirt and small rocks had been glued on the plywood to conceal the mouth of a cave. The massive contraptions were crudely built, yet when seen from a distance and covered by the afternoon shadow cast by the high bluff off the opposite wall of the ravine, the artificial cover blended right into the mountainside.

Jack searched for the space where the overlay came against the escarpment. Floyd and Eduardo came to help grip the edge of it, hoping to maneuver it to create enough leeway that they could squeeze into the hiding place. While Eduardo grimaced from the effort, Floyd winced and Jack stopped to rub a cramp in his leg. Floyd found the edge on the sheet of plywood only to discover it had been patched with Masonite. He pushed the panel, which fell without resistance, opening a window for him to peer inside.

Only darkness prevailed inside the cave.

Floyd pulled his pocketknife out and went to work on removing nails from the plywood. After pulling several nails out, Eduardo and Floyd managed to dismantle a section of plywood from the frame, leaving sufficient space for all three of them to crawl through to the inside. They held their breath as they waited for their eyes to adjust.

Lights flashed on, flickered two or three times, and then remained on, creating a nebulous atmosphere in the dim light.

"We've been waiting for you," a male voice said in Spanish.

All three men sought the location of the sound emanating from farther back in the cave.

"So who are you, you who've been waiting for us?" Floyd asked in Spanish as he struggled to focus in the shadowy light.

All three men saw her about the same time.

A child with a tousle of curly golden hair.

A child with a tousle of curly golden hair with a gun pointed at her head.

Holding the gun, a man stood to her side, the side farthest from the rescue team. Using the child as a shield, he kept the gun to her head.

"Right now, I'm in the business of raising ransom," the coyote responded.

The three men followed the voice again and saw the speaker. He held a location farther back in the cave, to the right side, creating a triangular space between where Floyd and his team stood and the spot to their left where the first man stood, the one who held the child at gunpoint.

Floyd detected a third kidnapper holding an automatic weapon. His positioning in the murky shadows on a mound of dirt gave him a better vantage point of the whole scene than the place the coyote occupied or the one maintained by the gunman with the child hostage. Floyd also detected what he took for an older woman, sitting on the cave floor several paces behind the coyote, sitting so still she hardly seemed real.

That can't be Nikki, he thought. *They would not leave her out as they negotiate.*

"You're in the business of raising ransom, so what merchandise do you have to offer?" Floyd asked.

"The prize several buyers want."

"Several buyers? Really? How many?" Floyd asked.

"Many. So if you want her, you must make the best offer."

"An offer?" Floyd asked. "If you tell me your price, maybe we can start negotiating."

"The last bastard offered me one million in U.S. currency. And, well, you can see, it was no deal."

"The last customer offered that much? Well, I need to inspect the merchandise first," Floyd said. "I can't imagine that much for a little girl. Let me walk up close to her and talk with her."

"Stay right where you are if you want to avoid what happened to the last customer, as you call him." The man laughed. "*Customers*, you mean those sons of bitches? Sí, esos hijos de puta. You have a sense of humor for a pinche gringo. You can see from where you're standing, the girl's in good condition."

"So what is your price and where do you want the money?"

"First, I want you to drop your guns on the ground. Chuck them a few feet away from you, to your left. One at a time. My assistant over there with the cuerno de chivo will take care of anyone trying anything stupid."

Floyd turned to his men and instructed them to do as they were told. Each one, including Floyd, took his turn and tossed his pistol on the dirt floor of the cave.

"How much do you want?" Floyd asked.

"Three million."

"If you expect me to have that kind of money, you're way wrong," Floyd said.

"The one I killed said the girl's father is willing to pay more than two million. He was a damn bajador. So I shot him and decided to wait for the girl's father to arrive."

"Where is that bajador now?" Floyd asked.

"Don't get cute on me, gringo pendejo. Unless you want to end up sharing a grave with him."

"So let's assume I can get some money, not three million, but maybe one point two million. I'll give it to you here, and I'll take the girl."

"Three million or no deal," the man said.

"One point two million. That's the most money you've ever seen. If you don't want it, sell her in the U.S. For a little girl like this one, you'll be lucky to get ten thousand."

Eduardo winced.

"Two million," the kidnapper said.

"I told you, I don't have that kind of money. One point two million," Floyd repeated. "Then you can retire from this business before the Federales get you and throw you in jail."

"The girl's father will pay more, so I'll wait for him, and in the mean-time—"

"I'm working for the girl's father. Whoever told you he'd pay more didn't know what he was talking about. The father will pay one point two million. It'd be a good idea to make this negotiation before the father gives up and calls the Federales. He's getting impatient."

"That'd turn into a bloodbath," the coyote said. "The girl might get killed. And you too."

"Don't forgot yourself. You better believe it," Floyd said without flinching.

"Pinche gringo," the coyote said. "I'll take one million, five. You've got a mobile phone. Make arrangements to transfer the money to my Guatemalan bank. Get your banker on the speaker phone and request the transaction."

"Wait a minute," Floyd said. "This is late Saturday afternoon—"

"So," the man said as he stood as still as a sentry on official duty, "my bank in Guatemala will receive wire transfers twenty-four hours a day, every single day of the year. You're not going to use the excuse of the weekend to avoid making a transfer. Not if you want the girl."

"Fine. I'll make an online transfer directly from my phone," Floyd said, "but before I do, I'll need for you to write your bank account and nine digit routing number on a piece of paper. After you hand that to me on a piece of paper, your people will need to put their guns down. We will dig a hole at the back of the cave and put all the weapons in there. Next, we will check each other to make certain we're not holding anything back. Only then, I'll make the transfer. You verify with your bank from your phone, and I take the girl."

"Oye, old woman, bring me a piece of paper and a pen," the coyote yelled.

The old woman stood up slowly and limped to the rear of the cavern. She disappeared, and in the interminable span of two minutes returned, trudging toward the coyote. She handed him the pen and a piece of folded paper.

Watching her intently, Floyd changed his opinion. It had to be Nikki. How had she managed to work herself in with them so closely?

The coyote started scribbling his account number.

The old woman turned to leave, and as she got slightly behind the coyote, she aimed her lipstick case at Goyo and pushed the button. She zapped him as hard as she could and with her free hand grabbed his gun, aimed for Bernardo's head, and pulled the trigger.

Reacting instantaneously to Nikki's attack, Floyd reached around to his waist line at his back, pulled the second gun he was carrying, aimed, and hit the assistant in the chest. The guy pulled the trigger on the automatic weapon just as the bullet pierced him. The burst of gunfire hit the roof, not hurting anyone. Split seconds later, he collapsed to the cave floor, his weapon falling away from him, the butt tumbling to the ground and rolling down the mound out of reach. Though injured, he attempted to crawl toward it. Floyd shot him again, in the leg.

Eduardo plunged to the ground, rolled over a couple of times, and grabbed the pistol he had thrown away a few minutes earlier. He visually checked on the assistant and saw both Floyd and Jack handling the fallen teenager. Eduardo rushed to help Nikki. She pointed Goyo's own gun at him to make sure he did not get up. The coyote, in a fetal position on the hard earth, lay both confused and in pain from the electric shock Nikki had given him. He twitched like he might get up, and she gave him one more blast from her lipstick case. As soon as Eduardo arrived at her side, she pulled out a short rope from one of the big pockets of her skirt and handed it to him.

"Man, you learned from Juana what to carry," he said as he took it from her.

"I got it when the coyote ordered me to bring the writing materials," she said. "I figured it might be useful."

Eduardo turned over the coyote, who was groaning. Using the rope, he secured the man's hands and arms behind his back. Taking the man's belt off, Eduardo used it to strap Goyo's feet together.

Eduardo stood, picked Nikki up in his arms, and she kissed him. As he put her on the ground, she broke loose from the embrace and flew to Bibi. The child, suffering from shock, simply stood there like a stone statue.

"Everything is going to be okay," Nikki said softly. "I'll get you back to your mother very soon."

Jack, in an expert fashion, had moved to check Bernardo's body, removed the gun gripped in the dead man's hand, and tucked the gun in his own belt. Without losing time, he dragged the corpse away, leaving Bibi and Nikki standing in the same spot where Bibi had been all along.

Nikki continued reassuring Bibi in soothing tones, telling her she would soon be safely home. Finally, the child threw her arms around Nikki, and the two embraced as Bibi started sobbing.

Floyd had already taken his own belt off and used it to tie the assistant's hands very tightly. Next, he removed the young man's belt and tied the guy's feet. To maintain security, he picked up the automatic weapon, removed the magazine, charged the weapon to make sure there was no cartridge left, and leaned it against the rock wall of the cave. Floyd returned to tend the young man's chest wound. With his pocket knife, he ripped a strip of his shirt to pack into the wound to make it stop bleeding.

To calm Bibi, Nikki started speaking about the world tree the Maya had carved into rock many centuries before.

"Are you still wearing the world tree necklace I gave you?"

"Yes," Bibi said, wiping her tears away. She reached into her blouse and pulled the necklace out. "I want to show it to my mother. I want her to know it brings good luck. It takes the bad guys away. Maybe it will bring me a puppy."

"Maybe, if you wish hard enough for a puppy," Nikki's hand reached out to smooth Bibi's hair a little, more in a loving gesture than to comb her unruly tufts.

"I've always wanted a puppy. Mom won't let me have one. She says dogs don't belong in a restaurant." Her sad eyes glanced at Nikki and then down at her necklace. "Maybe my necklace will give me a miracle."

"Let me tell you, Bibi, the necklace is a good luck charm. I'm afraid it won't get you a miracle. But talking with your mother about your reasons for wanting a puppy just might make a miracle happen."

"Oh, I don't think so," the child said.

"I think your mother will listen, and I'll also work to convince her. But we have a little job to take care of before we go back to your mother's house."

"What's that?" Bibi asked with hesitation.

"There's a bunch of children hiding in the truck at the rear of the cave. Remember?"

"Yes," Bibi said.

"We need to rescue them. Do you want to help me?"

Bibi nodded.

Nikki took her by the hand, and they walked toward the back of the cave. As they passed Eduardo, Nikki stopped to inform him that she and Bibi would release the other children. She let go of Bibi's hand, knelt down by Goyo, and looked up at Eduardo to ask him for help in removing the key from Goyo's pocket.

"The key is to the compartment where the children are locked up," she said.

"Okay, get the children ready. I'll come get all of you when Floyd says we're ready to leave," Eduardo said.

As they walked toward the trailer, Bibi started crying again.

"That man gave me a puppy, but he's a bad man. He took my puppy away," Bibi said.

Nikki stopped to comfort the child and took her hand again.

"Don't worry," she said. "I promise I will make sure your mother gives you a puppy."

They continued walking, and Bibi settled down.

When they got to the back of the cave, Nikki opened the swinging door to the multi-temperature trailer. It was subdivided into three compartments. The trailer was empty except for the children crammed into the first compartment, the small one located immediately behind the cabin. The third cargo bay, the one where Nikki had opened the swinging door, was scrubbed and meticulously cleaned, and its refrigeration remained off since that would only be needed after the payloads of meat and vegetables filled the other two compartments before crossing the border—to disguise Goyo's prize merchandize. Even then, he would probably leave the first compartment without refrigeration, only turning on the air fans and hidden vents to bring air into the human cargo component.

Nikki peered inside, as if she were seeing the space for the first time. When she had been loaded into the trailer that morning, she'd been too absorbed with the children to notice the installation. Now she knelt on the ground, creating a forty-five degree angle with her leg so Bibi could use it as a step, and hoisted Bibi's slender body into the cargo bay. As soon as the child was securely up, Nikki placed her hands on the bed of the trailer to leverage herself up as she took a small jump to lift herself into the trailer. As she stood, she reached for Bibi's hand, noticing Bibi was trembling.

"We are going to be okay. I promise you will be with your mother again soon," Nikki said as she stroked Bibi's hair.

Hand in hand, Nikki took Bibi through the large compartment, passing through the length of it. She noticed it came equipped with a dual rail hanging system for transporting sides and quarters of beef. At the rear of this compartment, Nikki recognized a hydraulic gantry, used to load and unload heavy carcasses. The floor was covered with a heavy-duty aluminum scuff liner often used in refrigerated units carrying meat products. As they passed through the middle unit, she saw it had wooden pallets already secured by pallet stops laid out on the floor, indicating its readiness for fresh vegetables. They carefully stepped their way across the wooden sections before reaching the door of the compartment where the children were holed up. Nikki noticed for the first time a movable metal curtain, like a sliding door, hanging from a track bolted into the roof. She looked down and saw a similar track bolted into the floor.

When that is closed over the door into the human cargo compartment, it conceals the doorway to the secret human hideaway, she thought.

As Nikki slid the key into the lock of the internal trailer door, the door that separated the unit where she and Bibi now stood from the one they had all been sardined into earlier that morning, she shivered as she reflected on how they had reached the cave.

It had all started once the group had finished eating breakfast that morning. All the children had been ushered to the trailer. As soon as Nikki and Angela had cleaned up and packed the remaining food, they too had been taken into the smallest of the three compartments and locked in with the children. Though not as bad as the fetid odor from the outhouses in the cave, the compartment had reeked with the malodor of bodies that had not bathed in several days. Plus, the buckets for human waste had unfortunately already been used by at least one child before Nikki and Angela were locked in.

Once everything and everyone was loaded, the truck had driven for several hours after it left the hideout in Zacatecas, but without windows or other means to tell where they were being taken, Nikki had assumed they were being transported north toward the U.S. border. She had been surprised when she saw they had all been transferred, after a very long morning of driving, to another cave, one more sparsely equipped, though it also had a small electric generator, as well as a kitchen and outhouses. Upon their arrival, Nikki and Angela had reheated the prepared food they'd brought with them from the cave in Zacatecas. When the entire group had been served, all the children, save for Bibi, had been sequestered in the trailer again. Nikki and Angela had also been shoved in with the kids. She had shuddered when she'd heard the sound of the key in the door as Goyo locked it.

Goyo had tried to take Bibi with him, but the child had started screaming. At that point, he'd unlocked the compartment door and had demanded Nikki come out and make the child stop wailing. As Bibi had continued crying, Goyo seemed ready to slap her, but Nikki had moved the girl two steps away from him and hugged her, which made Bibi stop crying.

At that point, Goyo had hesitated, and instead of hitting Bibi, he had locked the door, trapping the others inside. Then he'd placed the key in his pocket and ordered Nikki to take the girl to the mouth of the cave. She had taken Bibi's hand and headed toward the opening of the cave, not knowing what to expect, but had been thankful she had been let out to help with Bibi. Goyo and his two henchmen had followed a few steps behind them. Once they had arrived near the entrance, Goyo, like a general on a battlefield, had directed his troops. Nikki was to sit against the wall and not move unless he ordered it. Next, he'd placed his teenage assistant on the mound near the cave entrance to stand guard with his automatic weapon, and he'd stationed Bernardo next to Bibi. Bernardo had held an FN Five-seveN, the pistol of choice for the cartels, to her head and had told the child not to move.

Bibi had frozen in place.

Removing the key from the lock brought Nikki back to the present moment. She opened the door and entered the area of human cargo. The children were huddled into a corner around Angela. They all looked terrified. Just as terrified as Nikki had been when Goyo had locked her into the compartment and had taken Bibi with him. *Thank God Bibi had screamed*, Nikki thought. *It might be a different story if she had not.*

"We're going to be okay," Nikki said, looking at each one in turn and trying to reassure them through her confident manner as she spoke and took a quick headcount. "We are getting help, and we should all be rescued soon. If you need to use the outhouses or get a drink of water, do it as soon as you get off the truck. Return quickly to the rear of the truck so I can count you and get you out with us. Angela, I will need your help to make sure we have all the children when we leave."

⁓

Eduardo identified Nikki's tall silhouette near the trailer. She stood with a group of children surrounding her. She held Bibi close to her as she told the children they would soon be home with their parents. Eduardo stepped in behind her and put his arms around both of them. The strange man made her uncomfortable, so Bibi moved away and joined Angela. Nikki turned, nudged in closer to him, and placed her arms around his muscular shoulders. She relaxed as she squeezed her body tightly against his, as if she never wanted to let go.

Eduardo whispered in her ear. "Thank God, my undercover princess, you're okay. Let's get everyone out safely, Nikki, so you and I can get away from this nightmare."

"I'm so thankful you're here," Nikki said as her voice broke and tears filled her eyes. "But please call me Nita until this whole torment is over. Just in case."

"Before we leave, I need to check for the keys to the trailer. I'll need to drive this baby out."

Eduardo broke away from Nikki's embrace, walked to the cab, opened the door to the driver's side, and pulled himself up into the driver's seat. He quickly found the keys on the dashboard, pressed the ignition button, and started the engine. With a flip of the wrist, he turned it off again.

"Are you ready to leave, Nita?" he asked as he climbed out of the truck.

"Yes. All of us are. We're anxious to get away from this place," she said as she turned to gaze upon the children. "We're ready."

"Floyd wants you and Bibi to leave with him in the helicopter, and I'll drive the children in the truck. Floyd will call the Federales, and I'll turn the truck and the children over to them. A fellow by the name of Jack, a techy Floyd brought from Miami to track your locator chip, will help me."

"And where will I see you?" she asked, embracing him again.

"After Floyd gets you to San Miguel, he'll send the chopper back for me."

"In that case, I'll fly up when they come to get you," she said, "though I won't have time to take my body mask off or shower."

Eduardo leaned in to kiss her lightly on the lips and placed his hand on the side of her face before looking straight into her eyes.

"That'll be perfect. Now you and Bibi go find Floyd and get going."

"Let me tell Angela that she is to help you with the kids."

Nikki turned to look for Angela, who was leaning against the truck, holding Bibi's hand, and walked toward them.

"Follow Eduardo's instructions," she said to the group. "He's a good man and he'll get all of you back in the trailer to get you out safely. I'll try to catch up with you tomorrow. Angela, he is going to need your help especially to keep everyone together through this."

Angela looked as terrified as the younger children, but she nodded her head in understanding.

Nikki took Bibi's hand, and they headed toward the front of the cave, where Floyd waited for them.

CHAPTER 29

Mapimí Zone of Silence—Saturday, late afternoon, day four after abduction

The pilot climbed out of the helicopter with Fígaro in his arms. Floyd, Nikki, and Bibi ran toward them. The pup, upon spotting Nikki, went wild, squirming and wiggling in the man's arms. Nikki grabbed Fígaro and hugged him as Floyd helped Bibi inside the chopper and strapped her in before he settled into the copilot seat next to Santiago, who had also climbed aboard again and was fastening his seatbelt. Nikki got in and sat next to Bibi, handing the muzzled canine to her.

Floyd returned the Smith & Wesson to Santiago and thanked him for loaning the pistol to Jack. He also gave the pilot the FN Five-seveN Jack picked up from Bernardo's corpse and asked Santiago to deliver it to Fernando in Mexico City. Then Floyd looked back to check the status of the passengers.

"You can take that muzzle off Fígaro, but keep the leash on," he said, "until we are safely in San Miguel. Let me introduce Santiago, our pilot."

Santiago prepared for takeoff, but he smiled in their direction.

"And I'm Nita, and this is Bibi."

"You're still Nita?" Floyd asked as he chuckled. "You take your undercover persona very seriously."

"Yes, until I can explain everything to a precious little person." Nikki rolled her eyes toward Bibi as she spoke.

Bibi, totally engaged with Fígaro, hugged and kissed him. Despite the leash, he'd straightened into an upright position, sniffing and licking Bibi's face, and wagging his tail excitedly.

Santiago lifted the helicopter from the flat, sandy hollow formed at the entrance of the canyon. As he did so, he flew past the entrance of the cave. Nikki reached over, touched Bibi, and pointed to the truck below, showing Bibi that it had now left the cave and could be seen moving along the bottom of the canyon.

"The truck's so tiny. It looks like a toy," Bibi said, barely able to peer out from where she sat. "Are they going to be okay?"

"Everyone will be just fine. Eduardo will make sure of it," she said, though she noticed Bibi seemed uneasy after spotting the truck, despite holding Fígaro in her lap. "And we will make sure you'll be okay too. Your mother will be so happy to see you."

Floyd, ever vigilant, searched the barren landscape. Santiago followed the canyon to the natural opening between the two sides of the mountain range, and Floyd asked him to circle the area again.

Nikki, alarmed at his request, looked out the glass enclosure to see if she could find what he had seen. A growing cloud of dust trailed a black splotch racing across the ground, like a fountain pen etching a line into the desert, kicking up a sandstorm.

"Is that trouble?" she asked in a hesitant manner, afraid of the answer.

"Don't know yet," Floyd said. "But they can see us even better than we can see them. It could be the priest and his vigilantes, or it could be—"

"Priest and vigilantes?" Nikki asked. "What are you talking about?"

"Long story. When we landed out here, we came face-to-face with a pickup parked under a cottonwood tree. A priest and a young woman sat inside. The story is almost too preposterous to repeat, but the young woman said her name is Juana García."

"Juana García? Surely you're joking," Nikki said. "That's a setup."

"Let's follow the normal flight plan out and then make a big circle back," Floyd said, instructing Santiago on the course of action to take.

Floyd turned toward Nikki and resumed his conversation with her. "Now on the young woman, all I can tell you is apparently she is the daughter of the woman who called herself la Marihuana. But she thought her mother had died when she was five years old. Her father is Raimundo Beltrán, a cartel gangster. So her name is really Juana Beltrán García."

"How did you find all this out?" Nikki asked. "Something does not sound right."

"Eduardo is the one who started asking questions and dug all that information out of her and the priest. And by the way, they said they were going back to town to get extra people to help us, but they never returned. That may be them down there."

"It all sounds like a setup to me," Nikki said. "I don't believe that story for a minute. She must be in business with her father."

As the chopper flew over the area in a wide circle, the three adults watched as the distance diminished between the two trucks. The pickup kept going straight toward the trailer, as if it were on a purposeful collision course.

"Can't we do something? Like get in closer and see what's wrong with the driver of the pickup?" Nikki asked, her voice clearly showing anxiety.

"Not with you and the child here," Floyd responded. "But we are going to have to act somehow."

"Do it now," Nikki said, biting her lip, "before Eduardo is hurt or killed."

"Santiago, try buzzing past the pickup," Floyd said, "but do it from a safe distance."

Floyd saw the pickup stop short of hitting the trailer as it veered off at an angle. Then the pickup moved into a diagonal position to stop the trailer's continued advance, though the big truck's momentum took it within striking distance of the smaller one. Men jumped from both sides of the pickup, one holding a pistol and the other an automatic weapon, which they aimed at the cabin of the truck.

"Come in behind them," Floyd shouted at Santiago. He came up off his seat in the cramped cockpit and pulled a pistol out of the pocket of his cargo pants. "Head straight over the pickup, but from a secure height. To withstand attack. If we need to get closer, I'll tell you."

The pilot handled the directions with calm professionalism, and Nikki wondered what life-threatening situations he had faced before. Floyd struggled to climb around the copilot seat to get into position by the door. Once he got there, he struggled once more as he opened the door only a crack, yelling commands to Santiago over the sound of air gushing in.

"Fly the bird to the right and give me a straight line of sight to the point of danger," Floyd yelled as loudly as he could while he prepared his pistol to take aim at the intruders that had driven in from the desert. "Go lower so I can crush that guy."

As Floyd prepared his gun, the thug approaching the driver's side of the trailer, the one Floyd intended to take out, dropped to the ground. Santiago flew past and away from the vehicles, causing Floyd to lose the range where he could take action or even discern what was happening on the ground.

"Damn it, I can't see the guy. Give me another pass, just like that one, and be quick about it," Floyd instructed the pilot.

"Lo mataron," Santiago said loudly. "Somebody killed the guy."

"Then give me that same angle on the other side of the truck," Floyd yelled.

Nikki could not see the vehicles on the ground, but she could tell Bibi was terrified. The swooping of the helicopter and Floyd at the door with a gun was enough to scare anyone. She took Bibi's hand and held it as she explained the pilot and Floyd were protecting the children in the trailer below and helping to get rid of some bad guys. She did her best to hide her own fear and racing heart.

"If you will take care of Fígaro," Nikki said as she reached across and scratched the dog's head, "Floyd will save Eduardo and the children."

Bibi stared straight ahead and cuddled the pup, squeezing him against her chest.

Nikki peered out the glass enclosure to stare at the dangerous scene unfolding below. She saw the fallen man on the ground not far from the left side of the trailer's cabin.

But then she saw the second assailant, the one on the right side of the trailer.

Nikki saw the door of the trailer on the driver's side open, and Eduardo climbed out, gun in hand.

No! Don't get out!

Her fingers clawed at the glass enclosure of the helicopter in panic, like she had at the Abbot Northwestern Hospital in Minneapolis that night so many years ago when Robbie, her son, had been taken to that hospital. Being in the helicopter, looking down, provoked the same feeling of vertigo she'd felt that night. It overpowered her now.

I cannot faint. I cannot faint, she thought. *I must stay conscious to help Eduardo and Bibi.*

Santiago slowed the helicopter to a hover maneuver. Then he and Floyd watched the events unfolding below their vantage point.

⁓

Sitting in the cabin of the truck as Eduardo drove out of the cave, Jack pulled a handkerchief from his pants pocket to wipe his forehead. Then he chuckled.

"Man, that encounter with the kidnappers provided more excitement than I've ever seen in my work with Floyd. Usually, I'm doing electronic surveillance on people and money transactions. If I'm going to see action, I need more pay."

"That operation went pretty well. Too well, in fact. I was expecting much more resistance," Eduardo said as he pushed the gas pedal. "Glad Nikki had that Taser or it could have been a shootout."

The hardened desert road provided an excellent surface to drive on. It looked hardly used, and as a result, it was in good enough shape that Eduardo accelerated until the speedometer approached fifty miles per hour. Then a black shape and a plume of dust in the distance caught his eye.

"Do you see that truck coming this way?" he asked as his gaze focused straight ahead. "Maybe I spoke too soon."

"Not to worry," Jack said. "It's the priest and the young woman coming to help us now that we don't need them."

"Let's hope that's who it is," Eduardo said as he noticed the helicopter starting to circle. He guessed Floyd was making sure the pickup arriving out of nowhere was not going to be a problem.

With billowing dust trailing the pickup, it continued heading straight toward the truck. When the pickup's relentless race toward them persisted, Eduardo slowed to forty, but as the pickup kept coming, he slowed to thirty-five. There was no doubt in his mind now that this was not the priest or anyone coming to their aid.

When he realized he had to stop or risk crashing and possibly injuring the children in the truck, he stepped hard on the brakes, and the vehicle's momentum made it skid over the loose sand on the road's surface. The steering wheel jerked out of his grasp, but he quickly regained control and managed to stop, inches from the pickup which had blocked the road.

"Shit, we've got trouble. Get ready for a gunfight," Eduardo said.

He turned sideways to reach behind the seat to retrieve his own gun from the toolbox where he'd stored it, and he cursed when he could not immediately find it.

"They're going to kill us," Jack cried out, sliding to the center of the seat, as if that provided safety.

"Shoot them, damn it! Shoot!" Eduardo yelled at Jack as he saw a man coming up on his side of the truck, pointing a pistol at him.

"I don't have a gun!"

A bullet came through the window, shattering glass over the dashboard, with fragments showering Eduardo and Jack, who had hunkered down under the dashboard when the impact hit. Eduardo was still trying to maneuver his gun out of the toolbox behind the seat. He held his breath, expecting another bullet at any moment. When he finally got the gun in his hand, he looked out the window to gauge how best to defend himself. He quickly aimed for his assailant, but before he could pull the trigger, the man fell to the ground.

Eduardo's heart pounded. *How did that happen?*

For a split second, he wondered if Jack had somehow found a weapon and shot the man, but then he realized it must have come from elsewhere, maybe even the helicopter, as he became aware, for the second time, of the sound of the spinning rotors.

In the midst of the confusion, Eduardo tried to assess where the next assault would come from. He saw a man swinging an automatic rifle on Jack's side. Opening the door on the driver's side, Eduardo got out to take the man down, but he'd moved and Eduardo could not see him. A burst from the automatic weapon let Eduardo know the man was on the opposite side of the shipment container.

Oh, my God, he must be pelting Jack.

As Santiago continued to hover over the troubled area, Nikki saw several people, five or six, running down the mountainside. Her heart sank, and she couldn't breathe.

Eduardo cannot hold off so many assailants, she thought.

"See those men running down," Santiago said, his excited voice an octave or two above his normal pitch. "They could be vigilantes."

"Or they could be more bad guys," Floyd said.

The lone assailant on the passenger side of the truck was swinging his automatic weapon away from the trailer and instead appeared to be aiming at the people coming down the slope toward him. He pushed his spine up against the back part of the shipment container on the passenger's side. As he leveled burst after burst of automatic fire at the men who were still descending off the mountain, they took refuge periodically behind large boulders after taking shots aimed at the truck. Their shaky aim, caused by their running, missed the lone assailant every time, but one of them succumbed to the shelling as he appeared from behind a boulder to aim for the assailant. The man by the trailer stepped away from the vehicle to take aim at them and then darted back to hide by the trailer in an obvious effort at protection.

As Eduardo prepared to attack the assailant, he heard what sounded like several automatic weapons going off at the same time. When he heard a response from a single automatic rifle, he realized the man had moved all the way to the rear door of the shipment container.

It sounds as if he's using the back of the trailer to hide from someone shooting at him. Or is it someone coming to help him? But who could that be? Do we have more than one group vying to take the kidnapped children, or has the priest come back to help after all?

Eduardo inched his way to the back of the trailer, peered around, and realized the man hiding back there had moved to the long side of the container, on the opposite side from Eduardo. He knelt by the back panel for a better view. His line of sight passed between the two axles on the underside of the trailer.

After locating his target as he knelt by the shipment container, Eduardo stood, walked behind the truck, and took a single shot at the assailant. He then ducked back for safety, and with lightning speed, he aligned his body against the back panel, while also trying to make sure the truck's tires offered some protection to his lower extremities if his assailant turned on him.

The man responded by spraying bullets toward the rear of the truck, from where he must have assumed the single shot had come. The man inched his way forward toward the cabin. Eduardo peeked around the back end of the trailer and pointed the pistol at the man. The villain must have sensed that he was being targeted again because he turned his body to face toward the rear of truck. At the same moment the assailant turned back, Jack opened the door to the passenger side of the trailer's cabin and leapt out onto the assailant's back, knocking him down. Taking advantage of the element of surprise, Jack kept the man pinned to the ground and pushed his knee into the assailant's arm that still held the automatic weapon. Using his foot, Jack slowly managed to push the weapon away. The assailant, not a big man but strong and fit enough to continue the fight despite a visibly wounded arm, threw Jack off. He scrambled up and kicked Jack in the groin, knocking him flat. The man lunged after his weapon and positioned himself on the ground to unleash another burst of fire.

Instead of shooting and risking hitting Jack, Eduardo ducked behind the trailer as a stream of bullets hit the spot where he'd just been standing. He heard the whizzing sound of the slugs and a loud bang, probably a tire that was hit. Dust stirred up where the bullets hit the dirt not far from his feet.

Damn, Eduardo thought. *When I run out of bullets, we'll be sitting ducks. Maybe Floyd will land the chopper and come to our rescue. But that would endanger Nikki and the child, so that's not an option.*

Nikki stared in the direction of the action, though she did not have a full panoramic view the way Santiago did from the pilot's seat or the way Floyd could see from his crouched position near the door.

"Is Eduardo okay?" she asked in a quivering voice.

"Seems like those guys hiding behind the rocks are on our side," Floyd said. "I don't know who they are. Maybe Fernando sent a few Federales in."

"Not Federales, not those guys," Santiago said as he kept the chopper in a continual hover maneuver, though he changed the angle from time to time. "They're either vigilantes on our side, or they are bad guys, bajadores, here to take the children."

"Don't know for sure they're with us," Floyd said loudly, "but I know we need to act quickly if they turn on Eduardo or try to hijack the trailer. In fact, move farther away so we can be safe once they overpower that guy with the automatic rifle."

Nikki shifted her gaze to the helicopter's floor. She feared the outcome of the fight and could no longer bear to watch. She glanced at Bibi. The child sat motionless, staring at the back of the pilot's seat. Even Fígaro simply lay on Bibi's lap without moving.

Suddenly, Floyd shouted a strong hurrah, followed by Santiago echoing his sentiments.

"Bravo, bravo!!" the pilot cheered.

It was like they'd both witnessed an incredible show from the heights of their hovering position—a pantomime, without the traditional accompaniment of music.

"Those mountain people are our friends. They've just saved Eduardo and Jack," Floyd called back to her. "Let's land this bird."

Santiago took the chopper almost straight down from its seventy-five foot perch, and Nikki and Bibi both gasped as the dropping feeling hit their stomachs.

Before the dust even settled, Nikki unbuckled her seatbelt and opened the helicopter's door. She jumped out as soon as the blades rotated more slowly. Hunched over, and with her eyes almost closed to keep the sand out, she ran toward the trailer. Eduardo saw her and ran toward her. When they met, they folded into an embrace. Eduardo kissed her, touched her masked face, then kissed her again, this time searching for her tongue, and she responded with all the passion she felt for him. After almost a minute, he whispered his love in her ear. They kissed again and continued embracing as they swayed gently from side to side.

Floyd, still in the helicopter with Bibi, watched as two men tied up the assailant. After securing him, they walked up the slope to their own man who had been shot. They got him to sit up, and one stayed to tend to his wounds. The other vigilante returned to the injured intruder they had tied up. A third man walked around the truck to check on the body of the one who had attacked from Eduardo's side of the trailer.

Floyd took a look around, as if analyzing the level of danger. Then he glanced at Bibi.

"That is a mighty fine dog you've got there." Bibi looked up at Floyd without showing any expression. "That pup is Nita's friend, and he helped save both of you," he said, trying to get Bibi to respond to him.

"He belongs to a street lady where I live," Bibi said, finally responding to Floyd's prodding.

Looking flustered, Floyd reached out and scratched Fígaro's head.

"We can all get out if you promise to keep him on the leash," Floyd said.

He still didn't really know how to deal with the child, so instead, he unsnapped Bibi's seatbelt at the same time he told Santiago they should all get out of the copter and head toward the trailer.

Floyd climbed out, turned and faced into the chopper, took Bibi and the pup into his arms, placed them on the ground, and kept her tiny hand in his as they proceeded slowly toward the trailer, where several people were beginning to gather.

The vigilantes who had helped subdue the two assailants now surrounded Nikki and Eduardo, who continued in a passionate embrace. Floyd and his small entourage joined in the circle of onlookers. Santiago started applauding, and others quickly joined in.

Nikki and Eduardo finally realized what was happening. They broke their embrace and smiled at everyone as Eduardo put his arm around Nikki's shoulders and brought her in close to him.

"Thank you," Eduardo said. "Thanks to all of you for making it possible for me to be reunited with this headstrong and unmanageable woman whom I adore. She's the love of my life."

"They must think you like your women a whole lot older," Nikki said.

Eduardo turned to Nikki with eyes filled with love.

"It's you I love, not the way you look, though you are my beautiful undercover agent," he said.

Nikki pulled on Eduardo's hand, and together they walked up to Floyd. Nikki took Bibi's hand and brought her in for a hug.

"I told you everything would turn out okay. He has saved the children...Oh, my God, the children!"

Eduardo opened the back door to the truck and followed Nikki after she jumped into the shipping container. Goyo was tied against the wall of the large compartment he had intended to load with meat. He had a handkerchief around his mouth keeping him from talking, but his eyes blazed with hatred. Not far from him, Bernardo's body lay on the floor of the compartment, covered with a blanket Jack had found in the sleeping area of the truck. The young assistant lay tied in a fashion similar to Goyo's, except the assistant was stretched out on the floor and Goyo sat upright.

"Where are the children?" Nikki asked.

"In the small compartment up front," Eduardo said, leaning in to whisper in Nikki's ear. "I couldn't leave them up here. All of them are so afraid of Goyo, they could not be in the same area with him. I hate to say it, but I locked them up in the small compartment up front after Angela made a remark about Goyo not being such a bad man. I did not want to risk her untying him and we'd end up with problems again."

"You don't seriously think she'd do that?" Nikki asked.

"She's traumatized. Bonds can build between kidnappers and their victims, especially in the cases of sexual abuse."

"You're right. Like Stockholm syndrome. Of course. Better to be safe, just in case. Now let's get the kids out."

Floyd stood apart from the other people milling around outside the trailer and held Bibi's hand again. Jack stood next to the captured assailant as the men celebrated that they had liberated a truckload of children.

Still holding Bibi's hand, Floyd speed-dialed Fernando, asking him to send Federales. It was late afternoon, and he located Fernando still working in his Mexico City office. Floyd agreed to wait with the children until the federal police arrived.

After hanging up from that call, he asked Bibi if she would like to talk to her mother.

"Mia madre?" Bibi asked as she jumped up and down and showed real emotion for the first time. "Sí, sí, sí!"

As Bibi spoke on the phone to her mother, Jack approached Floyd.

"One of the vigilantes and I are going to change the flat tire on the truck. A bullet hit it and we've checked and there is a spare. They are double tires and the truck is empty, but it'd still be best to change it."

"Good idea," Floyd said, grinning. "Have fun."

Nikki and Eduardo descended from the shipping container. They both helped the children get down and stretch out from being cooped up in the compartment. Nikki pointed to a nearby boulder and gave Angela instructions about taking all the girls behind it to take care of the call of nature, but she kept her eye on Angela as she led all the girls, save for Bibi. Nikki told Eduardo she was going to take Bibi to the bathroom in the opposite direction and asked him to go with them to stand guard. As she took Bibi toward a couple of large rocks, two figures waved as they walked down the slope of the mountain. She scrutinized the figures and saw they were carrying assault rifles. She squeezed Eduardo's arm in fear.

"We have company again," she said.

"That's a priest and a young woman—"

"Juana's daughter?" Nikki asked, interrupting Eduardo.

"You know . . . ?"

"Floyd told me."

"Yes. One of them probably took out the assailant on my side of the truck," he said as he stepped between Nikki and Bibi and took each one by the hand, Nikki on one side and Bibi on the other. Bibi also held Fígaro's leash as he sniffed around on the ground. "Let's catch up with them."

Nikki signaled to Floyd to tell him to keep an eye on the girls, who were heading toward the rock boulders on the opposite side.

"Where have you been?" Eduardo asked as they stopped to greet the newcomers. He introduced them, explaining that Juana's daughter used her nickname, Ana. "I need to thank you both for saving my life."

"It was Ana who saved you," Father Abelardo said. "We think she got rid of a Colombian who joined up with Arturo Béjar, a well-known extortionist and wannabe trafficker."

"We thought you'd abandoned us," Eduardo said.

"We got here with minutes to spare," the priest said. "When we returned to Ceballos to get reinforcements, an informant confirmed Goyo was hiding in one of the canyons out here."

"The informer worked for Arturo," Ana said, "until recently when they had a disagreement and he turned on him. He said Arturo had been tracking the original kidnapper to get a specific child. When we were told Arturo was driving out here from Zacatecas, we took a northern route, a longer route, to avoid Arturo seeing us."

"We did not call because our informant said Arturo carries special equipment to intercept calls," the priest added.

Ana seemed pensive. "We didn't want to give away the location of the children to Arturo and the Colombian. We didn't know exactly where the kids were hidden, but we knew where Predator had gone down, so we—"

"If you were here, why did you let us handle the cave on our own?" Eduardo asked.

"We figured Goyo was in a cave," Father Abelardo said, "but we didn't know the exact location until we saw the helicopter on the ground. You were obviously already inside the cave. That's when we took our positions. Ana and I on one side, and the five vigilantes on the other side."

"When we saw Floyd leave in the helicopter with you," Ana said, gesturing toward Nikki and Bibi, "we waited to make sure the coast was clear, as they say. We watched as guardian angels, in case the bajadores arrived. This scene has played out far too frequently in recent years. Plus, we wanted to catch those malditos bastardos in the act of taking the children. That's the only way to put an end to their trafficking."

"That's when we saw the dust from Arturo's truck," the priest said, "and then the attack began."

Ana looked at the dog and kneeled down to scratch his head.

"What's his name?" she asked.

"Fígaro," Bibi said.

"The pup belonged to your mother," Eduardo said to Ana. "Would you like to have him?"

Ana smiled and picked him up in her arms while Bibi held the leash.

"I'd love to have my mother's dog," she said as she cuddled Fígaro.

Bibi moved a step away and dropped the leash, her head hung low.

"But I think this puppy is already bonded with this girl, and he's her dog now," Ana said. She smiled as she put him back on the ground, picked the leash up, and handed it to Bibi. "He's a cute puppy, and he needs you. The two of you need each other. I'd like to visit the both of you in San Miguel. If you invite me, that is."

Bibi nodded, a small smile on her face.

"Let's gather the group so we can get out of here," Eduardo said.

"Even though he was a thug, I'd like to say a few words over the dead man," Father Abelardo said, clearing his throat. "We need to start the forgiveness process so we can heal."

"There's another dead body in the back of the trailer," Eduardo said. "We'll turn over three men for questioning—Goyo, his assistant, and the man with the wire-frame glasses. Did you say his name is Arturo?"

As the group approached Floyd, they heard the familiar sound of a helicopter in the distance.

"Must be the Federales," Floyd said as he looked up at the sky, searching for the government-owned chopper. He turned to shake hands with both the priest and the young woman. "Thanks for getting your people out to help us. Now we'll turn the children and the criminals, both the dead ones and the live ones, over to the federal police."

"We want the Federales to take the children from you and then officially grant us responsibility for them," Father Abelardo said. "They can take the criminals, and we'll take the children."

"I don't know if they have authority to do that," Floyd said as he pulled his mobile phone out. "I'll call my contact to see if we can make that happen out here."

After consulting with Fernando over the phone for a minute, Floyd asked the priest to pose for a photo.

Perplexed, Father Abelardo half-smiled at Floyd's phone. Floyd sent the photo to Fernando and waited for a response.

The government helicopter started its landing maneuver.

"Okay, we're good to go," Floyd said. "Fernando will contact his people to let them know they have approval to transfer temporary custody of the children to Father Abelardo."

"That helps us get started on processing each child's return to their families. We are grateful," the priest said as he shook Floyd's hand.

"I'm the one who is grateful," Floyd said, yelling to make sure the priest heard him over the sound of the chopper. "As soon as we turn everyone over to the Federales, and you get the children back, my entire team can return to San Miguel."

CHAPTER 30

San Miguel de Allende—Saturday evening

The sunset's last rays reflected on the helicopter's glass canopy as Santiago brought the chopper in for a perfect landing on San Miguel's small airstrip. Timothy stood under a dark-colored awning with Sofía, Paolo, and Chiara. He reminded them Sofía needed the time and space to welcome Bibi home first.

"Bibi's been through a lot of trauma," Timothy said. "She does not know that her grandmother and her father also await her return. After Sofía explains that to her, both of you can join them."

As the chopper's engine stopped and the blades slowed down, Timothy nodded to Sofía. She walked out onto the tarmac and waited for the passengers to alight from the helicopter, wiping the palms of her hands on her skirt.

Eduardo got out first, and Nikki followed. Bibi appeared at the door, with Fígaro in her arms, and waited for Eduardo to put his hands around her waist and help her down. Bibi placed the Pomsky on the ground and held his leash. Then Nikki took Bibi's free hand and headed toward Sofía. As they got closer, Bibi let go of Nikki's hand and started running toward her mother, with Fígaro trotting right beside her.

The two embraced so hard and for so long that the Pomsky decided to get in the picture too. He jumped on Bibi's legs and, despite his pint size, he knocked her slightly off balance.

"Cos'é questo?" Sofía asked, taking notice of the dog for the first time.

"Il mio cucciolo," Bibi said.

"Your puppy?"

"Yes. A nice lady gave him to me."

"That's good. Our ristorante needs a watchdog. And what's his name?" Sofía asked.

"Fígaro."

"Lovely. We need to introduce Fígaro to a couple of people who came to see that you're okay."

"My teachers?" Bibi asked as she looked around.

"No. Your father and your grandmother, Chiara. Yeah, your father and grandmother came from Italy to make sure you got safely home. They are over by the building. Go over to see them, and take Fígaro with you."

At first, Bibi hesitated, but when she saw her father, she walked toward the group under the awning.

Nikki and Eduardo approached Sofía, who looked confused by her old-lady appearance.

"Sofía, I'm Nikki in disguise. I'm wearing a full-body mask."

Sofía stared for two or three seconds, shaking her head.

"It's a shock. You fooled me, yeah. You look so different. I do recognize your voice, though." She threw her arms around Nikki. "Thank you so much for saving my daughter."

"Nikki went undercover to rescue Bibi," Eduardo said. "She called herself Nita. She did an extraordinary job. And we need to talk about Bibi. I'd recommend you get a good counselor for as long as she needs it to make sure she recovers completely from the trauma she's been through."

"Timothy was explaining that to me," Sofía said. "Yeah, explaining that kidnap victims experience terrible things. Atrocities, at times. I hope that was not the case for Bibi."

"We hope not too," Eduardo said. "Take her to your medical doctor as soon as possible for a complete check-up." He placed his arm around Sofía and patted her back in a reassuring manner.

"Yes, good idea," Sofía said, looking like she might become emotional again.

"The important thing is, Bibi is okay," Eduardo said, trying to sound positive. "She may display withdrawal symptoms or even memory loss for a while. It's the way the human brain deals with trauma. She may also experience irrational fears at times. She'll need professional help if that happens, so she can overcome her fears."

"Changing the subject," Nikki said, "I'd like to add that Bibi knew me by the name of Nita, and she only saw me in this full-body mask. We need to explain that I'm not Nita. I dressed like this so I could rescue her. I'd like for her to be present when I remove the facial mask and she can learn my real name."

Sofía reached for Nikki's hand and held it.

"You told me you'd find my daughter," Sofía said. "I'll never be able to repay you for bringing her home safely."

"I know you didn't much care for Juana la Marihuana," Nikki said, "but we located Bibi from information she gave us before she was killed."

"She was not a bad woman," Eduardo added, "simply eccentric and living in a lot of pain. Her reason for using marihuana and other drugs."

Floyd walked up with Santiago and joined the group, interrupting their conversation. He introduced the pilot to her.

"Why don't you all come over to the house," Sofía said. "Yeah, Paolo and his mother will be there."

"Paolo's mother? She's here?" Floyd asked, surprised.

"Yes. Bibi is talking to both of them right now," Sofía said as she gestured with her hand toward Bibi.

"I thought you didn't like your former mother-in-law?" Floyd asked skeptically.

"I never have liked her." Sofía sighed. "But she's Bibi's grandmother, and she has apologized for the way she has treated me. Yeah, she has apologized profusely. They're both spending a few days at my house."

Floyd shook his head. "Are you sure you want that at this time? You need to get your life, and your daughter's, back to normal. You even accused your ex and his mother of being the masterminds of the kidnapping."

"Well, she flew over from Italy once she knew how bad it was, yeah, you know, when we couldn't find Bibi. All those years she called me a bad mother, she's told me she'd been wrong about that. She's still Chiara Lombardi, thinking she's Italian royalty, but she's Bibi's grandmother, and I've accepted her apology. So she's welcome to stay with us."

Floyd glanced at Eduardo and sighed.

"Nikki, can you . . . may we call you Nikki again?" Floyd asked.

"As soon as I have a little talk with Bibi," she said as she turned to Sofía. "Can we get Bibi and take her to the restroom so I can explain about my mask?"

"Take care of your mask, and I'll speak with you later," Floyd said. "Then we can go to our hotel. It's been a long day."

As Nikki and Sofía started walking away, Floyd stopped them as he scratched his head.

"Sofía, why are Paolo and his mother staying at your place tonight?"

"He's her father, after all. It might be helpful to Bibi. Even though I don't like Chiara, she told me she lost her nephew Matteo recently. Said she didn't want to talk about it, but it made me feel sorry for her. Yeah, she loved that boy like her own. Besides, if her royal bones don't mind sleeping on an inflatable bed, she can stay."

Floyd considered telling her about the suspicious conditions surrounding Matteo's death, but there were still so many unknowns. Would it be wise to restart a family drama that seemed to be healing? He decided to wait until he had more details.

"Tomorrow we'll stop over to pick up our equipment and personal stuff," he said instead. "We have several issues to wrap up before this job is complete. Returning the helicopter I've leased, and more importantly, finding out what the federal police have managed to get out of those criminals we turned over to them."

Nikki took Sofía by the arm, and together they walked to get Bibi. When Sofía asked her daughter to join them for a trip to the bathroom, Bibi showed her mother the world tree necklace.

"Nita gave this to me. It's very special," she told her mother, taking her hand. "It saved my life. And one more thing, it got me Fígaro." She smiled down at him as he sat patiently next to her.

"It's really Ms. Nita who saved your life," Sofía said as she pulled the door open and they stepped into the restroom. "She made a very big sacrifice for you. What she did was pretend to be Nita so the man who stole you would take her along in the group, but Nita is really a wonderful woman by the name of Nikki."

Bibi's eyes went from looking at her mother to staring at Nikki.

"I don't understand. You're not Nita?"

"Don't be scared," Nikki said. "It's just like wearing a costume. I'm going to take it off now."

Nikki removed the face mask and wasn't surprised her skin was irritated from having worn the mask so long. When she looked at herself in the mirror, she noticed the bruise on her right cheek, where Bernardo had struck her, looked smaller than she had expected. Her entire semblance was red and puffy. Turning the water faucet on, she leaned over the sink and, using both hands, splashed water on her face. Then she tore a paper towel from the dispenser and blotted her face to dry it.

"This is what I really look like," she said as she turned to talk with Bibi. "Well, mostly. The redness will go away. If I had not worn a mask over my face, the bad man who took the dog away from you would never have allowed me on the trip with you. I had to wear a mask to save you. I also have a mask on my body, which I'll take off when I take a shower at my hotel. I'll see you tomorrow morning, and you can ask me questions if you want."

"I have a question," Bibi said. "May I keep the world tree?"

Nikki smiled. "Of course."

"You can keep Fígaro too," Sofía said. "Shall we take your new puppy home? I'll bet you're both hungry."

"Great idea," Nikki said. "Let's all leave."

"Vedrete la vostra nuova casa presto," Bibi whispered to Fígaro as she picked him up in her arms.

"Bibi told Fígaro that he'll see his new home soon," Sofía said, translating for Nikki.

Bibi seems to be taking everything in stride, Nikki thought. *Now I need to get to my suite and take a shower. I'll be so happy to take this body mask off.*

Sofía had her arm around Bibi as they joined Paolo and Chiara under the awning, and all four of them walked toward the street.

Eduardo took Nikki into his arms. "My God, you look gorgeous."

"Wait till I've taken my body mask off and showered. I'll really be irresistibly gorgeous then," she said, smiling. "This ordeal is over, and we can return to our vacation. It feels good to know Bibi and the other kids are safe."

Eduardo kissed her.

COYOTE ZONE

"Hey, love birds," Floyd said, "let's get out of here."

With six people, including the pilot and himself, Floyd had too many for one taxi, so he hired two cabs to take them to the B&B where Charlotte had made reservations for all of them. The same boutique guesthouse where Nikki and Eduardo were staying.

As Floyd stepped into his cab, he noticed a large black car, a Mercedes stretch limo, also parked at the curb picking up passengers—Sofía and her group.

What an impractical car for San Miguel's narrow streets, he thought, *but I guess Chiara Lombardi needs to be chauffeured in style.*

CHAPTER 31

San Miguel de Allende—Sunday, early hours

A ringing phone awakened Floyd.

"What the shit...? Who the *fuck*...?"

He reached out to the night stand and fumbled the phone in the dark. It fell to the floor, and the ring tone blared on the terra cotta tile.

When he finally grasped the phone in his hand, his sleepy voice answered without checking the Caller I.D.

"Fernando, what's up?" he asked after hearing Fernando apologize for disturbing him.

When he heard Fernando's answer, Floyd leapt out of bed.

"In León, Guanajuato? What's the name?"

Floyd listened for a response.

"Do you think we have time to stop—?"

He listened again.

"Thanks, I'll see them there."

As soon as he hung up, Floyd checked the time. Four fifteen a.m. He dialed Nikki's number.

When her groggy voice answered, he said, "Get Eduardo up. Meet me outside in ten minutes. We need to get to work. Fernando believes Bibi's been kidnapped again."

Twenty minutes later, Eduardo and Nikki stepped out of a taxi in front of Sofía's ristorante. Eduardo asked the driver to wait for them. Nikki had dialed Sofía on the short drive to the ristorante and awakened her. A semiconscious Sofía, dressed in a royal-blue robe and uncombed hair, waited by the door.

"Have you checked on Bibi in the last couple of hours?" Nikki asked, as she hurriedly descended from the taxi.

"She's in her bedroom. No, I have not, but she's in the room next to mine."

"May we come in and verify all continues to be safe?" Nikki asked.

Sofía's semblance showed fear, but she let them in. The three of them walked through Sofía's bedroom. As she passed through the door into Bibi's room, Sofía turned the light on.

The bed was empty.

Sofía screamed.

Fígaro whined and scratched on the door to the hallway bathroom, where he had been locked up.

"Listen to me, Sofía," Eduardo said. "Everything will be all right. Floyd got a call from the person who is responsible for the interrogation of the kidnappers—"

"This can't be happening again. Not again," she said as she collapsed on Bibi's bed.

"We know where Bibi is," Eduardo said.

"The Federales questioned those criminals involved in the kidnapping," Nikki said. "For several hours, past midnight, they questioned them. They purposely exhausted them, and one of them confessed he'd purchased plane tickets for an Italian woman and a child. He also produced fake passports and other documents. The woman is posing as—"

Paolo appeared. He was barefoot, wearing a white terry cloth robe with a monogram embroidered in gold.

"What's going on?" Paolo inquired, looking at the three adults. When he glanced at the bed, his face registered shock. "Where is Bibiana?"

"We think your mother has taken her," Eduardo said.

"My mother? Where would my mother take her at this hour?" Paolo asked, shaking his head. "Have you searched the rest of the house?"

Sofía pointed to the inflatable bed on the floor where Chiara was supposed to sleep.

"She's stolen her again."

"Chiara's taking her to Italy using false documents," Nikki said. "They're booked on a flight to Naples."

Paolo turned to leave the room, yelling his daughter's name.

Sofía followed after him, shouting in Italian, "Don't be a hypocrite. You criminals, you've planned it this way!" Her yelling gave way to sobs.

Paolo stopped and faced Sofía.

"If you think I had anything to do with Bibi's disappearance this time or the first time, you're dead wrong," he said in a menacing whisper. "But if my mother is behind this, she will pay. By God, she will pay."

After picking up his clothes from the chair next to the inflatable bed in the parlor, Paolo went into the bathroom and slammed the door behind him. It took thirty seconds for him to throw on his clothes and shoes and meet the other three congregating in the parlor.

"Floyd and the pilot should already be on the helicopter heading to the airport in León," Eduardo said. "They'll stop Chiara from boarding the plane—"

Unable to stand it any longer, Sofía interrupted Eduardo. "Why must you tell Paolo what the plan is? So he can notify his mother? Yeah, so she can abscond with my daughter?"

Sofía clenched her hands into fists and starting pounding Eduardo in the chest.

He grabbed her hands and in a calm voice asked her to be reasonable. "We are doing everything in our ability to stop Chiara, but we need your cooperation."

The distraught woman used the cuff of her robe to wipe her nose. Nikki grabbed tissues from the box on the side table near the doorway and handed them to Sofía.

"Don't you know extradition for kidnapping cases between Mexico and Italy is almost impossible?" Sofía said, her voice scared yet firm. "If she gets Bibi on Italian soil, it will be the end of the story. I'll never see Bibi again."

"That's why we need to get to the airport. A taxi's outside," Nikki said.

"And why Naples if she lives in Milán?" Sofía asked.

"There's a flight departing at six fifty-five this morning from the León airport directly to Naples," Eduardo said. "There may not be a flight to Milán, and she wouldn't have had time to arrange a private plane."

"We'll never make it in time," Sofía said, groaning and on the verge of tears again. "It's over an hour drive."

"Floyd should be there shortly," Eduardo said.

"Are you certain it's that airport?" Paolo asked. "Are you certain of your information? How do you know?"

"We're acting on good intel," Nikki said. "Get dressed, Sofia, the taxi's waiting."

⁂

"Can't find them," Floyd said as Nikki ran up to him at the airport. He looked worried. "Can you check the women's bathrooms in the VIP lounge?"

"Isn't the plane about to leave?" Nikki asked.

Out of breath, she'd run from the terminal entrance to the area outside the airport's only VIP lounge. Floyd had texted his location within the newly remodeled and expanded terminal. Despite the recent work done to improve Del Bajío International Airport, it provided only one working runway, and its lone terminal was rather small for an international airport.

"Yeah, I'm going all the way to the gate. I have one of Fernando's people covering that area. After you check the VIP bathroom, join me at gate seventeen. Two more restrooms are located between the lounge and the gate."

"What about other airports?" Nikki asked. "Isn't it possible this one is being used as a decoy while she leaves through another one?"

"It's possible," Floyd responded. "Fernando is taking care of that angle. He has people staked out at several airports. My gut tells me it's here."

Floyd left Nikki and rushed to the gate. When he arrived, the Alitalia plane was boarding. Since the airport had insufficient gates with jet bridges, this flight was using a movable staircase to load passengers directly from the tarmac. As the passengers filed past the ticket reader before stepping outside, Floyd scrutinized everyone, especially those with children.

Nikki arrived at the gate to see the last passengers climb the stairs to the Alitalia plane. Floyd was busy talking on the phone. When he finished his conversation, he contemplated Nikki with a hint of despair evident in his eyes. His jaw was clenched tight.

"Fernando's people traced Chiara's two tickets on this plane under her assumed name, Claudia Piti. Boarding passes have been issued, yet their seats are vacant. She's obviously fooled us."

"Do you think we should—?"

"It'll be a mess to try to get that child back if Chiara gets her to Italy," Floyd said. "It would change the whole case, making it an international incident, and Sofía would have to file kidnapping charges against her ex and former mother-in-law. The Mexican government would need to work through Interpol. It could take years."

"Paolo may not be involved," Nikki said.

"Somehow I don't believe that," Floyd said. "By the way, where is he?"

"I left him with Eduardo and Sofía in the parking garage. I told them they had to wait there. Eduardo will keep Sofía from killing him."

"Fernando has made sure people are watching other departures to Italy from Mexico City, Querétaro, and all major airports in Mexico, but my guess is that woman has vanished. She's probably taken a flight through the U.S. or Spain or wherever under a different assumed name." He sighed heavily as he put his phone back in his pocket.

Nikki stood next to him, not speaking. She stared through the floor-to-ceiling windows toward the plane. The strong morning sun reflected off the silver-colored siding of the movable stairs. To conceal her disappointment, she took her sunglasses out of her purse and put them on. They both watched as two employees wearing noise reduction headsets started pulling the stairs away from the aircraft.

"So what do we do next?" Floyd asked. He sounded like he was thinking out loud more than addressing the question to Nikki.

As Floyd waited for an answer from Nikki or an insight from his own brain, a flash of sunlight reflected off the windshield of a long, black Mercedes limousine that suddenly appeared behind the plane. It drove around the tail of the plane, whipped around it, and with squealing tires, the limo came to an abrupt stop and parked parallel to the Alitalia jet.

"My God, there they are," Nikki said.

"Let's go."

Floyd grabbed Nikki by the arm and signaled to a federal policeman standing ten feet away. The officer pulled paperwork from his pocket and showed it to the airline employee standing by the ticket scanner. Then the three of them charged through the door to the tarmac.

Out on the runway, the chauffeur stepped out of the limo and dashed to the other side of the car to open the door for his passengers. From the open airline door, a flight attendant signaled the airport employees to push the stairs back against the aircraft for loading the late passengers.

Chiara, struggling to pull Bibi along with her, rushed from the car and started ascending the staircase. When she couldn't drag the child, the elegant woman got behind Bibi and forcefully pushed her. Bibi cried and hung onto the handrail of the portable stairs.

Floyd and Nikki sprinted to the boarding stairs, the policeman following at their heels. Floyd took the steps two at a time and grabbed Chiara's arm, squeezing until she had to let go of Bibi. Nikki was right there to take Bibi's arm and accompany her down the stairs. The federal policeman helped Floyd subdue Chiara.

Bibi, sobbing, cried out for her mother.

"Your mother is in the terminal," Nikki said. "If you will run with me to the building, we will find your mother in there."

Once inside the terminal, Nikki dialed Sofía. As soon as she answered, Nikki told her Bibi was safe, and she handed Bibi the phone to talk to her mother.

While they talked, Nikki turned to look outside and saw Floyd and the federal policeman had restrained Chiara. They were walking her down the stairs. The woman had a very stern look on her face, but she held her shoulders up and her head high. She never gave up her regal posture as they continued to escort her to a second car that had arrived. A car not nearly as elegant as Chiara's limousine.

Floyd returned to the terminal through gate seventeen. He looked for Nikki and Bibi and spotted them farther down the wide hallway. He sprinted and caught up with them.

"Where are they taking her?" Nikki asked as all three resumed walking toward the garage to find Bibi's mother.

"Chiara's been charged with attempting to abduct a minor," Floyd said. "For now, she's going to a federal lockup in Mexico City."

"Federal charges?" Nikki asked.

"Yes."

"Uh, I would not want to be in her feet tonight."

"In her feet? What's that mean?" Floyd asked.

"Since she'll be in jail, she won't like the shoes they'll give her, so I can't use the expression 'I don't want to be in her shoes.'"

"Okay," Floyd said, not really trying to comprehend the logic behind Nikki's comments. "Is Sofía still waiting in the garage?"

Nikki nodded.

When they reached the elevator to the garage, Bibi refused to get in. The small space terrified her, so instead, the three of them walked up the stairs.

Standing by the elevator on the second floor, Sofía, Paolo, and Eduardo waited for Bibi to arrive. As soon as she reached the top of the stairs, Bibi dropped Nikki's hand and ran toward her mother, calling to her as she ran.

"Mamma! Mamma! Mamma!"

Sofía opened her arms wide, and Bibi flew into them. Sofía came down on one knee to be closer to her daughter's height. The two embraced until Bibi stopped crying. It became obvious to the adults, Bibi did not want to let go of her mother again.

Paolo had tears in his eyes, but Floyd asked the father to step aside with him for a private conversation.

"Your mother has been charged with a federal offense," Floyd said. "Unless you post bail, she will spend the night in jail."

"She can rot there forever for what she's done," Paolo said. "Look at Bibi. My daughter is traumatized. My mother put Bibi's life at risk. I've never understood my mother, but this is the worst act she's ever committed. Chiara's always been strong-willed and determined to get her way in life, without concern for others, but this time she's gone too far. It's time she pays for all the suffering she has brought on others."

"But Chiara has the money to post bond for herself," Floyd said.

"I'm not so sure she does," Paolo said. "My father failed to put enough constraints on her trust fund, and she's spending it at a fast clip."

"Be honest, Paolo, did you have a hand in all of this?"

Paolo looked Floyd straight in the eyes before responding.

"In the abduction? No, I did not. I know it looks like I'm guilty by association. After all, my mother and my cousin committed a crime, but I didn't even know she was in Mexico until she arrived at Sofía's in that Mercedes. I should have known better, but she convinced me she regretted treating Sofía so badly over the years. Bloody hell, she convinced Sofía herself."

"But you filed a lawsuit against Sofía for shared legal custody of Bibi, didn't you?" Floyd asked.

"Yes. My attorney advised a strategy so I could get her in Italy for the full summer. He recommended asking for six months so we could settle on three."

"What about Matteo?" Floyd asked.

"He was more important to Chiara than I was. I don't know that she loved him. I don't know that she loves anyone. But she manipulated him, and they depended on each other."

"And he allowed it?" Floyd asked.

"He needed her money."

"And now Matteo is dead."

"That's another investigation. The Mexican authorities will have to determine if she has any culpability in his murder," he said in his very British-Italian accent.

Sofía left Bibi with Nikki and approached Floyd, interrupting his conversation to ask him if they could be driven home.

"I can do better than that," Floyd said. "We still have the helicopter. We'll pay the taxi driver, and I'll call Santiago to get the chopper ready to fly us to San Miguel."

"I don't like the fact Paolo is going with us," she whispered. "He should be turned over to the police too."

"Sofía, you've surely heard the expression 'Keep your friends close and your enemies closer.' That's what we want to do here. But we don't know if he's part of the conspiracy or not. He will be interrogated by the federal police later today. I'm convinced, though, that he did not know about Matteo."

"Matteo?" Sofía asked, looking perplexed. "What about Matteo?"

"You don't know he was killed by Bibi's kidnapper?" Floyd asked.

"Oh my God. No, no," she said, looking like she might faint. Floyd reached out to steady her. "They could have killed my daughter."

"Bibi is safe now," Floyd said.

"I thought Matteo had been killed in Italy. Chiara made it sound to me as if it had happened a few months back. Why would she lie to me?"

"The obvious reason," Floyd said. "To keep you from being suspicious of her. And now, shall we go to the helicopter?"

CHAPTER 32

San Miguel de Allende—Sunday, late morning

In the ristorante's elegant dining room, Sofía served cappuccino she'd made at the patio bar. She also served pastries and left extra croissants at a side table. Though they were all tired, Floyd's entire investigative group enjoyed the late morning Italian-style breakfast. Paolo also sat with them, looking as comfortable as an unwanted dog, but Sofía had invited him to share in the breakfast after the helicopter had brought them back to San Miguel.

Timothy and Jack had packed their gear and left it by the front door. They sat at the table gulping their coffee and devouring chocolate croissants while they waited for a taxi to drive them to the airport. When Sofía announced their car had arrived, she took them through the covered patio to the front door. She hugged both men, thanked them, and stepped outside to give instructions to their driver.

Back in the dining room, Paolo reached into his shirt pocket and handed Floyd a check for the work his team had performed.

"I assume a check is okay for you to deposit in Miami," he said. "If not, I can arrange a bank transfer."

"A check is fine," Floyd said. "I get paid from international locations all the time." Turning to Eduardo, he added, "I'll transfer your consulting fee to your account in Miami, but I'll need your bank data."

"Instead of paying me, I'd like you to donate that money to Father Abelardo," Eduardo said. "Normally, I don't agree with vigilante tactics, but the work he does with the children is needed so much."

"If the government does not prevent human trafficking, then citizens do take matters into their own hands," Nikki said, shaking her head. "It's a sad situation. In our case, I'm happy the vigilantes helped."

"I'm going to follow Eduardo's example," Paolo said, glancing at Floyd. "Can you provide me with the priest's information? I will also make a donation."

Sofía returned to the room with a caffè latte, stopped at the side table to get a croissant, and sat down again with the group. An arm's reach away, a Spanish-style fountain built into the floor contained bright-red rose petals floating on the water in both basins.

"Your cappuccino is the best I've ever tasted," Nikki said as Sofía joined them. "And I love the elegance of this dining room. The fountain adds such a romantic touch with the rose petals gliding on the surface of the water."

"My housekeeper, the only one of my employees who started working again this morning, put fresh rose petals in today. She does it every morning." Sofía turned and dipped her fingertips in the water to test the temperature. "The cool water keeps the petals looking great for twenty-four hours."

"I never thought I liked religious art," Nikki said, "but the icons in this room, coupled with the rich, wooden furniture, the hand-hewn pine beams in the ceiling, and the white stuccoed walls create a tranquil and inviting atmosphere. I've changed my mind about religious art."

"It's typical San Miguel décor," Sofía said. "San Miguel can get wild in its decorative style, but even at its most playful, there is always a reference to religion and to pre-Colombian myths. I love it. You should visit me in November for the Day of the Dead festivities. You won't believe all the decorations."

"And I love Bibi's paintings in that alcove," Nikki said. "How is she doing?"

"She's sleeping now. My little angel was so tired."

"I'd encourage you," Eduardo said, "to make sure she continues to paint, especially as she recovers from the trauma. It will help her readjust. Besides, her talent is incredible."

"My favorite painting of hers," Sofía said, "is the one of the plain, white calla lilies in the decorative Mexican vase where the water has spilled on the table and the flowers are reflected in the puddles of water. I have another favorite Bibi painting in the patio. The relaxed, indoor and outdoor living is one of my favorite aspects of being here. Where else can you live like this?"

"In Southern Italy," Paolo said. "Maybe you should return to your native country. You can set up a San Miguel style ristorante. And it's safer there."

"No, thanks," Sofía said. "I feel perfectly safe right here. I love this lifestyle. Besides, once your mother gets out of jail, Bibi and I would not be safe in Italy."

With that, Sofía left the dining room, crossed the patio, and entered the private family quarters to check on Bibi. Sofía had asked her housekeeper to stay in Bibi's room while the child slept. She gazed upon her daughter with loving eyes. Fígaro's face, visible over the white sheet, looked as if he felt right at home.

Back in the living room, Floyd was sipping his second cup of cappuccino when he received a phone call from Fernando in Mexico City. He excused himself and left the room to talk in private. Upon his return, he informed Paolo the federal police would arrive soon to interrogate him about Bibi's kidnapping.

"I have nothing to hide," Paolo said. "They can ask me whatever they want."

Fifteen minutes later, the Federales knocked on the door, and Paolo joined them at the patio bar, where the housekeeper served coffee to them.

Nikki walked to Bibi's bedroom to tell Sofía that Floyd needed her in the dining room. After the two women returned, Floyd launched into the specific details of the abduction for them and Eduardo.

"Fernando called. He has a good grasp on everything that happened. The evidence and signed confessions by the kidnappers show Chiara and Matteo as the masterminds."

"What about Paolo? Was he involved?" Sofía asked.

"Apparently not. Chiara asked Matteo to pose as an Italian Mafioso to get the name of a person in Mexico to carry out the kidnapping. Matteo got a reference from a corrupt federal agent and flew that person, whose name is Arturo Béjar, to Naples. Attempting to disguise their true identity,

Matteo promised Arturo the opportunity to run Camorra operations in Mexico."

"Yeah, Camorra is an Italian Mafia," Sofía said. "That sounds like Chiara. She always manipulated Matteo. She always felt above the law too."

"Now it gets interesting," Floyd said. "Arturo also happens to work for Paolo's attorney in Mexico City—"

"You see, Paolo is involved," Sofía jumped in, "but you won't—"

"Hold it, Sofía, let me get through the entire story. Arturo told the Federales he was trying to break into the big time since Héctor Sánchez, the attorney, did not pay him enough. So when Matteo offered him an opportunity he could not refuse, he seized upon it. Matteo told Arturo that his first assignment would involve the kidnapping of a specific child in San Miguel."

"Can't you see Paolo is also involved?" Sofía said. "If he's paid you for the work I hired you for, that does not prove his innocence. Yeah, I hired you, and I will pay you."

"Sofía, can you please listen with passionate indifference?" Floyd begged. "I know this is emotional for you, but I ask you not to jump to conclusions without evidence to back them up. Shall I continue with the facts?"

"Yes, please," Nikki said.

"Arturo acted cautiously," Floyd said. "Instead of abducting Bibi himself, he hired a known child trafficker. Arturo did not dirty his hands with the actual kidnapping so he wouldn't lose the attorney's work if he messed up. The problem got compounded when Goyo asked for more money once he had abducted Bibi. Then Goyo disappeared."

"This guy, Arturo, is the one who followed us here in San Miguel," Nikki said, turning to Eduardo, "the night la Marihuana was killed. He was the one with the thin-rimmed glasses. The one who drove the pickup after you left the cave. The vigilantes called him a bajador."

"Yeah, I put that together too," Eduardo said.

Floyd continued with his facts. "Arturo knew he'd kissed away his opportunity with Camorra when Matteo arrived in Mexico and discovered Arturo did not have the child. That's when Arturo decided to ask Sofía for ransom money, though he continued working with Matteo to recover Bibi. Arturo still considered Matteo a member of the mob."

"Was Matteo also in on the ransom request?" Nikki asked.

"We don't know that. But Matteo had given Arturo all of Sofía's information, making it easy for him to try to extort money, and Matteo had provided him with an Italian burner phone when they met in Naples," Floyd said.

"So Arturo was triple dipping," Nikki said. "He worked on this case for the attorney in Mexico City, he worked on Chiara's and Matteo's sinister plot to kidnap Bibi, and he also extorted seventy-five thousand dollars in ransom money from Sofía. What a dirty bastard, he did not even have a thief's sense of honor."

"By then, Goyo had gone rogue with the idea of extorting as much money as possible," Eduardo said. "But what made him wait to make a deal with the father, as he stated at the cave when you were negotiating with him?"

Floyd shrugged. "Goyo realized he was holding on to a child whose father could pay big bucks. He saw too much interest in that one child. Maybe Matteo said something, but we will never know for sure."

"So he killed Matteo and the older man," Nikki said, "the one who had been at the scene of the accident when Juana was killed. It's all making sense now." She put the story together before Floyd could finish.

"That's right, Nikki. After killing the two men, he then moved operations from the Zacatecas cave to the one in the Zone of Silence. It's more isolated. He told the interrogators he could control the situation more from that location."

"That explains everything, except for Paolo," Sofía said. "He would have paid ransom. He will pay your fee, Floyd, just to appear innocent. Yeah, to keep himself out of jail."

"Now listen, Sofía, I have interrogated Paolo. I honestly think he's telling us the truth. It's doubtful he knew about his mother's scheme. The federal police are interrogating him right now, so we may learn more shortly. There is one more item about this I have not told you."

"And what's that?" Sofía asked, the expression on her face between total disgust and bitterness.

"When the police interrogated Chiara, she gave them nothing. So they are going to keep her in jail. The chief said she'll be ready to talk by tomorrow."

"Keep her in a Mexican jail overnight?" Nikki asked. "That woman will post bail and be out in no time."

"Not if the bail is set at the equivalent of seventy-five million U.S. dollars," Floyd said.

Nikki and Eduardo raised their eyebrows in unison.

"God only knows what that woman is worth," Sofía said, "but between her and Paolo, they can make that amount. Yeah, he will get that cagna released."

"The last item Fernando told me," Floyd said, "is that the Federales will be interrogating her tomorrow morning at the city jail in Mexico City. If we claim to be her 'relatives,' he can get three of us in to watch as she is questioned. We will observe through a one-way mirror. Nikki and I should be there for sure. Sofía, do you want to be the third person?"

"Absolutely. Yeah," Sofía said with a determined toss of her head. "I would love to see her squirm after a night in jail."

<hr />

Bibi came in, holding her father's hand. Her golden curls framed her tranquil, smiling face. Fígaro followed them, bouncing along—sniffing at the floor, the French doors, and the legs of a chair. Then, discovering someone he knew, the pup ran to Nikki, wagging his tail in excitement.

"I think he needs to go outside," Nikki said. She picked him up and invited Bibi to go with them to the backyard, the area used by valet parking.

Bibi turned to her mother with an expression of "May I do this?" on her face.

"Go, my sweet. Take him outside. Nikki is right. Yeah, Fígaro needs a bathroom break. Pronto." Sofía waved her hand to emphasize taking Fígaro outside quickly.

Bibi stopped by the side table where there was one last croissant. She picked it up and crammed half of it in her mouth as she and Nikki left the room.

Floyd asked Paolo to sit down and handed him a piece of paper.

"Here's the information you asked for on the priest." Then Floyd shifted his gaze toward Eduardo. "Nikki told me the two of you are scouting for venues to hold a wedding. When you find a location you like, maybe Father Abelardo can perform the ceremony."

"That's funny. We talked about it last night," Eduardo said.

"Finding a venue or asking Father Abelardo to officiate? Which one?" Sofía asked.

"Nikki wants to wait until next year to get married," Eduardo said, "but when we came on vacation to the Yucatán, we thought we'd look at possible locations."

"So you want a beach wedding?" she asked.

"No, not at all," he said. "We were thinking more about an archeological site for the ceremony, but then we'd need a place to hold the reception. We do want an exotic location, though."

"Tulum is an archeological site on a beautiful beach, if you invite guests who like the beach," Sofía said.

"Tulum is beautiful, but that's not what we want. We're only starting to think about what we'd like," Eduardo said.

"What about San Miguel?" Sofía asked. "A lot of exotic places in this town for the ceremony, and I'll do the reception here. I'll do a very nice party for you. Yeah, very nice, using the patio and the dining room."

"Thanks," Eduardo said. "I'll talk it over with Nikki."

CHAPTER 33

Mexico City—Monday, late morning

Floyd stood between Nikki and Sofía as the three of them crammed into a small, dark, musty space that felt more like a closet than an observation room. Except for the one-way, see-through mirror, it could have served as a closet. They waited about twenty minutes before Chiara was brought into the small interrogation chamber.

Escorted by two detectives, Chiara sat down at a beat-up wooden bench facing a narrow metal table in full view through the mirror. Sofía suppressed an expression of surprise when she saw Chiara's bruised face.

"Must have been a rough first night in jail," Floyd observed out loud. "Either that, or her inquisitors got aggressive last night."

Both interrogators sat on folding metal chairs, facing Chiara from the opposite side of the table. One was middle-aged, and the other one was an older man. The older man initiated the conversation in Spanish.

"You must have run into a problem last night," he said, motioning vaguely at her face. "We have a few questions. If you answer them, we can begin the process to get you out of here."

Chiara stared at her investigator.

"Why did you attempt to take that child out of the country illegally?" he asked.

"I want my attorney here," Chiara said.

"You left a message with your attorney yesterday, and he has not come to see you yet. But we have the right to ask you questions because you broke the law—"

"I will not speak unless my attorney is present."

"Well, since your attorney is not here for this questioning session, we will return you to the cell block. It may be a few days before your attorney can be present for you. His office called to say he's traveling."

The two men got up.

Chiara lifted her head a little higher and faced the older man.

"If I answer your questions, you will let me out?"

"If you answer our questions, we will start the process to release you," the man said.

"I want out of here," she said. "I'm only answering if you promise to release me on bond. I'll get my son to arrange bond."

"All I can promise is that we'll start the process. But if you don't cooperate, we will keep you indefinitely."

"You cannot do that," she said.

"Until you post bail, we can keep you as long as we need to. A couple of years, if necessary. Until you talk."

"You bastard," she said, her voice, full of venom, breaking as she spoke. "Look at my face." She pointed at her black eye. "This is an uncivilized country."

"Why did you try to leave the country under an assumed name?"

"It suited me."

"Why did it suit you?" he asked.

"So the mother of my granddaughter wouldn't know we were leaving."

"And why were you taking your granddaughter with you when you have no authority to do so?"

"She has a terrible mother."

Sofía raised her fist. If she had been in the same room as Chiara, Nikki was sure she would have attacked her and blackened Chiara's other eye.

The investigator asked Chiara to describe why the child's mother was terrible.

"She is not raising her correctly."

"Give me specifics," the older interrogator asked.

"She's not a good mother," Chiara insisted.

The interrogator turned to the younger man. "Let's take her back to the cell block. Maybe she'll cooperate tomorrow."

"You cannot put me back there."

"Yes, we can. And we're taking you back right now."

Both men stood and walked to either side of her.

"Two women beat me last night," Chiara said. "They called me a rich foreign bitch and threatened to ..." Chiara looked at the older man, who by now had his hands around her upper arm to physically remove her from the room. When the two men started to pull on her arms, Chiara stood on her own.

"Wait. I'll give you the reason I tried to save my granddaughter."

The two interrogators let go of her arms.

"This had better be good," the older one said.

"My granddaughter is coming into an inheritance shortly. Her mother cannot and will not take care of that money my husband worked so hard for all his life. My husband would have wanted our granddaughter to be raised with proper manners. Now it's up to me to ensure she becomes a good adolescent."

"So you think you can raise her better than her mother can? What does the mother do that's so terrible?" the interrogator asked.

"I'll send her to the Anglo-Italian International School to improve her manners," Chiara said, looking with contempt at her interrogator.

"With your attitude, it's no wonder you got attacked last night," the younger man said.

San Miguel de Allende—Monday, late afternoon

Back at Sofía's, Floyd interrogated Paolo one more time. Nikki and Eduardo were with them as they all sat around the same table in the dining room where they'd had coffee and croissants the day before.

"Why didn't you tell me Bibi is coming into an inheritance?" Floyd asked.

"Inheritance?" Paolo asked, confused.

"That's what your mother said when the Federales interrogated her today. An inheritance from your father."

"Oh, you mean the trust. When my father died, he left a sizeable trust for Bibi, his only grandchild. Bibi's not eligible yet, but it will be held in trust until she turns twenty-one. To ensure Bibi gets a first-rate education, the trust instrument contains a clause to allow Bibi's custodian, that'd be Sofía, to access funds for Bibi's health, education, and welfare. That provision goes into effect once Bibi turns twelve."

"But why would she kidnap Bibi if she can't get at the money?" Nikki asked.

"Chiara, maybe I should call her *mother*, would stop at nothing to get her hands on that part of my father's estate. If she managed to get Bibi, she probably had a plan devised to eventually get custody of her. If that ever happened, she would control the trust. She'd then deplete it over time for her own selfish benefit."

"But what about you?" Floyd asked. "Under that scheme, wouldn't you be the one to have custody?"

"Yes, but look, Chiara put my dad into an early grave. Matteo is dead as a result of her actions. If something happened to me, Chiara could get custody, as long as Bibi were in Italy. It's hard to believe she'd be so evil, but my father must have thought so, the way he arranged the trusts, especially for Bibi and me, to protect us from my mother."

"Chiara is livid her plan has been thwarted," Nikki said. "She planned to place Bibi in a boarding school in Naples, the Anglo-Italian International School. When Bibi comes into the inheritance—"

"Inheritance?" Sofía asked as she walked into the room, surprising them. "You're discussing the inheritance Bibi will get from her grandfather?"

"Yes, I'm updating Paolo," Floyd said.

"Chiara kidnapped Bibi so she could control that trust fund," Sofía said. "Yeah, she doesn't care about Bibi at all. It was all about getting her hands on the money."

"Greed. That pretty much sums it up," Floyd said.

"She caused all this suffering to get Bibi's inheritance," Sofía said. She shook her head, not understanding her former mother-in-law's malice. "If Chiara had asked, we would have signed it over to her. Yeah, if she'd leave us alone, I'd sign it all over to her. And you too, Paolo. Leave us alone, and I'll sign the transfer. Yeah, just leave us alone."

"Sofía, let me make you an offer," Floyd said. "You and Paolo need to work through this issue. The consequences for everyone affected by the kidnapping are not over, but the two of you should be on amicable speaking terms for the sake of your daughter."

"I'm happy to cooperate," Paolo said. "Sofía, I'm going to reimburse the seventy-five thousand dollars you transferred to that extortionist—"

"I'll stay and serve as a mediator over the next three days to help get you there," Floyd said. "Can you each commit to three days of working sessions? I'm not a psychiatrist, but I am a certified mediator, and I think I can help."

Paolo agreed, but Sofía bit her lower lip and looked at Nikki to borrow more time to think about it before responding. Nikki nodded her head, but Sofía still took another minute to agree.

"Unless you need us," Nikki said, "Eduardo and I plan to take the bus to Zacatecas today, get the rental car we left at the hotel, pick up the rest of our clothes there, and check out of our room tomorrow morning. Eduardo tells me Juana's pet crow is in a cage, so we'll take Sebastián with us to visit Father Abelardo and Ana on Tuesday morning. I think she'll want the crow her mother rescued."

"I'm afraid you'll fall in love with Sebastián once you see him," Eduardo said.

"I probably will, but our lifestyle does not make it possible to have pets. Finding good homes for both Fígaro and Sebastián is better for them than trying to take them with us," Nikki said as she turned her attention back to Floyd. "Eduardo will consult with Ana and the priest about the orphanage, and I want to say goodbye to the other children from our operation."

Floyd nodded his agreement. "You were on vacation when I called you, Nikki. You and Eduardo take the next three weeks to relax and recharge your batteries. Oh, and make an appointment for styling your short hair. The office will pay for it since you chopped it off in the line of duty."

"Great idea, thanks," Nikki said. "Late Tuesday, we'll fly to the Yucatán, if you don't need us."

Nikki and Eduardo walked to the living quarters to spend a little time with Bibi before they left. The child sat in front of a desktop easel in her bedroom, painting a portrait of Fígaro.

"He won't sit still," she said, complaining about the pup. "But I love him, so it's okay."

COYOTE ZONE

When Nikki explained she and Eduardo would be leaving, Bibi pulled her world tree necklace out from under her blouse.

"Thank you for my good luck tree. But most of all, thank you for making sure my mom's okay with Fígaro."

Bibi hugged Nikki. Then she picked the pup off the floor and placed him in Nikki's arms.

"Your mother will come to love Fígaro," Nikki said.

She ruffled up the hair on the Pomsky's neck, put him back on the floor, and scratched his belly.

CHAPTER 34

Palenque—Wednesday, midday

Sitting on the top step of the Pyramid of the Inscriptions, Nikki looked at the scene in front of her and sighed.

"What are you thinking about?" Eduardo asked.

"The magic of this place," Nikki said. "There's only one other time in my life I felt so absorbed in the magic of life, the universe, the . . ."

"When we made love this morning," Eduardo said, completing her sentence.

"Well, that too," she said as she squeezed Eduardo's hand and glanced at him with a loving glint in her eyes, "but Palenque reminds me of two trips I made to Barcelona when my parents were still alive."

"Barcelona is magical," Eduardo said, touching Nikki's face in a loving manner.

"We stayed with my mother's sister," Nikki said. "She lived near a large apartment complex, called Casa Milá, built by Gaudí the famous Catalán architect. I get mystical feelings in Palenque, especially as I look at the Palacio tower, which somehow reminds me of the rooftop of Casa Milá. On my first visit, she arranged for us to visit the famous rooftop terrace. Its surreal chimney and skylight structures resembling Darth Vader fascinated me. They were interesting sculptures, like the Palacio tower right over there."

"Casa Milá, also called La Pedrera. People say those sculptures scare the witches away," Eduardo said, standing up. "But I can't believe this. When were you there?"

"The first time, when I was about nine or ten. About Bibi's age. Then we visited my aunt when I was fifteen. That was the last time I was in Barcelona."

"On the rooftop, when you were about ten, did you play hide and seek with a younger kid?" he asked.

"My brother, yes," Nikki said slowly, looking questioningly at Eduardo.

"Did a kid a couple of years older join you, and you got in trouble for hiding inside one of the fanciful chimneys, the one with the cluster of Darth Vader look-alikes?"

Nikki pulled slightly away from Eduardo and looked at him with a confused expression.

"My mother was furious," she said, "but the crawlspace had a grid in it so there was no way I'd fall down the flue. But I don't remember telling you about that experience."

"I'm not sure if your mother's concern was for your safety or for being inside that tight space with an older boy who might lead you astray."

Nikki stared at Eduardo with open-mouthed astonishment.

"How do you know about that?" she asked.

"I was there. That was me. That must be why I fell in love with you the day I met you in Colombia. I'd been in love with you since we were on that rooftop as children. The vision of that girl with the adventuresome spirit, the one who climbed into the chimney with me, remained embedded in my brain for years."

"This is surreal, like I'm in a dream," she said. "Can you pinch me?"

"We took that trip two months before my dad died," Eduardo said, his voice turning a bit solemn.

"My brother and I lost our parents in a car accident after our second time we were in Barcelona."

"I only visited once. What an incredible coincidence that we met as kids. We should plan a trip to Barcelona and also tour the caves in Northern Spain and Southern France."

"Caves?" Nikki asked caustically. "No, thanks. I've had enough caves for now."

"These are very special caves. It's the Altamira and Dordogne areas with cave art dating back thirty thousand years. If we're going to be archeological junkies, we should—"

Nikki's mobile phone rang.

"It's Floyd," she announced, looking at the screen.

"Not again," Eduardo said, sighing. "Don't answer, Nikki. Please don't answer. We already wrapped up everything when we visited with Ana and Father Abelardo yesterday."

"I have to. He's my boss, remember?"

Eduardo shook his head and focused his gaze near the Temple of the Cross, where he'd purchased the world tree necklace for Nikki.

"Hi, Floyd. What's up?"

As Nikki listened to Floyd, Eduardo retrieved his own mobile phone from the side pocket of his cargo pants and scrolled through his photos.

"Yes, we had a terrific visit with Ana and the priest," she told Floyd. "They are doing amazing work with the children, and Eduardo promised to help them with a bit of consulting. Then we returned the rental car at the airport in Zacatecas, and we arrived in the Yucatán last night. And now tell me, what's happened with the Matteo investigation?"

As Floyd talked to her, Eduardo took a couple of photos of the Palenque grounds. Then he stood up and went down a few of the pyramid's narrow steps, turned to face Nikki, and framed her body against the shrine at the top of the pyramid before snapping a few photos of her.

After talking with Floyd for fifteen minutes, Nikki finished her conversation. She turned on the camera and snapped a few pictures of Eduardo with the tower, the one that reminded her of the Casa Milá rooftop structures, in the background.

"You can't be the only paparazzi," she said, laughing.

"What assignment is Floyd sending you on now?" Eduardo asked.

"We're on vacation for three weeks, remember?"

"No dangerous assignment, Ms. 007?"

"Come up here again, and I'll update you on the latest," she said.

Eduardo climbed the twenty or so steps to rejoin Nikki.

"Floyd said Chiara is still in jail. Sofía and Paolo are on good speaking terms, and she isn't accusing him of masterminding the kidnapping anymore. He has agreed to short, supervised visits with Bibi for the next three years because he understands Sofía's fears. The good news is, Bibi is doing well. Floyd said she and Fígaro have bonded."

"I'm glad Bibi is doing well," Eduardo said. "What else is going on?"

"Matteo's death is being investigated. Goyo is the obvious suspect. And the last news is that Floyd wants us to take a trip."

"What?" Eduardo asked. "I thought he said no assignments except vacation."

"Wait till I finish. When the Federales questioned Arturo more intensely, he told them he'd been hired by Matteo to kidnap Bibi. Matteo masqueraded as a member of the Camorra Mafia to convince him. Arturo, in turn, hired Goyo, who then wanted more money so he kept Bibi, guessing she came from a family with money."

"The kidnapper went rogue. We figured all of that already," Eduardo said, putting his camera back in his pants pocket.

"There's more. Arturo hired a couple more people, including the old man at the scene where Juana was killed. He was Antonio Enríquez, and after Juana was dead, he sought Josefina out to question her on Bibi's whereabouts. That's who killed her when she was not forthcoming with info."

"Yeah, that's the old man I found in the mass grave at the cave. I'm sure Goyo killed him," Eduardo said.

"Oh, for sure. But there's still more. The guy who jumped out of his pickup to go after you in the trailer was a Colombian national Arturo had hired earlier that week. He employed him as a favor to a Colombian drug trafficker living in Mexico. But the trafficker had an ulterior motive—to get rid of me. That trafficker's name is Cristóbal Arenas . . ."

"Good God, Nikki, you're in danger," Eduardo said. "That was Manuel Del Campo's fellow trafficker in Colombia. That guy in San Miguel did intend to kill *you*, not Juana."

"That's precisely why Floyd wants us to leave Mexico tomorrow. I told him we'd be happy to fly to Spain for three weeks. On vacation."

"Are you serious? We need to get you out right away. Like right now."

"Floyd will arrange our tickets to Barcelona under aliases, to make sure we're safe getting out of Mexico. He will send documents to our hotel tonight, and we'll leave early tomorrow."

"Documents?" Eduardo asked.

"Yes. Passports, driver's licenses, and airline tickets. Mine will be in the name of Nicolasa Torres, which, by the way, is my maiden name. I never liked Nicolasa, so I legally changed it to Nikki when I became an American citizen."

"And who am I?" Eduardo asked.

"Maximiliano Garza."

"Maximiliano, like the emperor of Mexico? Not a bad name. I like it."

"I like it too, Your Majesty."

Eduardo took Nikki into his arms and kissed her.

"Maybe we can scout out a wedding location in Spain," he whispered in her ear.

"Caves are not feasible venues to consider, no matter how much prehistoric art they contain," Nikki said.

"We should visit Casa Milá," Eduardo said, still hugging her. He held her very close for more than a minute. As they started walking down the narrow pyramid steps, Eduardo stopped Nikki and gazed at her intently. You know, I like your short, gray hair."

"You're joking. I'll get it colored after we get to Barcelona," Nikki said. "Now about Casa Milá, maybe we can arrange a wedding on the rooftop."

Eduardo took Nikki's hand and looked at her with a serious expression on his face that quickly dissolved into a smile.

"I like that idea. But there's a problem. Now that we have aliases, does that mean I need to propose to you all over again?"

"We can buy a cigar at the hotel, and you can use the band to place on my finger, like you did in Cartagena," Nikki said, laughing.

"Let's do it," he said. "Let's head back to our hotel, but before we leave Palenque, I want to buy you another world tree necklace. It never hurts to have good luck on our side."

THE END

But wait . . . there's more!

Bonus! A FREE chapter of the first Nikki García Thriller, *Waking Up in Medellín!*

Pinnacle Award in Fiction
Fall 2016

Killer Nashville Silver
Falchion Award 2017
Best Fiction Book of the Year!

HANDSOME COLOMBIAN MEN AND LIFE-THREATENING DANGER were not normally a part of Nikki's auditing job, but this assignment was anything but normal. Despite her emotional wounds, she accepts the challenge as a way to overcome the loss of her young son in a tragic event.

In the midst of the male-dominated business world in Colombia, she investigates mismanagement allegations and uncovers a sinister plot involving fraud . . . and possibly murder. She also discovers an attractive man who seems to have feelings for her. As her relationship with him grows deeper, so does the level of danger she finds herself in. When the guns come out, Nikki realizes it will be up to her to find a way to survive . . . **BUT IS SHE UP TO THE TASK?**

Excerpt from *WAKING UP IN MEDELLIN*

If only that man would speak to me, I could be on my way.

Waiting exasperated me. The man's bombastic voice gave final instructions to a subordinate in the hallway behind me.

"Tell them we can ship to Singapore and have it there in six weeks. Or they can pay for air freight if they can't wait that long," he said.

I turned and saw Manuel Del Campo standing outside the double doors of his office. The molding of the oversized doorway framed his muscular and impeccably-dressed physique. He wore a crisp, highly-tailored, bone-white suit—appropriate to the climate, yet contrasting conspicuously with the concept of steel mills.

I sat in Del Campo's plush office near Medellín, Colombia, waiting for him to answer a few questions for me. Fidgeting with my nails, I contemplated the multiple reasons I'd accepted coming here to do this job. I was having second thoughts, but it was too late. Now that I was on-site, it was better to just get on with it.

I'd flown in last night. A weather delay before I left Minneapolis, plus the five-hour flight to the José María Córdova Airport in Medellín, gave me ample time to think about corruption in Latin America—corruption so widespread that individuals across the workforce, from police officers on the street to the back offices of low level government officials, supplemented their incomes inappropriately. When dishonesty exists openly at the street level, it always emanates from the top and permeates all of society. In countries like Colombia, drug related crime adds more layers of complexity to unscrupulous behavior. To their credit, the Colombian people had fought against traffickers in a convincing manner. I was fortunate not to be investigating drug traffickers. I was only here to probe into possible mismanagement of a steel mill.

My eyes scanned the top of a carved mahogany desk directly in front of me. A photo stared back at me of Del Campo himself, wearing the same bone-white suit he sported today. Del Campo entered the room, his tone of voice tempering to lower ranges, apologizing for the delay in meeting with me.

"I have time," I said. I assumed he never arrived late for business appointments with men, but since I was a woman, he had been purposely rude.

He walked to his carved desk, preceding our meeting with pleasant Latin platitudes as he flipped open a cherry wood humidor, his initials engraved on the top, and selected a seven-inch Churchill. He cut the cap with a double guillotine cutter and lit a narrow strip of Spanish cedar with an old-fashioned butane lighter he retrieved from the top drawer of his desk. Cigar in mouth, he slowly rotated it in the spill's flame as he pulled air in gentle puffs to ensure an even burn. The spicy-sweet aroma of good hand-rolled tobacco mingled with the scent of the burning cedar, making me crave a cigar. But Del Campo was not about to offer a cigar to a woman and certainly not to one who was a lowly auditor. Manuel could ignore the ban on indoor smoking that worldwide headquarters in Minneapolis had issued. After all, Medellín, Colombia, was a long way from Minneapolis.

He looked at his cigar and rolled it around between his fingers. Without lifting his eyes, he abruptly turned the conversation to the purpose of my visit.

"So you're here to investigate me." His voice hardened as he spoke.

"I'm here to investigate allegations of wrongdoing reported to headquarters," I said.

"I'm completely transparent about managing this company," Del Campo said. He puffed on his cigar. "Everything here is on the up-and-up, like in a game of fencing."

"Fencing? What does that have to do with managing a company?"

"You don't go for perfection," Manuel said. He puffed on his cigar, blew out three smoke rings, and stared at me as the rings slowly dissipated. "You just go for solid returns."

"I don't know much about fencing. I've seen it televised at the Olympics. But let me ask a few routine questions about the mill."

"Women stand to learn a lot about business if they learned the game. In the context of fencing, it's all about the frame you set up." He took the photo of himself, set off by a gilded frame, and fidgeted with it until the angle of it set straight ahead of me.

"Frame?" I asked, confused.

"Let me explain. If you tell yourself your opponent is weak, and you play the game believing you are better, you create a psychological advantage. On the contrary, if you are afraid of your opponent, you will see yourself ambushed."

"That philosophy is true in life. In the weeks to come, you can explain the game to me. Right now, though, I need to get some information from you about the company."

"I'm listening," he said, leaning back in his chair.

For the next hour, I asked a lot of questions. He lit up a second cigar. The more he spoke, the longer he drew on each puff. He held the seven-inch Churchill between his thumb, middle, and index fingers, like an aficionado. I continued probing. He continued blowing smoke rings.

"If everything is above board, as you say, why did your employees call the Corporate Security Office to report misappropriation of company assets?" I asked.

He switched the cigar to his left hand. The inch-long ash fell in one piece on the highly-polished mahogany. His right hand, fingers cupped, pushed the ashes across the desk in a semicircle and onto the floor in one sweeping motion.

"It's probably a disgruntled employee trying to discredit me. Or a competitor," he said.

"You think one disgruntled employee would be so persistent?" I asked, my voice firm.

"One angry person can easily try to incriminate another, especially behind the veil of anonymity. Why believe a caller who won't give his name?" Manuel asked, his voice playful.

Almost immediately, he swiveled his chair, moved forward, and looked me straight in the eye.

"Look, Ms. Corporate Auditor Nikki Garcia, I'm tired of your insinuating questions. I find your tone accusatory. If corporate headquarters is not happy with my performance, they can fire me. They can trust me and stop this god-damned investigation, or they can fire me. You tell them that."

His voice became heated; his face turned fire red. He looked at me as if it was all he could do to control his anger. If I'd been a man, he may have taken a swing at me.

"I thought the game of fencing was about dealing psychologically with the opponent," I said.

He took what remained of his cigar and crushed it against the ashtray with such force I thought the ashtray might break. His face became purple with anger, and he stood, signaling our meeting was over. As I got up, his demeanor relaxed. He escorted me out of his office, smiling like a man accustomed to getting his way through temper tantrums. He cleared his throat, as if the cigar had irritated it.

"If you need anything while you're here on assignment, Nikki, just speak with my assistant. She'll arrange it for you. We want to make your visit to Medellín as pleasant as possible," he said. He closed the door to his office, officially ending our conversation.

I stood by the door, once again livid with the corporate policy of informing high-level executives when they were the object of a review for fraudulent activity. No one ever told lower level employees when they were the target of an audit, a tactic to ensure they didn't have time to cover up or destroy evidence. So why inform executives?

That man, manipulative as he seemed, had been president of Amazonia Steel for twelve years. He had taken control of a small company, which manufactured for the Latin American market, and grown it into a vast enterprise that exported around the globe, and he had been relentless in building his empire. His name had been tossed around at headquarters as a successor to the aging worldwide CEO, but Del Campo himself had taken his name out of contention, preferring, he claimed, to live in his native country.

I looked at the lavish furnishings around me in the office Del Campo's administrative assistant occupied. I'd met Theya, his assistant, that morning before she left at noon for personal reasons. The entire building was impeccable, but the elegant setting of the executive suite made me feel as if I were in upscale offices in Upstate New York instead of Medellín, Colombia.

I walked to the window to calm my anger at corporate policy before I talked with anyone else. Five floors up, I had a splendid view of an artificial lake that sparkled in the sunlight like a jagged and vast aquamarine. Occupying several acres, the lake had a bridge spanning the two shores at their narrowest point. The bridge curved gracefully over the lake, ending at a small, treelined parking lot to the right side of the front entrance to the building. Trees sprinkled along a pathway circled the circumference of the lake. Beyond the lake and across the highway were low, rolling hills. The vacant land, lake, and neatly-tended lawns around the company gave the entire complex a country club atmosphere. The steel mills were tucked out of sight half a mile away.

Amazonia Steel was one of the most profitable affiliates in the Globan family of companies. Globan International, where I worked, had worldwide holdings in steel, mining, energy, and large scale construction. I'd been sent to "la ciudad de la eterna primavera," City of Eternal Spring, after the Globan Corporate Security Office received fifteen anonymous phone calls on the Sarbanes Oxley Hotline claiming the president was defrauding the company.

Sarbanes Oxley was the law that resulted from several large accounting and fraud scandals in corporate America, including giants like Enron, Tyco, and WorldCom. Though the law is complex, multinational companies instituted telephone hotlines as part of their internal policing function to comply with a small part of the legislation. Employees could report malfeasance anonymously on these hotlines.

Calls to Globan's Security Office Hotline gave few details on the accusations against Del Campo. *I could be chasing a hoax.* Yet that thought quickly evaporated as I focused on Manuel's behavior at our meeting. Still gazing out the large window in Theya's office, I glanced at my watch. It was time to call it a day.

Get your print or ebook copy or read the rest of

chapter one now at

www.Pen-L.com/WakingUpInMedellin.html

ACKNOWLEDGEMENTS

I am indebted to countless individuals who kindly expressed words of encouragement for me to continue writing Nikki García's story. It's impossible to name the many friends, family, and fans deserving specific mention, including the members of books clubs from Texas to North Carolina to Pennsylvania who sponsored me. A few people are mentioned by name since they contributed directly to *Coyote Zone*.

Pattie Hogan and Bob Hurt, for walking the cobblestones of San Miguel for three days with me, an incredible sacrifice! Especially on the uphill portions toward Montes de Oca and Tianguis del Martes.

Philip Calkins, my son, for his technical advice on helicopters.

Pete Palmer, former CIA and security advisor, who guided me on the Mexican federal police and matters of private investigations in Mexico.

Nancy Miller, Janet Tuohy, Brenda Gottlieb, and Fred Childs—my beta readers—for their excellent suggestions.

Lowell Mick White, my mentor, for his guidance and recommendations, which I have listened to and consequently have become a better writer.

Ken Mayfield, banker and CPA, for his insights on international money transfers.

Dean Herr, Dan Rich, Andre Edwin, Ralph Bivins, and Roger Stacy—my writing group in Houston—whose suggestions improved this book.

Cliff Hudder and Hipólito Acosta—their encouragement and support of my writing provides me with great impetus to continue this path.

Becki Borth and Pattie Hogan—Fígaro and Sebastián are included for you.

Rachel Leigh Little, top hair stylist, who provided ideas for Nikki's hair in her undercover persona.

Jenna Cooper, LMSW, for advice regarding victims of human trafficking.

The many fans and friends who kept asking for Nikki's next adventure—thanks for waiting!

A special thanks to my publishers, Duke and Kimberly Pennell of Pen-L Publishing, and to Meg Welch Dendler, my editor, who tied all the loose ends together.

Kathryn Lane
2017

DISCUSSION QUESTIONS FOR COYOTE ZONE

Coyote Zone is the second novel in the **Nikki García Thriller Series**. This novel, like the first one in the series, is a mystery. For those of you who have also read *Waking Up in Medellín*, you will be able to compare Nikki and her accomplishments between the job she performed in Colombia and the assignment in Mexico. You will also have the advantage to detect the differences in plot, characters, story, and settings between the two novels. Although *Coyote Zone* covers a dark topic, this book offers a strong female protagonist in a dangerous situation, with two robust yet insightful and understanding male characters who work with her.

Danger and Adventure

1. What kind of man, while on a long-anticipated trip full of adventure accompanied by the love of his life, is willing to wait as she goes on an assignment that not only halts their adventurous sojourn but also requires him to assist her in a job that might include danger for both of them? Why would he do this?

2. Nikki realizes she will encounter elements of danger by going undercover. Once she has taken the plunge, she feels twinges of remorse and, at times, deep remorse. Do you think her remorse is a passing emotion, or will it change her attitude toward her relationship with Eduardo? If so, in what ways?

3. Does her resolve to find Bibi waver after going undercover? If so, why?

4. Who is the greatest danger to Nikki in her underground persona— Goyo or Bernardo? What is the biggest risk to the entire operation?

5. Do the light-hearted parts of the story provide momentary respites from the more serious parts?

International Setting

1. Does the international setting add excitement to Nikki's work? What aspects of the story are different in an overseas location than they would be if the story were set in the U.S.?

2. With regards to the legal ramifications of doing undercover work in a foreign country, is Nikki's job easier or harder in the international location? Provide examples of each.

3. What is your opinion of Juana la Marihuana? And what about Sofía?

4. Do the World Heritage Sites Eduardo and Nikki visit make the foreign country more interesting or more realistic? Give examples to support your opinion.

Comparison of *Coyote Zone* with *Waking Up in Medellín*

1. Has Nikki's character changed from the first story to the second one? Explain your answer.

2. Has Nikki matured as a character in the second novel? Provide examples.

3. What do you think of her transition from fraud auditor to full-blown private investigator?

4. What about Eduardo? In what ways has he changed?

5. Is Floyd's role as important to the story in *Coyote Zone* as it was in *Waking Up in Medellín*? What about Eduardo's role—is he as important?

Other Items to Consider

1. Who is the real hero or heroine of *Coyote Zone*?

2. What about Fígaro? What role does he play?

3. Is there psychological tension between any of the characters in this story?

4. What items in the plot took you by surprise? Explain.

5. What type of adventure do you think will await Nikki in the next novel of the series?

ABOUT THE AUTHOR

Award-winning author Kathryn Lane writes fiction inspired by Latin American cultures she experienced during her career as an international finance executive and in her life growing up in Mexico. Her debut novel, *Waking Up in Medellin,* was recognized with a Killer Nashville Silver Falchion for Best Fiction Book of the Year 2017 and a second Silver Falchion for Best Fiction Adult Suspense 2017. The novel also received a Pinnacle Achievement Award in Fiction. She is a 2017 finalist for the RONE Award in the Mystery category. In 2017, the novel was also released in Spanish, under the title *Despertando en Medellín.*

An anthology of Kathryn's short stories entitled *Backyard Volcano and Other Mysteries of the Heart,* which explores the fusion between fantasy and reality, was published by Alamo Bay Press (2017).

Association of Writers and Writing Programs featured Kathryn on the *Arriba Baseball!* panel in Seattle (2014). She has been recognized in her community with a Montie Award for Excellence in the Arts, and as a member of the Rotary Club, she has twice been honored with the Paul Harris Award. She lives in Texas with her husband Bob Hurt, where she serves on the Montgomery County Literary Arts Council.

Dear Readers,
If you enjoyed this book enough to review it for Goodreads, B&N, or Amazon.com, I'd appreciate it!
Thanks, Kathryn

Find more great reads at
Pen-L.com

CPSIA information can be obtained
at www.ICGtesting.com
Printed in the USA
LVOW10s0719300318
571752LV00018B/466/P